BATTLE HYMN

ACE BOOKS BY WILLIAM C. DIETZ

AMERICA RISING SERIES

Into the Guns
Seek and Destroy
Battle Hymn

MUTANT FILES SERIES

Deadeye
Redzone
Graveyard

LEGION OF THE DAMNED SERIES

Legion of the Damned
The Final Battle
By Blood Alone
By Force of Arms
For More Than Glory
For Those Who Fell
When All Seems Lost
When Duty Calls
A Fighting Chance
Andromeda's Fall
Andromeda's Choice
Andromeda's War

DRIFTER SERIES

Drifter
Drifter's Run
Drifter's War

SAM MCCADE SERIES

Galactic Bounty
Imperial Bounty
Alien Bounty
McCade's Bounty

SAURON DUOLOGY

DeathDay
EarthRise

JAK REBO SERIES

Runner
Logos Run

JAK CATO SERIES

At Empire's Edge
Bones of Empire

Freehold
Prison Planet
Bodyguard
Where the Ships Die
Steelheart

AMERICA RISING

BATTLE HYMN

william c. dietz

ACE
New York

ACE
Published by Berkley
An imprint of Penguin Random House LLC
375 Hudson Street, New York, New York 10014

Library of Congress Cataloging-in-Publication Data

Names: Dietz, William C., author.
Title: Battle hymn / William C. Dietz.
Description: First edition. | New York : ACE, 2018. | Series: America rising ; 3
Identifiers: LCCN 2017012871 (print) | LCCN 2017018389 (ebook) |
ISBN 9780698184459 (ebook) | ISBN 9780425278741 (hardcover)
Subjects: | GSAFD: Science fiction.
Classification: LCC PS3554.I388 (ebook) | LCC PS3554.I388 B38 2018 (print) |
DDC 813/.54—dc23
LC record available at https://lccn.loc.gov/2017012871

First Edition: February 2018

Printed in the United States of America
1 3 5 7 9 10 8 6 4 2

Cover art by Paul Youll
Cover design by Sarah Oberrender
Book design by Kelly Lipovich

This one is for Marvin Mack . . .
gin connoisseur, science fiction aficionado, and friend.

CHAPTER 1

You take the front line when there is danger. Then people will appreciate your leadership.

—NELSON MANDELA

EAST OF ALBUQUERQUE, NEW MEXICO

It was three in the morning. The past two days had been spent infiltrating troops into the hills east of Albuquerque, New Mexico. It would have been impossible without the snowstorm. But, thanks to the poor visibility, Union forces had been able to enter the area without being spotted. And one of those soldiers was the President of what had once been the United States of America.

However, even though Samuel T. Sloan was commander in chief of all armed forces, Captain Nick Black was in command of Charlie Company, 1st Battalion, 2nd Infantry Brigade from Fort Carson, Colorado. Because, as Sloan's military attaché put it, "You aren't qualified to lead a squad, much less a company." And Sloan knew it was true.

So why was he there? Crouched under a tree? Waiting for the signal to attack rebel-held Albuquerque? Because it was important to walk the walk, that's why. He was popularly known as the "Fighting President," even though he could just as easily be called "the accidental president" since he had never run for political office.

The global disaster took place on May Day 2018, when sixty-plus meteors streaked through Earth's atmosphere. Some struck the Pacific Ocean, sending tidal waves surging east and west. Others continued on, and one of them exploded over Washington State. The force of the blast was twenty to thirty times more powerful than the explosion that had leveled Hiroshima during WWII.

The secondary effects were even *more* devastating. Especially the widespread dispersal of particulate matter into the atmosphere. So much dust that the amount of sunlight reaching the surface of the planet was reduced by 15 percent. Plants died, the animals that fed on the plants died, and the humans who relied on both died. Millions upon millions of them.

America was hard-hit. Not only by the stuff in the atmosphere, and the effect that it had on crops, but by the meteors that struck Denver and Washington, D.C. In the blink of an eye, the top echelons of the federal government were annihilated, and Secretary of Energy Sloan became president.

Sloan had been in Mexico on May 1. And by the time he made it back and managed to assume the presidency, his badly shattered country had descended into chaos. There were pockets of civility. But large swaths of the country were controlled by warlords, religious groups, or no one at all. And that opened the way for a group of Libertarian oligarchs to form a new government in the American South. The Second Civil War followed.

Now, after many months of conflict, the Union Army was about to drive the Confederates out of Albuquerque. That was the plan, anyway. And some of the necessary groundwork had been laid. Thanks to arms supplied by the Union Army, a chief named

Natonaba and a thousand Navajos had put the squeeze on the Confederate supply line that led up from Texas—and into New Mexico.

As a result, the rebs had to send heavy armor up Highway 285 north every time one of their convoys headed for Albuquerque. And, because the city was well within the reach of the Union Air Force, the Southerners couldn't fly the supplies in either. All of which meant that the Confederates were running short of everything. That included food, fuel, and ammo.

The bastards did have one thing going for them, however—and that was the civilian hostages who were being held at key locations in the city. A situation that kept Union forces from bombing Confederate troop concentrations—and forced them to attack on the ground.

Sloan's thoughts were interrupted as his platoon leader spoke on the radio. "This is Archer-Six. Move out. Watch those intervals and rotate the people on point every fifteen minutes. Over." Sloan knew that the person on point would have to break trail for those who followed. That made it necessary to rotate people through the one slot in order to spread the work around. Not to mention the risk since the person on point was more likely to trigger an IED or catch a bullet.

Of course the lieutenant colonel in command of the battalion knew that. So, rather than send her people down the network of trails that could easily be booby-trapped, Barkley ordered each platoon to find its own way to the extent that was practical. And thanks to the mostly low, scrubby growth that covered the hills, her strategy was working.

To ensure that her troops didn't get lost, Colonel Barkley had assigned local guides to each platoon. They were supposed to occupy the two slots right behind the point man and in front of the platoon leader.

As for Sloan, he was number eighteen in a twenty-six-person platoon, five of whom were Green Berets assigned to protect him. That in spite of Sloan's opposition to any form of executive privilege. But Secretary of Defense Garrison and the rest of the cabinet were adamant. Sloan could accept the bodyguards or they would quit en masse. White House Chief of Staff Wendy Chow had been selected to deliver the message. "If you get yourself killed, or if the rebs manage to capture you, everything we've worked for will go down the toilet. So accept some bodyguards or run the administration by yourself." Sloan had no choice but to agree.

Thanks to his night-vision gear, Sloan could see the soldier in front of him as she passed between snow-laden trees and circled a snowcapped boulder. Sloan's snowshoes kept him from sinking into the powdery stuff. But they were clumsy, and his knees were starting to ache.

About three miles. That's how far the platoon had to go in order to reach Kirtland Air Force Base, which was located adjacent to Albuquerque's International "Sunport." Kirtland had been home to the Materiel Command's preimpact Nuclear Weapons Center a couple of months earlier.

But when it became clear that the rebs were going to capture Albuquerque, it had been necessary for air force personnel to destroy key parts of the facility as they withdrew. The ruins would make a good place to rally, however, and prepare for the final push into the airport, where more than a hundred civilian hostages were being held.

What were conditions like? Were the prisoners being fed? And what about the children? At least a dozen of them were being held in the main terminal, according to intelligence reports. Assuming all went well, this would be their last night in captivity.

Sloan had hoped to free Albuquerque earlier in the war but

couldn't do so without pulling much-needed soldiers out of the east, where General Hern couldn't win without them. But thanks to recent successes, troops were available.

Sloan saw a flash of light and heard a loud bang. He raised the M4 but couldn't spot any targets. "This is Archer-One," Lieutenant Orson said. "We have a man down. No medic required. Keep moving."

It seemed that the platoon's point man had been killed by an IED, or a mine, in spite of the decision to stay off established paths. But where *were* the paths? Under many inches of snow, that's where . . . And it looked as though the platoon had strayed onto one of them.

Had the enemy heard the explosion? Or seen the flash? Perhaps. But the curtain of steadily falling snow might have been sufficient to conceal the flash and muffle the sound.

Sloan winced as he slip-slid past the point where the charge had gone off. A body lay in a patch of blackened snow—and a badly mangled arm pointed the way. Sloan felt something cold clutch his stomach. Would *he* be next? *Why not me?* Sloan asked himself. *Maybe it's my turn.*

As soon as the platoon arrived on level ground, it began to move more quickly. Speed was of the essence. Especially if the enemy knew they were coming. A hill rose to the right and forced them to circle around it. There were still no signs of an enemy response, which gave Sloan reason to hope that the explosion had gone unnoticed.

His knees were on fire by then, and Sloan wanted to rest. Five minutes would be enough. But no, that wouldn't be possible until they arrived at Kirtland. And there was no way in hell that he would request something the other soldiers couldn't have.

After crossing a large open area, the platoon arrived at an unplowed road. Sloan had studied a map of the area and knew it was

Pennsylvania Street NE, a street that would lead them to Kirtland AFB. And that was good. The fully loaded pack and TAC vest were starting to make themselves known, and Sloan's shoulders had begun to ache, a sure sign that he should work out more often.

Not Lieutenant Orson, though . . . he fell out of line occasionally and let the rest of them pass before shuffling up to the head of the column again. *Why?* To check on his soldiers, that's why. Because they were his responsibility. And Sloan admired him for it.

Finally, after what seemed like an eternity, the vague outlines of buildings began to appear through the veil of steadily falling snow. There were what might have been fuel tanks off to one side. And even though the very top of the com tower was lost in the grayness up above, Sloan could make out the bottom third of the structure, along with the equipment shed nearby.

The only tracks were those left by the people in front of Sloan, and that was promising. If the enemy knew the force was there, surely they would have come out to fight by now?

Orson led the platoon through a shattered door into what had been a fitness facility. After posting sentries, the platoon leader told the rest of his soldiers to take a bio break. It felt good to remove the snowshoes. A couple of Green Beanies followed Sloan as he went out to take a pee. It was annoying, not to mention intimidating, but there was nothing he could do about it.

By the time Sloan reentered the gym, the rest of the battalion was preparing for the final push. He wanted to pester Colonel Barkley but knew it would be counterproductive and managed to restrain himself.

Sloan took the opportunity to mingle instead. All of the troops knew who he was, and most were willing to talk. And that was part of the mission Press Secretary Besom had given him. "Shoot the shit with the troops," Besom said. "They'll write home about it, some of their anecdotes will appear in the hometown paper, and you'll score some points."

Sloan knew that "points" were important with an election coming up in a few months. But he *wanted* to talk to the soldiers and took pleasure in doing so. He was busy chatting with a tech from Iowa when Colonel Barkley appeared at his side. "Sorry to interrupt, Private . . . Can I borrow the president for a moment?"

"Yes, ma'am," the soldier replied, and drifted away.

Barkley was a little under six feet tall. Sloan figured the officer was in her forties. But she looked older because of her prematurely gray hair and the damage that years spent in the field had done to her face. Barkley's eyes were gray and fearless. "So far, so good, Mr. President. Thanks for making the rounds. The troops like you, and no wonder. Lots of politicians claim to love the military but wouldn't dream of risking their own lives."

"It's an honor to be here," Sloan replied. "Are we running on schedule?"

Barkley nodded. "The other battalions are in position and ready to move out. After we depart, we'll double-time our way up to the main terminal. Chief Natonaba and his people will launch a feint on my command. Then, if everything goes as planned, the attack will pull most of the rebs over to the north side of the building. That's when we'll force our way in." Barkley shrugged. "Who knows how things will go after that."

"Yeah," Sloan said. "Who knows?"

Barkley smiled. "So, you're ready?"

"As ready as a desk jockey can be."

"Good. Please do me a favor, Mr. President."

"Sure, name it."

"Don't get killed. It would be bad for my career." With that, Barkley turned and walked away.

Sloan laughed, and was still grinning, as Orson led the platoon out into the snow. They began to jog. The local guide led the way through a maze of buildings and over onto what Sloan knew to be the airport's north runway. A single set of tire tracks was visible. A perimeter patrol? Yes, that would make sense. But, thanks to the poor visibility, the rebs hadn't been able to spot the white-clad invaders.

There were no indications that planes had been arriving or departing, however. And that was to be expected. The airport was shut down except for the rare C-17 loaded with critical supplies. The platoon passed a wrecked plane, though . . . A passenger jet perhaps? Caught on the ground when the city fell? Most likely. A white shroud covered its remains.

Sloan was tired by then. He was a runner . . . But most runners don't carry fifty-pound packs. His breath came in short gasps, and it was hard to keep up with the 120-pound private in front of him. She was carrying fifty pounds, too . . . And showed no signs of flagging.

The runway lights were off, consistent with the citywide blackout imposed by the Confederates. But cracks of light could be seen around the edges of the terminal's windows and hinted at life within. Sloan was trying to imagine the scene inside the building when muffled explosions were heard. He knew that was the diversion . . . The one intended to pull rebs over to the north side of the terminal building.

Night turned to day as the airport's lights came on. Suddenly, the column of soldiers was fully lit and exposed to machine-gun fire that originated from the top of the terminal building and some ground-level pillboxes. Soldiers fell as streams of tracer converged ahead of Sloan. He went to one knee and returned fire. A rooftop machine gun fell silent as a rocket struck it.

"Follow me!" Lieutenant Orson shouted as he led the platoon

to a door. A noncom ran forward. He was armed with a shotgun and fired two breaching rounds into the lock. The door sagged, and the sergeant pushed it out of the way.

Orson was the first person through the doorway, and the first to fall, as a reb fired half a magazine into the officer's lower extremities. The next soldier killed the Confederate, only to be cut down himself.

That was when Sloan found himself standing in the entryway. He'd fought before and been to the range since. The M4 carbine seemed to fire itself. Someone was screaming epithets at the Confederates as they fell. And it wasn't until all of them were down that Sloan realized the truth. The steady stream of obscenities had originated from *him*.

Now, with no one in front of him, Sloan yelled, "Follow me!" A flight of stairs led to the first floor. And Sloan was halfway there when two Green Berets passed him. A body came tumbling down as one of them fired upwards.

Then the Union soldiers hurried up to the main floor, where a metal door barred further progress. "I have the code," the sergeant with the shotgun said. Three blasts from the twelve-gauge were required to get the job done, and Sloan was the fourth person to enter the terminal through the door marked GATE 11. He expected to encounter resistance, but the waiting area was empty. The persistent rattle of gunfire could be heard in the distance, however, and Sloan's thoughts were with the hostages.

A number of experts had been consulted during the planning phase of the mission. All of them agreed that there were two possibilities. If the rebels who controlled the airport were fanatical followers of the so-called New Order, they would probably slaughter the hostages in order to terrorize the North.

But if the rebs were regular rank-and-file soldiers, they would be hesitant to kill civilians. Even if they were ordered to do so. Especially since they'd been members of a unified army six months earlier and been trained to avoid inflicting civilian casualties. And everyone believed that the second proposition was the more likely of the two. But were they correct? Sloan was about to find out.

He signaled for silence and led the platoon down a hall, past a row of empty food stalls, and through a security door. And that was when Sloan saw them. The hostages were an island of humanity sitting in a sea of trash. Airline blankets, empty food containers, and cast-off water bottles were strewn everywhere.

Children were crying, and adults had their hands clasped behind their heads, as two soldiers stood guard. They were armed with assault weapons and looking south, toward the sounds of fighting. What to do? Call on the soldiers to surrender? And run the risk that they would open fire on the prisoners? Or shoot them?

They're regular soldiers, Sloan reminded himself. *Good people in a bad place. They don't want to commit mass murder. Stick to the plan.*

Sloan looked left and right. The platoon was waiting for him to make the first move. He stepped forward. "Union Army! Place your weapons on the floor and take two steps back."

The rebs raised their rifles as they turned, saw all of the weapons aimed at them, and stopped. "Don't shoot!" one of the rebs said. "I'm putting my rifle down."

Sloan heaved a sigh of relief, and was about to move forward, when a hostage stood. She had frowsy hair, a full figure, and was wrapped in a winter coat. She yelled something incomprehensible. That was followed by a loud bang and a flash of light. The woman ceased to exist. The force of the explosion threw Sloan onto his back. And that's where he was, staring at the ceiling, when a Green Beret bent over him. "Mr. President? Were you hit?"

Sloan ran a quick inventory. "No, I don't think so. Help me up."

Once on his feet, Sloan was confronted with the worst carnage he'd ever witnessed, and that included the bloodbath in Richton, Mississippi. A bright red bull's-eye marked the spot where the woman had been standing. The individuals closest to her had been ripped to shreds. Body parts were strewn everywhere. Many of the people who were farther out from the explosion had been wounded, and Union soldiers were applying first aid. The horror of it stunned him. Sloan saw a hand lying nearby. A child's hand. His stomach heaved, and he threw up. Once the nausea passed, he straightened up and made use of a sleeve to wipe his mouth. "Why?" Sloan demanded of no one in particular. "*Why?*"

"Because the people in charge knew the soldiers wouldn't want to kill the hostages," Colonel Barkley said as she arrived next to him. "So they planted a fanatic in the crowd. It's supposed to teach us a lesson."

Sloan looked at her. "What lesson is that?"

Barkley's expression was hard. "Even if you win, you lose. That's what they want us to believe."

The firing had stopped. The colonel's radiotelephone operator (RTO) spoke to her. "The airport is secure, ma'am."

Sloan should have felt a sense of satisfaction. He didn't. "Even if you win, you lose." That was a good description of the war, *any* civil war, and the reality of that threatened to crush him.

BILOXI, MISSISSIPPI

Rest and relaxation. R&R. That was the mission Major Robin Macintyre and 1,326 other members of the military had been sent to the recently "liberated" town of Biloxi, Mississippi, to accomplish. Except the people of Biloxi didn't believe that they'd been liberated. No, they were pretty sure that they'd been *conquered*, and the knowledge didn't sit well. And that was evident in the hotel clerk's surly manner. "Your room will be ready in an hour or so. Perhaps you'd like to check your bag and take a stroll through town. You own it, after all."

Mac raised an eyebrow. There was no point in responding to the barb, and she didn't. "Okay . . . Who should I give the bag to?"

"Henry will take care of it," the clerk replied as he brought his hand down on an old-fashioned bell. "Enjoy your stay."

He didn't mean that, of course, since the clerk was clearly a loyal Confederate, who hoped that Mac would die and join the rest of her kind in hell. Mac forced a smile. "I will."

Henry was a wizened old man who might have been in his eighties. Could he be a Union sympathizer? Based on the wink Henry gave her, Mac thought he was. She followed him across the lobby to the bell stand on the far side. Massive columns supported a coffered ceiling, potted plants served to define separate conversation areas, and louvered windows were open to the outside. But even though the room *looked* as if it had been there for a hundred years, Mac knew the hotel had been built just after Hurricane Katrina, back when real estate was cheap.

After placing Mac's overnight bag in a storage room, Henry gave her a claim ticket and a card that had his name scrawled on it. "If you want some good gumbo, go to Louie's," he said. "Tell the front man that Henry sent you and give him this. The gumbo won't be any cheaper, but the cook won't spit in it."

It was, Mac decided, a valuable lesson in political reality. Even though the North had been able to reclaim New Orleans and establish a foothold in the Deep South, they had a long way to go before winning the hearts and minds of the people who lived there.

Biloxi was untouched by fighting and surrounded by Union troops, so stepping out of the hotel was like entering a bubble, a place where things *looked* normal even if they weren't. Most of the people on the street were soldiers, about 70 percent of whom were male and eager to find some female companionship. But outside of the bars and beach casinos, there wasn't much for them to do other than walk up and down the main drag.

Mac wasn't interested in the bars. But she *did* want to do some shopping and was disappointed to discover that items like shampoo, quality underwear, and chocolate bars simply weren't available. Because of shortages? Perhaps. Or maybe the shop owners didn't want the Union soldiers to have them. *No,* Mac thought, *that's silly.* But the idea persisted.

Mac was able to buy a top, shorts, and sandals, however . . . And went back to the hotel to put them on. The third-floor room was large, and a tiny balcony looked down onto the street.

After donning her new clothes, Mac returned to the first floor and left the hotel. She was hungry by then. It took fifteen minutes to find Louie's. The reception was cool at first. But, after giving Henry's card to the maître d', Mac was shown to a nice table that looked out onto the street. Her drink arrived quickly, soon followed by a nice salad and a big bowl of gumbo. Sans spit? She hoped so. And it was a welcome change from the steady diet of Meals Ready to Eat (MREs) that she had grown accustomed to.

After paying an exorbitant bill with a wad of OC (Occupation Currency), Mac exited the restaurant and began the trip back to the hotel. Soldiers hit on her, and one of the street vendors attempted to hang a necklace around her neck. That was when Mac felt the familiar itch between her shoulder blades. It was the same sensation she'd felt in nightclubs when some guy was checking her out, and on the battlefield just before somebody took a shot at her.

So she turned to check her six. There was nothing to see other than the constant flow of soldiers.

You're battle happy, Mac told herself as she made her way up the street. *A good night's sleep will put you right.*

Once she was back in her room, Mac took a long shower and reveled in the seemingly limitless supply of hot water. Then it was time to don a tee shirt with ARMY emblazoned across the front and a pair of pink socks.

Mac brushed her teeth, removed the baby Glock from her AWOL bag, and checked to ensure that it was loaded. The habit of sleeping with a pistol had begun shortly after the meteor strikes turned everything upside down and wasn't likely to go away anytime soon.

Mac turned the lights off and crawled into bed. It was not only huge, but soft, in marked contrast to the surfaces she'd slept on for months. Mac enjoyed the feeling at first.

But, after tossing and turning for fifteen minutes, she realized that the mattress was *too* soft. For her, anyway. So Mac got up and pulled the coverlet off the bed. After laying that and a pillow on the floor, she lay down and pulled the comforter up around her shoulders. She fell asleep three minutes later.

Mac was somewhere pleasant, with someone she liked, when the noise awoke her. It didn't take much. Not for a soldier who'd been on the front line for months. Her hand went to the Glock as she heard the creaking sound again. It was coming from the direction of the door that opened onto the balcony. Or *was* it? Maybe she was hearing noise from the street or the room next door. *You're wound tight,* Mac told herself. *Get a grip.*

There was a streetlamp outside. And as the door swung open, a silhouette appeared. He, or she, paused as if to look around. Then the intruder raised a long-barreled pistol and fired. The reports were muffled. A suppressor? Yes! All of those thoughts flashed through Mac's mind as she fired the Glock three times. It was loud by comparison, and as muzzle flashes strobed the room, the figure slumped forward.

Mac rolled free of the comforter and stood with the pistol pointed at the balcony door. Were *more* gunmen about to enter? Mac backed up to the point where she could access a wall switch. Light flooded the room.

The would-be assassin had fallen forward over the foot of her rumpled bed. Black-edged holes marked the bullet holes in one of the pillows. It appeared that the jumble of bedclothes had been enough to give him the impression that she was in bed. Shit! What the hell was going on? Was she looking at a thief? Someone banged on the door. "Security! Are you all right? Open the door."

Mac went over to stand next to the door. Her training kicked in. Never assume. *Was* it security? Or was a backup team trying to get in? "A man tried to kill me," she said through the door. "I shot him. He's dead. If you are who you say you are, you have a master key. Use it . . . And come in with your hands on your head."

Mac heard a click, saw the door open, and stood ready to fire as a man entered. Then she remembered how she was dressed. Or *wasn't* dressed. But it was too late. "I'm Enrique," the man said. "Please point the pistol somewhere else."

Mac lowered the Glock. "Okay, sorry about that. But it pays to be careful."

Enrique was thirtysomething and wearing a blue blazer with khaki slacks. Just like all the other security guys she'd met. He looked from the body and back to her. "What happened?"

"It's like I told you. That bozo came in off the balcony and tried to kill me. Look at the pillow. You can see the bullet holes. His nine mil is on the floor."

Enrique frowned. "Why are you still alive?"

"I was sleeping on the floor."

Enrique eyed Mac as if to make sure she was serious, looked at the comforter, and nodded. "You're military?"

"Army."

He nodded. "I am going to reach inside my coat and remove my cell phone. Then I'm going to call the military police."

Mac smiled thinly. "Go for it."

As Enrique made the call, Mac took the opportunity to enter the bathroom and put a uniform on. For the sake of modesty, yes, but for another reason as well. If Mac was going to deal with some MPs, she wanted to do so as a major, rather than a girl wearing a tee shirt and panties. So she was fully dressed by the time the MPs arrived.

"I'm Sergeant Kirby," the lead investigator said. "This is Corporal Kinney, and that's Private Nagata." Kirby had dark skin, a round face, a slim body. He looked from the body to Mac. "So, Major . . . What happened?"

Mac told the story again as Nagata pulled a pair of latex gloves on and began to search the body. Light strobed the walls as Kinney took photos. "Here's something interesting," Nagata said, as Mac's narrative came to an end. "Check it out."

"It" was a piece of much-creased paper, which Kirby handled with great care. He scanned it, did a double take, and turned to Mac. "Look, Major, you're famous!"

Mac could hardly believe her eyes. The flyer said, "WANTED DEAD OR ALIVE!" across the top. And there, immediately under the header, were the words: "Major Robin Macintyre, Commanding Officer Mac's Marauders, for war crimes."

That was followed by a photo which, surprisingly enough, was quite current. And no wonder. She'd seen it in the *New York Times* a month earlier. What the hell? After scanning the flyer, Mac read it again. The description was accurate. She had been born in '93, she was twenty-seven, and her mop of hair was brown.

As for the text under the heading "Criminal Record," some of that was true and some wasn't. Mac *had* been court-martialed, found guilty, and sentenced to four years in prison. President Sloan had pardoned her as part of a plan to return low-level offenders to military service and the battlefield. Had favoritism been involved? Yes, most certainly, since she had saved Sloan's life—and he'd been forthright about his interest in her.

But the rest was grade-A bullshit. Especially the line that read: "After being pardoned by Union president Samuel T. Sloan, Macintyre and her band of criminals committed numerous crimes, including kidnapping and the murder of her sister, Confederate major Victoria Macintyre."

The truth was that Victoria had been killed by a crazed Confederate deserter two weeks earlier. As for kidnapping, Mac had been involved in snatching the Confederacy's Secretary of Energy, but that was a legit thing to do during a war.

Then there was the reward. "Upon delivery of Major Robin Macintyre to the proper authorities, or DNA evidence proving her death, the government of the New Confederacy will pay a reward equivalent to $100,000 in gold or silver."

That was bad enough. But the *real* shocker was down in the left-hand corner of the page in small font. "By order of General Bo Macintyre, Chairman of the Joint Chiefs, Confederate Army." Bo was her father! Her estranged father, yes, but the wanted poster still came as a shock.

Bo and Victoria had always been close. To some extent, that was the result of a natural affinity based on two similar personalities. But there was something more going on as well, and that was

Victoria's determination to secure *all* of her father's affection, by any means necessary. It was a need that put Victoria at odds with both her mother and her sister. And Mac's insistence on going her own way had done nothing to close the gap with Bo.

But a death sentence? That represented a new level of hostility where Bo was concerned. Did he actually believe that his youngest daughter was responsible for his oldest daughter's death? Communications weren't perfect due to the war, and Mac *had* been present when her sister died. So maybe he did.

There was another possibility, too . . . Bo was Chairman of the Confederacy's Joint Chiefs. Maybe he was under pressure to disown the daughter who not only fought for the North but had gained a considerable amount of notoriety for saving President Sloan's life? Would Bo Macintyre sacrifice Mac for his career? She couldn't rule it out. That realization triggered a flood of sorrow. The kind of grief she might have felt had her father been killed. And, in a way, he was dead to her. Or maybe he always had been. "So what do you think?" Kirby demanded.

"I think I'm worth *more* than a hundred thou," Mac replied. "And I want a different room. This one is too messy."

SOUTH OF WINSTON-SALEM, NORTH CAROLINA

General Bo Macintyre was standing on one of the four landing pads that were clustered around the topmost section of Confederate Defense Tower 26. The structure was three hundred feet tall, and located just south of the New Mason-Dixon Line. It, like the identical towers located to the east and west, had been constructed *before* Bo was named as Chairman of the Joint Chiefs.

Had Bo occupied that position when the idea was initially put forward, he would have reminded President Lemaire and his cronies of *another* chain of fortifications that were supposed to keep enemies out. And that was the ill-fated Maginot Line. It consisted of concrete bunkers built all along France's borders with Switzerland, Germany, and Luxembourg.

Unfortunately, the seemingly impregnable defenses had a weak spot near the Ardennes Forest, a flaw the Germans were not only aware of but eager to exploit. Doing so allowed them to split the French-British defensive front, leading to the famous evacuation at Dunkirk. The French surrendered six weeks later.

And defensive towers like the one Bo was standing on were proving to be equally vulnerable. Six had been bypassed or destroyed, allowing Union forces to push down along both banks of the Mississippi River and link up with an amphibious force in New Orleans, the same city where, Bo was convinced, his daughter Victoria had been murdered by her sister. Bo winced and pushed the thought away.

The point was that the Union had been able to effectively split the Confederacy in two. And that's why Bo was in North Carolina. He was there to boost morale and keep the eastern half of the country in the fight. If they could continue to hold, Bo believed that the Yankees could be driven out of the South. Unfortunately, winning, as in conquering the North, was no longer a realistic possibility. A fact that President Lemaire and his sycophants had yet to accept.

That was the *big* picture. But as Bo brought a pair of binoculars up to his eyes, he was thinking about the brigade arrayed in front of him. According to the reports that Bo had read, the Union forces were under the command of Major General Suzanne "Bunny" Smith. She'd been two years behind him at West Point, and while Bo didn't know Smith well, he was familiar with her reputation.

The nickname "Bunny" stemmed from the fact that Smith was so physically attractive that her male classmates thought she could qualify as a Playboy Bunny. But that had everything to do with nothing. From what Bo had heard, Smith was competent, hard, and aggressive. So why was Bunny sitting on her butt? *Because she's waiting for something,* Bo concluded. *Something I won't like.*

And that prediction was borne out when his aide, Major Brian Arkov, arrived. He was slightly out of breath. "It's time to pull out, General . . . They're sending a helicopter up from the Dungeon."

Bo knew that the men and women stationed on Tower 26 routinely referred to the windowless complex underneath the central column as "the Dungeon." He lowered the glasses. "Time to go? *Why?*"

"Union paratroopers are landing south of us, sir. It looks like they're the anvil, and General Smith is the hammer."

"The Hammer," would be a much better nickname for Smith in Bo's opinion. "Cancel the helo, Brian. We're going to stay."

Arkov wore rimless glasses, and he looked like a stern headmaster at an elite school. He frowned. "Is that wise, General? If you were to be captured, or killed, it would be a severe blow to the war effort."

"Thanks for the vote of confidence," Bo replied. "But I can assure you that I won't be captured. As for killed, well, there are plenty of generals in Houston. One of them will step in. Think about it, Brian . . . If we leave, how would that look to a private? Or to the citizens of North Carolina?

"Besides," Bo added. "Colonel Katz is rolling north with two cavalry battalions. And once he gets here, we'll be able to push Bunny back across the New Mason-Dixon Line. All we need to do is hold on."

Arkov looked doubtful. "Sir, yes, sir."

"Pass the word," Bo said. "This ain't over till it's over. Tell the CO that I want every clerk, cook, and tech geared up and ready to defend this installation."

Bo's self-confidence was contagious, and Arkov grinned. "Yes, sir. I'll tell him."

"Good. And one more thing . . . I want him to launch every attack helicopter he has. I want them in the air, and I want them to hit those paratroopers hard. That will force the Yankees to slow down and soften them up for Katz."

Arkov tossed Bo a salute, turned, and ran toward the elevators located in the central column. Bo walked out to the edge of the platform, looked down, and eyed the berm that Smith's troops would have to cross. It was defended with machine guns, mortars, and 20mm Gatling guns. And that wasn't all. The tower's C-RAM system stood ready to detect and destroy incoming artillery, mortar, and rocket rounds *before* they could cause damage. And a surface-to-air-missile battery was located on the next platform over from where Bo stood. It swiveled left and right every now and then, like a dog sniffing the air. Bo turned his gaze to the north. *Come on bitch,* Bo thought. *Let's see what you've got.*

CHAPTER 2

> Let me tell you something that we Israelis have against Moses. He took us 40 years through the desert in order to bring us to the one spot in the Middle East that has no oil!
>
> –GOLDA MEIR

PINE KNOT, KENTUCKY

It took Marine One less than an hour to make the 150-mile trip from Fort Knox to the Union penitentiary near Pine Knot, Kentucky. Or more specifically, the recent addition to the McCleary Prison, which was often referred to as "Supermax South," because of the large number of high-ranking Confederates being held there. They were officials and military officers for the most part. Meaning people who had intelligence value or could be swapped for Union prisoners.

Sloan stared out the window as the VH-60N "White Hawk" circled the low-lying complex and settled onto the pad that bore the big letter "H." It wasn't every day that the president dropped in to visit a supermax inmate—and shotgun-toting guards were visible everywhere.

Sloan released his seat belt as the helo touched down. Secretary of Treasury Martin Tyler was seated beside him. Tyler had light brown hair, a cheerful demeanor, and an eidetic memory. As Tyler followed Sloan off Marine One, he was absorbing everything he saw. Two Secret Service agents followed along behind.

Warden James Gladfelter was there to greet the incoming dignitaries. He was balding, a bit pudgy, and much given to dry washing his hands. "President Sloan! And Secretary Tyler! I'm James Gladfelter. I hope you had a good flight."

Sloan endured a damp handshake and forced a smile. "It's a pleasure to meet you, Warden. The trip down was pleasant. Thank you. Is the prisoner ready?"

"Yes, of course," Gladfelter responded. "Please follow me."

A concrete path led away from the pad, took a number of sharp turns, and delivered them to what looked like a one-story bunker but was actually more. A guard opened the door, and more security people waited within. The first floor was devoted to office space, meeting rooms, and a lounge for staff. But most of the supermax was underground.

An elevator took the party down to level 3B, where the doors opened onto a sterile lobby. Sloan noticed that the lights were unusually bright, and everything was made of concrete. That included a bench, the walls, and the highly polished floor. The air was so chilly that Sloan chose to keep his overcoat on.

"We're standing in the core," Gladfelter explained. "The facility has three levels, each of which is ringed by twenty-four cells, for a total of seventy-two. Each floor has two interview rooms—and one of them is set up for you. Once you're ready, I'll send for the prisoner. Would you like coffee or tea?"

"No, thanks," Sloan replied. "Go ahead and send for him. We'll settle in."

After showing Sloan and Tyler into a small, sparsely furnished room, Gladfelter disappeared. "Check this out," Tyler said as he sat down. "My chair is bolted to the floor."

"The ceiling feels low," Sloan observed. "And there aren't any windows. Plus, based on what I've heard, the food sucks. I feel sorry for Sanders. But not sorry enough to send him home."

Confederate Secretary of Energy Oliver Sanders had been captured during a daring raid deep into the heart of Texas and subsequently brought north. He'd been "ripening" in the supermax ever since. The prisoner had been less than cooperative during the days immediately following his capture. Had his attitude changed? Sloan and Tyler were going to find out.

Secretary of Energy Sanders was shown into the room the way any prisoner would be. He was dressed in a baggy prison uniform, had cuffs on his wrists, and wore shackles on his ankles. They rattled as he walked.

Sanders was well under six feet tall, had a medium build and a sallow face. It registered surprise as a guard ordered him to sit down. "*President* Sloan? I guess I'm more important than I thought I was. Are you going to trade me for a Union prisoner?"

"Nope," Sloan replied. "What I am going to do is give you a chance to do the right thing. And that could be helpful when you go on trial after the war."

Sanders made a face. "Fuck you."

"My, my," Sloan responded, as he withdrew a packet of photographs from an inside pocket. "Such a potty mouth. I brought you a present. Here, have a look." Sloan pushed the photos across the table that separated them.

Sanders looked down at them, up at Sloan, and down again. He didn't touch them. "There's nothing to be afraid of," Sloan assured him. "They're pictures of your wife and children. They were taken two weeks ago."

That brought Sanders's head up. Sloan could see the wheels turning. The implications were clear. A Union spy knew where the Sanders family lived! And, if the agent could take pictures of them, he or she could do other things as well. Like shoot them. Would Sloan order such a thing? No, of course not. But Sanders didn't know that. He'd been part of a government that did use such tactics.

Gingerly, as if handling something very fragile, Sanders examined each photo with care. Then he put them down. A look of resignation appeared on his face. "If we win, I will request permission to shoot you in the face."

"And, if you win, flying pigs will fill the sky," Sloan replied. "Now, let's get down to business. The gentleman to my right is Secretary of the Treasury Tyler. We're going to ask you some questions about the Strategic Petroleum Reserves that you and your henchmen stole from the United States government. Specifically, we want detailed information regarding how much oil has been sold to other countries, who represented them, and how much money changed hands.

"And, before we begin, please make a note. Both Secretary Tyler and I have an intimate knowledge of this subject. And we have the means to verify most, if not all, of what you tell us. So don't waste our time with lies. You'll regret it if you do. However, *if* you cooperate, that will factor into the way you're treated after the war."

Sanders nodded. "Understood." And while Sanders didn't volunteer any information, his answers were consistent with what the two men knew or believed that they knew.

Finally, as the interview came to a close, Sloan shuffled the photos like a deck of cards. Then he pushed them across the table. "You can keep them."

A look of gratitude appeared on Sanders's face. "You won't hurt my family?"

Sloan wanted to say, "No, of course not." But that would be stupid. So Sloan was careful to hedge. "That depends, Oliver . . . It depends on *you*."

Sloan turned to the guard standing next to the door. "We're done. Take Mr. Sanders back to his cell."

"So," Tyler said once Sanders was gone. "What do you think?"

"It's pretty obvious that Lemaire and his friends are using the oil reserves to pay for the war, *and* they're skimming money off the top as well. But that isn't the worst of it. We will need that oil to rebuild the country."

"What are you going to do?" Tyler inquired.

"I'm going to take the oil reserves back," Sloan replied. "And recover as much of the money as I can. Come on, let's get out of here. This place gives me the creeps."

NEW ORLEANS, LOUISIANA

The Bayou Choctaw Strategic Petroleum Reserve wasn't much to look at. Not from twenty-two miles above the surface of the planet. But seventy-two million barrels of crude oil were stored in the former salt mine, and that was a big deal.

Such were Mac's thoughts as she eyed the satellite photo from the back of a crowded meeting room at the Holiday Inn hotel. What she saw was a large section of light-colored soil surround by lush greenery. The site included two storage tanks, some widely separated sheds, and a maze of pipes. None of it meant anything to her. But that's why Captain Hines had been brought in. It was his job to brief Marine Colonel Natasha Walters and her officers on the reserve. Hines was a tall man with reddish hair, a ruddy complexion, and a tendency to wave his laser pointer like a wand. He'd been teaching geology before the government called him back to active duty.

"The Bayou Choctaw site contains about seventy-two million barrels of crude oil," the engineer said for the second time. "And it's connected to the St. James Terminal on the Mississippi River by a thirty-seven-mile-long, thirty-six-inch pipeline." Mac watched the red dot trace a path from the reserve, through some green fields, and over to a tank farm that was located adjacent to the river.

"That's how the reserve looked *before* the war," Hines continued. "*This* is the way it looks now." A new photo appeared. It was similar to the first one except that new features had been added. A defensive berm surrounded the site now, watchtowers had been added at each corner of the complex, and all sorts of defensive weaponry were visible.

But, being a cavalry officer, what grabbed Mac's attention were the Strykers parked in separate revetments. The presence of such vehicles suggested that the rebs weren't going to be shy. They planned to go out and do battle with Union forces when the time came. "So," Hines concluded. "The site is very well defended. And before you attack it, you'll have to fight your way through ninety miles of Confederate-held territory. We will try to provide air cover, but aircraft are in short supply, and there are likely to be times when you'll be vulnerable. Do you have any questions?"

"Yes," a Marine captain said from the first row. "Is it too late to join the Coast Guard?"

That produced some laughs, and Colonel Walters had a smile on her face as she replaced Hines at the podium. "Request denied, Captain . . . The Coasties will have to get along without your services. How about it? Are there more questions?"

There was. A platoon leader stood. "Yes, ma'am . . . The rebs at this site are cut off. Is that correct?"

Walters nodded. "It is."

"So," the lieutenant continued. "Why attack? We could starve them out."

It was a good question. Walters turned to Hines. "Captain Hines?"

Hines stood. "The people up the chain of command were concerned that it would take too long. Our citizens need the oil stored in those caverns."

Mac considered that. How high had the decision gone? All the way to Sloan? And, if so, had it been difficult for him? Did Sloan realize that he was going to trade lives for oil? But what choice did he have? The North had some oil wells but not enough . . . And what did her Strykers run on? Oil by-products, that's what . . . Not to mention heating oil for homes and all the rest of it.

There were more questions. And once they'd been answered, Walters thanked Hines before turning back to the audience. "Okay, let's talk about how to get this job done. The brigade's table of organization looks like a pig's breakfast. It includes a battalion of Marines, a battalion of soldiers, a medical unit on loan from the navy, drone operators supplied by the air force, *and* the civilians who are supposed to operate the reserve once we capture it. And that *is* the plan . . . We are supposed to capture the facility, not destroy it. Please keep that in mind during the days ahead."

Walters was almost six feet tall, lean, and had chosen the Marine Corps over the navy after graduating from Annapolis. Her eyes scanned the room. "Now hear this . . . Even though we represent different branches of the military, we have a common objective, and we've got to function as a team. I will have zero tolerance for interservice-rivalry bullshit. If I see it, hear it, or smell it, you will be sorry. Don't disappoint me.

"Here's how it will go down . . . At 0600, drone operators are going to eyeball both sides of Interstate 10. Major Macintyre's Strykers will take the point at 0630. The rest of the brigade will follow at 0645. We'll spend the night near the town of Sorrento, which is about halfway to our goal. So brief your troops, check everything twice, and check it again. That will be all. Battalion commanders will remain. The rest of you can rejoin your units."

As most of the officers left, Mac made her way to the front of the room, where she joined Walters, Marine Major Joe Corvo, and Marine Captain Misty Giovani. "I'm going to tweak the table of organization," Walters told them, "so we'll have as much clarity as possible. Let's start with you, Joe. You have some LAV-25s. True?"

"Four of them," Corvo replied.

"Right. Assuming you have no objection, I would like to transfer them to Mac's Marauders on a temporary basis. I think you'll agree that it makes sense to put all of our armor under a single officer."

Mac could tell that Corvo didn't like it. But what could he say? There was only one possible answer. "Yes, ma'am."

Mac knew that while the Marine Corps LAV (Light Armored Vehicles) *looked* like eight-wheeled Strykers, there were some differences, including the fact that the LAVs could "swim" rivers and lakes.

But Mac had been around long enough to know that everything comes at a price. So it was too early to celebrate her good fortune. And sure enough, Walters was turning her way by then. "*You* have two companies of infantry," Walters said. "For the purposes of this mission, I'd like to place them under Major Corvo's command."

Mac didn't like it any more than Corvo did. And, like Corvo, she had no choice but to acquiesce. "Yes, ma'am. One thing, though . . . I need to keep my Stryker crews, techs, and mechanics."

"Of course," Walters said as she made a note. "That brings us to you, Captain Giovani. I'm putting *all* of the support functions under you, and that includes responsibility for the civilians."

Giovani looked worried, and for good reason. Walters was asking her to integrate the supply and transportation functions of two dissimilar battalions and to accomplish it overnight. She swallowed. "Yes, ma'am. I'm on it."

Walters grinned. "The three of you look like mourners at a funeral! Buck up, it will work. I promise."

Mac's Marauders were parked on the first two floors of the five-story parking garage located next to the hotel. That was less than perfect since the rebs could bomb the shit out of the structure, but the garage did keep them out of sight and offered some protection from strafing attacks. Shortly after Mac arrived, she sent for her senior noncoms and officers.

There was a chorus of groans as Mac delivered the news. None of her people wanted to be seconded to the Marines—no matter how temporary the assignment might be. Or, as one sergeant put it, "If I wanted to be a jarhead, I would have joined the fucking Marine Corps."

Mac felt some sympathy but had to push back. "I understand how you feel, but Colonel Walters is correct. In order to take our objective and minimize casualties, we need a clear chain of command. One in which everyone knows who's in charge of what.

"Captain Overman, please make sure that our troops are briefed. Once you accomplish that, report to Major Corvo for further instructions. The techs, mechanics, and Stryker crews will remain with me. Are there any questions?

There were lots of questions. Process stuff mainly, most of which had yet to be addressed. And since Mac didn't have a lot of answers, the best she could do was to take notes and promise to follow up.

She could answer one question, however. It was posed by a platoon leader. "Since we won't be riding in the Strykers, what sort of transportation will we have?"

Mac understood the officer's concern. If she and her soldiers had to ride in soft-sided trucks, they'd be extremely vulnerable. "That's a good question," Mac responded. "You and your troops will ride in Marine Corps AAVs (Assault Amphibious Vehicles). You can expect leather seats, stereo, and a wet bar."

Most of them laughed because they knew that while the so-called amtracks could hold more troops than a Stryker, they were anything but luxurious. Not only that, but the tracked vehicles were slow compared to the eight-wheeled Strykers, and that could be a problem depending on the situation. Still, the AAVs had good armor and mounted heavy weapons.

"All right," Mac said. "Make me proud. Let's get to work. Captain Wu, a moment of your time please."

Wu was Mac's supply officer and, more than that, one of the people who had been freed from prison as part of President Sloan's Military Reintegration Program. And, like all good supply officers, Wu could be *very* resourceful when she needed to be. Which was most of the time. She was small and intense. "Permission to speak freely, ma'am?"

"Go for it."

"Reporting to a Marine sucks."

"Do you feel better now?"

"Yes, ma'am."

"Good. There's something I want you to do for me before you report to Captain Giovani."

"Which is?"

"Find two dozen multispectral combat beacons for me. The special ops people might have some."

Wu was clearly curious, but since Mac hadn't chosen to say why she needed the beacons, the supply officer let it slide. "Yes, ma'am . . . I'll see what I can do."

Mac thought about the coming day. Her Strykers would be on point—the tip of the spear, the first to fall. But damned few of them would if Mac had anything to say about it. She went to work.

SOUTH OF WINSTON-SALEM, NORTH CAROLINA

Confederate Defense Tower 26 was surrounded and under attack. Meanwhile, high above, the cowardly sun was half-hidden behind a screen of striated clouds. The nonstop boom of artillery, the thump of mostly futile mortar rounds, and the occasional crack of a long-range rocket blended together to create a symphony of war sounds.

But most of the incoming shells and rockets ran into the wall of metal that the tower's twin C-RAMs threw out and were instantly neutralized. *Most*, but not all. Some managed to get through, and there were casualties as a result. And that's why Major General Suzanne "Bunny" Smith continued to fire them. After dropping paratroopers south of the tower, she was determined to wear the defenders down.

What Smith didn't know, or General Bo Macintyre *hoped* she didn't know, was that two battalions of Confederate cavalry were racing north to kick her ass. So his task was to hold and keep holding. And he was all in . . . Meaning that Bo was going to stay until the battle was over. Trenches ran out to the twelve-foot-high berm like spokes on a wheel. Most were one-way. Some ran *in*, so that the wounded could be taken belowground for treatment, and others ran *out*, enabling personnel and supplies to reach the wall.

And it was understood that everyone, regardless of rank, was to grab something and bring it with them if they were headed out to the berm. Bo grabbed a can of 7.62mm ammo and lugged it along as he followed a couple of privates toward the east side of the perimeter.

Craters could be seen where artillery and mortar rounds had managed to penetrate the C-RAMs' defensive fire, and one of them partially overlapped the trench. Bo winced when he saw a dark stain on the dirt. It was surrounded by cast-off bandages. Someone had been hit and taken away.

Stairs led up to a circular platform that wasn't much different from similar structures that Bo had seen in the ancient fortresses of Europe. And that made sense since the functions were similar. Soldiers had to stand on something if they were going to fight, regardless of whether they were armed with a machine gun or a crossbow.

Bo paused to place the ammo can next to some others before beginning his tour. He was bareheaded, so everyone could see who he was, and armed with a golf club. The putter was part of his persona now. He had taken one into action in Afghanistan and become known for it. Now the club was a useful gimmick. The kind of thing that was sure to generate stories. "And there the general was," a private might say. "Strolling around with a putter on his shoulder, cool as a cucumber, while the bullets flew over his head."

That was bullshit, of course, since Bo was as frightened as anyone else. But, unlike some, he knew how to hide it. And the club was part of the act.

"How's it going?" Bo demanded as he came upon a surprised mortar team. He knew that they, like most of the machine gunners, had yet to fire a shot. "Don't worry," he told them. "You'll get your chance before long . . . And when you do, give 'em hell!"

And so it went as Bo made his way around the circuit with Major Arkov and his bodyguards in tow. Every now and then, Bo would climb up on top of the berm and make a production out of peering through his binoculars. Arkov didn't like it, but the troops did, and that was the point.

A sniper fired at him, and a bullet kicked up a geyser of soil next to Bo's right boot. The report followed a fraction of a second later. "The bastards can't shoot," Bo remarked as he forced himself to remain on the wall for an additional three seconds.

That got a laugh from the team assigned to a .50 caliber machine gun and gave Bo a chance to jump down. A lieutenant saluted him, and Bo made use of the putter to return the gesture of respect. *That was close,* Bo thought as he strolled away. *I'm one lucky son of a bitch.*

The tour continued. And Bo was about halfway around the circumference of the berm, and shooting the shit with a master sergeant, when Arkov interrupted them. "Excuse me, sir . . . But I have a message from the CO. He wants you to know that Union tanks are approaching the tower from the west. Lots of them."

Lieutenant Colonel Fields was down in the underground command center, where he was supposed to be. And there were lots of cameras and sensors mounted on top of the three-hundred-foot tower. So if tanks were coming, he could see them.

Maybe this was it. After doing what she could to wear the Confederates down, Bunny Smith had decided to launch a full-scale attack. Or had she? Something felt wrong. "Ask Colonel Fields to take a look all around," Bo said. "A *careful* look."

Arkov nodded and spoke into a handheld radio. What seemed like a long thirty seconds dragged by. Then Bo saw Arkov's eyebrows rise. "Really? Holy shit. I'll tell him."

Arkov turned to Bo. "Colonel Fields says that motorcycles are coming in from the east! At least fifty of them."

Bo's mind was racing. *Motorcycles . . . What the?* Then he had it. The engineers who designed the towers had been in a hurry . . . And rather than build two *vertical* retaining walls, and fill the space between them with earth, they settled for a steep slope. A slope that could be used as a ramp! One the bikers could use to jump the defensive berm.

The weapons on the parapet would cut down most of the motorcycle riders before they could do that, of course . . . But if Smith sent enough bikers, some would get inside. To capture the tower? No. To kill people and cause confusion while the tanks rolled in. All of that flowed through his mind in an instant. "Tell Fields to put out the word: Kill the bikers *before* they can jump the berm and land in the compound. Come on!"

Bo began to run along the top of the wall. The rest of them had no choice but to follow. The noise generated by the motorcycle engines blended with the sound of outgoing gunfire to create an asynchronous roar. The four soldiers were halfway to the east side of the compound when a biker managed to pass through the hail of bullets unscathed and soar into the compound.

The bike landed hard, and the rider was thrown clear. He came up shooting and managed to kill a couple of unsuspecting soldiers before a third put him down.

Bo swore as he followed a flight of stairs down into the compound below. Bo's bodyguards were firing their assault weapons by then, and one of them managed to smoke an incoming soldier *before* his motorcycle could touch down.

A Union solider was lying on his back clutching his leg when Bo shot him in the head. The situation was critical, the biker still had the capacity to fire his weapon, and Bo didn't have the resources to guard prisoners. A different biker saw the execution and fired his machine pistol at Bo. The bullets cut Arkov down as one of Bo's bodyguards shot the Yankee in the throat.

Bo knelt next to Arkov to check for a pulse. There was none. He took the major's radio. It looked as though the motorcycle attack was over. "This is Macintyre . . . We're making progress in the compound. What's the situation outside the wall? Over."

"Our armor arrived," Fields responded. "They're duking it out with the Union tanks. So far so good."

"Glad to hear it," Bo replied as he fired at a Union soldier. "Keep your doors locked."

"They're sealed," Fields assured him. "And our helicopters are on the way back."

After being sent away, the command's Apaches had been ordered to land and wait for orders. Now they were about to swoop in, and just in time, too, since surface-to-air missiles were flashing off the top of the tower, a sure sign that Smith's aircraft had joined the fray.

The contest for control of the compound was over fifteen minutes later. The larger battle raged on for more than two hours. But when it was over, and Bo looked out over the battlefield from the top of the tower, he liked what he saw. General Smith's forces had been forced to retreat northwards, leaving a hundred wrecked vehicles behind them. Some continued to burn. The threads of gray smoke came together to throw a pall over the ravaged farmland that surrounded the tower.

Bo heard intermittent bursts of gunfire as unspent rounds of ammunition cooked off in the burning vehicles. Tiny figures limped north. Some were carrying stretchers, and Bo wondered if he knew some of them. Probably. Not that it mattered. He turned his back on the scene and walked away. A battle had been won. Others waited to be fought.

NEW ORLEANS, LOUISIANA

The Strykers left at precisely 0630. There was a hint of light in the east, and Mac could see her breath, as she stood in the **DOOBY DO**'s forward hatch. Strykers came in a variety of flavors, and the **DOOBY** was an ESV, which stood for Engineer Squad Vehicle. A tractor-style blade was mounted on the front of the truck. And, based on previous experience, Mac knew the specially equipped vic could be useful for pushing stalled cars out of the way, something that might come up. Ten Strykers were lined up behind the ESV. The rest were at the very tail end of the column, where, should it be necessary, they could turn and fight.

Meanwhile, an air force Predator drone was flying ahead, searching for any signs of a blockage or ambush. Thousands of feet higher, a pair of F-15 Eagles had been assigned to provide air cover. And that was important in case the AWACS (Airborne Warning and Control System) plane circling to the south detected enemy aircraft. All of which was good. So, Mac asked herself, why am I worried?

Because you're always worried, her inner voice replied. *No one can move a brigade without someone noticing. How will the rebs respond?*

The question went unanswered as the ESV threaded its way through narrow streets and followed an on-ramp up onto I-10. It was a squeeze point, and Mac wouldn't have been surprised to encounter trouble there. But the way was clear, and traffic was light. That made Mac feel optimistic as the **DOOBY**'s TC drove along the elevated section of I-10 that bordered Lake Pontchartrain on the right.

After ten minutes or so, the freeway veered to the northwest, and Mac turned to look back. The good news was that her Strykers were maintaining the correct intervals. The bad news was that they couldn't exceed 30 mph without leaving the Marine amtracks behind.

Mac's thoughts were interrupted by a bright flash of light and a thunderous BOOM. The noise came as a shock. Mac felt a stab of fear and was glad that no one could see her face. *Don't feel, think,* Mac told herself.

By some miracle, none of her vehicles were damaged by the blast. It blew a big chunk out of I-10, however, and more explosions followed. One of them was *behind* her. Mac turned to see that a huge crater was blocking the way. The **DOOBY**'s truck commander stomped on the brakes, and the ESV jerked to a stop.

There was all sorts of radio chatter by then, but Mac's attention was elsewhere. Her responsibility was to think before giving a command but to do it quickly. What caused the explosions? IEDs? No, Mac didn't think so. Because a bomb-disposal team had been sent out to check the highway an hour earlier.

What then? Not aircraft . . . The AWACS plane would have warned them about that. What remained? Cruise missiles, that's what . . . Fired by a Confederate sub somewhere in the Gulf of Mexico!

Okay, but *why*? Cruise missiles cost more than a million each. So the Confederates had spent more than eight mil attacking the convoy so far. That was a very expensive way to destroy a column of vehicles. Unless there was another purpose. What if the rebs were attempting to chop the brigade up into smaller pieces? So they could defeat it in detail? A variation on the old divide-and-conquer strategy. Mac keyed her radio. "This is Marauder-Six. Prepare to receive infantry attacks from both the left and right flanks. Over."

No sooner had Mac spoken than mortar rounds began to fall

on the road. Each explosion produced a crumping sound, a geyser of asphalt, and a hail of shrapnel. The fire appeared to be coming from the Maurepas Swamp on her right. And as Mac looked back, she saw that the Marine amphibs were under attack as well.

Walters was calling for the Zoomies by then, and Mac hoped the planes were carrying full loads of rockets and bombs. If so, they would be able to suppress the mortar fire in short order.

But Mac had a more immediate problem to deal with as Confederate soldiers began to fire on the column from the tree line on her right. "Cross over to the other side of the freeway!" she ordered. "And turn toward the enemy. Keep your vics low, but make sure your weapons can fire on the woods. Over."

Wheels spun as the ESV crossed the median and turned. Like most highways, I-10 was higher in the middle so that water would run off and into the ditches that bordered both sides. So once the Strykers had taken up their new positions, all the enemy soldiers could see was the top third of each vehicle. "Hit 'em hard," Mac ordered. "Over."

Mac wanted to check on the rest of her command at that point but couldn't as dozens of rebel soldiers emerged from the tree line, ran forward, and took cover in the newly created craters. Bullets rattled against the **DOOBY**'s armor as the ESV's 40mm grenade launcher began to chug. The vic's gunner could see the enemy on her remote-weapons-system screen and fire without exposing herself. A line of explosions marched along the highway, and the volume of incoming fire began to drop off.

Mac continued to fire short bursts from the pintle-mounted machine gun. It wasn't bravery so much as a single-minded determination to get the job done. Then something struck the back of Mac's knees. That caused her legs to buckle, and she fell into the cargo compartment below.

Mac was pissed . . . And that must have been visible on her face because medic Larry Moody raised a hand. "Don't give me any shit, Major . . . This ain't no movie, and you sure as hell aren't John Wayne."

Moody had a tendency to be outspoken at times and occasionally insubordinate. But he was the best medic in Mac's battalion, and at more than two hundred pounds, a hard man to ignore. "I'm going to court-martial your ass," Mac told him, as bullets continued to ping the Stryker's armor.

"It's too late for that," Moody replied. "They already did! And *you* got me out of prison. So I may be a fuckup, but I'm *your* fuckup. Live with it."

Mac grinned. "Yeah . . . Thanks."

Both of them looked up at the ceiling as the Stryker shook, and a dull boom was heard. It was the F-15s! Providing close ground support.

Mac stuck her head up through the hatch just in time to see black smoke billow up into the sky. A second run followed the first. Then a combined force of Marines and soldiers swept past. The ensuing firefight lasted for fifteen minutes, and by the time it was over, the surviving Confederates had been forced back into the swamp. The drone operators had failed to spot them. *Why?* Because shit happens, that's why. Maybe it was negligence. Or maybe the rebs were good at concealment.

Sadly, two Strykers and two Stryker crews had been lost along with an amtrack carrying twenty-one people. Had the Confederates won? Or had they lost? Judging from the number of bodies that lay scattered about, Mac felt sure that the enemy had suffered most of the casualties. But the Union Army had been delayed. And maybe, in rebel minds, that was a victory.

Casualties were loaded onto helicopters for transportation to the navy hospital ship a few minutes away in New Orleans. Then the convoy got under way again. It was midmorning by then, and everyone felt jittery. Mac was no exception. What else did the rebs have up their sleeves?

The answer was snipers. It was impossible to tell if the sharpshooters were members of the military or civilian resistance fighters. Nor did it matter. A bullet is a bullet. And while most of the projectiles failed to find flesh and bone, they hit the Strykers with enough regularity to keep everyone on edge.

So Mac felt a sense of relief as the column pulled into Sorrento and took possession of an athletic field. The next hour and a half was spent setting up a defensive perimeter, which was reinforced by carefully positioned Strykers and amtracks.

Once that chore was completed, tents were erected to provide shelter for the brigade command post, the first-aid station, and the troops themselves. One of the shelters was assigned to Mac. It served as battalion HQ and a place where Mac could meet with what remained of her command structure.

And finally, after all of the outstanding issues had been discussed if not resolved, the tent was hers to sleep in. But first Mac went over to check in with Walters—and wound up eating an MRE with the CO. Then it was back to the tent for a sponge bath before hitting the rack. The cot wasn't very comfortable. But Mac was so tired, she could have slept on a sheet of plywood. And that's where she was, dreaming about a sandy beach, when an enormous weight straddled her.

Mac opened her mouth to scream only to have a wad of fabric shoved into it. A battery-powered night-light was sitting on the storage module near the entrance to the tent. But it was dim. And as Mac looked up, she couldn't make out a face. A knife cut her tee shirt open. She could smell the man's sweat as huge hands mauled her breasts. Mac tried to push him off. He chuckled. "No way, whore . . . We're gonna have some fun . . . Then I'm going to cut you."

Mac recognized the voice. Larry Moody! The *same* Moody who had forced her down out of the hatch earlier that day. All two hundred pounds of him. The Glock then . . . It was half-hidden by her pillow and close to her left hand. But that was pinned to the edge of the cot as Moody leaned forward to suck on an exposed nipple. Mac *could* wrap her fingers around the nine mil's grip, however. She pulled the trigger three times as Moody bit her.

Moody hadn't been hit but jerked as if he had and straightened up. Mac saw the glint of polished steel as Moody raised the knife, but that was when light flooded the tent, and a male voice yelled, "Freeze!"

Mac expected Moody to stab her. But, much to her surprise, the ex-convict kept his hands raised. Mac pulled the wad of cloth out of her mouth with her right hand as she brought the Glock up under the medic's chin. She spoke through gritted teeth. "Get off me, or I will blow your fucking brains out."

More soldiers had arrived by then, and they took Moody away. Mac pulled a shirt on, sat on the cot, and began to shake uncontrollably. Then the tears came. But they were silent tears because people could hear, and Mac was supposed to be strong.

CHAPTER 3

To a surrounded enemy, you must leave a way of escape.

—SUN TZU, *THE ART OF WAR*

SORRENTO, LOUISIANA

It was raining, and Mac could hear the pitter-pat of raindrops hitting the tent over her head. More than five hours had passed since Moody's attack. She was the only patient in the first-aid tent because Colonel Walters had ordered the medical personnel to ". . . take a break." *Why?* Because the Marine wanted to speak with her privately. And, judging from the expression on her face, Walters was angry. "They tell me you're going to be okay," Walters said. "And that's good because it means I'm free to chew you out."

Mac was confused. "Chew me out? For what?"

"You held out on me," Walters replied. "Explain *this*."

Mac winced as Walters pushed a much-folded piece of paper across the table. It looked as if it had been kept in someone's pocket. Moody's pocket? Yes. Now Mac understood. The ex-con had been determined not only to rape *and* kill her but get paid for it. "I filed a report."

Walters stared at her. The words were icy. "With whom?"

"With Colonel Russell. He's the officer I report to."

"He's the officer you report to *on paper*," Walters replied. "You could have copied me, and you didn't. *Why?*"

Mac looked away and back again. "I was afraid that you would give my battalion to someone else and send me north."

The expression on Colonel Walters's face softened slightly. "I get that. So, are the accusations true? Did you kill your sister?"

"No, but I was present when she died. There were a lot of witnesses."

"But your father thinks you pulled the trigger."

"Yeah, I guess he does."

Walters frowned. "This is a first so far as I know. And, since there isn't any precedent to follow, I can handle the situation as I see fit."

Mac searched the other woman's face for some sign of what she intended to do. "And?"

"And I need you . . . But other people may know about the reward and come after you."

"I know that," Mac replied. "But they might come after me *anywhere*, and that includes cities north of the New Mason-Dixon Line. What are you going to do with Moody?"

"I'm going to send his ass up to Leavenworth, where his original sentence will go back into effect. Then they'll court-martial him all over again," Walters replied. "We're leaving in an hour. Do you feel up to it?"

Mac stood. "Yes, ma'am."

Walters smiled. "Good. So get the hell out of my first-aid tent. The swabbies want it back."

GRAND CAYMAN ISLAND, THE CARIBBEAN SEA

The clouds had parted, the sun was out, and President Samuel T. Sloan still felt slightly seasick as the landing craft came alongside the tender pier. Grand Cayman had been a regular stop for cruise ships back before the May Day disaster. And untold thousands of tourists had been sent ashore in brightly colored tenders to stroll through Georgetown before going back to their respective ships for dinner.

But rather than the usual mélange of professional greeters, hopeful taxi drivers, and food vendors, a company of Marines was waiting to greet the president as he stepped off the boat and onto the platform. It felt good to stand on something solid and, as the rest of his team disembarked, Sloan paused to look around.

A visitor center was located directly in front of him, and Georgetown lay beyond. Sloan had never had a reason to visit the Cayman Islands but knew they were home to secretive offshore banks. And that was why he was there . . . To pry the banks open and recover the money that had been stolen from the American people. "Mr. Higgins is here," a Secret Service agent announced. "He claims that you requested a meeting."

Sloan was about to reply when a pair of navy F-35 fighters roared overhead. They were flying low, no more than five hundred feet, and going extremely fast. Overlapping booms were heard as the planes broke the sound barrier.

Sloan grinned. "Shock and awe." That's what the boys and girls at Fort Knox called it . . . And if the citizens of Georgetown had been unaware of the invasion before, they sure as hell knew about it now. Sloan turned to find that a portly man in a tropical-weight suit was waiting to speak with him. "Mr. President? I'm your consular agent. My name is Brian Higgins. Welcome to Grand Cayman."

Sloan had never heard of consular agents until the previous week. That was when Secretary of State George Henderson explained that the Caymans were too small to rate a consulate, much less an embassy. So Higgins had been hired to handle whatever issues might arise. The businessman had a round face, two chins, and a tendency to sweat. After removing a document from an inside pocket, he offered it to Sloan. "My bill," Higgins explained. "I haven't been paid since the meteors fell."

"I'm sorry to hear that," Sloan said as he tucked the document away. "I will ask the State Department to pay you immediately. Now . . . Call the premier, tell him that I'm here and that I want to meet with him."

A look of horror appeared on Higgins's face. "We need an appointment! He would never . . ."

"Call him," Sloan said. "Tell the premier, or his gofer, that if the big Kahuna fails to arrive within the next hour, we're going to drop a two-thousand-pound smart bomb into his swimming pool. And yes, we know where he lives. As for me, I understand there are some nice bars a block away, and I'm going over to have lunch. He can join me there."

Higgins fumbled a cell phone out of his pocket and was dialing as Sloan and his bodyguards walked away. It didn't take long to discover that Georgetown had fallen on hard times. Except for a dozing dog and two boys on bikes, the main drag was deserted. Most of the previously thriving businesses were closed.

One of the few exceptions was the garish-looking Margaritaville Restaurant. Sloan waved his entourage forward. "Come on, lunch is on me." The interior was nearly empty, and the staff was eager to seat such a large group of customers.

Sloan was seated at a table, and halfway through an order of chicken quesadillas, when he heard a commotion out front. The premier? Yes. And his bodyguards, all of whom were immediately disarmed.

Finally, after being cleared by Sloan's Secret Service detail, Higgins was allowed to escort Premier Alfred Campbell into the part of the restaurant where Sloan was seated. He stood and went forward to greet Campbell. The premier was a big man, with black hair and coffee-colored skin. Judging from the look on his face, Campbell was pissed. *No surprise there,* Sloan thought. *He's seen the steel . . . So it's time for the velvet.*

"Premier Campbell! What an honor . . . Thank you for agreeing to meet with me on such short notice. Please, have a seat. Will you join me? The food here is excellent . . . But I'm sure you know that."

Campbell, who was clearly prepared for a contentious meeting, looked confused. "Yes," he said. "There are many fine restaurants in Georgetown. I'm glad you like it."

"I certainly do," Sloan assured him, as the premier sat down. "I'm sorry about the planes, the troops, and all that . . . Please rest assured that we have no intention of occupying your country, harming your citizens, or interfering with the running of your government. We could use some assistance where some illegal banking transactions are concerned, however. Once that's been taken care of, we'll be on our way. But let's eat first. There will be plenty of time to talk business later."

Sloan's friendly manner, combined with his assurances, were enough to take the edge off. Campbell seemed to relax, and the ensuing conversation centered on the devastating loss of income from tourism *and* international banking the Caymans had suffered since the meteors fell. And, according to Campbell, the civil war was making a bad situation worse. He wanted to know when the war would end.

The opening was too good to ignore, and Sloan didn't. "The

war will end when the Confederacy surrenders," he said. "Which I believe will happen within the next six months. In the meantime, there are certain financial arrangements that we need to put right. And, if you can find a way to help me, that will serve to strengthen our already positive relationship."

||||||||||||

Campbell was no fool . . . And he had no difficulty translating Sloan's flowery bullshit into real-speak. What the Union president meant was that he could assist the Americans or they would take whatever they wanted. Yes, the UK was supposed to protect the islands, but it was on the other side of the Atlantic. So he was tempted to cave in. But what about his Confederate friends? They'd gone to considerable lengths to support his faltering economy. Because they had large quantities of money stashed in the Caymans? Yes, but some of their representatives seemed to have a genuine affection for the colony as well.

How would the Confederates react if he were to cooperate with Sloan? Not well, Campbell reasoned. And that put him in a bind. Should he remain loyal to his Confederate clients? Or place a risky bet on a Union victory? Perhaps there was a middle course. He could cooperate with Sloan, but drag his feet and hope to continue the positive relationship with the Confederate government. "So," Campbell said. "Tell me more. What 'arrangements' were you referring to?"

||||||||||||

Sloan smiled. He could read Campbell's mind, or thought he could, and liked the way things were going. "I believe you know Oliver Sanders," Sloan said.

"You kidnapped him," Campbell said. "That's what it said in the *New York Times*."

Sloan chuckled. "That's what the article said. But you know Oliver . . . And you know the man is no fool. And when Oliver saw how the war was going, which is to say poorly for the South, he chose to defect. What you read in the *Times* was a cover story and nothing more. But that's just between us, right?"

Judging from the expression on the premier's face, Sloan could see that he was hooked. He wanted proof, though . . . Something to hang his hat on. "Really? How do I know that's true?"

"Oliver's living in Kentucky now," Sloan replied. "I went down to visit him a week ago. He told me about the fishing trip that you took him on. According to Oliver, he caught a two-hundred-pound yellowfin tuna, but that seems hard to believe."

"It was every bit of two hundred pounds," Campbell replied. "That was a very enjoyable day."

The truth was that Sanders had shared the tuna story with another prisoner, who had been quick to share the anecdote with Warden Gladfelter in return for some extra phone calls. Sloan smiled agreeably. "I'm sure it was. Anyway, according to Oliver, he was ordered to pump oil out of my country's petroleum reserves and dump it onto the open market. And each time one of those transactions took place, some money was taken off the top and deposited in bank accounts belonging to President Lemaire and other prominent officials. Guess where those bank accounts are located? That's correct, they're *here*. In your country. And I want that money back. Not for me, not for the Union, but for the United States of America."

Campbell's seafood salad had arrived by then but sat untouched. He took a sip of white wine. "I wasn't aware of that," the premier said. "Or involved in it," he added. "And, now that I understand the issue more clearly, I realize that I can't help you. In order to recover your funds, it will be necessary to sue the officials in our courts and win. At that point, you can approach the appropriate banks and request payment. I would be happy to provide you with a list of reputable lawyers."

Sloan frowned. "Okay, Al . . . I was hoping to do this the nice way. But now I realize that you're a cretin. Call your wife. Tell her that she has ten minutes to take the kids and get out of the house."

Campbell's eyes grew larger. "*Why?*"

"Because we're going to drop a bomb on that motherfucker. Or, if you prefer, you can help pry our money loose. It's your choice, option A or option B. Which one is it going to be?"

"If you drop a bomb on my house, England will view that as an act of war!"

"Where were the Brits when Canada tried to invade my country?" Sloan demanded. "I'll worry about them later. Option A or option B. You choose."

There was a long moment of silence. Campbell appeared to be ill. "I'll take option B."

"An excellent choice!" Sloan said as he raised his glass. "To a short and mutually beneficial relationship! Oh, and by the way, don't try to communicate with your buddies in Houston. We seized control of your communications an hour ago. That includes the submarine cables that connect you with the Eastern Caribbean Fiber System and the UK. It sucks, doesn't it? Finish your salad, Al. We have work to do."

PLAQUEMINE, LOUISIANA

It was the beginning of what was likely to be a long, bloody day, and Mac wondered how it would end. Would she be alive when the dimly seen sun set? Or zipped in a body bag? It could go either way.

After leaving Interstate 10 near Gonzales and traveling west on Highway 30, the convoy entered Plaquemine on Highway 1. It had been a pleasant riverfront town of seven thousand people before the war. Now it was a ghost town filled with deserted buildings, empty streets, and the charred wreckage of a fire that no one had been present to fight.

And the reason for that was apparent. To protect the nearby Bayou Choctaw Strategic Petroleum Reserve, the Confederates had placed thousands of mines in the communities of Plaquemine, Morrisonville, and Crescent. And the strategy had been successful. Before Colonel Walters could proceed, she had to send for mine-clearing vehicles.

Two days passed while the M1 Panther IIs were brought forward. That gave the rebs a lot of time to prepare, but it couldn't be helped. The brigade was forced to settle in, assume defensive positions, and wait.

Finally, on the third day, the Panthers rolled down off their flatbed trucks. It took most of that afternoon to prepare the machines. The results were anything but pretty. Each vehicle consisted of an M1 tank hull, minus the gun turret, which had been replaced by a low-profile lid.

Rollers were mounted on the arms that extended out in front of each tank. The rollers were designed to rise and fall with the terrain and trigger any mines they encountered. Working side by side, the Panthers could clear a two-lane swath of land at a speed of 15 mph. Assuming that the rebs weren't able to stop them with artillery, tanks, or rockets.

Each Panther had a two-person crew. They could ride in the vehicle itself, or control it remotely, via a briefcase-sized CCTV system. And that was the way they chose to proceed.

But clearing a path into the mine-free zone that lay beyond the edge of town was only the first step in what promised to be a difficult process. Assuming the brigade managed to get through the minefield, it would still have to face whatever the Confederacy threw their way *before* they could attack the petroleum reserve. And that wouldn't be easy.

As the Panthers rolled forward, two Strykers followed along behind them. Both were buttoned up for safety's sake, and Mac was riding in the **DOOBY DO**. The Stryker's other passengers included the tank's two-person crew and Mac's RTO, Private Yancy. Sergeant Lang was operating the Panther via the CCTV rig sitting on his lap. Perez was taking a nap.

Earlier, while preparing for the mission, Mac asked Lang to describe how reliable the demining vehicles were. Lang said, "One hundred percent." But Perez, who had been standing slightly behind him, shook her head. So it *could* happen.

If the **DOOBY** ran over an antipersonnel mine, that wouldn't matter too much because Strykers had good armor. But antitank mines? Like an M-15 or an M-19? Either one could blow a track off a Panther or destroy a Stryker. So if the Panthers failed to detonate a large mine, the workday was going to end early.

Mac didn't like being cooped up in a steel box but knew it wouldn't be safe to stand in the forward air-guard hatch, so all she could do was sit and stew while the Confederate mines began to blow. There was a hollow place at the pit of her stomach. "Here we go," Lang said, as a dull thump was heard. "It's showtime!" Lang's remote-control rig consisted of a single joystick, which he pushed forward.

The explosions came in quick succession, and in some cases overlapped each other, as the tanks worked in concert. The **STEEL BITCH** was following the second Panther and hanging back as far as it could. The Stryker's truck commander had to remain inside the remote-control system's 250-foot range, however, or the tank commander would lose control. Metal clanged on metal as shrapnel fell from above.

Stop thinking about that, Mac told herself. *Focus on what you're going to do on the other side of the minefield.* That would depend on what the enemy did, of course . . . But the colonel's orders were clear. Mac had responsibility for seven Strykers and four Marine Corps LAV-25s. Eleven vehicles in all. And her job was to push the rebs back, and keep them back, so the amtracks could crawl forward. Would that be difficult? The answer was obvious.

Suddenly, a *new* sound was added to the now-rhythmic thud of exploding mines. "We have incoming artillery," the truck commander said tightly. "The rebs are aiming for the Panthers—but we're right behind them."

For the first time in her military career, Mac found herself hoping that the enemy gunners were good shots. Because if a 155mm artillery shell landed on top of the **DOOBY DO**, the Stryker would pop like a balloon. Lang must have known that. But the hand on the joystick was rock steady—and Perez had started to snore. Ladylike snores, to be sure, but Mac resented them. She was scared and firmly believed that everyone else should be scared, too. And Yancy *was.* Mac could see it in his eyes. "Call the colonel," she told him. "Tell her that we're taking artillery fire." Walters knew that, of course, but the message would give Yancy something to do and help steady his nerves.

"Well, that sucks," Lang said. "Tank two lost a track . . . We're on our own now."

Lang was wearing a headset that allowed him to communicate with his peer in the other Stryker. And he was correct. The loss of tank two meant the amtracks would be forced to proceed single file rather than two abreast, effectively doubling the time required to squeeze the brigade through the minefield. And who was supposed to hold the rebels off while that took place? Her battalion, that's who. Yancy's eyes were huge. "Let the colonel know," Mac ordered. "And tell the *Steel Bitch* to fall in behind us."

Yancy made the call, listened to the response, and turned back to her. "The colonel says that the Confederate Strykers are coming out to play."

Mac nodded and knew that her truck commanders were listening in. "Tell the colonel that we're going to kick their asses."

The brave words were meant to make Mac's crews feel good. Unfortunately, victory was anything but certain. Not once during Mac's training had any mention been made of how to conduct a Stryker-on-Stryker battle. And there was no reason for it to come up. American forces were the only ones who used Strykers, and since they weren't going to fight each other, why prepare for a situation that wouldn't occur?

It wasn't the first time Mac had considered such a scenario, however. The possibility of such an engagement had occurred to her back in New Orleans during the briefing from Captain Hines. That didn't mean that her outfit was ready, though . . . Not by a long shot. Especially since there had been no opportunity to train with the Marine LAV crews. So there was plenty to fear . . . Including the possibility of failure. Which would cost a lot of lives. Maybe her own. Mac knew her hands were shaking, so she was careful to fold her arms.

"All right," Lang said as he looked up from the CCTV screen. "I think we're through. Hey, Perez! Wake up, damn it . . . We need to inspect the tank. I'm going to be pissed if those bastards dinged my paint."

That was when Mac realized that she hadn't heard any explosions for *what*? A minute or so? And that included the incoming artillery rounds. *Why?* Because the enemy Strykers were entering the area, that's why . . . And the Confederates couldn't fire without running the risk of hitting their own vehicles. It was showtime.

After grabbing her brain bucket and fastening the strap, Mac stuck her head up through the forward air-guard hatch. The air felt cool after the warmth of the Stryker's cargo bay, gunmetal-gray clouds hung low over the northern horizon, and green fields lay all around. It felt good to escape the steel box.

The **DOOBY** had paused so that the tank crew could exit through the back. The ramp came back up as the **STEEL BITCH** pulled alongside. The rest of her Strykers were passing through the minefield and spreading out to either side of her.

"This is Marauder-Six," Mac said. "Kill your IFF (Identification Friend or Foe) systems and switch to the multispectral combat beacons. Friendly vehicles are blue. You can shoot at everything else. Watch your aim, though . . . We can't afford to overshoot, undershoot, or miss. Keep it tight. Over."

Mac heard a flurry of clicks as she turned to scan the area ahead. Confederate Strykers were emerging from the distant tree line—and Mac was reminded of the roles that cavalry played during the first civil war. They'd been used for reconnaissance and for harassing the enemy as they tried to retreat. But above all else, the cavalry had been called upon to fight delaying actions. And that's what the Confederates were doing now.

Based on the fact that the rebs were coming out in a line abreast, Mac figured their CO was planning on a largely static long-range duel in which each formation would try to pound the other into submission. That was stupid. A Stryker's greatest asset was its mobility. And there was no way in hell that Mac was going to sit still while the enemy shot at her. "Lay smoke!" she ordered. "And get in there!" The words were brave enough . . . But her mind was filled with doubt. What if she was wrong about the enemy's intentions? There were no do-overs in war.

Each vehicle was equipped with four M6 smoke dischargers. And since there were four tubes in each discharger, a vic could launch up to sixteen grenades. Mac figured that would be enough to do the job. She made a quick count. The rebs had *fourteen* vics to her eleven! Not the best odds, but what was, was.

A gray fog closed in around the battlefield as the Union Strykers raced toward the rebel line, passed through the gaps between the Confederate vehicles, and turned. That was the plan the TCs had agreed to follow if the battalion was faced with a line abreast. But it was the full extent of what Mac could do. The rest was up to the individual truck commanders, like the corporal in charge of the **DOOBY DO.**

His name was Roy Rogers. His parents thought it was funny. But Rogers had been taking shit for the moniker ever since he entered grade school, and eventually acquired the handle "Cowboy." It suited him well. Part of that had to do with his Gary Cooper good looks. But the nickname referenced Rogers's run-and-gun persona, too, and it matched the situation. Because there wasn't going to be enough time for Mac or anyone else to give Cowboy orders.

Nor would it be possible for Cowboy to choose targets. His gunner's name was Maggie, or "Mags." And because of the thick smoke, Mags would have to use thermal imaging to "see" the vehicles around her, sort them out, and reserve her fire for the enemy.

Under normal conditions, Mags would have been able to use the standard IFF system for that. However, since the reb vics had the *same* IFF system, Mac wasn't sure whether the enemy Strykers would appear as friends or foes. She hoped the "outlaw" multispec beacons would not only provide her people an important edge but prevent friendly-fire incidents, too.

The key to winning the battle would be individual initiative and judgment. Who would prove to be better at that? The rebs? Or her ex-cons and their Marine Corps buddies? They were about to find out. Action was an excellent antidote for the fear that crept in whenever there was nothing to do. But being up top, Mac had nothing to rely on other than what her eyes could see, and was grateful for her goggles as the smoke swirled around her. Suddenly, she was a machine gunner instead of a battalion commander, and that was no easy task.

A Stryker with a 105mm cannon appeared to her right, and knowing that none of her vehicles had a long gun, Mac fired the LMG (light machine gun) at it. The relatively light 5.56X45mm rounds couldn't penetrate the other vehicle's armor, but rebs would hear the bullets ping their hull, and the sound might distract them.

Then Cowboy turned to the left and Mags began to fire the **DOOBY**'s 40mm grenade launcher at a target Mac couldn't see. She could *hear*, though . . . And a hellish symphony it was. Mac heard the crack of grenades exploding, as well as the intermittent chug, chug, chug of multiple .50 caliber machine guns, overlaid with the harsh bang, bang, bang sound produced by the LAVs' chain guns.

The **DOOBY** threw Mac sideways as Rogers made a tight turn. An enemy Stryker appeared out of the smoke with a Confederate flag flying. Was that a matter of pride? Or a way to identify the unit? Mac fired at it, watched the vic veer away, and saw another truck in the distance. It was flying a flag, too . . . So maybe the enemy CO harbored the same concerns she did.

Something slammed into the **DOOBY**'s right flank and lifted the truck up off that set of wheels before gravity prevailed. A 105 round? If so, Mac was lucky to be alive as Cowboy put his boot down. The response was slow. Was that due to the dozer blade mounted up front? Or had the DOOBY been damaged? Mac feared the latter, and Rogers confirmed it. "Two of our right-hand wheels were destroyed, Major . . . So we're limping a bit."

"Do the best you can," Mac told him. "We'll make it."

Because Strykers have eight-wheel drive Mac figured that the DOOBY could continue to mix it up on a limited basis. And the more moving targets the rebs had to deal with, the better.

Mac was forced to duck as a vic pulled alongside and fired its fifty. The big slugs were hammering the hull, and eating their way in, when she heard a muffled explosion. A triumphant shout followed: "*Semper fi*, motherfuckers!"

And when Mac stuck her head up again, she saw why. Because there, in the DOOBY's wake, was a burning Stryker. An LAV was doing victory laps around it as a Marine fired his LMG into the wreckage.

The smoke was drifting away by then . . . And Mac was desperate to see what had taken place. Had the battle been won or lost? Gradually, as DOOBY circled the battlefield, a picture started to emerge. Nine of the enemy machines were little more than burning hulks, and a handful of rebs stood with their hands raised. The rest of the Confederate vehicles were nowhere to be seen and had presumably withdrawn.

That was the good news. The bad news was that two of her vics had been destroyed, two of her soldiers had been wounded, and three were dead. Some machines, like the DOOBY, were badly shot up. Those realities were enough to counteract any feelings of jubilation that Mac might have otherwise felt. "This is Marauder-Six," she said over the radio. "You are the best group of crazy people that ever wore whatever uniform you're wearing. *Hooah!*"

What came back over the radio was a mutual "Hooah," intermixed with "Oorahs" from the Marines. Mac couldn't help but grin. The Marauders might be a badly mismatched bunch, but they were hers, and she was proud.

Mac was kneeling next to Cowboy, and they were inspecting one of the **DOOBY DO**'s badly mangled wheels, when Colonel Walters arrived. Engines roared as Marine amtracks churned past them. Walters was forced to shout in order to be heard. "Good job, Major! I watched the whole thing via our drones. What I could see through the smoke, anyway. Strykers on Strykers! That was a battle for the textbooks."

"My truck commanders were outstanding," Mac replied. "Take Rogers here . . . It turns out that he *can* drive and chew gum at the same time."

Cowboy had a huge wad of pink gum in his mouth. He blew a bubble, and it popped. "Thanks, Major . . . I appreciate the feedback."

Walters laughed. "It looks like your Stryker needs some repairs, Corporal. As for *you*, Major Macintyre, there's no rest for the wicked. I want you and any vehicles that are operable to follow the troops in. Major Corvo will show you where to put them. The rebs had lots of time to prepare. Maybe they'll sit tight, or maybe they'll come out to play. If so, the weapons mounted on your Strykers could make the difference."

"Yes, ma'am," Mac replied. "The LAVs did a great job, by the way . . . Maybe the Marine Corps isn't so bad after all."

Walters grinned. "I'm gratified to hear it. I'll see you later." And with that, she was gone.

Mac ran a quick check, determined that seven of her vehicles were functional, and ordered them to follow the **STEEL BITCH**. She had taken some hits, but her TC swore that she was good to go.

Mac climbed aboard and rode up top as the Stryker passed between two widely separated houses. The LAVs had left deep track marks in the soil, and so all they had to do was follow them. A large retaining pond blocked their path, forcing the trucks to turn and follow the amtracks north.

That led the vehicles to an access road. Mac brought her binoculars up as the **BITCH** turned left. Corvo's amtracks could be seen in the foreground and were splitting into a Y formation that was calculated to envelop the Confederate base.

Beyond the personnel carriers, Mac could see the low-lying oil reserve. Concrete barriers had been set up to slow incoming vehicles, rolls of razor wire had been laid along the bottom of the berm, and a steel gate guarded the entrance. It was going to be a tough nut to crack. Fear began to seep back into her belly again. Fear of dying, fear of failing, and fear of fear.

Planes and or helicopters could have laid waste to the facility in fifteen minutes. But that wasn't going to happen. The brigade had orders to capture the reserve intact, or mostly intact, so that the Union could access the oil stored there as quickly as possible.

Mac heard a boom, followed by the scream of a ranging shot, and saw a column of dirt leap into the air just short of an amtrack. The second phase of the battle had begun.

HOUSTON, TEXAS

General Bo Macintyre sat slumped in the backseat as the black SUV threaded its way through downtown traffic. His phone vibrated every now and then, but Bo chose to ignore the incoming messages in order to focus on an important problem. Lots of problems, actually . . . But only one that kept him up at night. And that was what he perceived to be a lack of will on the part of the people who were in charge of the government.

President Lemaire and his backers had been full of piss and vinegar when the war started. But after some setbacks, and a half year of fighting, it felt as if he was going through the motions. Meanwhile, people were dying. But what if Bo was wrong? What if the president and his staff were gung ho?

So Bo was going to have lunch with Orson Selock, who was not only a friend but Secretary of the Army. They'd gone to West Point together. And if anyone could give him the straight scoop, Selock could. But *would* he?

Selock had been passed over for general, had retired as a colonel, and was working for a government contractor when the war began. Thanks to his military background and a carefully nurtured network of contacts, he'd been named Secretary of the Army.

So what *was* Selock? A soldier at heart? Or had he gone over to the dark side? By which Bo meant civilians who liked to talk the talk but couldn't walk the walk.

The SUV pulled in under the formal portico in front of the Four Seasons Hotel. One of Bo's aides got out to open the door for him. Both were dressed in civilian clothes. "I'll be a while," Bo told her. "Grab some lunch. I'll call when I'm ready to leave."

The major who opened the door was young for her rank and bore a vague resemblance to Victoria. Had that influenced his decision to select her? No, of course not.

The major said, "Yes, sir," and closed the door behind him.

Bo had been to Quattro Restaurant on previous occasions and knew the way. The maître d' welcomed Bo and led him past tall windows and paneled walls to a table located in the back of the dining room. It was large enough to seat four but set for two, and half-hidden by a bushy plant. There was nothing unseemly about the Secretary of the Army having lunch with the Chairman of the Joint Chiefs. But Bo had no desire to advertise it.

After shaking hands and taking their seats, the men spent some time socializing. Selock congratulated Bo on his upcoming marriage to his longtime secretary and on the successful defense of Tower 26. "You kicked Bunny's ass fair and square," Selock proclaimed. "I'll bet she's still feeling the pain."

Then the drinks arrived, and the conversation turned to the crappy weather, Selock's fading golf game, and his son's latest DUI. "The boy's an idiot," Selock finished bleakly. "He's in a line outfit. Maybe the Yankees will kill him for me."

"Or maybe he'll wise up," Bo said dutifully. Although he knew that was extremely unlikely.

The food arrived shortly thereafter and, after a bite or two, Bo began to steer the conversation in the direction he wanted it to go. He had to be careful, however . . . If Selock *had* gone over to the dark side, he might report the conversation to the Secretary of Defense. And while that wouldn't be fatal, it wouldn't be helpful, either. "Tell me something," Bo began. "How would you describe morale?"

"You've seen the polls," Selock replied. "The number of people who approve of the war, and think we're going to win it, fell off when we lost New Orleans. But the majority of our citizens still support the president and what he's doing."

Bo nodded. "Right. But what about higher up? How's the morale within the administration?"

Selock frowned and put his fork down. "What's on your mind, Bo? It isn't like you to weasel word around."

Bo did his best to appear nonchalant. "I'm not as close to such things as you are, Orson. So there's a good chance that I'm wrong.

But I feel as if the overall sense of urgency has fallen off a bit . . . Almost as if certain people have given up."

Selock looked left and right before taking a sip of his drink. "You're very perceptive, Bo . . . Of course you always were. That's one of the reasons you made general.

"Yes, I think our failure to secure a quick victory, followed by our inability to wall the Union off, had a negative impact on executive morale. But the Cayman Island thing put an end to that. The people you're referring to are all in now, and you'll feel the difference soon."

"The Cayman Island thing"? What Cayman Island thing? Bo knew he was onto something, but he had to proceed with care. "Yes," he lied. "I heard whispers. But nothing specific."

Selock nodded. "It's hush-hush, needless to say . . . But certain officials had substantial sums of money stashed in the Caymans. Escape money, if you will, to use if we lost the war.

"But President Sloan put an end to that when he invaded the islands and forced the banks to divest the money in the accounts that belonged to the board of directors, the president, and members of his cabinet. Now, if the Confederacy were to fall, those officials would be SOL."

Bo stared at him. "I see. So what you're saying is that their backs are to the wall. And that means they're going to fight harder."

Selock drained his glass. "Yes. Sloan made a serious mistake."

"Perhaps," Bo agreed. "Tell me something, Orson . . . Did *you* lose some money?"

Selock looked away, waved to a waiter, and held his empty glass up for the man to see. Then he turned back. "Enough shop talk, Bo . . . How 'bout those Astros? They won't have to play the Yankees, thank God."

Bo had his answers. Lemaire and his cronies had been preparing to run, and that included Selock, a man who'd been a warrior once. There was some news to savor, however. The rats were trapped on the sinking ship, and they'd be forced to fight if they wanted to survive. He raised his wineglass. "To the Astros . . . Long may they prosper."

CHAPTER 4

There are known knowns. These are things we know that we know. There are known unknowns. That is to say, there are things that we know we don't know. But there are also unknown unknowns. There are things we don't know we don't know.

—DONALD RUMSFELD

FORT KNOX, KENTUCKY

Sloan entered the executive conference room to discover that a large number of his closest associates were already present. The group included his military attaché, Major Sam McKinney; Secretary of State George Henderson; Secretary of Defense Frank Garrison; and Chairman of the Joint Chiefs Four-Star General Herman Jones. They were seated at a circular table and stood as he entered.

Sloan paused, looked down at the sheet of paper with his schedule on it, and back up again. "Wow, there's a lot of brainpower in this room . . . And I see a lot of serious-looking faces. Please take your seats. Now, what is Operation Exodus?"

There was a scraping of chairs as everyone except McKinney obeyed. He positioned himself next to a screen. Sloan found himself looking at an aerial photo of *what*? A fort? A ghetto? It was impossible to tell. "Operation Exodus concerns 296 Union POWs," McKinney said. "All of whom are being held in Detention Center One, near the town of Ascensión, Mexico."

"Mexico?" Sloan demanded as he sat down. "What the hell are they doing there?"

"That's a good question," McKinney said. "And the answer begins with *this* man."

Sloan saw the visage of a grim-faced man appear on the screen. "As you know," McKinney continued, "General Bo Macintyre is General Jones's peer within the Confederacy's military structure."

Sloan knew him all right . . . Or knew *of* him. Bo Macintyre was Robin Macintyre's father. How could such a wonderful woman be related to such an asshole? Sloan forced himself to concentrate. "Okay, keep going."

The photo of Macintyre was replaced by the likeness of a gaunt brigadier general. "This is General Marcus Lorenzo," McKinney explained. "He reports to General Macintyre—and has responsibility for feeding, housing, and looking after our POWs. And, in keeping with the Libertarian principles that guide the Confederacy, Lorenzo chose to privatize his area of responsibility. And like any good conservative, he took the work to the lowest bidder who, in this case, was located in Mexico. The same country that is currently sending mercenaries to fight for the Confederacy."

Secretary of State Henderson had a jowly face and a compact body. "We submitted numerous protests to the Mexican government," he said. "But they were ignored."

"So the POWs are being held in Ascensión, Mexico," Sloan said slowly. "Where, exactly, is *that*?"

Secretary of Defense Garrison had wispy hair and wore wire-rimmed glasses. He was cleaning them with a handkerchief. "It's about 120 miles southwest of El Paso," he answered. "In an area known for its lawlessness."

"Exactly," McKinney agreed. "In fact, the woman who runs the detention center is a well-known drug smuggler. Her name is Rosa Alvarez Carbone. But she's better known as '*La ángel de la muerte*,' or the Angel of Death. The name stems from both her angelic appearance and the fact that she is responsible for killing at least 182 people, thirty-seven by her own hand.

"So, as you might expect, our POWs have been subjected to all sorts of abuse. Some were killed during a mass-escape attempt, there's no medical care to speak of, and they're starving."

Sloan looked from face to face. "I assume you have a plan."

General Jones had a buzz cut, brown skin, and a chestful of ribbons. "We do," he said gravely.

"I'm all ears," Sloan replied. "Lay it on me."

They did. And Sloan smiled when the presentation was over. "It won't be easy . . . But you're well aware of that. I want our people back."

BAYOU CHOCTAW STRATEGIC PETROLEUM RESERVE

Mac knew she wasn't going to die—and felt a mix of emotions. Happiness, guilt, and relief all battled each other for dominance. After surrounding the Bayou Choctaw Petroleum Reserve, the brigade settled in for a night of psychological warfare. Flares went off at random intervals. Mortar shells fell occasionally. And a cheesy recording of "Yankee Doodle Dandy" blared through portable speakers. Anything to keep the Confederates on edge. Unfortunately, that cut two ways and, after spending the night in a Stryker, Mac was exhausted.

An MRE was followed by a predawn staff meeting with Colonel Walters. And that was when Mac learned that Major Corvo was going to lead all of the troops, hers included, up and over the defensive berm. Or try to anyway . . . Because the outcome was anything but certain.

And that's why Mac *wasn't* going to die, and why she felt guilty about it. Her job was to lead Mac's Marauders, not stand on top of a Stryker and watch the battle like a spectator at a football game.

But Walters was not only insistent but fundamentally correct. Corvo didn't need a spare major looking over his shoulder. So Mac was left to peer through a pair of binoculars as the sun rose behind her, and the infantry advanced. The brigade's redlegs fired the first shots. Their 155mm howitzers were stationed five miles back from the Confederate base, and the first shell produced a rumbling sound as it passed overhead. That was followed by a dull thump, and a column of smoke, as the round exploded somewhere within the enemy compound. More shells followed.

Would the artillery fire destroy the facilities the brigade was supposed to preserve? Maybe. But Walters didn't care if the brass slapped her wrist. Not if the strategy worked. Mac admired the Marine's style. Walters was an asskicker . . . No doubt about that.

The artillery barrage ended as suddenly as it had begun. And, like attacks launched on behalf of countless causes over the last three thousand years, soldiers charged forward. Never mind what kind of weapons they carried. The essence of the assault was no different than Wellington's attack on the city of Badajoz. There had been artillery, a wall, and a storm. Just the thought of it seemed to summon the rain.

Like the French, the Confederates were standing on top of the wall, firing down. Automatic weapons rattled, and grenades exploded, as the Union soldiers surged forward. They were able to take cover behind the concrete traffic barriers, which, ironically enough, had been put in place by the rebs. *I'll bet someone feels stupid now,* Mac thought, as her Strykers and LAVs opened fire on the defenders.

Grenade launchers weren't appropriate for the situation, but the big fifties had a lot of reach, and so did the Marine Corps' chain guns. *Keep their heads down,* Mac thought, as the vic's fifty began to chug. Red tracers drew a line between the **STEEL BITCH** and the top of the wall. And that was important because the Union troops were going to be extremely vulnerable as they made their way up the rain-slicked slope.

And the strategy worked. As Mac panned her binoculars along the top of the berm, not a single head was visible. So Mac felt a new sense of optimism as the soldiers continued to climb. Then she heard what sounded like hundreds of firecrackers going off as flashes of light rippled across the front surface of the slope. Union soldiers were hurled backwards as the rebs detonated dozens of M18AC Claymore antipersonnel mines. Smoke rose like an evil mist. Badly mangled bodies slid downhill as *more* people fought their way up and over them.

Now the heads appeared as the Confederates fired down on the soldiers, and the assault stalled. Mac watched in horror as the attackers were forced to pull back under fire. Stretcher parties rushed forward only to stagger and fall.

There was counterfire though . . . A rocket exploded on top of the wall and sent bodies flying. But it wasn't enough. *The attack is about to stall,* Mac concluded. *No, the attack has stalled. And our wounded are dying.* Mac felt an overwhelming need to do something.

"This is Marauder-Six," Mac said. "All units will continue to provide fire support as they move forward to evacuate the wounded.

Trucks one, two, and three will split left. Four will lead the remaining vics to the right. Let's go. Over."

None of the battalion's Strykers were M1133 Medical Evacuation Vehicles. But all of them could be pressed into service for that purpose. The berm seemed to grow taller as the **STEEL BITCH** got closer to it. The TC was a corporal named Provo. Bullets kicked up geysers of mud all around a stretcher party as Provo came to a stop between the soldiers and the incoming fire. Mac felt a stab of fear as a projectile snapped by her right ear. She shouted into her boom mike.

"This is Marauder-Six . . . Put their heads down!" Then, as if to demonstrate what she meant, Mac aimed bursts of machine-gun fire at the top of the wall.

The fifty began to thump as the **BITCH**'s ramp went down and soldiers hurried to load stretchers into the cargo bay. "Get them to the LZ (landing zone) as fast as you can," Mac ordered. "Seconds count."

Mac removed her headset and jumped to the ground. There were more wounded to care for and not enough medics to go around. For the next twenty minutes, Mac was just another grunt, trudging through the mud and comforting the wounded. All the while waiting for the hammer blow—and the long fall into darkness.

"Don't worry," she told the soldiers. "You'll be fine." Some nodded, and one kid called her "Mom," just before the light faded from his eyes. Unrestrained tears ran down her cheeks as Mac turned away.

By the time the last casualty had been evacuated, and the last body bag had been loaded into an LAV, Mac was physically and emotionally spent. What felt like five pounds of mud clung to each boot as she slogged back through the brigade's perimeter and collapsed next to a wounded private. A bloody bandage was wrapped around his head and his eyes stared at her without any sign of recognition. "Emilia, is that *you*? They killed Tom."

"I'm sorry," Mac told him as she put an arm over his shoulders. The soldier's body shook as he cried. Mac held him until a navy corpsman arrived to lead the Marine away.

She wanted to stay there and let the cold rain wash her face, but there were other soldiers to tend to. *Her* soldiers. And they needed her.

Mac spent the next hour tracking the Marauders down, doing what she could to comfort them and restore morale. Most were okay, but some had been killed, and others wounded in ways that would never heal.

Mac was on her way back to the tent that had been assigned to her when she saw Colonel Walters. The Marine officer was sitting under a tarp, staring at the patch of mud between her boots. "Colonel?"

Walters looked up. Her face was drawn, and for the first time since they'd met, Mac saw despair in the other woman's eyes. "Major . . . Thank you for pitching in to help the wounded. I won't forget."

Mac felt a lump form in her throat and managed to swallow it. Here, even in defeat, Walters was doing her job. "Permission to speak freely, ma'am?"

Walters pointed to a crate. "Sure . . . Take a load off."

Mac sat down. "It wasn't your fault, ma'am."

"Thanks," Walters replied. "But that's bullshit. I should have thought of Claymores. I should have, but I didn't. People died. End of story."

Mac nodded. "Okay, but ask yourself this . . . Did I think of Claymores? Did Major Corvo alert you to that possibility? There was no negligence involved, Colonel. And, until an all-knowing commanding officer shows up, the job is yours. I, for one, wouldn't have it any other way."

Mac saw what might have been a look of gratitude in the other woman's eyes. "Thanks, Robin, that means a lot. You look like hell, by the way . . . Try to set a better example for the troops."

Mac grinned, stood, and delivered a textbook-perfect salute. "Yes, ma'am. I'll do my best." And with that, she did an about-face and left.

The rest of the day was spent encouraging the mechanics who were trying to complete field repairs on the vics, requisitioning more of everything, and plowing through all of the usual paperwork.

But throughout it all, there in the back of Mac's mind, a simple question waited. Was there a way to enter the rebel base without taking so many casualties? Could paratroopers do the job? What about some sort of special ops mission? Or attacking the berm with enormous tractors?

Each scenario had advantages, but each had weaknesses as well, like the tractor concept. Sure, earthmovers could dig a path through the berm. *If* the rebels allowed them to do so. But they wouldn't. What to do? The problem continued to plague Mac as she crossed a sea of mud to the area where her vehicles were parked.

The sun was setting, and Sergeant Lang was sitting on the front deck of his mine-clearing tank, smoking a pipe and reading a book. It was a peaceful scene at the end of a very bloody day. And as Mac walked past, something clicked. The result was an idea. But what kind of an idea? A good idea? Or a bad one?

Mac turned, stepped over a puddle, and arrived below the point where Lang was seated. He saw her and stood. "As you were," Mac said. "I'm sorry to interrupt, but I could use some help."

"Sure," Lang replied. "What's up?"

"I have an idea," Mac told him. "But I don't know if it's feasible. I'd like to pitch it to you. Then, depending on what you think, I might take it to the CO."

Lang nodded. "Shoot."

"I want an honest evaluation," Mac cautioned.

"You'll get it," Lang promised.

So Lang listened as Mac explained what she had in mind. And once she was finished, he nodded. "It would take some prep. But if we set it up the right way, I think it will work."

"You're sure?"

"Hell, no," Lang answered with a grin. "But I think it's worth a try."

"Okay," Mac said. "Let's run it up the flagpole and see if anyone salutes."

Colonel Walters was in a meeting when the twosome arrived at the brigade's HQ tent. That left them with no choice but to sip bad coffee and wait. The occasional pop of a flare could be heard, along with the faint strains of "Yankee Doodle Dandy," and an occasional rifle shot. The snipers were working late.

It was well after 2000 hours by the time Walters was free to speak with them. "So," Walters said, as her guests perched on stools that had been "liberated" from a nearby house. "I understand you have a proposal. Fire away."

"We need a way to enter the Confederate compound while suffering only minimal casualties," Mac began. "And maybe we have it. What if we took one of Sergeant Lang's mine-clearing tanks, mounted a two-thousand-pound bomb over the front rollers, and pushed the payload up to those steel doors?"

Mac watched the idea sink in. Walters was tired, so it took her a moment to process it. But it wasn't long before her expression started to brighten. "Holy shit! I like it . . . But the explosion would destroy the tank. And what about the driver?"

"I'll be in a Stryker," Lang told her. "Operating the tank by remote control and following along behind it."

"That's right," Mac agreed. "And once we blow the door, my gunner will fire *over* the remains of the tank and into the compound as troops rush the entrance."

Mac could see the wheels turning as Walters began to expand on the idea. "Maybe we'll use *two* bombs . . . Let's see what the experts say. And we can launch a feint at the west side of the berm while the tank goes in . . . That should draw some of the bastards away from the gate."

Mac grinned. "So, it's a go?"

"Hell yes, it's a go. Make it happen."

Thus began a long, sleepless night. There was a lot of work to do. It was necessary to stretch a huge tarp over the tank to conceal it from rebel drones, Captain Wu had to obtain the necessary bombs from the air force, and a team of mechanics were ordered to fabricate the bulletproof boxes that the explosive charges would ride in. Because if the bombs were detonated early, the entire effort would be for nothing.

Mac collapsed on her cot just after 0300 and got up three hours later. After a quick trip to the latrine, a mug of coffee, and a can of peaches, it was time to inspect the tank.

Twin boxes were mounted over the roller assemblies. What would the Confederates make of them? Would they assume the boxes contained weights? Which were part of a strategy to detonate mines? Or would one of them divine the truth? Fortunately, it didn't matter so long as the modified M1 managed to complete its mission.

Other changes were apparent as well. Messages had been spray painted onto the tank. They included, "To the Confederacy with love," "For Mindy," and "Payback is a bitch."

The nameless machine had been transformed into a vessel for the brigade's sorrow and hate. Was that a good thing? What if the attempt failed? But it was too late for such concerns. Colonel Walters had a weapon, and she was going to use it.

The area was suffused with a sense of grim purpose as engines started, sergeants ran last-minute gear checks on their soldiers, and Mac made her way up the ramp and into the **STEEL BITCH**. She couldn't stand in the air-guard hatch this time. Not initially.

As soon as the modified M1 tank appeared and began to make for the gate, the rebs would throw everything they had at it. And once the Abrams blew, shrapnel would fly every which way. Like it or not, Mac would have to sit in the cargo compartment and sweat the trip out.

Sergeant Lang was already aboard, as was Perez, who was busy painting her nails. Mac couldn't figure out if Perez was brave or simply crazy. One thing was for sure, however . . . The army didn't allow soldiers of either sex to have painted fingernails. But, given the fact that Perez might be dead within half an hour, Mac decided to cut her some slack.

Provo and her gunner were running systems checks as Private Yancy entered the cargo bay. Mac knew that he'd been sent to ensure that Walters could communicate with the Stryker even if its com system went down.

"I brought you this," Yancy said shyly as he offered a thermos. "It's full of coffee. Just the way you like it."

That was when Mac realized that Yancy had a crush on her. Was it a case of hero worship? Or did the RTO have a thing for older women? It didn't matter. "Thanks, Yance . . . That was very thoughtful. Some caffeine would hit the spot."

Yancy looked pleased, and Mac was sipping coffee when the order came down. "Thunder-Six to Marauder-Six. Go get 'em. Over."

Mac made eye contact with Yancy. "Tell her we're on it." Then, after turning to Lang, "You heard the lady . . . It's time to rock and roll." Lang nodded and went to work.

There was a pause while the M1 got under way. Then, once the correct interval had been established, Provo put the **STEEL BITCH** into motion. Both vehicles were traveling at about 10 mph, which meant that it would take fifteen minutes to reach the oil reserve and approach the gate.

Time seemed to stretch as the modified tank churned through the mud. *How many times?* Mac wondered. *How many times will I do this before my number comes up? I hope it's quick.*

Then bullets began to ping the M1's armor, mortar rounds fell, and geysers of soil flew up into the air. Lang was talking to his tank. "You can make it, hon . . . A little to the left, that's right babe, you're looking good."

What were the rebs thinking? Mac wondered. Maybe they assumed that the Abrams was going to be used as a self-propelled battering ram. And that wasn't far from the truth. But regardless of the M1's specific purpose, the enemy knew the machine was a sixty-ton threat, so they threw everything but the kitchen sink at it. Machine-gun fire raked the hull and AT4 rockets flashed as they struck. But, unless they managed to destroy a track, there was nothing the Confederates could do to stop the behemoth.

Rank hath privilege. And even though Provo might not appreciate Mac's presence, she went forward to peer over the truck commander's shoulder. From that vantage point, Mac could see the back end of the tank as well as the looming wall beyond. The rebs were starting to panic by that time, and most of the M1 was obscured by smoke as the incoming fire enveloped it. "We're close," Provo said. "So far so good."

Mac turned and went back to sit next to Lang. An unlit pipe jutted from his mouth as he made a small correction to the M1's course. By looking at his screen, Mac could see every scratch and ding in the steel doors that protected the rebel base. The tank stopped. "I have contact," Lang announced.

"Blow it," Mac ordered, and he did. Even though Mac was inside a Stryker, the explosion was still extremely loud. The **STEEL BITCH** rocked as the pressure wave hit her, shrapnel clanged against the hull, and Provo produced a whoop of joy.

Perez blew on her nails. "There goes seven million dollars," she observed coolly. "I hope it was worth it."

Mac stepped up onto the seat, opened the hatch, and stuck her head through the hole. It *had* been worth it. To her, anyway. The twin explosions had reduced the once-powerful M1 tank to a burning hulk. "Hey, Kolo," Mac said. "Fire through the smoke . . . Keep them back."

The fifty started to chug as troops surged past both sides of the Stryker. Then Kolo had to let up as the soldiers poured through the shattered gate and into the compound beyond.

Most of the Confederate heavy weapons were pointing *out*. And there was very little time in which to turn them around as Union troops began to shoot the gunners from behind. The rebs fought bravely, but the effort came too late. The Confederates had no choice but to surrender. Mac felt a sense of relief.

She entered the compound on foot. There wasn't much to look at other than some damaged storage tanks, a shattered shed, and a lot of mangled pipes. Bodies lay where they had fallen. As for the oil that so many people had died for, that was somewhere under her feet. Was it worth the suffering on both sides? Mac hoped so.

||||||||||||

An hour later, Mac was seated in her tent, finalizing a letter to a dead soldier's parents, when Colonel Walters arrived. Mac began to rise. Walters said, "As you were," and lowered herself into a rickety lawn chair. Mac's miniscule staff withdrew. "I'm sorry to interrupt," Walters said. "But no good deed goes unpunished. And you've been good lately."

Mac forced a smile. "Uh-oh, what's up?"

"Major Corvo's people found a list of the soldiers assigned to the base, and three rebs are missing."

"There were lots of body parts lying around the compound," Mac said. "Maybe they add up to three people."

Walters shook her head. "No, I'm positive that they ran. And that's one of the reasons why we won. The CO, the XO, and a doctor left their people to die."

Mac winced. "That's terrible . . . But why do we care?"

"Because they took all of the records with them. That includes how much oil was pumped, where it was going, and the name of the person who authorized the transaction. All of which would be useful after the war."

Mac could imagine it. The trials would involve hundreds of defendants and last for years. "Roger that. Thanks for sharing. I hope Corvo finds them."

Walters chuckled. "Nice try, Macintyre . . . But this plate of shit has your name on it."

"No offense, ma'am . . . But that's crazy. How would I find the bastards? They could be anywhere by now."

A smile appeared on Walters's face. "I have good news for you, Major . . . We have a very good idea where Lieutenant Colonel LeMay and his officers are."

"LeMay was the CO?"

"Yes, he was. And when you blew the west gate, he and his buddies fought their way out through the *east* gate. They were in a Stryker, and quite possibly headed for a town called Frogsong."

"'*Frogsong*'? Seriously?"

"Seriously. That's where LeMay's family farm is located. It was a plantation prior to the first civil war and, according to Lieutenant Everson, it's partially fortified. It seems LeMay is a hard-core every-man-for-himself Libertarian. So grab some sleep, gear up, and go to Frogsong. I want those records. Everson agreed to accompany you."

Mac groaned. "Oh, goody . . . A POW to keep track of."

"Stop whining," Walters replied. "It sets a bad example."

Mac made a face. "Yes, ma'am."

Walters turned to go and turned back again. "One more thing."

"Yes?"

"I put you in for a distinguished service medal." Then she was gone.

Mac was tired but curious as well. So after consuming most of an MRE, she went looking for Lieutenant Everson. Much to her surprise, the Confederate officer was being held with the other POWs in a makeshift jail. The "pen," as the MPs referred to it, was located inside the recently liberated compound. It consisted of a double-wide trailer that had originally been used as an office, plus some chain-link fencing scavenged from another part of the facility, and rolls of razor wire that had been on top of the berm.

Mac's reaction stemmed from the fact that Everson was being held with the other rebs. They were bound to be at least somewhat cognizant of the fact that he had been cooperating with their captors, and that being the case, he was likely to be regarded as a traitor. Except that he wasn't. And the reason for that became clear when Everson was brought out to meet her.

The officer had sandy-colored hair, freckles, and slightly protruding ears. The salute was parade-ground perfect. "Lieutenant Mark Everson, ma'am . . . Confederate Army. May I make a request?"

"That depends on what it is," Mac replied. "I'm Major Macintyre."

"Yes, I know," Everson replied. "Everyone does. If you have no objections, I would like to speak to you next to the fence. So my soldiers can hear what's said."

That *was* a surprise, but it made sense. Everson was operating in the open, which implied that the other prisoners knew and approved of what he was doing. Why were they willing to cooperate? Because Lieutenant Colonel LeMay had betrayed them, that's why.

"Sure," Mac replied. "Let's see if the MPs can round up some chairs. I'm glad it isn't raining."

Once two beat-up lawn chairs were in place, Mac and Everson sat down only inches from the cyclone fence. Everson took a moment to introduce the delegation of five Confederate soldiers who had volunteered to listen and share what they heard with the other prisoners.

"Okay," Mac said, once the preliminaries were taken care of. "We're here to discuss how to locate and capture a deserter named Lieutenant Colonel LeMay. Tell me everything you think I should know. My task force will depart in the morning."

The language was necessarily formal given the unique nature of the situation and made no mention of Mac's *real* mission, which was to recover the records that Colonel Walters had described. As the meeting came to an end, Mac thanked the Confederates and asked if they were getting enough to eat.

After being assured that they were, Mac went back to her tent, where she collapsed on her cot and fell asleep. It felt as if only minutes had passed when the alarm sounded seven hours later. After a frigid shower, followed by two mugs of coffee and a chicken noodle MRE, Mac was ready to depart.

Marine Lieutenant Maureen Collins and the rest of Mac's team were waiting next to the team's vehicles. The force consisted of Collins, a squad of Marines, and an equal number of soldiers under

Staff Sergeant Mick Preston. There were eighteen people in all. The plan was to split them up between two Strykers and two Marine LAV-25s.

After introducing herself to the troops, and explaining the mission, Mac asked Collins and Preston to join her as she inspected each vehicle. Knowing that the unit might have to fend for itself for up to five days, Mac wanted to ensure that Task Force Longarm had plenty of everything, with an emphasis on food, ammo, and fuel. And thanks to good planning by Collins and Preston, Mac could find very little to complain about.

At that point, it was time to mount up, drive to the holding pen, and sign for Everson. Mac chose to put the rebel officer in the **STEEL BITCH** with her and assigned two privates to keep an eye on him.

After providing Provo with some preliminary directions, Mac sat next to Everson in the cargo compartment. A map was spread out in front of them. "Show me where we're going," Mac instructed.

"Frogsong is here," Everson said, as a grubby index finger stabbed the map. Mac saw that he was pointing to a bend in the Mississippi River located north and west of Baton Rouge. That put the community in the so-called disputed zone. Meaning the stretch of river that the Union didn't fully control yet. And based on her experiences up around Vicksburg, Mac knew that could mean trouble. The key was to get in, grab what she needed, and get out quickly.

According to what Everson had told her, LeMay was likely to go home because he couldn't rejoin the army. Not without explaining why he wasn't dead or being held captive in a Union POW camp. As for how Everson came to know about Frogsong, that stemmed from the fact that he and some of his fellow officers had been guests at the farm a month earlier, when Mrs. LeMay held her annual cotillion. War be damned.

The task force had to clear multiple checkpoints as it passed through Baton Rouge. There hadn't been a lot of fighting there as far as Mac could tell, and that was a good thing.

Highway 61 took them north and slightly to the west. Traffic was light, the weather was relatively good, and all Mac had to do was enjoy the view as they rolled through a succession of small towns. Then came verdant farmland, which was dotted with well-kept houses and barns. Mac looked back every once in a while and was pleased to see that the other vehicles were maintaining the proper intervals.

About an hour outside of Baton Rouge, Everson told Provo to turn off the highway and onto a country road. That was the point where the possibility of trouble increased. Union forces were in firm control of the highways. But the areas to either side of them? They were up for grabs.

And there was another threat as well. It didn't seem likely given the circumstances. But what if Everson was flat-out lying? And more than that, leading the task force into a trap? It was a possibility that Mac and Walters had discussed. So unbeknownst to Everson, a Predator drone was scouting the route ahead. Lieutenant Collins was responsible for maintaining contact with the operator—and would let Mac know if there were signs of trouble.

But there weren't any alerts as the Union vehicles ventured out into the countryside. "This is Longarm-Six," Mac said. "We're in the zone. Keep a sharp lookout. Over."

Mac heard a flurry of clicks before ducking down into the cargo area below. The rest of the passengers turned to look at her. "So," Mac said, as she sat down. "We're getting close. What's next?"

"We're going to pass through the town of Frogsong," Everson replied. "It was founded by ex-slaves immediately after the first civil war. Then we'll enter the farm. According to what I was told during my visit, it's about half the size of the family's original holdings. But it still includes something like a thousand acres of land and swamp."

"Okay, and then?"

"Then we'll drive to the center of the farm. Union troops burned the original mansion to the ground. When the war ended, Colonel LeMay's great-grandfather built a new home on an island in the middle of Snake Bayou where, in Mrs. LeMay's words, 'the Yankees couldn't get at it.'"

"We'll see about that," Mac said dryly. "So LeMay is on the island. How can we reach it?"

"There's an old drawbridge," Everson replied. "But the colonel is likely to raise it. Maybe we can locate some boats."

Both of the LAV-25s were amphibious, and could "swim" out to the island, so long as there was a beach to launch from. But Mac saw no need to explain that and didn't. She went forward to stand in the hatch again.

The vic passed dilapidated houses from time to time, along with empty fruit stands and a run-down church. Then the column entered Frogsong. There weren't many people on Main Street, and those who were stood and stared. Mac figured they hadn't seen much of the war and weren't sure who the vehicles belonged to.

Judging from the brick buildings that lined both sides of Main Street, Frogsong had been a bustling place at one time. But those days were over. At least half the stores were empty and hung with FOR SALE signs. The sidewalks were sagging, weeds grew in the neglected street planters, and the clock on the bank was more than four hours off.

After passing a defunct Ford dealership, the task force entered the leafy tunnel formed by two rows of ancient oak trees. The passageway delivered the convoy to a formal gate with an overarching sign: FROGSONG FARM. The soldiers had arrived.

The gravel road went past a rusty tractor and a tumbledown barn before turning north. Mac caught a glimpse of the Mississippi off to the left but lost sight of the river as thick trees blocked the view. Rays of sunlight streamed down through broken clouds to splash the land with pools of liquid gold. *No wonder the LeMay family loves this place,* Mac thought. *I would, too.*

The road narrowed as water appeared on the right. Snake Bayou? Probably. And that meant the task force could run into trouble at any moment. LeMay had a lot of employees according to what Everson had told her, some of whom were so-called swamp rats, and excellent shots.

That's what Mac was thinking about when she spotted the vehicles parked up ahead. There were cars, pickup trucks, and a bus. People were milling around but none appeared to be armed. It wasn't what Mac expected to see, and she told Provo to pull over. Then she asked Yancy for his mike. "This is Longarm-Six actual. We're pulling over. Gunners will remain at their stations. Longarm-One, Longarm-Four, and I will go forward to check the situation out. Longarm-Five will be in command while I'm gone. Maintain situational awareness. Over."

The back ramp was down by the time Mac dropped down into the cargo compartment, and Sergeant Preston was waiting outside. "Bring three soldiers," Mac told him. "Whoever you'd like to have around you if the shit hits the fan."

With her M4 at the ready, Mac led them up the road. A well-kept cemetery bordered the road on the left. It was surrounded by a wrought-iron fence on which wreaths of flowers had been hung. A man in a black suit was helping an elderly woman out of an ancient Cadillac. Mac paused to speak with him. "Excuse me. I'm Major Macintyre, Union Army. What's going on here?"

The man had short black hair, dark skin, and a dignified manner. "Welcome to Frogsong, Major . . . I'm Mayor Cummings. This is my mother, Natalie. We came for the funeral."

"May I ask who died?" Mac inquired, as people entered the cemetery.

"Of course," Cummings answered. "We're here to say good-bye to Colonel LeMay. This was his farm."

LeMay was dead? Mac could hardly believe it. "What happened? Did he have a heart attack?"

"Oh, no," Cummings replied. "He deserted, and Mrs. LeMay shot him. Then she planned the funeral."

Mac stared at him. "You're serious?"

"Yes, ma'am."

"So, Mrs. LeMay is in jail?"

"No, ma'am," Cummings answered. "The sheriff says the army should deal with it. He means the Confederate Army, but they left the area. Maybe you can handle it. Would you like to meet Mrs. LeMay?"

"The locals don't want to charge her," Everson observed. "They think Mrs. LeMay did the right thing."

Mac knew that her father would agree. And, because she was his daughter, she had similar feelings. Would *she* shoot a deserter? No. Maybe. She wasn't sure. "Thank you, Mayor. Please lead the way."

The Union soldiers followed Cummings through the gate and up the aisle, which, according to the names on the monuments, served to divide the LeMays from everyone else. They included in-laws, servants, and a Great Dane named Duke.

And there, at the end of the corridor, about fifty folding chairs had been set up. And as the mayor arrived, a woman in a knee-length black dress came forward to greet him. "Mayor Cummings! How nice of you to come! And Mrs. Cummings . . . I do hope you brought some of your famous peach pie for the wake. It's a pity, isn't it? The peach crop was only half what it should have been. Peach trees don't like waterlogged soil.

"And Lieutenant Everson! What a wonderful surprise. That was such a beautifully written note that you sent us. Please allow me to apologize for the colonel's actions. His father is buried right over there, and I can hear him rolling over! There's no excuse for cowardice, none at all, and I'm sure the Lord will explain that to John when they meet in heaven."

Mrs. LeMay's bright blue eyes were alight with patriotic fervor, or was it madness? Regardless of that, Mac could feel the power of Mrs. LeMay's personality as the other woman turned to confront her. "I don't believe we've met, Major. Union Army, I presume?"

"Yes," Mac replied. "My name is Macintyre. I was sent to find your husband."

"Well, mission accomplished," Mrs. LeMay said as she directed a nod toward the ornate casket. "He's right there." The coffin was sitting on two sawhorses draped with bunting. "Macintyre you say . . . I met a general named Macintyre about three months ago. Are you related?"

"He's my father."

"And you're fighting for the *North*? How extraordinary. That must be very difficult for him."

"I wouldn't know," Mac replied. "We haven't spoken to each other in a long time."

Mac cleared her throat. "Please accept my apologies, ma'am, but I need to look in the casket. More than that, we'll have to take photographs and a tissue sample."

Mrs. LeMay's eyes grew larger. "You can't be serious."

"Oh, but I am," Mac insisted. "For all I know, that casket is filled with rocks, and your husband is at home sipping bourbon."

Everson looked at Mac with a newfound sense of respect. "I never thought of that."

Mrs. LeMay made no attempt to conceal her disgust. "Daddy was right . . . Yankees *are* pigs. Go ahead. Do what you will. I have no choice, do I?"

"No, you don't," Mac agreed. "And it will be necessary to search your home as well."

Mrs. LeMay turned away. "Take my arm, Natalie. You've been standing for too long. I have a nice chair waiting for you. Would you like a glass of water?"

Mac looked at Sergeant Preston. "Open the casket."

The noncom obeyed. And, as the lid was lifted, a body was revealed. It was that of a middle-aged man dressed in a blue suit. A blue-edged hole marked the exact center of his pale forehead. Mac turned to Everson. "Well? Is that Colonel LeMay?"

Everson nodded. "Yes, ma'am. That's him all right."

Mac turned to Preston. "Take photos and cut his left ear off."

Preston was aghast. "You're kidding?"

Mac frowned. "Why don't people believe the things I say? No, I'm not kidding. Stand with your back to the crowd so people can't see what you're doing."

To Preston's credit, he was fast. Once the photos had been taken, he cut LeMay's left ear off and wrapped a battle dressing around it. The package formed a bulge in a cargo pocket. "Okay," Mac said. "Let's return to the vehicles."

It seemed as if Mrs. LeMay's anger was contagious, because the soldiers were on the receiving end of some nasty looks as they exited the cemetery. "What about Mrs. LeMay?" Everson inquired. "Aren't you going to arrest her?"

"The colonel got what he deserved," Mac said, without looking at him. "We'll let the sheriff handle it."

The **STEEL BITCH** preceded the other vehicles to the turnaround at the end of the road. Three vehicles were parked there, including a Stryker that bore Confederate markings. The one LeMay used to escape the battle? Of course.

And the fact that LeMay had chosen to leave it at the turnaround suggested that it was too heavy for the wooden drawbridge. Or LeMay thought so, and Mac saw no reason to question his judgment.

With that in mind, Mac left half of her tiny command at the parking area, with Lieutenant Collins in command, and led the rest of them across the bridge. The house was a stately two-story affair, complete with white columns and a sweeping porch.

The front door was unlocked, and when Sergeant Preston pushed it open, a bell jangled. That brought a woman in a maid's uniform out from somewhere deep within the house. She frowned. "This is Colonel LeMay's home! You have no business here. Get out."

"I'm sorry," Mac told her. "We won't be here long. Lyons, take this woman into custody. Sergeant, search the house. You know what we're looking for. I'll check the study."

The office was to the left off the foyer. It was furnished with an ancient desk, walls hung with memorabilia, and shelves loaded with books. It took Mac less than a minute to locate a briefcase that contained a laptop, a thick sheaf of Excel spreadsheets, and a variety of other documents pertaining to LeMay's battalion.

Mac placed all of it in a cardboard box, which she carried out into the hall, where the angry maid was waiting. Sergeant Preston looked out of place as he descended the broad staircase. A couple of soldiers followed. "There's nothing of interest upstairs, ma'am."

Mac nodded. "Let's haul ass before people arrive for the wake."

"Roger that," Preston said enthusiastically. "They might come after the ear."

The trip back to the Choctaw Oil Reserve went smoothly. Not a shot was fired. *Maybe,* Mac thought, *they'll send us north to keep the peace in a city like Vicksburg. Or, better yet, leave the battalion where it is. A vacation so to speak . . . While the war plays itself out.* The idea pleased her, and Mac smiled.

CHAPTER 5

Who Dares, Wins

—MOTTO OF THE BRITISH SPECIAL AIR SERVICE (SAS)

FORT KNOX, KENTUCKY

Sloan was seated at his desk staring at page 12 of a tasking order titled: "Operation Exodus." He'd read every word of it three times. More than that, he'd studied the text looking for anything that didn't make sense or might be missing. Like the extra helicopter that could have made the critical difference during the Iran hostage-rescue attempt in April of 1980.

Eight helicopters had been sent to the first staging area, but only five arrived in good condition. One developed hydraulic problems, a second was exposed to a cloud of extremely fine sand, and a third had a cracked rotor blade. Or what *might* have been a cracked rotor blade.

During the planning stage, it was decided to abort the mission if fewer than six helicopters remained operational, even though it was agreed that four aircraft would have been sufficient to carry out the mission. But when military commanders asked President Carter for permission to abort, he agreed.

Then, as the rescue team prepared to depart, a helicopter crashed into a transport loaded with military personnel and jet fuel. The resulting inferno destroyed both aircraft and killed eight servicemen. It was the sort of disaster that Sloan feared.

But no, the president told himself. *This mission is risky, but it's well resourced.* Did that mean it was a slam dunk? Of course not. There were lots of variables, not the least of which was the way that Mexico's government might respond. Maybe they didn't care what happened to the so-called Angel of Death and her private prison. Or maybe they did and would decide to take offense when sovereignty was violated. That was one of the reasons why Sloan was hesitant to sign the order.

The other reason had to do with the person that his advisors agreed was best qualified to lead the mission: army major Robin Macintyre. Sloan was in love with Mac. Or *believed* he was in love with her, even though they'd never been on a date or shared a kiss. And *if* he signed the order, and *if* his signature resulted in Mac's death, Sloan knew he would never forgive himself.

But if he *didn't* send her, and the rescue attempt failed because of poor leadership by another officer, what would become of the POWs? Slowly, and with great reluctance, Sloan scrawled his name on the sheet of paper.

THE BAYOU CHOCTAW STRATEGIC PETROLEUM RESERVE

They came for Mac in the middle of the night. As a dark figure entered her tent, he ran into the waist-high string that pulled a coffee can full of rocks off the top of an upended crate and dumped them onto the plywood floor.

The ensuing clatter was more than enough to wake Mac. She was trapped inside of her sleeping bag as she rolled off the cot, hit hard, and brought the pistol up. The red dot wobbled across the man's chest. His voice was desperate. "Don't shoot!"

"Why not?" Mac inquired as she kicked the bag off.

"Because if you shoot him, I'll have a lot of paperwork to do," Colonel Walters replied. A boyish-looking lieutenant was pinned in the glare of her flashlight as she entered the tent. "I told him to wait for me, but he didn't," Walters added. "They get dumber every day."

The red dot vanished as Mac got to her feet. She was dressed in a baseball shirt and a pair of running shorts. The air was cold, and Mac shivered as she looked from the lieutenant to Walters. "What the hell is going on?"

"The boy genius arrived on a helicopter twenty minutes ago," Walters said. "He has orders for you and, as far as I can tell, they're legit."

The intruder had lowered his hands by then and was struggling to regain some measure of dignity. "I'm Lieutenant Baker," he said stiffly. "I'm sorry about barging in . . . I didn't realize . . ."

"Get out," Mac said. "I'll talk to you outside."

Walters laughed as Baker left. "I wonder if he peed his pants."

"I damned near peed mine," Mac said as she kicked the shorts off. "Why couldn't they send orders down through the chain of command?"

"I asked," Walters replied. "And Baker told me that I don't need to know. He's from the Joint Special Operations Command, which would suggest that some kind of spookery is afoot. And you were chosen to take part in it."

"But I don't *want* to be part of it," Mac said as she pulled her pants up.

"Nobody cares what we want," Walters replied. "If they did, I would be allowed to retain your services. You'd make a halfway-decent Marine."

"Only *halfway* decent?" Mac inquired as she tied her bootlaces.

"You don't say the word 'fuck' frequently enough to qualify as a *real* Marine."

"I'll work on that," Mac said as she put her jacket on. "Right after I find out what the fuck is going on."

"That's better," Walters said agreeably.

Baker was waiting outside. He gave Mac an envelope. "Your orders, ma'am."

"To do *what*?"

"You have been temporarily assigned to the Joint Special Operations Command. That's all I can tell you because that's as much as I know. Please pack your gear. A plane is waiting for you in New Orleans."

"That's it? There's nothing more?"

Baker nodded. "Yes, ma'am."

Mac turned to Walters. "What about my battalion?"

"I'll try to hold it together while you're gone," Walters replied.

There were all sorts of instructions that Mac wanted to give her subordinates, and it would have been nice to say good-bye. Walters would try to keep the outfit intact, but *could* she? The brigade was a temporary entity, so anything was possible.

But orders were orders. And there was nothing Mac could do but go into the tent and pack. She'd done a lot of packing over the last few months and gradually reduced her belongings to the bare minimum. All that remained was her sleeping bag, two sets of camos, and her combat gear. Everything fit into a large duffel bag. Mac lowered the TAC vest over her head, put her helmet on, and was ready to go. It was second nature to grab the M4 on the way out. Walters gave her an awkward hug. "Take care, Robin . . . I'll see you soon."

Mac hoped that was true as she followed Baker to a Black Hawk helicopter. He tossed her bag up to the crew chief and stood to one side. Once inside, she sat where the crew chief told her to, which was all the way in back, facing the cockpit.

Mac held her M4 muzzle down as she listened to the engines wind up. The helicopter wobbled as it left the ground, steadied, and sped away. The doors had been removed, and Mac was thankful for her jacket, as a rush of cold air pummeled her body. A scattering of lights was visible below as the helo continued to climb. The city of New Orleans glowed in the distance. How many people had chosen to ignore the official blackout? Damned near all of them, judging from appearances.

Mac felt lonely . . . And frightened. Where was she going? And *why*? She was like a cog in a machine too large to comprehend. A younger her would have been excited. But a lot of people had died since then, and Mac was tired. She closed her eyes. Faces came and went. Most of them belonged to ghosts.

It was a short flight, and when the Black Hawk landed, Mac realized that the Louis Armstrong International Airport was operating under military control. That made sense since the North and South were still fighting for air supremacy, and it wouldn't be safe for commercial flights to come and go.

The helicopter skimmed past two tubby transports before landing next to a sleek Learjet. No sooner had the wheels touched down than Baker threw her duffel bag to a dimly seen person on the tarmac. Mac thanked the crew chief before jumping down onto the ground. And there, waiting for her, was a friendly face.

The first time Mac had met Major Sam McKinney was in Richton, Mississippi, where President Sloan's attempt to establish an airhead had gone terribly wrong. Her company of Strykers had been sent south to rescue as many survivors as possible. McKinney had been Sloan's military attaché—although "mentor" might have been a more accurate title.

But now Major McKinney was sporting the silver oak leafs of a lieutenant colonel. "Welcome to New Orleans, Major," he said. "I wish we could go out and grab a good meal, but we don't have time."

Mac smiled as she shook his hand. "Congratulations, sir. I'm glad they made an honest 05 out of you."

"Rank comes quickly during a war," McKinney observed. "As you are well aware. Come on . . . The Learjet is for you! And breakfast is included."

The plane's interior was luxurious compared to life in a tent, and Mac wished that her boots were clean. But they weren't, and there was nothing she could do about it.

Once her helmet, TAC vest, and M4 were stowed—Mac took a seat across from McKinney. There was a lot of catching up to do, and they were still at it, when the jet reached cruising altitude. "We're headed north," McKinney informed her. "Up to Missouri, west to Colorado, and south to New Mexico."

Mac frowned. "*New Mexico?* Why?"

McKinney was about to reply when the civilian flight attendant brought their breakfasts. The food was precooked but steaming hot, and Mac was surprised to discover how hungry she was. Twenty minutes passed while they ate, and McKinney brought her up to speed on the war effort. The good news was that the North was winning. The bad news was that it was taking forever. And people were dying every day.

Once they were finished, Mac poured the last of the coffee into their cups. "Okay, give. Why are you taking me to New Mexico?"

Mac listened intently as McKinney explained how the general who was in charge of all Confederate POW camps had decided to outsource a prison to a Mexican drug dealer named Rosa Alvarez Carbone, AKA "*La ángel de la muerte*." Or the Angel of Death.

Mac frowned. "Who does General Lorenzo report to?"

"Your father."

Mac winced. Even though she and Bo were fighting for different sides, she knew what his core values were. Or had been. The man she'd grown up with would never countenance treating POWs the way Carbone was treating the men and women under her control. But people change . . . And, since her father had chosen to side with the Libertarian oligarchs, maybe he approved of handing POWs over to the lowest bidder.

"So," McKinney concluded, "your job is to lead a rescue team into Mexico, free our people, and bring them home. *How* you accomplish that is up to you. A lot of resources have been assembled at Antelope Wells. And, if you need something more, I'll get it for you. That's why the president sent me . . . To make sure that no one roadblocks you. And he told me to give you *this*."

As Mac accepted the envelope, she saw that her name was written on it and recognized the scrawl. "Nature calls," McKinney said. "And, like General MacArthur, I shall return."

Did McKinney believe, as so many did, that she and the president were lovers? Probably. And he was giving her a moment of privacy to read whatever was contained in the envelope.

Mac tore it open and read the note.

Dear Mac,

I am sending you into danger. I do so with a heavy heart because I want to protect you from harm. But our first responsibility is to the 296 prisoners being held in Ascensión, Mexico. Unfortunately, my military advisors believe that you are the best qualified officer to get our people out. As always, my thoughts and prayers will be with you.

With deep affection,
Sam

Mac read the note again before tucking it away. The message was short but spoke volumes. If only they were normal people, Mac thought to herself. What would it be like to sit across from Sam in a restaurant and share a meal? It was a simple thing for other people but impossible for them.

"So," McKinney said as he returned to his seat. "Did the president have some advice for you?"

"Yes, he did," Mac deadpanned. "Drink bottled water."

McKinney laughed. "He should know. Given his long trip home from Tampico. Grab some sleep, Mac . . . The moment we land, everyone will want something from you. Attention if nothing else."

Mac knew that was true and was happy to discover that the Lear's seats could fold down, offering a narrow bed to sleep on. After throwing a blanket over Mac and dimming the lights, the flight attendant went forward. Mac felt good stretching out, knowing that she was momentarily safe.

Sleep came quickly and ended with a thump as the wheels touched down. Mac glanced at her watch. She'd been asleep for three hours. It would have been nice to have more, but something was better than nothing.

Mac sat up and peered out through a window. She saw a radar installation flash past, followed by tents, then vehicles parked under camo nets. Then the installation disappeared, and a stretch of open desert appeared. The Lear slowed, turned, and taxied back.

"Welcome to Camp Freedom," McKinney said, from the other side of the aisle. "I hope you like the airstrip. We made it just for you." Mac had her boots on by the time the plane came to a stop, and the door opened. A shower would have been nice, along with a fresh uniform, but they would have to wait.

It should have been hot outside, but it wasn't. The globe-spanning high haze was responsible for that. But it was bright, and Mac had to squint as she made her way down the stairs to the point where two people stood waiting. McKinney followed behind her.

A sharp-looking captain stepped forward to offer a salute, which Mac returned. He had deeply sunken eyes, gaunt features, and a rapier-thin body. "Good morning, Major. My name is Alan Roupe. I'm your XO."

Mac shook his hand. "It's a pleasure, Captain."

"This is Command Sergeant Major Lester Deeds," Roupe added as he stepped to one side. Deeds was wearing a green beret. He had bright blue eyes, high cheekbones, and brown skin. Mac returned his salute and could feel the man's strength through his handshake. "Tom Lyle claims that you know your shit," Deeds told her. "And that means it's true."

Lyle was a special operator Mac had worked with in the past. She smiled. "I'm glad he's okay . . . And I like who you hang out with. So give it to me straight, Command Sergeant Major . . . What kind of soldiers do we have?"

"The best, ma'am . . . I chose them myself."

"Well done," Mac replied. "I'd like to meet them as soon as possible."

Mac saw something click behind the bright blue eyes. Approval? Yes, she thought so. All the gear in the world didn't mean jack shit without good soldiers—so that was something they agreed on. "Okay, I'm sure we have lots to do. What's up first?"

The last thing Mac wanted to do was step off the plane and walk into a staff meeting. But Roupe and the rest of them were all jacked up and eager to get going. And Mac knew it was important to harness that energy.

Roupe led the way. And as they passed some Strykers, each safe within its own revetment, Mac saw the mobile radar unit in the distance. It consisted of a tan-colored truck, a mast with a rectangular antenna fastened to it, and two boxy trailers. "What's the radar for?" Mac inquired. "Is there reason to believe that we'll be attacked by the Mexican Air Force?"

"That's our cover story," Roupe explained. "The rebs are sure to spot Camp Freedom from the air and wonder what we're up to. So we're doing what we can to make the base look like it's part of an early-alert detection system."

"That makes sense," Mac replied. "Although there is the law of unintended consequences to consider. What if the Mexicans decide to attack it?"

Roupe frowned. "That's a possibility I guess. But why bother? Unless they're planning to side with the Confederates."

It was a reasonable answer, and Mac knew that Roupe was correct. The Confederates would almost certainly spot Camp Freedom from space, a spy plane, or a drone. Or maybe they had.

Mac was on the receiving end of numerous salutes and curious stares as they passed the tents where her soldiers were living. She was pleased to see how organized everything was and wondered who deserved credit for that. Roupe? Deeds? Or had the two of them been working as a team? The third possibility would be best.

The house trailer was long and narrow. The interior was divided into an admin section, a meeting space, and an office for Mac. The meeting area was set up for a briefing. A large map and numerous photographs obscured one of the windows. "I thought we could begin with a sitrep," Roupe suggested, "and take it from there."

"This is an excellent time to brief you regarding Captain Roupe," McKinney interjected. "He's the only person to escape from Detention Center One and live to tell about it. That's one of many reasons why he was chosen for this mission. Alan knows everything there is to know about the layout of the prison, the way Carbone runs the place, and the appalling conditions there."

A faraway look appeared on Roupe's skull-like face. "I was lucky," he said. "Better people died trying to escape that hellhole."

"I'm glad you made it," Mac said as she approached the bulletin board. "Is *this* the building you escaped from?" The structure she was referring to was shaped like a square, with a central courtyard located at its center.

Roupe nodded. "Yes, ma'am. It was supposed to be a regional hospital. But after the meteors struck, construction came to a stop. About a month later, Carbone leased the building from the government for $1,000.00 per month. Money changed hands under the table, you can be sure of that, since it's worth more.

"It isn't clear whether she had a deal with General Lorenzo at that point," Roupe added, "or was hoping to get one. Nor does it matter. The building is two stories high, and each of the four wings was designed to accommodate 40 patients, for a total of 160 people max.

"But, since Carbone and her gangbangers chose to occupy *all* of the east wing, only 120 slots remain. That's if the structure were used as a hospital. At this point we estimate that 296 POWs are being held there, although the actual head count fluctuates as people die and new prisoners are brought in."

"Which raises an important question," Mac put in. "What can

we expect? How many prisoners will be able to walk? And how many will need to be carried?"

"If it's like it was on the day I left, about 80 percent will be able to walk, albeit slowly," Roupe answered. "The rest will require stretchers."

Mac looked at Deeds. "That suggests a lot of medics in addition to our combat personnel. Let's put a number on that." Deeds nodded and made a note.

Mac turned back to the photo. "Tell me about the central courtyard. Could helicopters land there?"

"No," Roupe replied. "Carbone thought of that. You can't see them in the photo, but steel wires crisscross the central courtyard at roof level."

"That sucks."

"Yes," Roupe agreed. "It does."

As the briefing continued, it soon became clear that Roupe had done his homework. He knew about the roads in and out of Ascensión, where the nearest army unit was located, and more. Roupe even had a full-on mission plan ready to go. All of it was contained in the thick packet that he handed to Mac.

After promising to read the material, Mac asked Deeds to show her around. She could have chosen Roupe. But Mac wanted to assess how Deeds interacted with the troops and signal the noncom's importance.

There were a number of stops on the tour, along with opportunities to chat. And, for the most part, Mac liked what she saw. She could tell that although Deeds was popular, he kept the right amount of distance between himself and the troops and was quick to identify discrepancies. As for the rank-and-file troops, morale was high. In fact, most of the soldiers were champing at the bit. They wanted to free the POWs and do it yesterday.

Once the tour was over, Mac thanked Deeds and went to her tent. Her duffel bag, TAC vest, and helmet were waiting there—along with the M4. It was midafternoon, and Mac was in need of a nap. She closed the tent flap, lay down, and pulled a blanket up around her body. Sleep came quickly, and it was nearly 1730 by the time she woke up hungry. There was no chow hall. So Mac went looking for an MRE and wound up having dinner with three of the Stryker crews. All of them were aware of Mac's Marauders and peppered her with questions. The most common was, "How can I get a transfer?"

Then the conversation turned into a full-on bullshit session and storytelling fest, complete with a lot of anecdotes. Some were true, and some weren't, but all of them were funny.

It was dark by the time Mac thanked her hosts, borrowed a flashlight, and took an unannounced stroll around the perimeter. It consisted of a cyclone fence, well-sited machine-gun emplacements, and a central mortar pit that could provide 360-degree fire support if the base came under attack. The sentries were pleased to see her, and Mac knew why. Sentry duty was boring as hell . . . And it was nice to see that the CO cared.

After the walkabout, it was back to the tent for a cup of instant hot chocolate and her homework. All of the shelters had power thanks to the portable generator that ran twenty-four/seven, so a reading light sat on Mac's folding table.

After eyeballing a variety of maps and photos, Mac settled in to read Roupe's plan. She was impressed by the fact that her XO had the initiative required to write one. But the good feelings ended there. The way Roupe saw it, the task force would depart at 0500, enter Mexico via the border-patrol checkpoint in Antelope Wells at 0530, and follow Highway 2 to the town of Ascensión.

Then, after what Roupe assumed would be a brief fight, Carbone would surrender. All of which was hopelessly naïve because Mac figured the Angel of Death would hear about the gringo column five minutes after it left the United States. Or what had been the United States. That would give the bitch plenty of time to get ready, and rather than surrender, she'd fight like hell.

Roupe's exit plan wasn't any better. Having won the battle in Ascensión, Roupe planned to put the POWs aboard a fleet of trucks and ambulances. Then, with Strykers acting as escorts, the column would return to Camp Freedom. The whole thing was laughable. But *why*?

Mac was pretty sure that she knew the answer, and that was a straightforward lack of talent. Mac knew officers who were very good at implementing plans but not all that good at coming up with them, and it seemed as though Roupe fit the second description. So her task would be to make the plan better without eroding her XO's self-confidence.

The process began the next morning when Mac requested that Deeds, Roupe, and his platoon leaders join her in the trailer. McKinney was present as well. Mac stood next to the improvised bulletin board. "First, I'd like to compliment the entire group regarding your efforts to get this unit ready for combat. Thanks to the fact that the company is well organized, and our morale is high, we'll be able to launch this mission quickly. And that's important because our POWs are suffering, as Captain Roupe can attest. I read the preliminary mission plan last night and, as all of you know, any document submitted to the commanding officer will be changed. That's what COs do when they aren't playing golf."

Most of them laughed. Roupe was the single exception. *Uh-oh*, Mac thought. *He's pissed. I'm off to a bad start.*

"For starters," Mac continued, "the mission will take place at night. There are a number of reasons for the change. First, our soldiers have night-vision equipment and, as far as we know, Carbone's people don't. Second, our Strykers are equipped with thermal-imaging gear. So while the enemy pickup trucks have headlights, that's the extent of their night-fighting capabilities." Most of them chuckled, but Roupe frowned.

"Third," Mac said, "is the matter of the Confederates. They have the capability to see us at night, but will they be looking? And if they *are* looking, and they see heat signatures on the move, how quickly will word of that reach Carbone? There's no way to know for sure, but I think there could be some lag. If so, that will be helpful.

"Finally, in order to take full advantage of our capabilities, we're going to sleep during the day and train at night."

Roupe cleared his throat. "Can I ask a question?"

"Of course," Mac replied. "Shoot."

"What about security? Who will guard the camp during the day?"

It was a sensible question even if Mac wasn't entirely certain of Roupe's motive in asking it. "I asked Colonel McKinney to request a platoon of MPs," Mac replied. "They're scheduled to arrive by 0600 tomorrow. Once they set up, they'll assume responsibility for security. And, if we return with civilian prisoners, the MPs will be here to receive them."

Roupe's plan made no mention of Mexican prisoners or how to handle them. And Mac could see the look of consternation on his face. She scanned the crowd. "Maneuvers will begin at 1800 tomorrow night. The goal will be to strengthen teamwork, hone our night navigation skills, and give our platoon leaders an opportunity to shine. And that's important because there's no way to anticipate what we'll encounter in Ascensión. If things go poorly, it could be necessary for each platoon to fight independently. Are there any questions?" The lieutenants looked solemn and shook their heads.

"Good," Mac said. "Here's what I have in mind. On the first night, Command Sergeant Major Deeds will organize a game of capture the flag. Platoon leaders will be in charge of the opposing teams. Colonel McKinney will serve as referee. The victors will win a cold, wet prize, which I predict will be to their liking." The announcement drew cheers and some enthusiastic hooahs.

"During the second night, the Command Sergeant Major will host two or three games of hide-and-seek. One platoon will hide, and the others will try to find them. As before, prizes will be awarded to those who are deserving." That set off a second round of applause.

"And on the *third* night," Mac said, "we are going to bring our brothers and sisters home."

That announcement produced the biggest celebration yet. Mac grinned. "Tell your people what I told you. Keep them in the loop. That will be all. Colonel McKinney . . . Could you join me for a moment?"

McKinney could and did. After getting cups of coffee, they took them into Mac's office. Her desk consisted of a sheet of plywood resting on two sawhorses. The red plastic chairs were better than nothing. "The night exercises are a great idea," McKinney observed as he sat down. "Although trying to play capture the flag with eight Strykers and sixty soldiers will result in total chaos."

"And total chaos is what we're likely to encounter down south," Mac said. "So here's hoping they learn how to deal with it in two days." Mac eyed him over her coffee mug. "You said you could get me whatever I need. True?"

"True," McKinney said. "Assuming it makes sense. What do you have in mind?"

"I need four C-17 transport planes plus a backup," Mac replied.

McKinney's eyebrows rose. "*Five* C-17s? What the hell for?"

"The first bird will bring a load of medics into Ascensión," Mac replied. "Deeds figures we'll need about fifty of them. And rather than add all the vehicles required to haul the medical personnel across the desert, I prefer to fly them in. As for planes two, three, and four, they'll be used to evacuate the POWs who can walk. The fifth Globemaster is a backup. Assuming that all goes well, it won't need to land."

"And the POWs who can't walk?"

"We'll put them aboard the plane with the medics," Mac replied.

"That's smooth," McKinney said. "Very smooth. But there's a problem. A *big* problem."

Mac nodded. "I know what you're thinking. Ascensión has an airstrip called *Amp Aeropuerto*. It's fine for light planes and helicopters, but the runway is short. And a Mexican Army detachment is quartered right next to it. So, even if the seventeens *could* land there, the Mexicans would be likely to object."

"Exactamundo," McKinney said. "So? What's the solution?"

"The C-17s will land on Highway 2," Mac replied. "According to aerial photos, the section leading into town is straight as an arrow and two lanes wide. Plus there's plenty of shoulder on both sides. There is a row of telephone poles, but we'll drop them if we need to."

"Shee-it! "McKinney said enthusiastically. "A whole flock of four-engined jets landing on a highway! I'd like to see that. If the Globemasters can land on unimproved runways, then a highway should be a fucking piece of cake. I'll get on the horn to General Jones. Once he's on board, the rest will be easy. One thing, though . . . How about our task force? How does it get in and out?"

"We'll use Strykers," Mac replied. "And rather than follow

Highway 2 down, we'll drive cross-country, which will cut forty miles off the trip. We'll come back the same way we went in. It would be a good idea to have some helicopters on call, though . . . Just in case."

"That makes sense," McKinney agreed as he stood. "I'll get to work."

"Me too," Mac said. "If this operation is classified—how come the paper pushers know where to send all of their bulletins, memos, and instructions?"

McKinney grinned. "Because we work for *them* . . . Not the other way around." And then he left.

FORT BENNING, GEORGIA

Four-Star General Bo Macintyre was seated in the reviewing stand waiting to welcome more than a thousand soldiers into the Confederate Army. And that was good because the casualty rate was high. But there was a dark side to the occasion as well. The young men and women arrayed in front of him were conscripts rather than volunteers. And draftees were less reliable than people who joined on their own.

Even worse was the fact that the need for replacements was so high that it had become necessary to shorten basic from ten weeks to eight. Two weeks was no big deal. That's what his public-affairs officers had been ordered to say. And that was grade-A bullshit.

But new bodies were required to feed the Confederate war machine, and time was critical. Hopefully, after pushing the Union back, the army would be able to reinstitute the previous standards.

And Bo took comfort from the fact that the board of directors had approved a nationwide draft. That was clear evidence of a renewed commitment to the war. Secretary of the Army Orson Selock was correct. After losing their secret bank accounts, people like President Lemaire had to win the war or live like everyone else.

The thought brought a wry grin to Bo's face as the current speaker mentioned his name. "So, it is my pleasure to introduce the Chairman of the Joint Chiefs, General Bo Macintyre!"

Bo heard a simultaneous "Hooah!" as he took the podium and knew that it had been rehearsed. A sea of faces stared up at Bo as he began his speech. It was standard stuff for the most part. They were special . . . They should be proud . . . And they were about to embark on a grand adventure.

Then it was time to transition into the material supplied by the newly formed Office of Morale Management. Bo's voice boomed through loudspeakers as his eyes swept the formation before him. "As you take your place among the ranks of soldiers sworn to defend our country, know this . . . After failing to win the war on the battlefield, the enemy has chosen to terrorize our families with acts of unprecedented barbarity. A week ago a unit of the Union Army entered the community of Macy, South Carolina, and executed every male over the age of twelve."

That wasn't true insofar as Bo knew . . . But if lies would help to win the war, then he was willing to tell them. The assembled soldiers uttered a mutual gasp of horror, which elicited a loud "As you were!" from a drill sergeant.

Bo nodded. "Yes, I know what you're thinking. You want to punish those Yankee bastards. Well, don't worry. You'll get your chance. Kill those sons of bitches for your family, kill them for your hometown, and kill them for your country! And may God bless the New Confederacy!"

A noncom shouted, "Atten-hut!" The band played "I Wish I Was in Dixie," and a sergeant yelled, "Dismissed!"

The officer in charge of the training facility was an aging colonel named Mundy. He was waiting to shake Bo's hand. "That was an excellent speech, General. I hadn't heard about the massacre in Macy. Damn those bastards to hell!"

Bo said all the right things, left as quickly as he reasonably could, and entered the waiting SUV. It took him to the airfield, where a small jet was waiting. His next stop was Houston. But what should have been a three-hour flight, would take three times that long, because the plane would have to circle out over the Gulf of Mexico before turning north. The trip would give him time to work on administrative tasks, however, and take a nap.

The flight went smoothly, but there was a lot of traffic in Houston, which was virtually untouched by the war. That was clearly a matter of choice since the Union had the means to bomb the shit out of the place if they chose to. And, had Bo been fighting for the North, he would have done so by then.

But most of his peers agreed that President Sloan was too pragmatic to kill thousands of civilians, and by doing so, create the kind of hatred that would make it impossible to put America back together again. And that was fine with Bo since it made his life easier.

Bo's destination was the new command and control center located south of Houston and adjacent to the Bryan Mound Strategic Petroleum Reserve. Or in the words of one critic, "as far from the fighting as the brass could go without getting their feet wet."

But the location made sense because it was well away from the civilian population and practically on top of something the Union wanted to protect, which was the Bryan Mound Reserve. The facility was vulnerable to stupidity, however, including meetings like the one Bo had been ordered to attend. Bo's motorcade consisted of three SUVs. Their grill lights flashed as the lead driver used burps of sound from her siren to clear a path. But in spite of her best efforts, the one-hour trip still took an hour and a half.

After passing Freeport, the motorcade paused at Checkpoint Alpha, where all personnel, Bo included, had to show their IDs before passing into the half-mile-deep "restricted zone." It was crisscrossed by prepared fighting positions and connecting trenches.

Then the procession had to stop at Checkpoint Bravo and show IDs again. After being cleared, the party was allowed to pass through the twelve-foot-tall steel-reinforced blast wall that surrounded the CCC on three sides. The Gulf of Mexico bordered the center's south flank, where all manner of naval defenses had been put in place to protect it.

Most of the complex was belowground, so the motorcade had to follow a circular drive down to the third level before Bo could exit the vehicle. Bo didn't have enough time to stop by his new office, so he went straight to the Executive Center's Reagan Room, where the most boring meetings were held. This one was titled "Succession Planning," which typically meant "We're about to dump the Secretary of XYZ and replace him with someone equally incompetent."

But as Bo entered the room, he noticed that the mood was different. The side conversations were muted, and being a political animal himself, Bo could smell blood in the air. But whose? *His?* No, he didn't think so. But someone was on the bubble. Bo could feel it. And the people in the room had been summoned to witness whatever was about to take place.

Bo sat next to Selock, and both of them watched the president's cabinet enter the room, closely followed by the man himself. And as Morton Lemaire stepped up to the podium, Bo could see it on the president's face. *He* was the one! Holy shit, Lemaire was going to step down! That was a big deal.

It quickly became apparent that Bo's assumption was correct. After mentioning what Lemaire saw as his primary accomplishment, which was the creation of ". . . a great nation," the president cleared his throat. "However," he added. "I'm sorry to say that my health has taken a turn for the worse, making it necessary for me to resign the presidency. Fortunately, we have a very capable vice president who is ready to take over. Please join me in an offering of universal support for the vice president, soon to be the president, Martha Stickley!"

Bo stood with all the rest of them and joined in the applause. *Martha Stickley,* he thought. *The so-called Iron Maiden.* A nickname that stemmed from the fact that if Stickley had a sexual preference, no one knew what it was—as well as the fearsome coffin-like devices of the same name.

So what did Stickley's ascendency mean to *him*? Not a great deal, Bo concluded. Stickley was neither friend nor foe. And, to the extent that she had the balls that Lemaire lacked, Stickley might be the jolt the sagging Confederacy needed. The board of directors clearly thought so because they called the shots. And when they told Lemaire that he was too sick to serve, he had the good sense to feel ill.

Stickley rose to say a few predictable words. Then her chief of staff announced that a press release had gone out fifteen minutes earlier, talking points had been sent to each person via e-mail, and it was important to abide by them.

The meeting was adjourned after that, and Bo was relieved to see Stickley leave the room. The last thing he wanted to do was line up to kiss her ass. There were no negative comments as people filed out into the hall. That sort of thing was best saved for conversations with close confidants.

It was getting late by then, and Bo had promised Kathy that

he'd come home for dinner. So he checked out by phone, retrieved his Land Rover from the fifth subbasement, and left the complex. A circular route took him out and around the Brazosport area to the Coast Guard station located in the community of Surfside. And that was where, by virtue of his position, the Chairman of the Joint Chiefs was allowed to park for as long as he wanted to.

A phone call was all it took to summon a water taxi, which took him along the coast to Galveston's upscale Cedar Lawn neighborhood. That was where he and his soon-to-be second wife, Kathy Waters, had purchased a three-bedroom ranch-style house.

Kathy was a middle-aged blonde who kept herself in good shape. She'd been Bo's secretary and companion for many years, and he was lucky to have her. The look of pleasure on Kathy's face was plain to see as Bo came through the front door and gave her a kiss. "Dump the briefcase," she told him, "and meet me on the deck. Your drink will be waiting."

Bo said, "Yes, ma'am, right away, ma'am," and made his way down the hall to his office. It was supposed to be a bedroom, but it had a wonderful view of the Gulf and was large enough to meet his needs. They were still moving in, but Kathy was starting to spread things around the house, and his study was no exception.

And as Bo eyed the row of framed photos Kathy had arranged on his credenza, one of them came as a shock. Because there, sitting next to a picture of her mother, was a photo of Robin! That in spite of his negative feelings about her.

The picture was no accident. Bo knew that. Kathy was a peacemaker by nature and, in spite of Victoria's death, insisted that Bo should regard Robin as being innocent unless she was proven guilty. So Bo hadn't told Kathy about the bounty. Why upset her? Especially with their wedding day coming up.

He stared at the photographs for a moment. Robin was the

spitting image of her dead mother who, in spite of the conflict that characterized their marriage, Bo still loved. More than he loved Kathy? Yes, probably. But Kathy was a lot easier to live with.

As for Victoria, well, she'd been his favorite. The son who never came along and, more than that, a younger *him*. Slowly, carefully, Bo placed the picture of Robin facedown on the credenza. Kathy would find it there and get the message. Bo had *one* daughter, and she was dead.

CHAPTER 6

Always do everything you ask of those you command.

—GENERAL GEORGE S. PATTON

NEAR ANTELOPE WELLS, NEW MEXICO

The sun was a bloody smear in the western sky as darkness fell, and the waiting ended. Mac was standing outside the command trailer drinking black coffee from a ceramic mug. Three days had passed since she had arrived, and the company was as ready as it could be under the circumstances. They were going to leave in one hour. Had she considered everything? Were the Confederates staring down from space? Was she going to die in Mexico?

"Robin?"

Mac's body jerked at the sound of Lieutenant Colonel McKinney's voice. Had he noticed it? She tried to sound casual. "Yes, sir . . . What's up?"

McKinney's face was a white blur in the dim light. "We're good to go . . . And we have a message from the president. 'Good hunting, and Godspeed.'"

Mac thought about Sloan. "I'm sending you into danger." That's what his note said. "Thank you, sir. Did you pass the word?"

"Yes. The troops are raring to go."

Mac knew it was true. Because even though the mission was going to be dangerous, every man and woman in her command wanted to rescue the POWs. Mac emptied the last of the coffee onto the bone-dry ground. "All right, Colonel," she said. "I'll see you in Ascensión."

McKinney was going to fly in aboard the first C-17. He nodded. "Take care out there." Then he was gone.

The vehicles were lined up with their parking lights on. Firefly-like headlamps moved from place to place as drivers carried out last-minute checks on their Strykers.

Mac heard occasional bursts of static and the faint strains of a country-western tune as she passed the **BETSY ROSS**. Platoon Leader Susan "Sixgun" Evers was there to greet her along with Sergeant Major Deeds. "Good evening, ma'am," Evers said. "My platoon is ready for inspection."

Archer Company had been divided into two platoons, each consisting of three nine-person squads, plus a two-person crew for each of the six Strykers. That added up to sixty-six people plus Mac, Roupe, and Deeds. Would the force be sufficient? Mac thought so. More people would lead to additional complexity and the likelihood of mistakes.

But what if they were outnumbered? *We have night-vision gear,* Mac reminded herself. *And the Mexicans don't. Plus, we'll have a Predator drone circling overhead. So less is more.* "Thank you, Lieutenant," Mac said. "Let's take the tour."

The final inspection was more for the purpose of interacting with the troops, and maintaining morale, than finding flaws. So things went smoothly. After Mac chatted with the members of the first platoon, she moved on to the second platoon. It was led by Lieutenant Ron Okada. And because Captain Roupe was slated to accompany the second platoon, he was present as well.

There wasn't much light. But what there was had an orange glow. Even allowing for that, Roupe's countenance had a sickly appearance. Was he ill? Or simply frightened? He certainly had every right to be. Going back to the place where he'd suffered so much wouldn't be easy.

But Roupe was the only person who knew his way around the prison. And, if something happened to Mac, it would be his duty to take over. Would he execute *her* plan? Or switch to his own? Mac would never know. Roupe's salute was perfect. Mac tossed one in return. "Captain . . . Lieutenant . . . Are we ready to roll?"

"Yes, ma'am," Okada said confidently. "The *California Girl* was running rough, but the issue was resolved."

"Good," Mac replied. "I'd like to say hello to the troops."

The members of the first squad were standing next to their truck, shooting the shit, when Deeds barked, "Atten-hut!"

Mac said, "As you were," and paused to chat before moving on to the next squad. And so it went until the inspection was complete.

Mac paused for a private word with Roupe. "You know the drill, Alan. Complete the mission should I fall. And one more thing . . . Watch our six. There's no reason to believe that Carbone and her people are onto us. But what if the rebs are watching from orbit? And what if they tipped the Angel off? The bastards could be hiding out there, just waiting to roll in behind us."

"Don't worry, Major," Roupe assured her. "We'll keep a sharp eye out. There's no way in hell that they're going to surprise us."

"Good," Mac replied. "I'll see you in Ascensión."

Roupe produced a jerky nod followed by a second salute.

Mac returned it, thanked Okada, and made her way back toward the head of the column. Deeds was by her side. "Permission to speak freely, ma'am."

"Of course. Go."

"Captain Roupe has been through hell. I think it would be a good idea to keep an eye on him."

Mac turned to look at Deeds. If there was an expression on his face, she couldn't see it in the murk. The comment seemed to suggest that someone should protect Roupe. But it could also be interpreted to mean that Deeds considered the XO to be unstable. And if that's what the noncom meant, he was taking a lot on himself. Many officers would have instructed Deeds to back off. But Mac had faith in Deeds and said as much. "I hear you, Sergeant Major . . . Use your own judgment."

"Yes, ma'am," Deeds replied. Then he was gone.

As Mac returned to the head of the column, she was wearing her TAC gear minus the helmet, which was hanging from the **BETSY ROSS**. Mac put it on. Her RTO was a kid named Harmon. She nodded to him. "Tell the company to saddle up. We roll five from now."

The **BETSY ROSS** was in the one slot. The Stryker was equipped with a 105mm gun, and Mac was counting on gunner Alfie Thomas to clear the way if an obstruction appeared.

As Mac made her way through the cargo compartment on her way to the air-guard hatch, she paused to speak with the driver. Her name was Ronda Smith, or Smitty to her peers, and she had an infectious grin. "Hey, Major . . . You like my whip?"

"I do," Mac assured her. "Lieutenant Evers says you're one helluva driver."

"She got that right," Smith said proudly. "Don't you worry none . . . I'll get you there."

"I'm counting on it," Mac said. "And I'd like to come back, too."

Smith laughed as Mac turned to climb up into the hatch. The squad was on board by that time, and seated knee to knee in the equivalent of a metal box. Mac's presence, plus Harmon's, made the cargo bay even more crowded.

But rank hath privilege, and Mac was free to stick her head up through the hatch and savor the cool air. There was no moon, a high haze was blocking the stars, and the only lights were those that belonged to the other vehicles. They went out one by one. That entailed some risk, of course . . . But the truck commanders had thermal-imaging gear and could use it to avoid running into each other. Just one of the skills they'd honed while playing capture the flag during the hours of darkness. Even though Harmon was on board, Mac could communicate with the company directly if she chose to. "This is Archer-Six. Watch those intervals . . . Let's move out. Over."

Mac heard the characteristic whine that all Strykers made as the **BETSY ROSS** got under way. She took the opportunity to turn her night-vision equipment on. Her surroundings glowed green, but she could see quite well and was grateful for that.

Smith and the other drivers had been studying the route for days, and any one of them could lead the column if necessary. The plan was to drive southeast through the desert, cut across a large farm, and enter Ascensión via a secondary road.

That would theoretically enable the company to catch Carbone by surprise. The biggest problem was the need to separate friend from foe to avoid the possibility of a friendly-fire incident. Fortunately, based on Roupe's account, the prisoners wore bright orange jumpsuits. That would help, but there would still be room for accidents. Her troops would have to be careful.

It was a smooth ride until the **BETSY ROSS** was forced to slow down and waddle through a dry creek bed. But, thanks to the vehicle's muscular eight-wheel drive, the Stryker was able to lurch up and out of the arroyo without difficulty.

Mac couldn't see any obstructions as she eyed the countryside ahead. Smith had the **ROSS** up to thirty miles per hour by then—and that was likely to be the column's top speed as it traveled south. If so, the company would arrive in Ascensión within the hour.

Off to her right, Mac could see the cluster of lights that represented the tiny town of El Berrendo, Mexico. Soon after they disappeared, Mac spotted a second set of twinkling lights on the right. They marked the location of a sizeable farm, which, when viewed from above, consisted of buildings surrounded by irrigated crop circles.

So far so good. Next up would be the hills that Mac thought of as "Dos Amigos." The column would pass them on the left as it angled down to Ascensión. And sure enough . . . Mac spotted the smaller *colina* a few minutes later. Smith was following a dirt road at that point. It was the type of backcountry track often used by drug smugglers and illegals as they tried to enter the United States. Except that the flow of *ilegales* had slowed to almost nothing since the beginning of the war.

They had passed the two amigos, and were making good time, when Okada spoke. "This is Archer-Two. Half a dozen vehicles are approaching the column from the west! They were hiding between the hills. I see two gun trucks . . . The rest of them are dune buggies. Over."

Six vehicles coming in fast . . . It was a no-brainer. One might represent a farmer. Maybe two. But *six*? Hell, no. Mac felt a sense of apprehension followed by fear. Carbone knew they were coming. The how could wait. "This is Archer-Six actual," Mac replied.

"The second platoon will turn west and engage. The first platoon will form a line abreast and prepare to deal with an attack from the south."

The attack from the south might or might not occur, but Mac planned to be ready in case more vehicles were streaming north from Ascensión. Mac turned back in time to see flashes of light as the gangbangers opened fire, and Okada's platoon turned to face them.

It was no match. The **CALIFORNIA GIRL** was equipped with a 105mm gun. It produced a loud boom. Something exploded, and as it did, flames lit the surrounding desert.

In the meantime, the **UNCLE SAM** and the **MOLLY WONKER** were firing as well. The entire engagement lasted no more than three minutes. Okada's report said it all. "This is Two . . . All enemy vehicles destroyed. Casualties, zero."

That was good . . . As was the fact that no one had attacked from the south. But the overall situation was bad. Very bad indeed. Mac could turn back, which would make sense given the circumstances, or continue on. In spite of the fact that the assholes knew the Union soldiers were coming. Mac was weighing her alternatives as Roupe spoke. "Archer-Five to Six. Should the second platoon turn around? And lead the way back to the base? Over."

It was a perfectly reasonable if somewhat leading question, and left no doubt as to what Mac's XO wanted her to do. And why *was* that? Mac would have expected the ex-POW to be super gung ho. But there was the possibility of PTSD to consider. Perhaps Roupe was maxed out.

Suddenly, and in spite of Roupe's expressed preference, Mac made her decision. "This is Archer-Six actual. The second platoon will fall in behind the first. The fact that the enemy didn't attack in force means they believe that we'll turn back. And if they believe that, then imagine their surprise when we knock on the door! Let's roll. Over." Mac heard the sound of cheering from the troops below and grinned.

Now that the decision was made, and the column was under way again, doubts began to surface. *Did* Carbone think the company would turn back? Or was the Angel of Death's failure to throw more resources into the attack part of a clever trick? A way to draw the norteamericanos in? If so, Mac was about to lead her people into a trap. That possibility filled her with dread. *Don't panic,* Mac told herself, as the Stryker hit a rough spot. *Think.* Mac looked up into the sky. She couldn't see the drone but knew the drone was there. And it was carrying *two* Hellfire missiles. That could even things up.

Mac's radio might or might not reach the base. So she ducked down into the cramped cargo compartment and looked at Harmon. "I need to speak with Colonel McKinney . . . Get him on the horn."

Harmon nodded. And the other soldiers got to listen in as Mac spoke with McKinney. "They know we're coming, sir. So let's give them a big dose of shock and awe. The bad guys live in the east wing of the prison. Let's feed them a Hellfire missile. Who knows? Maybe we'll get lucky and kill Carbone! But even if we don't, we'll grease some of her gang members and mix things up. Over."

"I like it," McKinney replied. "But what if some POWs are in the east wing for interrogation? Or to mop floors?"

"It's a risk," Mac admitted. "But what about our troops? We need to give them an edge. And the missile strike would do that."

There was a period of silence while McKinney considered it. And when he spoke, the soldiers sitting around Mac could hear him. "We'll be in some deep shit if this goes wrong, Major . . . But if I were sitting in one of those cells, I'd say, 'Go for it.'"

Sergeant Kris Riker nodded. "Damned straight."

Her troops produced a loud "Hooah," which caused Mac to smile. "Roger that, sir . . . We're about fifteen minutes out. I recommend that you wait ten, fire one Hellfire, and keep the other in reserve."

"Will do," McKinney promised. "Keep me informed. Over."

Mac gave the mike to Harmon and was about to return to her perch when Riker spoke. She had eight years in, and a no-nonsense attitude. "The colonel was right, Major . . . And so were you."

Mac forced a smile. "Thanks, Sergeant . . . Please leave some gangbangers for the second platoon. They'll get all pissy if you don't."

That got the predictable laugh, and Mac felt guilty as she stuck her head up through the hatch. They trusted her, but *should* they? Especially since she didn't trust herself.

The lights of Ascensión were visible at that point. And the glow was so bright that Mac was able to turn her night-vision gear off. Would Carbone attempt to stop them at the city limits? Or was she prepared to defend the prison?

Mac was scanning the area ahead, looking for any indication of a roadblock, when a flash of light strobed the city. The boom was like an afterthought. The Hellfire! *That'll give them something to think about,* Mac thought to herself. But what if there had been a mistake? What if the missile struck the *west* wing instead of the east wing? What if a hundred POWs were dead?

Such fears continued to plague Mac as the **BETSY ROSS** entered town, left the dirt road for a paved street, and took a right turn. That was when Mac saw the police roadblock and realized what she should have known from the beginning. The *policía* were on the Angel's payroll and had orders to stop the column.

The cops were hiding behind a couple of black-and-whites, and they scattered as the **BETSY ROSS** bore down on them. The Stryker was surrounded by a so-called birdcage, which was supposed to protect the vic from RPGs (rocket-propelled grenades). And when the slat armor struck one of the cop cars, it sent the vehicle spinning away. Mac heard Smith's war cry over the intercom and was glad the cops were okay. The mission was to rescue POWs rather than kill policemen.

Flames lit the area ahead, and because most of the buildings were no more than two stories high, Mac could see the structure that was on fire. And it was the prison. A sudden explosion sent debris upwards, and the resulting boom rolled across the city. *There goes Carbone's ammo supply,* Mac thought to herself. *We lucked out.*

Or so it seemed until gunfire converged on the column from every direction. Most of it was small-caliber stuff that rattled and pinged as slugs flattened themselves against the truck's armor. But it quickly became apparent that the gangbangers had some fifties, too . . . And rocket launchers. RPGs began to explode against slat armor.

Mac's first thought was to get on her LMG and fire back. But the volume of incoming fire was too heavy, and she was forced to drop into the compartment below. Sergeant Riker's soldiers could hear the rounds pounding the hull and knew they would have to leave the comparative safety of the Stryker soon. Their faces were grim. Mac smiled at them. "Hey there . . . I'm hungry. Does anyone have a candy bar?"

All of them smiled as the **BETSY ROSS** came to a stop, and gunner Alfie Thomas went to work. The truck lurched as the 105mm gun fired. "That's one," Thomas said. And Mac heard servos whine as the cannon began to traverse.

"Here," a private said as he gave Mac a chocolate bar. They heard a thump and felt the recoil as Thomas fired again.

"Thanks," Mac said. "I hope you don't mind waiting while we

tidy up." That produced the predictable laugh—and Mac began to chew the candy bar as she listened to the radio traffic.

"This is Archer-One," Lieutenant Evers said. "Put some fire on the white van . . . Nice work! Bad man dead. Over.

"Look alive truck three. There's a guy with an RPG launcher on the roof south of you . . . Grease him. Over."

And Okada was equally active. "See the bozos by the gate? Give them some forty mike-mike to chew on. And put some on the door, too . . . Make a hole, people—we're going in. Over."

Mac felt a sense of pride as her platoon leaders not only did their jobs but did them with the sort of panache that was a boost to morale. As the incoming fire began to fall off, Mac issued the order the company was waiting for. "This is Archer-Six actual. Truck commanders will drop their ramps. Let's go in and bring our people out. Over."

As the ramp dropped, Mac was there to lead the squad out and around the **BETSY ROSS**. The surrounding streetlights were on—which made it easy to see and be seen. But Mac had an app for that. "This is Archer Six . . . Kill those lights."

The lamps went out one by one as a succession of rifle shots were heard. But the east wing was still on fire, and that meant there was plenty of light. A possibility Mac should have considered but hadn't.

She ran toward the entrance. Mangled bodies lay sprawled in front of the steel doors, but the barriers themselves remained intact. Evers was standing there with a Colt Python in her right fist. It wasn't reg, but Mac didn't give a shit what kind of pistol the platoon leader carried so long as she got the job done. Two of her soldiers were busy placing charges against the steel doors. "It's time to pull back," Evers said, and followed her own advice.

Carbone's people began to fire down on the soldiers from above as the officers took cover behind the **BOLO II**. The incoming stopped as the LMG gunner on the **CALIFORNIA GIRL** sprayed the second floor with machine-gun fire.

There was a loud explosion as the demolition charge went off, and Mac stepped out from cover to take a look. The door on the left remained intact, but the one on the right was slightly ajar. "Nice job," Mac said. "Where's Captain Roupe?"

"Right here," Sergeant Major Deeds said as he gave Roupe a shove.

As the XO tripped and managed to recover, Mac saw that he was disheveled and unarmed. She turned to Deeds. "What's going on?"

"The bastard tried to run," Deeds replied grimly. "Sergeant Haskins caught him."

The obvious question was *why?* Was Roupe suffering from PTSD? Or was he a coward? But that would have to wait. Roupe was supposed to lead the company into the prison, and he was going to do it.

Roupe stared at her. "Please! Don't make me go in there."

Mac turned to Deeds. "Take this piece of shit into custody and put it on point."

Deeds grabbed hold of Roupe's TAC vest and jerked the officer to his feet. "Start walking, *sir* . . . We're counting on you."

Roupe whimpered as Deeds shoved him toward the steel doors. Mac and the rest of the first platoon followed. Half of Okada's people fell in behind them. The rest remained outside to provide security.

The steel doors opened onto a passageway that led to the central courtyard and a scene straight out of hell. Flames continued to lick around the edges of the hole in the opposite side of building, and they were reflected in the windows that still had glass in them.

And there, at the center of the courtyard, was a scaffold. A body was dangling from it. Soldiers streamed past as they went looking for the POWs. Shots were heard as they came into contact with the surviving guards.

Mac turned to Roupe. "Where is she? Where is the bitch who runs this place?"

"I-I don't know," Roupe said miserably. "Carbone knew we were coming. She could be fifty miles away by now."

Mac figured that was a real possibility. But if there was any chance of taking the Angel of Death north, she wanted to do so. Certain people, her father included, would have to stand trial after the war. And Carbone would be part of that. "Did she have an office of some sort? A place where she might hole up?"

"Under the east wing," Roupe replied. "In the basement."

"Take us there," Mac said as she prodded him. "On the double."

Roupe led the way, closely followed by Mac, Deeds, and Harmon, as the sounds of fighting came from the second floor. Smoke drifted in the air, empty shell casings littered the floor, and one of them made a tinkling sound as a boot struck it.

Mac could hear Evers and Okada giving orders over the radio, and it sounded as though they were making progress. A short jog took them to an entrance well away from the flames. Roupe stopped next to the door, pushed it open, and waited to see if he was going to die. He didn't.

Roupe entered the hall. The lights were out. The corridor turned green as Mac switched her night vision on. A fire alarm continued to bleat as they followed some twists and turns to what had once been a sizeable storage room. It was a chilling place. A wooden riser was located in front of a metal desk. A wooden chair was bolted to it and, judging from the restraints, it had been used to interrogate prisoners.

Was Roupe familiar with the chair? Yes, judging from the way he turned his back on it. "Grab what you can," Mac instructed as she scooped a stack of printouts off a corner of the desk. "There's no telling what may have value. Then let's get out of here."

Harmon found a canvas shopping bag that the others filled to overflowing before herding Roupe into the hall. The central plaza was a madhouse. Some of the POWs stood in groups. Others lay on makeshift litters, awaiting transport. Evers hurried over. Her eyes flicked from Roupe to Mac. "We have all of them, ma'am . . . We checked and checked again."

"Good. How many?"

"Two hundred and seventy-seven," Evers replied. Mac swallowed the lump in her throat. Two hundred and seventy-seven out of an estimated two hundred and ninety-six. She'd been hoping for more. "Have you heard from the colonel? What's the ETA on the planes?"

Evers opened her mouth to reply but was interrupted as a scarecrow-like POW uttered a scream and came rushing at them. He had a knife, taken from a guard perhaps, which he held high. "Roupe! You traitorous bastard!"

Deeds was fast. So fast that he was able to step in and disarm the man in a matter of seconds. Roupe turned and tried to run. Harmon tripped him. "Guard him," Mac ordered. "Kneecap the bastard if you have to."

Mac knelt next to the POW. He was lying on his back with a massive boot on his chest. "I'm Major Macintyre . . . You know Captain Roupe?"

"All of us know the rotten, stinking son of a bitch," the man said bitterly. "The guys were planning a breakout. A *big* breakout. And Roupe ratted them out. So the Angel let him go. But not before she ordered the guards to execute fourteen prisoners. He stood by her side as they died." The POW struggled at that point and tried to push the boot off his chest.

Though shocking, the news made sense. No wonder Roupe's rescue plan was flawed. He *wanted* the strategy to fail. And how had Carbone known that the company was coming? Because Roupe told her. Mac looked up at Deeds. "You can remove your foot, Sergeant Major . . . And help him up."

Mac's eyes went to the POW. "Don't worry, soldier . . . You'll get a chance to take Roupe down. But not with a knife. Your testimony will help put him away for good."

The man blinked. "Thank you . . . I've been praying for this day."

Evers was waiting as Mac stood. Her voice was grim. "We've got trouble, Major."

"Yeah? Like what?"

"According to the Pred operator, the local army unit left their quarters next to the airport, and they're rolling toward Highway 2. We're talking four French-made Jaguar EBRCs along with two Humvees and a couple of trucks."

Although Mac had read about the French vehicles, she'd never seen one. She knew they had six wheels and were roughly the same size as a Stryker but more heavily armed. Whereas the **BETSY ROSS** mounted a 105mm gun, Jaguars were equipped with 40mm cannons, *plus* side-mounted medium-range antitank missiles. Any of which could reduce a Stryker to a pile of burning scrap.

What's more, the Jags were equipped with day/night vision, nuclear, biological, and chemical (NBC) protection, a laser warning system, a threat missile-detection system, *and* they carried gear that could jam radio communications. So the Jaguars were a threat Mac couldn't take lightly. But why were they headed for Highway 2? Was that a matter of coincidence? Or were the Mexicans acting on intelligence provided by Carbone? The answer seemed obvious. All of it flashed through Mac's mind as she looked at Evers.

"Congratulations," Mac said. "You're the XO now . . . I'm going to take some Strykers and intercept the Jaguars. Tell the colonel that the C-17s need to circle the city while we secure Highway 2. In the meantime, set up a defensive perimeter, prepare the POWs for transportation, and secure the prisoners. Got it?"

Evers nodded. "Yes, ma'am."

"Good. Come on, Harmon . . . Let's go." Time was of the essence, so Mac began to jog. Harmon followed. They passed a group of prisoners who wore hoods and were seated on the ground, with their hands secured behind their backs.

Once outside, Mac keyed her handheld radio. "This is Archer-Six actual to trucks one, two, and three. Mexican armor is heading down Highway 2 to intercept our planes. We're going to stop them! Crank 'em up and let's move."

Mac led Harmon into the **BETSY ROSS** and ordered Smith to head for Highway 2. Mac fell sideways into a seat as the Stryker jerked into motion. Harmon sat across from her. "Get that Pred operator on the horn," she told him. "Pronto."

Harmon did as he was told and gave the handset to Mac. "This is Archer-Six actual," Mac said. "We're going to intercept those Jaguars. But the surface-to-surface missiles they carry can kill any one of my vehicles in a matter of seconds. I want you to smoke the lead vehicle with your remaining Hellfire. Here's hoping the officer in charge is riding in it. Then I want you to crash the Pred into Jag two."

"That's a roger regarding the Hellfire," came the response, "and a negative on the Pred. Those suckers cost four million each. Over."

"I don't give a shit what they cost," Mac replied. "You *will* crash that Predator into Jaguar two—or I will fly to Colorado, find the fucking basement that you live in, and blow your brains out! We're trying to rescue some POWs, and money doesn't mean jack shit. Over."

Another voice chimed in at that point. "This is Victor-Six actual," McKinney said. "You have your orders . . . Carry them out now! Over."

Harmon's eyes were wide. "What are we going to do?" he wanted to know.

Mac forced a smile. "After our buddy in Colorado kills those Jags, we'll tackle the others . . . And we outnumber them."

Harmon's expression brightened. "Okay then. We have this."

The BETSY ROSS lurched as Smith rounded a corner. Mac hoped that her optimism would be justified. She keyed the radio attached to her vest. "Archer-Six actual to trucks one, two, and three. Prepare to operate independently if necessary . . . The Jaguars may be able to jam our radio transmissions. The key is to get in close and hammer the bastards! Don't let up. Over."

Mac heard a series of clicks as she made her way over to the bench where she could access the air-guard hatch. Most of what happened next would be up to Smith and her gunner. But Mac wanted to see, and firing the LMG would give her something to do.

Mac arrived up top just in time to see a flash of light and the crack of what sounded like thunder. The Hellfire! But was it on target? Harmon's voice crackled through her earbud. "This is Archer-Nine . . . The Pred operator confirmed a bug splat. Over."

Mac knew that a "splat" was a hit. She opened the intercom. "Aim for the flames, Smitty . . . That's where the bastards are."

A second boom was heard, and Mac saw the explosion. It was smaller, however . . . As if fueled by the Predator's propellant rather than the gas in the Jaguar's tank. "This is nine," Harmon said. "The second target was damaged but not destroyed."

Ah well, Mac thought. *It's better than nothing . . . I'll take it.*

That was when a Mexican missile hit the **DON'T TREAD ON ME** and obliterated it. Mac felt the pressure wave hit her from behind and heard a thunderous BOOM. She turned, saw that the burning hulk was falling away behind them, and knew that both of the Stryker's crew members were dead. *Shit, shit, shit.*

Engines roared as the remaining Strykers raced past a brightly lit cantina and out onto Highway 2. Mac stood ready to fire the LMG as she eyed the brightly illuminated area ahead. The lead Jag had been reduced to a pile of burning scrap. But beyond it, and still headed for the section of road where the C-17s were going to land, she could see the other vehicles. And they were turning to face her! The enemy was going to fight.

Mac keyed her mike. "Step on the gas! Get in close! What are you waiting for, Thomas? Smoke the bastard."

The criticism was unfair. Thomas fired as Mac spoke, the **BETSY ROSS** lurched, and Mac heard a loud clang as the empty casing hit the street behind the vic and tumbled away. The 105mm shell landed short of the lead Jaguar but just barely.

The enemy unit's 40mm cannon began to chug, and the **BETSY ROSS** shook as a burst of shells exploded against the front of the vehicle. The armor held, but Mac knew that it was just a matter of time before the incoming rounds found their way in. As Mac dropped into the cargo compartment, Thomas uttered a loud whoop of joy. "Got the bastard!"

Two to go, Mac thought to herself as she climbed back up. The situation had changed. Now the surviving Jaguars were turning off Highway 2 in an attempt to escape the Strykers. And, thanks to some aggressive driving, the range was closing fast. Could the Mexicans fire their missiles at a target located behind them? Mac hoped they couldn't.

The damaged machine was trailing smoke. And even though the Jag's gunner should have been able to spin the 40mm gun around, it was facing forward. Was that the result of incompetence? Or had the turret jammed?

That became a moot point as Thomas fired again and scored a direct hit. The shell hit the Jaguar where its armor was the thinnest and punched a hole through it. The resulting flash of light strobed the surrounding buildings. And as pieces of fiery debris fell out of the sky, the surviving vehicle sped away into the desert.

"Let them go," Mac ordered as she watched the surviving Mexican vics drive away. "Harmon . . . Get on the horn. Tell the colonel that the planes can land and tell Evers to get ready."

"Yes, ma'am," Harmon replied.

Mac keyed her mike. "This is Archer-Six actual . . . It's time to set roadblocks at both ends of the landing strip. Truck one will block Highway 2 at the Del Carmen intersection, and truck two will block the road at Farm Road 3. Don't let anyone pass in either direction."

The BOLO II rolled past as Smith turned out into the road. Ideally, they would have had some soldiers along to manage the roadblocks, but they didn't. So it was up to Mac and Harmon to handle things at the first checkpoint, while the BOLO's two-person crew took care of the second. Fortunately, it was late, and there was very little traffic.

Mac jumped down onto the highway and looked up at the sky. She could hear the C-17s, but she couldn't see them. Not until the first plane's landing lights came on. The big four-engine jet transport was very low—and approaching from the northeast.

According to Mac's calculations, there was enough room for the Globemaster to touch down on the center of the highway *and* clear the telephone poles that ran along both sides of it. And those numbers had been checked and double-checked.

Still, what if something had changed since then? What if a wing clipped a new billboard? The plane might crash, killing the crew and leaving the POWs without a way out.

That concern plagued Mac as the plane came straight at her and roared over her head. The rush of air associated with the Globemaster's passage was so powerful that it almost knocked Mac off her feet. Tires screeched as the C-17 touched down, and the thrust reversers came on. They slowed the plane and reduced the possibility that foreign objects would be sucked up and into the engines.

No sooner had the cargo jet rolled to a stop than the rear hatch opened, lights appeared, and a ramp was deployed. Mac felt a sense of pride as a specially equipped bus loaded with medics rolled down onto Highway 2 and pulled away from the plane. An Air Force Combat Control Team had deplaned and had taken charge of the makeshift runway. The first C-17's engines began to scream as it took off and *another* plane came in for a landing.

Mac turned to Harmon. She had to shout. "Tell Evers to send two Strykers. We should provide escorts for the buses."

A Globemaster landed, delivered a bus, and took off again. The **MOLLY WONKER** and the **UNCLE SAM** had arrived by then and took up protective positions at both ends of the column, which departed seconds later. The prison was ten minutes away, and the operation was running on time.

Mac debated whether to return to the prison or remain in the landing zone, and decided on the latter as the fourth C-17's pilot cranked the thrust reversers up—and *backed* her plane up the highway. It was something to see, and Mac was staring at the strange sight, when Lieutenant Colonel McKinney materialized out of the gloom. There was a big grin on his face. "Hello, Major . . . Fancy meeting you here."

They exchanged salutes and spent the next few minutes bringing each other up to speed. McKinney was sorry to hear about the loss of the **DON'T TREAD ON ME**, but pleased to learn that the prison had fallen, and the evacuation process was proceeding smoothly.

The officers were still talking when the medical bus arrived from the prison, rolled in behind the C-17, and propelled itself up into the ramp. Once the vehicle was inside the cargo bay and properly secured, the jet's ramp came up. The noise produced by the C-17's engines increased. Moments later, the transport was thundering down the makeshift runway even as *another* Globemaster landed to pick up *another* bus loaded with POWs.

After the prisoners were loaded onto the last plane, and Mac's personnel were assembled next to the highway, she shook hands with McKinney. "Take care, sir. I'll see you soon."

"I'll be waiting for you," McKinney told her. "Watch your six."

CHAPTER 7

Desperate times call for desperate measures.

—OLD ENGLISH PROVERB

THE TIERRA DORADA RANCH, CHIHUAHUA, MEXICO

It was early afternoon, and all the members of President Luis Salazar's hunting party were comfortably ensconced in a hillside "hide" waiting for a herd of African blesbok to pass through the defile below. A shooting bench ran across the front of the bunker—and tripod-mounted rifles were aimed at the killing ground. General Bo Macintyre was sitting between a white-clad businessman from Ecuador and a natty drug dealer from Colombia. They were discussing the lamentable shortage of Cuban cigars.

Bo's weapon was a Nosler M48, which, judging from the box sitting next to it, was loaded with .308 Winchester ammo. It was a big-game rifle to be sure. And, according to Jorge, Salazar's executive assistant, a favorite with a certain Hollywood actor.

Bo didn't give a shit *who* liked the weapon but was careful to act like he did since flattery was free. And if Salazar thought the actor was a big deal, then fine.

Bo sipped his drink, and a woman laughed as Salazar delivered the punch line to a dirty joke. The key, according to the pretrip briefing he'd been given, was to shoot well but not *too* well. "Kill a buck if you can," the briefer told him. "But don't drop more than two. Don Salazar will smoke three or four animals on an average outing, and it's bad form to top his score."

"Says *who*?" Bo had inquired.

"Says Salazar," came the response. "And he's the one you need to please."

And that was true. Because the war wasn't going well for the Confederacy, and he'd been sent down south to negotiate a deal. "Places everyone!" Jorge announced. "Get ready to fire! The herd is nearly here."

There was a murmur of conversation and the scraping of furniture as guests turned to face the horizontal opening. Shooting antelope as *vaqueros* herded them past an air-conditioned hide was far from sporting. Not in the conventional sense, anyway. But Bo knew the occasion would call for some good marksmanship nevertheless. For one thing the "hunters" would be firing at a downward angle, the animals would be in motion, and none of the guests had fired their weapons before. And that meant something since every rifle has an individual personality.

Then there was the social pressure involved. He was the Chairman of the Joint Chiefs. So if he missed, it would not only reflect poorly on the Confederacy's military, it could put him at a disadvantage during the negotiations that lay ahead, all of which upped the ante. Bo checked to make sure that the weapon was loaded, that the safety was off, and that the tripod was operating properly. When he glanced at the digital readout mounted over the bench,

Bo saw that a one-mile-an-hour breeze was blowing south to north through the valley. Still another thing to remember as he took his first shot.

Bo *heard* the blesbok before he saw them. Their hooves created a dull thunder as they sought to escape the shouting *vaqueros*. Then the herd appeared. It looked like an undifferentiated mass of heaving horns at first. But as animals approached the hide, Bo could distinguish the antelopes' white faces, pointy ears, and tan bodies.

Bo spotted a big buck toward the front of the herd. One of his horns was missing. *Lead him*, Bo told himself, *just like a deer*. The trigger seemed to squeeze itself, the rifle butt thumped his shoulder, and the blesbok stumbled. Then Bo saw a puff of blood mist appear over the animal's hindquarters and realized that the animal had been shot by someone else as well.

When the buck disappeared, there was barely enough time to trigger a second shot. It was right on the money. And Bo was pleased to see an antelope go down with a bullet through the heart. Then the blesboks were gone, leaving twelve bodies behind.

A camera drone was circling the scene, and as Bo turned to look at the monitor, he spotted one-horn lying on its side. "Congratulations!" Jorge said enthusiastically. "Almost all of you scored at least one kill. Please make your way up to the parking area, where vehicles are waiting to take you to the Casa de Salazar, where you'll have time to freshen up before dinner."

Bo allowed himself to be led past the bar, down a hallway decorated with beautifully executed murals, to a small elevator lobby. Two trips were required to get everyone up to the covered loading area located on the east side of the ridge. Three Range Rovers were waiting. All of them had green paint jobs and bore the Tierra Dorada's distinctive rising sun logo.

Bo was ushered into the second Rover. He slid in next to the driver. A female fashionista and a Japanese businessman were in the back. They were discussing sushi, a subject that Bo had zero interest in since the thought of eating raw seafood was disgusting. That left him free to enjoy the scenery.

The Tierra Dorada ranch was huge. According to the glossy brochure in Bo's room, the estate included more than four million acres of land, employed some eight hundred people, and was home to half a million cattle. Never mind the four hundred thousand sheep and sixty thousand horses that grazed on the grasslands as well.

But even though Salazar was wealthy, most Mexicans weren't so fortunate. Prior to America's Second Civil War, the total value of goods imported to and exported from Mexico totaled more than 530 billion U.S. dollars. But now, as a result of the fighting, cross-border trade had dwindled to 10 percent of what it had once been. And tourism was in the tank for the same reason.

The result was widespread unemployment and increasing levels of civil unrest. So Mexico needed to bring in some cash and get unemployed people off the streets. Especially unemployed males under the age of thirty-five. Because if they rose up, Salazar and his cronies would be in some deep shit. Would those factors be enough to fuel an advantageous deal? Bo believed that they would.

As the convoy rounded the side of a barren hill, the Salazar residence was revealed. Huge blocks of what looked like white adobe had been stacked so as to balance each other out. Except that what appeared to be adobe was actually steel-reinforced concrete.

Having been there for a day, Bo knew the house had twenty-four bedrooms, thirty-two bathrooms, an Olympic-sized pool, a state-of-the-art workout facility, a huge living room, and a very attentive staff. But as the convoy paused at a checkpoint, other features were visible, too.

Bo's trained eye was drawn to the partially screened SAM (surface-to-air missile) launchers, tennis courts that could accommodate four helicopters, and a maze of landscaped retaining walls that would provide defenders with plenty of cover. It seemed that Salazar had reason to be concerned about his personal safety, even here at the heart of his empire.

After clearing the checkpoint, the convoy followed a curving drive up to the house and the shade provided by a portico. Servants hurried to open the doors, and as Bo got out, a boy was there to offer a glass of well-iced lemonade. He took a sip from it as Carla appeared to welcome him home. She was the hostess assigned to Bo's suite and made the peasant outfit look good.

After conducting a quick assessment of Bo's current needs, Carla led him back to his room. It was quite large and included both a king-sized bed and a luxurious bath. "Dinner will be served at six," Carla said. "Can I get you anything?"

"No, thank you," Bo replied. Carla bowed and backed out of the room in much the same way that a geisha might have.

It would have been nice to call the office on his sat phone. But Bo felt certain that the room was bugged. So he took a nap followed by a shower. Then it was time to get dressed. A dark suit and tie were mandatory according to the "Guide" on Bo's dresser, and tuxedos were welcome. No mention was made of uniforms, but Bo decided to wear his on the chance that Salazar would be impressed.

Once he was ready, Bo made his way down to the main level, where his fellow guests were gathered in front of a sleek, modernistic bar. The bartenders were backlit by a spectacular fish tank, and soft music was playing in the background, as Bo ordered a bourbon.

That was when the fashionista sidled up next to him. She had predatory eyes, a sculpted face, and was wearing a simple black dress. A cloud of perfume wafted around Bo as she fingered one of the ribbons on his chest. "Tell me about this one, General . . . How many people did you kill to earn it?"

"None," Bo replied. "Some guy with an AK-47 shot me."

The woman was undeterred. Her finger moved to another ribbon. "And this one?"

And so it went until Jorge rang a silver bell. "Dinner is being served in the dining room. Please follow me."

The dining room was beautifully furnished, in keeping with the rest of the house. A long slab of black granite rested on chrome legs, and was flanked by high-backed chairs.

The table settings were equally modern and laid out with the sort of precision that any general would approve of. Outside, beyond the glass, hundreds of carefully placed lights turned what would have otherwise been a black hole into a twinkling fantasyland.

Jorge was in charge of seating, and Bo found himself sitting between the drug lord and the Ecuadorian businessman. The crime boss was the more interesting of the two, and Bo was quizzing him about the war's impact on the drug trade when Salazar arrived.

The president was wearing a beautifully tailored tux and went straight to the head of the table, where a glass of cold champagne was being poured for him. As Salazar raised his glass, he invited his guests to do likewise. *"¡Viva México!"*

"¡Viva México!" the guests replied in unison. Waiters appeared as Salazar took his seat. Dinner began with a small tossed green salad, followed by lentil soup and blesbok steaks. The antelope meat was a first for Bo, and he liked it.

"Nothing goes to waste here," Salazar assured them. "The rest of the meat was distributed to my employees and their families." That produced some polite applause although Bo got the feeling that his fellow guests weren't concerned about what happened to the rest of the meat so long as they had theirs.

Once the meal was over, Salazar led his guests into the living room. It was a large, carefully decorated space, with all the charm of a hotel lobby.

Bo heard a whirring sound as a screen was lowered from a recess in the ceiling. "I thought you would enjoy watching footage of today's hunt," Salazar told them. "Especially those of you who actually hit something!"

The statement was framed as a joke, but Bo knew Salazar took the subject of marksmanship seriously and felt reasonably sure that his own performance had been adequate.

The opening shot consisted of an aerial shot captured by Salazar's drone as it flew over the undulating herd. That was followed by tighter shots captured from a variety of angles, and cut together with the skill one would expect of a world-class TV production company.

But most amazing, to Bo's mind, was the way in which Salazar's people had been able to grab a shot of a person firing their weapon followed by video of the hit. *If* they had a hit—which was not always the case.

The guests appeared one by one, often accompanied by commentary from their host. "That was a very nice shot," the president said, admiringly, as the fashionista dropped a buck with a bullet to the head. "Maybe next time," Salazar said, when the Japanese businessman missed. And so on.

Then Bo saw himself. And, according to what appeared on the screen, he proceeded to shoot a blesbok in the ass. "Oops!" Salazar said, as the slow-motion blood mist floated away. "It looks as though General Macintyre is a bit rusty! But never fear . . . He drops the next one with a clean shot through the heart." The guests chuckled.

As Bo watched the second animal fall, he knew that he'd been had. His bullet had killed the first animal even as another shooter put a bullet in its butt. Salazar perhaps? Firing quickly, so as to kill more blesbok than anyone else? Yeah, Bo would have been willing to bet on it.

Had Salazar directed his staff to misrepresent what actually occurred? Or did they routinely cover up for him? Bo would never know. Nor, in all truth, did he give a shit. What Bo wanted to do was cut a deal . . . And to go home.

Once the video review was complete, and the screen had been retracted into the ceiling, a pianist appeared. She was no more than sixteen years old but very talented. As the girl played, Salazar worked the crowd, telling jokes and slapping backs. Bo's included.

"So," Salazar said. "Do you smoke cigars?"

Bo didn't but said that he did. "Good," Salazar replied. "Follow me . . . We'll light up, enjoy the evening air, and discuss the war."

Bo felt a rising sense of excitement as he followed Salazar into the adjoining study. The president took a humidor off his desk, flipped the lid open, and offered the contents to Bo. "Cuban," Salazar said, as if that was all his guest needed to know.

"Thank you," Bo replied as he took a cigar. "These are hard to come by."

"That's true for most people," Salazar replied as he returned the humidor to the desk. "But for men such as ourselves? Anything is possible. Come . . . We'll light up outside. My wife hates the smell."

Sliding doors led out to a dedicated patio, which was home to some high-end deck furniture and lit with wall sconces. Salazar made a production out of clipping his cigar, passing it under his nose, and lighting up. Bo followed suit. Shadows moved as bodyguards patrolled the grounds.

"So," Salazar said, once their cigars were drawing properly. "Have a seat. The Confederacy sent its top general down to see me. *Why?* Is your Secretary of State on vacation?"

Bo smiled. "No, Mr. President. I'm here because this is a military matter—and the civilians figured we could discuss it general to general."

Salazar *was* a general in his country's reserve force, although to the best of Bo's knowledge, Salazar had never participated in anything more dangerous than a parade. Still, maybe some flattery would work. It did.

"Yes," Salazar agreed. "What do civilians know? It's our task to advise them."

"Exactly," Bo agreed. "And that brings me to the purpose of my visit. The Confederacy is winning the war, albeit slowly." That wasn't true of course, but how good was Mexican intelligence? And it was the kind of thing the Mexican president would expect him to say.

"So," Bo continued, "President Stickley wants to speed things up. And when she called on me for advice, I suggested that we examine the possibility of an arrangement with Mexico."

"What sort of arrangement?" Salazar wanted to know.

Bo blew a column of smoke out into the night. "The Confederacy would like to hire four divisions of Mexican troops to help bring the war to a speedy conclusion."

The tip of Salazar's cigar glowed cherry red as he drew on it. Smoke dribbled out through his nostrils. "I see," he said noncommittally. "Four divisions . . . What is that? Sixty thousand men?

Tell me, General . . . What would the Confederacy offer my country in return?"

"Half a billion Confederate dollars for twelve months of service," Bo answered. "Plus the supplies required to support your troops."

Salazar had heavy eyebrows and a Tom Selleck mustache. His eyes narrowed. "You must be joking."

Bo had arrived ready to negotiate. But the contempt in Salazar's voice took him by surprise. Some ash dribbled onto his right pant leg. He brushed it away. "Joking? Why do you say that?"

"Because the price is too low," Salazar replied. "Contrary to your claims, the Confederacy is *losing* the war, and losing it badly. What? You think that all of the mercenaries you hired are what they seem? Some of them work for our *Inteligencia Militar*. So, if you wish to secure our help, it will cost more. *Much* more."

In spite of the fact that the air was cool, Bo was beginning to sweat. "Okay, I might be able to scrape up another two hundred million or so."

Salazar threw back his head and laughed. "No, General . . . Mexico isn't going to take sides in your civil war for seven hundred million dollars."

"What then?" Bo wanted to know.

Salazar leaned forward in his chair. His eyes were unnaturally bright. "What we want is a large chunk of the land that was stolen from us during and after the Mexican-American War. Assuming the Confederacy wins, we want sovereignty over the states of California, Nevada, Utah, and Arizona. You'll notice we aren't asking for *all* of our territory . . . Just the section that is currently controlled by the North.

"And win or lose," Salazar added, "we want *two* tons of gold. One ton of which will serve as a deposit."

Bo felt his spirits plummet. Now he knew the answer to his question. Mexican intelligence was better than good—it was excellent. Because Salazar had not only known about the Confederate offer in advance, he'd been ready with a counter. And his demands made sense, from a Mexican point of view, anyway, which was the only thing Salazar cared about.

By taking control of the land Salazar was asking for, his country could not only regain what had been lost back in the 1800s, it could pocket some serious change and enjoy a measure of revenge for the anti-Mexican rhetoric American politicians had trafficked in for so long. All of which would be wildly popular with Salazar's constituents.

And who would be seen as the father of all that? Don Luis Salazar, that's who . . . And that's why the man across from Bo had a big smile on his face. "So," he said, "what's your answer?"

"I will take your proposal to the president," Bo replied stiffly. "We'll get back to you."

"Of course," Salazar said as he leaned back into his chair. "Take your time. Would you like some cognac?"

CHICAGO, ILLINOIS, THE UNION OF NORTHERN STATES

Sunlight streamed down through breaks in the cloud cover to bathe Chicago's Near North Side neighborhood in gold. The soldiers stood in ranks, feet apart, hands clasped behind them. They wore new uniforms and had been inspected twice. Of the 277 POWs rescued from the Confederate prison in Ascensión, Mexico, 212 had been cleared to take part in the parade that was about to begin. The others were still being treated for injuries, malnutrition, and/or PTSD in Colorado. "Listen up!" Sergeant Major Deeds boomed.

"You are going to ride in the buses parked behind you. You *will* wave, you *will* smile, and you *will* be happy. Do you read me?"

It was a joke, and the soldiers knew that. They replied with a loud "Hooah!"

Deeds grinned. "Good. Major Macintyre would like to say a few words. Major?"

Like her soldiers, Macintyre was wearing a dress uniform. When was the last time she'd had one of those on? For her court-martial? Yes. It seemed like a year ago even though only months had passed. Mac took three paces forward and stopped. A camera drone circled overhead. The craziness had begun.

"Good morning. The city of Chicago and the rest of the nation will be watching you during the parade and afterwards as well. So don't pick your noses. I'm looking at you Corporal Moses." The rest of the soldiers laughed, and Moses grinned proudly.

"Reporters will ask you questions," Mac told them. "They'll want to know what it was like in prison, the way you were treated, and how you managed to survive. Tell the truth.

"But remember, charges have been brought against Captain Roupe, and questions about his case should be referred to the public-affairs officer. She'll take it from there. Do you have any questions?" There weren't any.

"Okay," Deeds said to a staff sergeant. "Load 'em up."

As the ex-POWs boarded the double-decker tour buses, and climbed up to the top, where onlookers could see them, Mac led Deeds over to the point where the rescuers were assembled. They, too, had been asked to participate in the parade and the festivities that were to follow. The preboarding briefing that Mac gave them was nearly identical to the one that the ex-POWs had received. The soldiers were excited, and Mac knew why. Once the waving was over, they would be free to roam Chicago, the citizens of which were sure to wine and dine them.

Mac, along with Evers, Okada, and Deeds had been scheduled to lead the parade in a retro Cadillac convertible but elected to follow along behind so that the focus would be on the troops. It didn't work.

As a squad of motorcycle cops led the buses out onto the Magnificent Mile parade route, and dozens of cameras focused on the ex-POWs, even more photographers were busy grabbing shots of the Cadillac. Or more specifically, of Mac.

Because if the soldiers were interesting, then Major Robin Macintyre was even more so. Here was the officer who had rescued President Sloan from Richton, Mississippi, *and* defeated the Warlord of Warlords, prior to being court-martialed for disobedience.

Then, after a pardon from the president, Mac's Marauders had racked up a string of successes, many of which had been in the news. "Now what?" one of the news anchors wondered out loud. "The president is here, Major Macintyre is here, and both of them are going to attend the Freedom Ball this evening. Are the rumors of an affair true? Maybe we'll find out."

The Magnificent Mile had been closed to vehicular traffic, and onlookers lined both sides of what was normally a very busy street. Many members of the crowd were armed with American flags and waved them as the POWs waved back.

Then, as the buses passed between rows of high-rise buildings, a blizzard of red, white, and blue confetti began to fall. It was a sight to see—and President Sloan was watching from his suite in the Langham Hotel. He turned to Press Secretary Doyle Besom. "Nice job, Doyle . . . Where did the flags come from?"

"The America Rising Foundation paid for them." Besom answered. "This is an excellent time to remind people of the old flag. The *real* flag."

"Yes," Sloan agreed, as a drone-mounted camera zoomed in on

Robin Macintyre. She was still alive, thank God. And as beautiful as ever.

"There she is," a TV newswoman said. "Major Robin Macintyre. She led the raid into Mexico. But many viewers will remember that she rescued President Sloan, too, and was rumored to be having an affair with him, although no evidence has surfaced to support that allegation." *Because there isn't any evidence,* Sloan thought. *Robin says we should wait. But maybe, just maybe, I can change her mind.*

"Mr. President?"

Sloan could tell that he'd missed something. "Yes?"

"Mrs. Farrow wants to finalize seating arrangements for tonight's dinner. As it stands now, the Secretary of Defense, Senator Markley from Illinois, the House majority and minority leaders, Ambassador Zinski, and Mya Morrison are slated to sit with you."

Morrison was a well-known pop singer and one of Sloan's supporters. And, since she was going to sing, he couldn't move her. But Zinski? Mrs. Farrow would find another way to stroke the diplomat's ego. "Remove the ambassador from the list," Sloan instructed. "And add Major Macintyre."

Besom was fortysomething, a bit overweight, and famously wore his hair Ben Franklin style. He frowned. "That's asking for trouble, sir . . . You know what the press will say."

"Yes," Sloan replied. "I do. Is there anything else we need to discuss?"

||||||||||||

Mac had never been required to wear a blue mess uniform before. But, according to what she'd been told, that was what the occasion required. There was a full-length mirror in her hotel room, and she stood in front of it. The blue waist-length jacket had gold facings and was cut so as to reveal a black neck tab and a ruffled white blouse.

A black cummerbund was cinched around her waist and, below that, a full-length skirt hung to the floor. There was a lot of gold braid, too, not to mention her silver star and two medals that had been working their way through the bureaucracy until the day before. They included the Distinguished Service Cross and a Purple Heart.

Mac thought she looked pretty good but dreaded the prospect of having dinner with Sloan. People would talk. No, they *were* talking. Surely, Sloan knew that. And, judging from the invitation, he didn't care. Or he cared but was willing to take the heat.

Mac felt mixed emotions about that. On the one hand, she thought Sloan was being reckless, and on the other, she liked the fact that he would take risks to be with her. Mac felt a familiar tightness in her abdomen as she turned away. It was the same sensation she felt just before she entered combat.

IIIIIIIIIIIII

The Langham's gigantic ballroom was more than half-filled with linen-draped tables, each set with silver, and surrounded by formally attired guests. Sloan and two members of his security detail were waiting behind the blue curtain that ran all the way across one end of the room. The thing that Sloan liked least about his role as president was the endless pomp and ceremony. Yes, he understood the need for it but looked forward to a time when he could enter a room without being announced. "Ladies and gentlemen," a male voice said loudly. "It is my pleasure to welcome the President of the Northern States!"

Everyone stood and a band played "Hail to the Chief" as Sloan entered the ballroom and made his way over to a small podium. The applause was loud and sustained. "Thank you, thank you very much. Please be seated. And thanks for attending the America Rising Dinner and Ball. Our ex-POWs are here . . . As are the men and women who rescued them. Please welcome both."

The soldiers stood, and many of them looked embarrassed as the crowd applauded. Sloan smiled as they took their seats again. "There won't be any speeches tonight, my friends. Just good food, and good friends, followed by an opportunity to embarrass ourselves on the dance floor."

There was appreciative laughter as Sloan made his way over to the head table. He was careful to greet all of the people seated around it, but only had eyes for one of them. Mac looked every inch the army officer but beautiful, too, and when their eyes met, something special passed between them. Sloan felt like a schoolboy who, having been smitten by the prettiest girl in the seventh grade, has trouble speaking. "Good evening, Major . . . It's wonderful to see you again. Thank you for your service to our country."

||||||||||||

Mac felt the instant sense of connection. It was so strong that she feared the rest of the people at the table could sense it, too. "Thank you for *your* service, Mr. President. I like the tux by the way . . . You have a James Bond thing going on."

The people at the table chuckled, including Secretary of State Garrison, who was seated on her left. "It's wonderful to have you back, young lady. There were some worried faces in the Situation Room. Especially when those Jaguars arrived on the scene. I want you to know that the president called for air support the moment they appeared. But, by the time the F-35s arrived over your position ten minutes later, you had the situation under control."

The possibility that Sloan had been watching over her hadn't occurred to Mac. It should have. Sloan would monitor such a mission no matter who was in command. But the fact remained, he'd been there for her even if it was from a long ways off.

Senator Markley was seated to Mac's right. He was a staunch member of the Patriot Party and peppered her with questions as courses came and went, so that by the time the cherry tart arrived, Mac was wondering if the interrogation would ever end.

Meanwhile, Mac hadn't been able to chat with the stunning Mya Morrison, the one person other than Sloan who she wanted to speak with the most.

Senator Markley was in the process of formulating his next question when the MC stepped up to the podium. He had white hair, a runner's physique, and the practiced manner of a game-show host. "And now, after a fabulous meal, it's time for some entertainment. The Grammy-winning vocal artist Mya Morrison is with us this evening . . . And she's going to sing her latest hit. Please give her a warm welcome!"

Morrison had carefully styled hair, dark-colored skin, and a great figure. Her blue dress was covered with hundreds of silver sequins. They glittered as Morrison made her way over to a raised platform, and the other guests clapped.

Mac joined the applause as the blue curtain parted to reveal Morrison's band. Once she was in place, they began to play. Mac was pleased to discover that the song had nothing to do with the war. It was upbeat dance music and a reminder of better times. The audience loved it and gave Morrison a standing O. "Now," the MC said, as the dessert dishes were cleared away. "It's time to dance! Mr. President? Are you ready?"

IIIIIIIIIIIII

Sloan *wasn't* ready. But he'd been taking lessons for the last five days in hopes of maintaining his dignity. Everyone applauded as he went forward to embrace Morrison and wheel the entertainer around the dance floor. Their performance lasted for no more than a couple of minutes. But it felt like an eternity, and Sloan felt a tremendous sense of relief once it was over.

More people filtered onto the dance floor as Sloan thanked Morrison, made way for the Assistant Secretary of Veterans Affairs, and returned to the table. Senator Markley was still there—and still bending Mac's ear. "Excuse me, Senator," Sloan said. "But I'm going to pull rank. Major, could I have this dance? Even though I may step all over your feet?"

Mac laughed. "At least you aren't wearing combat boots! Of course, it would be my pleasure. Senator, if you'll excuse us?"

Markley had no choice but to nod agreeably as the couple departed for the dance floor. "Thank you," Mac said. "There's only one thing worse than combat; that's sitting next to Senator Markley during a long dinner."

Sloan laughed as they came to a stop. "Welcome to my world, Major. Shall we?"

Mac entered the circle of his arms. "I prefer Robin while dancing."

Sloan grinned. "And I prefer Sam. Are you ready?"

Mac smiled up at him. "Roger that, Sam." Then they were off. Sloan was a better dancer than Mac expected him to be. And, as they circled the floor, Mac found that it was easy to follow his lead. The surrounding faces became a blur, and for that brief moment, Mac was free to be herself, without worrying about the people who reported to her. And it felt good.

So Mac felt disappointed when the music came to an end, and they stepped off the dance floor. People were staring, but none of them were close enough to hear. "I want to take you home," Sloan told her. "To the farm where I grew up. Will you come?"

"I'd *like* to come," Mac told him. "But we'd be crossing a line. People would talk. Cable news would work it twenty-four/seven. Your enemies would rehash my court-martial *and* the pardon."

"I know that," Sloan replied. "But it's a price I'm willing to pay. *Please*, Robin . . . Please come with me."

Mac paused for a moment. She didn't want to cause problems for Sloan, but the opportunity to spend some quality time with him was too good to pass up. And what the hell? He was a big boy and knew what would happen. "All right, Sam . . . I'll go. But only if we go there soon. I've been away from Mac's Marauders for too long. I need to get back to them. Plus, if I hang around for very long, people will accuse you of favoritism."

"That won't be a problem," Sloan told her. "You're going to receive an invitation to testify before Congress. Members of my party want to ask you questions, and being politicians, be seen with you. I will ask the Speaker to shoehorn your appearance into the schedule. And if you're here to testify, no one can complain. Thank you, Robin. You'll hear from me soon."

And with that, they were forced to part company as a middle-aged congresswoman in a red suit arrived. "Excuse me, Major . . . But it's rude to hog all the single men! How 'bout it, Mr. President? Shall we trip the light fantastic?"

"I'm ready to trip," Sloan said good-naturedly. "So be ready." He offered his arm, and the congresswoman took it. Mac looked, saw that the head table was momentarily empty, and took the opportunity to fade. Her evening was over.

A sharp-looking lieutenant delivered the "invitation" the following morning. And, according to the formally phrased document, Mac was to appear in front of the House Armed Services Committee at 1000 the next day. "Fortunately, you have some time to prepare," Lieutenant Newsome told her.

"For *what*?" Mac inquired.

"Committee members can ask you anything they want, ma'am," Newsome answered. "The chairman will try to keep things on the straight and narrow. But the members have the right to ask you questions about obscure weapons programs, military strategy, and morale if they choose to. So it's best to be ready for anything."

Mac didn't like the sound of that. But there was nothing she could do. The rest of the day was spent in a hotel meeting room prepping for the hearing. Newsome was there, along with other subject-matter experts, all vying to ensure that Mac would represent their particular discipline well. Mac had a headache by the time 1400 rolled around and had to go take some pain tablets before returning to the fray.

Mac had trouble getting to sleep that night. And once she did, her dreams were beset by all manner of fears and concerns. So that when Mac awoke, she felt no more rested than she had the evening before.

After brushing her teeth, Mac took a hot shower and dressed with care. And there were lots of reasons to do so. It was important to look sharp for the committee, but there was the military brass to be concerned about as well, not to mention the TV cameras. "*You're* the reason the networks want to cover the hearing," Newsome had told her. "So keep that in mind."

Mac met Newsome in the hotel's lobby, and they had breakfast together before going out front, where a black SUV sat waiting for them. A private was at the wheel. "Where are we going?" Mac inquired, as the vehicle pulled away.

"We're headed for what was the University of Chicago and hopefully will be again," Newsome replied. "The university was forced to close after the May Day meteor strikes. And when Congress decided to set up shop in Chicago, the campus was the natural choice.

"A lot of people think Chicago should be recognized as the new capital, but the president isn't one of them. He plans to rebuild D.C., or start the process, anyway, since the project will take a long time."

Mac thought about that as the SUV's driver wound her way through morning traffic. The problems that Sloan faced were not only numerous, but complex, and she was one of them. The thought amused her, and Mac smiled through rain-streaked glass.

The trip took twenty minutes. Newsome used the time to quiz Mac regarding the military minutiae she'd been force-fed the previous day. But eventually the SUV entered a side street and pulled over. "We'll have to hoof it from here," Newsome told her. "But don't worry . . . It's a short walk."

"I'll call you when we're ready to leave," Newsome told the driver, and she nodded.

A light rain was falling, and neither of them had an umbrella. They hurried through a passageway between two buildings and onto the path that led to Cobb Hall. There were no students to be seen—and for good reason. Most were fighting or working in a factory. There were plenty of bureaucrats, though . . . Most of whom had been wise enough to bring umbrellas to work.

The Cobb Lecture Hall was on the left. It was a Gothic-style structure with an imposing entrance. But unlike the exterior, the interior had a utilitarian feel. Newsome knew his way around. And as they arrived on the second floor, both of them had to show their ID cards and pass through a metal detector before being allowed to proceed.

After they cleared the checkpoint, Newsome led Mac down a corridor to the door labeled, HOUSE ARMED SERVICES COMMITTEE. A man left, and as the officers entered, they were intercepted by a young woman named Molly.

"I'm one of Congressman Hastings's aides," she informed them. "Please follow me." Thanks to the schooling she received the day before, Mac knew that Hastings was the chairman of the committee and one of Sloan's supporters.

Reporters yelled questions as Molly led the officers through the press section and into the area reserved for members of the public. It was packed, and Mac could feel their stares as she followed Molly to a table down front. Three officers were waiting to greet her, all of whom were used to dealing with Congress and could help her in a pinch. Had Secretary Garrison requested that? Or the president himself? Not that it made any difference.

Mac had never met the general, the colonel, or the major before—and wondered how they felt about having to take part. Were they annoyed? Probably. And that would make sense. Her testimony was a sideshow, and likely to be a boring one at that.

But what was, was. And all of them had to go through the motions. "Odds are that everything will go smoothly," General Overby told her. "But don't hesitate to stand up for yourself if those jerks get in your face."

Mac thanked the general for his advice and took her seat, knowing that Newsome, Overby, and the others were seated behind her and had her six. A nerve-wracking five minutes passed while committee members milled around, whispered to each other, and checked their cell phones before finally taking their places.

The session was called to order after that and, much to Mac's surprise, she was sworn in. Was that a mere formality? Or a hint of potential trouble? Mac was already nervous and felt even more so at that point.

The process began with a warm welcome from Hastings. He was a grandfatherly type from Maine and went to great lengths to thank both the ex-POWs *and* their rescuers before allowing others to speak.

Then, consistent with Newsome's warnings, Mac found herself fielding questions about strategy, the new Iron Shield defense system, and the increasing use of robotics on the battlefield. None of which were subjects that she knew much about.

Mac said as much, called upon what little she knew, and things were going fairly well until Congressman Will's turn rolled around. He had a crotchety manner and, according to what she'd been told the day before, was one of Sloan's most outspoken critics. And because of her relationship with the president, Mac knew the politician was likely to be hostile. That, as it turned out, was definitely the case.

Will cleared his throat. "Thank you, Mr. Chairman. I have a different type of question for you, Major. According to what I've read, your father, General Bo Macintyre, serves as Chairman of the Joint Chiefs for the New Confederacy. Is that correct?"

"I've read that," Mac replied carefully. "But I don't have personal knowledge of it."

Will tilted his head down so as to peer at her over his glasses. "So you don't communicate with your father?"

"No," Mac answered flatly. "We've been estranged for years. And, even if that weren't the case, such communications would be inappropriate at this time."

"I see," Will said as he played with a pen. "But what if your father found a way to contact you? And told you to act on behalf of the Confederacy? What would you do then?"

"I would tell him to fuck off," Mac replied. "Then I would report the contact to my commanding officer."

The audience tittered. Will had bushy eyebrows. They rose incrementally. "Please watch your language, Major. You aren't in a bar.

"Now, while you maintain that you would ignore an order from your father, I remain unconvinced. And I daresay that others share my concern about the possibility of a security breach where you and General Macintyre are concerned. Especially in light of the fact that you were court-martialed for disobeying a direct order."

"I was pardoned," Mac said flatly.

"By a man you may, or may not, have slept with," Will countered smugly.

A mantle of hopelessness began to settle over Mac. Will was using her to hurt Sloan, and there wasn't a damned thing she could do about it, unless . . . A possibility entered her mind. "One moment, please. I would like to submit a document that I believe is relevant to this discussion."

Chairman Hastings looked surprised. "Yes, of course."

"I object!" Will said loudly. "We need to make sure that the document is real before . . ."

Hastings brought his gavel down. "Never fear, the document will be verified."

Mac opened her purse, removed the piece of paper she kept there, and gave it to Molly.

Molly took the much-folded piece of paper up to Hastings, who flattened it on the table in front of him. A look of surprise appeared on his face as he read it. A thin smile followed. "This *is* relevant. Molly, please make copies for the rest of the committee.

"In the meantime," Hastings continued, "I will read the document out loud. 'Wanted Dead or Alive, Major Robin Macintyre, Commanding Officer Mac's Marauders, for war crimes.' "

Hastings went on to describe Mac's photo before reading the rest of the text. " 'After being pardoned by Union president Samuel T. Sloan, Macintyre and her band of criminals committed numerous crimes, including kidnapping and the murder of her sister, Confederate major Victoria Macintyre.

" 'Upon delivery of Major Robin Macintyre to the proper authorities, or DNA evidence proving her death, the government of the New Confederacy will pay a reward equivalent to $100,000 in either gold or silver.' "

Hastings paused at that point, as if to make sure that everyone in the hall was paying close attention. "And here, at the bottom of the page, is the following text: 'By order of General Bo Macintyre, Chairman of the Joint Chiefs, Confederate Army.' "

Hastings eyed the TV cameras. "I think that any questions regarding Major Macintyre's relationship with her father, and her loyalty to our government, have been answered." The gavel fell again. "This meeting is adjourned."

CHAPTER 8

To the victor belong the spoils.

—SENATOR WILLIAM L. MARCY

HOUSTON, TEXAS

A stiff breeze was blowing in from the southwest. It caused the water taxi to wallow as it turned into the channel that led into Brazosport.

It felt good to be back in Houston even if that meant Bo had to deal with the Iron Maiden. Still, based on what Bo had heard via his personal network, the newly confirmed president was doing a good job. "She's kicking ass and taking names," was the way one admiral put it.

And that, Bo reflected, would make for a nice change. Thanks to a combination of incompetence and laziness on the part of ex-president Morton Lemaire, the initiative had been lost during the early months of the war.

Once the launch was inside the channel, the waves disappeared, and it took less than five minutes to reach the Coast Guard station where Bo's Land Rover was parked. Colin Ferth turned the wheel and brought the boat in next to the dock with a gentle bump.

A skillful application of power kept the boat in place as Bo stood and handed the retired petty officer a silver coin with a likeness of Ayn Rand on it. "Thanks for nothing, Colin . . . That was a crappy ride."

Colin grinned. "Tell it to Mother Nature, General. She's in charge. What time are you going to head home?"

"I don't know yet," Bo replied as he stepped up onto the dock. "I'll text you later in the day."

Colin tossed a salute. "Yes, sir. Have a good one."

That seemed unlikely. But Bo could hope. It was a short drive to the command and control center, but a long wait was required to get in.

Finally, after working his way through a twenty-vehicle queue, Bo arrived at Checkpoint Alpha. A sharp-looking MP delivered a perfect salute, eyed Bo's ID, and waved him through.

Half a mile later, Bo had to stop at Checkpoint Bravo and go through the whole rigmarole again. The process was a pain in the ass, but a necessary one, to prevent Union agents from getting in.

After parking his car, Bo rode the elevator up to the floor where his office was located. Bo had been forced to select a new secretary once his engagement to Kathy was announced, and Emily was there to greet him as he entered the office. She was about ten years younger than Kathy, and though given to trendy clothing, had a style that was similar to her predecessor's. Which was to say that Emily was calm, cool, and magnificently efficient.

Emily handed Bo a list of the people who had called in descending order of importance as he passed her desk, and Bo read it as he entered his inner office, where the usual thermos of hot coffee was waiting. The next forty-five minutes were spent dealing with all sorts of pressing problems, including the raid on a contractor-run POW camp in Ascensión, Mexico.

A number of Mexican prisoners had been captured and taken north, where they would probably spill their guts. And that, according to a telephone conversation with General Marcus Lorenzo, was likely to be a problem. "If the North wins the war, they're going to hold trials," Lorenzo explained. "And we could be blamed for irregularities at the prison."

"*What* fucking irregularities?" Bo demanded.

"It seems that Senorita Carbone was feeding the POWs less food than the contract called for," Lorenzo told him, "which allowed her to skim money off the top. And, according to some, she was abusive."

Bo felt the anger boil up inside of him. "Listen, you son of a bitch, it was *your* job to make sure that Carbone honored that contract! I have to meet with the president in fifteen minutes," Bo added. "But if I didn't, I'd go down to your office and kick your ass!"

And with that, he slammed the receiver down. General Marcus Lorenzo didn't know it, but he was going to die fighting for his country, and in the very near future.

The command and control center's top floor was divided into meeting rooms. They were named after Confederate generals, and it seemed fitting that the meeting with President Martha Stickley was scheduled to take place in the Robert E. Lee Room. Bo and half a dozen of his senior officers were present when the helicopter designated as Rebel One circled the building and landed on the roof.

Ten minutes passed. Then a Secret Service agent entered, looked around, and spoke into a wrist mike. That prompted three additional agents to enter the room. They checked to make sure that the people in the room were who they claimed to be and conducted a brief search before allowing Stickley to enter.

The president was tall, thin, and impeccably dressed. She had dark shoulder-length hair and green eyes. They jumped from face to face as Bo made the introductions. Stickley had met most of the attendees before and, thanks to an eidetic memory, she remembered the date of each encounter. It was an impressive feat, and a surefire boost to needy egos, of which there were many in the room.

Once the pleasantries were out of the way, and everyone had taken their seats around the oval table, it was time to get down to the important business of waging war. "So," Stickley said as she placed a well-manicured finger on the binder in front of her. "This is the final draft."

Bo nodded. "Yes, ma'am."

"And the comma splice on page 112 was corrected?"

Bo wanted to say, "Who gives a shit about the comma splice," but managed to control his temper. "Yes, ma'am."

Stickley smiled. "Good. I assume the issues I identified in draft one have been resolved. So pitch me. Or repitch me as the case may be. Why should we enter into an alliance with Mexico? And how would it work?"

Bo, with help from officers representing all of the different branches of the military, spent the next fifteen minutes detailing the plan. And they did a good job, too. That's what Bo thought, anyway. But, judging from the expression on the president's face, she remained unconvinced.

"I agree that the influx of four divisions, no matter how untested they are, could make an important difference in the war effort. But the price is too high. Two tons of gold *plus* the states of California, Nevada, Utah, and Arizona is more than I can stomach. And, if that part of the deal were to become public somehow, the North would fight even harder."

Bo nodded. "I realize that, Madam President. But what you won't find in the written plan, or on the PowerPoint slides, is something called Operation Overlord."

Stickley looked skeptical. "Which is?"

"President Salazar's proposal is very specific," Bo responded. "His chain of command is to be left intact, his troops won't be allowed to serve side by side with ours, and we can't break the Mexican divisions down into their component parts. All of which makes sense from Salazar's point of view. He knows that the citizens of California, Nevada, Utah, and Arizona will fight back when Mexico declares sovereignty over them. And he'll need at least four divisions of battle-tested troops to keep the gringos in line.

"But Salazar's plan has a weakness," Bo added. "And it's this . . . By keeping his forces together, all in one place, he will make them vulnerable to weapons he can't defend against. Weapons that can lay waste to an entire division in minutes."

Bo watched Stickley take the idea in and process it. Her well-plucked eyebrows rose. "Let me see if I understand. We pay the deposit, Mexico sends troops, and we use them to win the war. Then we use tactical nukes to decimate Salazar's divisions *before* Mexico can seize any territory."

"Exactly," Bo replied. "And that might be sufficient. But remember that while Mexico would be severely wounded at that point, it would still have a pulse. And by killing something on the order of sixty thousand Mexican troops, we could create so much hatred south of the border that we would have to fight another war just months after winning the one with the North.

"To avoid that scenario, we recommend that the Confederacy pivot to the south as soon as the tactical situation allows us to, invade Mexico, and take *all* the territory north of the Panama Canal. Countries like Guatemala, El Salvador, and Nicaragua were doing poorly *before* the meteor strikes. They're even worse off now.

"Think of it as an extension of Manifest Destiny," Bo added. "Think of it as the country the United States could have been, *should* have been, reborn based on conservative principles."

The president was silent for a moment. Bo held his breath. What would it be? Yes to a glorious future? Or no to the plan that could win the war *and* pave the way to a twenty-first-century empire?

Stickley's eyes locked with his. "You amaze me, General . . . Finally, someone with vision. *And* the balls to make the vision real. I want every person in this room sworn to secrecy. I want a security detail for all of the participants, and I want everything pertaining to Project Overlord to be classified as top secret. We have a plan, people . . . Let's make it happen."

CHICAGO, ILLINOIS

After testifying before Congress, Mac returned to her hotel. And there, waiting at the front desk, was an envelope bearing the presidential seal. Mac took the envelope up to her room before opening it. Mac found a neatly typed itinerary inside along with a handwritten note from Sloan.

Dear Robin,

Nice job! It will be a long time before Congressman Will gets over that. As for your father, I knew the two of you were estranged but hadn't heard about the bounty. I'm sorry, Robin . . . This is a terrible war in so many ways.

Please review the attachment. If it's okay, then no action is required on your part. But if you want to make a change, call the number at the bottom of the page by 6:00 PM, and ask for Mrs. Farrow. Sadly, everything I do involves a lot of logistics. So last-minute changes can be difficult.

The press will find out about the trip. That's a given. But you know that. When we're together, we can discuss how to handle the inevitable flap. And oh, by the way, you're on leave. Just in case someone asks about your status.

I look forward to seeing you at O'Hare in the morning.

Affectionately yours,
Sam

Mac checked to see if she had any doubts regarding the trip. Was Sam the one she'd been waiting for? Yes, well, maybe. But she would never be able to decide without spending some time with him. Even if a price had to be paid.

Mac slept well that night, awoke feeling rested, and ordered room service. Then, after completing her morning routines, she got dressed. Not in a uniform but in some of the civilian clothes she had purchased the evening before. Mac had lost track of fashion many months earlier. Fortunately, the store had a professional shopper who was happy to help and professed to be a fan. Mac knew she had critics. A lot of them. But it was nice to have a fan.

Now, dressed in new clothes, Mac felt different. For once, the person in the mirror came across as a young woman instead of a military officer. An attractive woman? She hoped so.

Since her arrival in Chicago, Mac had not only acquired some civilian clothes, she'd been issued new uniforms as well, and stocked up on everything from toothpaste to shampoo. That forced her to purchase a rolling suitcase to carry her loot in. After completing an idiot check to make sure she had everything, Mac towed the bag out into the hall.

It was early, and there was only one other person in the elevator that carried her down to the lobby. A man in a black suit was holding a card with her name on it. Mac identified herself, and unlike all of the drivers she'd had in the past, this one demanded to see her ID.

Something else was different, too . . . Rather than offer to take Mac's suitcase, the man led the way unencumbered. In order to keep his hands free? If so, the security precautions weren't for her but for Sloan.

It was quiet in the back of the SUV. So much so that Mac figured the vehicle was armored and sealed against gas attacks. It took the driver forty minutes to work his way through traffic and arrive in front of an obscure gate at O'Hare Airport. The guards wore civilian clothes but had military mannerisms.

A two-person team ran a check on the vehicle, while a third checked the driver's ID, before coming back to request Mac's. After examining the card, the woman gave it back.

Then, before Mac had time to roll the window up, the guard came to attention. The salute he gave her even though neither of them was in uniform was parade-ground perfect. "Thank you for getting those POWs out of Mexico, ma'am. One of them was my brother." And with that, the MP turned and walked away.

After passing through the gate, the SUV followed a pickup equipped with flashing lights through a maze of access lanes to the location where a Boeing C-32 sat waiting on the tarmac.

The SUV stopped a hundred feet away from the roll-up stairs that had been pushed up against the plane. As Mac got out of the vehicle, the driver went back to get her suitcase. It made a rattling noise as he towed it forward, and Mac was about to take over, when an air force noncom appeared. "I'll take care of that," he said. "It will be available in the main cabin if you need it. The president is here . . . You're free to board."

Mac thanked both men before making her way up the stairs to the entry port, where a casually dressed attendant was waiting to greet her. "Major Macintyre? I'm Tim . . . Welcome to Air Force One. Please follow me."

As they went aft, Mac caught glimpses of a communications center, a galley, and a lavatory. Then came a section of seats followed by a private cabin. There were *more* business-class seats beyond that. Sloan rose to greet her. "Good morning! Have you had breakfast? No? Have a seat. Tim will fix you up. I need to go forward for a minute . . . But I'll be back as soon as I can."

Mac was sipping coffee by the time Air Force One took off. Tim brought breakfast shortly thereafter, and Sloan arrived two minutes later. He was dressed in a polo shirt, jeans, and a pair of beat-up cowboy boots. "How's the food?"

"Good, thanks," Mac replied. "I love the fresh fruit."

"It's coming back," Sloan said as he sat next to her. "Slowly, but surely, *everything* is coming back. It's only a matter of time now. The Confederacy is on its last legs."

"Good," Mac said. "The sooner the better."

"Yes," Sloan agreed. "But enough of that. I'm taking the day off, to the extent that such a thing is possible."

"You told me that we're going to the family farm," Mac said. "Where is it?"

"North of Omaha," Sloan replied. "I'm an only child. And when Dad passed away, Mom hoped that I would take over. But I had other ideas. So she hired a local man to run it. His name is Tom

Benson. Then, when Mom's health started to slide, I moved her to D.C. so I could keep an eye on her."

Sloan looked away at that point. "Mom's assisted-living facility was near ground zero. I went there as soon as I could. But there was nothing left."

"I'm sorry," Mac said as she placed a hand on top of his.

Sloan forced a smile. "Thanks. I was trying to protect her . . . to take care of her. And, if I'd left her in Nebraska, she'd be alive."

"All you can do is work with the information you have," Mac told him. "And there was no way to know that meteors were going to fall—much less exactly where they would strike."

"Yeah," Sloan agreed. "That's what I tell myself. Anyway, Tom continues to run the farm, and he's doing a good job. But that isn't the point of the trip. I want you to see the place where I grew up. *How* I grew up. And I want to escape the press for one glorious day."

The rest of the flight was spent talking about Sloan's childhood adventures, the summer vacations Mac had spent on her father's farm, and the steadily growing rift that came to separate them.

The trip to Offutt Air Force Base took a little more than an hour, and a Marine Corps VH-60N "White Hawk" helicopter was waiting on the ground when Air Force One landed. Marine One carried them over Omaha and up into farm country, where vast tracts of corn could be seen from both sides of the aircraft. "The crop is only half as tall as it should be at this time of year," Sloan observed. "Government scientists are working on that. In two, maybe three years, we'll have a variant that can flourish with less sunlight. That's when production will increase.

"The Whigs oppose that research by the way . . . Some of them believe that God sent the meteors to punish sinners—so bioengineering constitutes a contravention of God's will.

"Others suggest that I'm pushing the project because I own a farm. Meanwhile, the lobbyists for the big agro companies are all for it. They like me." Sloan sighed. "This stuff begins to wear on you after a while."

Mac changed the subject. "We covered your childhood on the farm. What about college? I have you down as a class-cutting, pot-smoking, girl chaser. Am I wrong?"

Sloan laughed. "You got two out of three right. I won't say which ones. Suffice it to say that I made it through, matured a bit, and went to grad school.

"How about you? According to one of the magazine articles I read, your father wanted you to attend West Point, but you entered OCS instead."

"True," Mac replied. "Dad pushed me, and I rebelled. But after taking some time off after college, I felt the pull. I guess the army is in my DNA. So I joined, but I did it *my* way, and it pissed him off. That and the fact that I sided with Mom prior to her death."

Sloan nodded. "I'm sorry, Robin . . . I wish things had been different for you."

The White Hawk had started to descend by then. Mac saw a curving driveway, a nicely kept farmhouse, and a handsome barn. All surrounded by shade trees and closely cropped grass. Cornfields stretched off into the distance. "It's beautiful," Mac remarked.

Sloan looked pleased. "Thank you. I thought about selling it at one point but decided not to. And a good thing, too . . . Now I have a place to go when the presidential gig is over."

Sloan was thinking about the future. A future without war. Mac tried to imagine it. What would she do? *Who* would she be? And what part, if any, would Sloan play in answering those questions? The ground came up to meet them, and there was a gentle thump as the chopper touched down.

"Come on," Sloan said as he freed his seat belt. "I'll say hello to Tom. Then, assuming you're up for it, we'll take a walk."

Benson wasn't the only person who was waiting for them. Four Secret Service agents were present, too, all of whom were sporting identical sunglasses, barn coats, and jeans. They formed a protective barrier around Sloan and stood facing out.

Benson was wearing a Levi's jacket, blue tee, and jeans. His gray hair was short, and there were creases around his eyes. Sloan took care of the introductions. "Robin, this is Tom Benson. Tom, this is my friend Robin Macintyre."

Mac could feel the calluses as Benson's hand closed around hers and could see the curiosity in his blue eyes. He'd known Sloan for a long time, after all . . . And had been friends with Sloan's parents.

Sloan had chosen to omit any mention of Mac's rank, thereby dropping any pretense that she was there in some sort of official capacity. That felt good. "It's a pleasure to meet you, Mr. Benson . . . Sam is a big fan of yours."

The praise caused Benson to beam. And as the men chatted about the corn crop, Mac circled the house. It was interesting to see Sloan in his natural element. And that, Mac realized, was his plan. He wanted to convey a sense of his actual persona minus the presidential trappings. It was helpful, even if he wasn't a farm boy anymore and never would be. Because, like it or not, Secret Service agents and a certain amount of notoriety would follow him for the rest of his life. "There you are," Sloan said as he came up behind her. "Are you ready for that walk?"

Mac was wearing expensive half boots purchased the day before and hoped they would survive whatever Sloan had in mind. "Sure," she said. "Lead the way."

"Every kid needs a hideout," Sloan said, as they entered a field.

It had rained the day before, and the ground was soft. Mac felt her boots sink in. "That's true," she agreed. "Especially if you have a big sister."

They were strolling between rows of corn by then. The plants were only waist high, and the tightly wrapped ears of corn were only half the size they should have been. "So you'll appreciate my fort," Sloan said. "It's a place where imaginary Indians and pirates couldn't touch me. There it is . . . Straight ahead."

The cottonwood was standing all alone and impossible to miss. Massive branches twisted and turned as they sought the sun, and thanks to the shade that the tree's canopy threw, the ground beneath the cottonwood was nearly bare.

"Dad wanted to cut it down," Sloan told Mac, as they paused to admire the tree. "He said we should plant corn there. But Mom said 'no.' She said the tree belonged to me and that I was the only one who could kill it."

Mac looked up at him. "And you didn't."

"No," Sloan replied. "I didn't. And I never will." He pointed. "Look up there . . . Can you see the platform? I built it."

Mac *could* see the platform. And she could see something else as well. She could see the essential goodness of the man standing next to her. Was he perfect? No. But neither was she.

Their first kiss was a tentative thing . . . little more than a gentle touch. Then Mac felt the pull she'd experienced before, and they kissed again. The second contact was more insistent and, had they been somewhere more private, would have led to further intimacies.

The moment was *so* compelling that neither of them was conscious of the Secret Service agents who stood with backs turned, staring out at the cornfields. Then something crashed through the foliage above them and clattered to the ground. Sloan turned towards the threat. "What the hell is *that*?"

"I'm sorry," one of the Secret Service agents said. "An unauthorized device entered the area . . . So one of our interceptor drones fired a burst of microwaves at it."

Mac went over to look at the device. The drone was about three feet across, had four motors, and was equipped with a camera. There were no visible markings on the device, but it didn't require a genius to know that it belonged to a TV network. Mac made eye contact with the agent. "Could a drone like this send a live feed?"

The agent nodded. "Yes, ma'am."

Mac turned to Sloan. "You know what this means."

He nodded. "We're busted. For real this time. Are you sorry?"

Mac remembered the kiss. "No. Never."

Sloan nodded. "Me either."

"I need to rejoin my unit. Especially after this. *Before* the shit hits the fan."

"Yes," Sloan agreed reluctantly. "That would be best."

Then he turned to the agent. "Head back to the helicopter . . . And take the rest of the detail with you. We'll be along shortly."

Murphy looked like he might refuse, seemed to think better of it, and spoke into his sleeve. All of the agents disappeared. Sloan took Mac into his arms. "Let's try that kiss again . . . Maybe we can get it right this time." They did.

HOUSTON, TEXAS

General Bo Macintyre looked up at the sky. It was blue, and the sun was shining. How long had it been since he'd seen *that*? A month? At least. And now, on his wedding day, ol' Sol was making an appearance. That meant Kathy was happy. And when she was happy, *he* was happy. Or happier, since a state of giddiness wasn't possible for someone of his temperament.

Bo went to the back of the Land Rover to get the groceries Kathy wanted. Most of it was items they already had, like mixed nuts, chips, and dip. But Kathy was concerned that they might run out. The sun was out, so more people would come. That was her logic. But Bo figured it would work the other way. People would want to play—and anyone who could bail out would do so. As for the rest of them, meaning the other members of the Joint Chiefs of Staff, they were screwed. Bo grinned. He'd been there and done that.

Bo carried the groceries up to the back door, turned the knob, and entered the kitchen. Guests would arrive soon, and the caterer was hard at work. The caterer turned to look at him. "Kathy says it's time to get dressed. Or else."

"Yes, ma'am," Bo said as he took an appetizer and popped it into his mouth. "Yum! Prawns rolled in bacon! Save ten of those for me."

"You'll have to negotiate that with the boss," the caterer replied. "Those kind of decisions are above my pay grade."

Bo laughed and left the room. There weren't going to be any uniforms. Kathy had been clear about that. So his tuxedo was laid out on the bed, and Bo knew that Kathy was in the bathroom. He was tying his shoes when she emerged. She had chosen to wear a peach-colored dress. It looked good against her tanned skin.

Bo went over to give Kathy a kiss, and she raised a hand. "Oh, no you don't! I just put my makeup on. Your tie is crooked. Hold still while I fix it."

Bo held still. He was lucky, *very* lucky, and wanted to tell her that. But such things were difficult for Bo. Maybe, had he been able to communicate more freely, his first marriage would have been more successful.

Forget that, Bo told himself. *It's over. Margaret is gone, just like Victoria, and you have to live in the now.* Just thinking about Victoria was enough to choke him up.

"There," Kathy said. "Slip into your jacket, and you'll be ready." Then, by way of a concession, she kissed him on the cheek. "I love you," Kathy said. "Now get out there and mingle!"

The ceremony was going to take place on the large terrace located next to the house. A buffet-style dinner would follow. In the meantime, guests were starting to gather under the umbrellas out front. That's where the bar, the appetizers, and the view were. Sun sparkled on the Gulf. And as Bo stepped onto the deck, a warm breeze caressed his face.

Kathy appeared shortly thereafter, and the next twenty minutes were spent socializing. Bo didn't care for such occasions as a rule. But, with Kathy to keep things going and a couple of drinks under his belt, Bo had to admit that he was having a good time.

The ceremony was classy but short. And by the time it was over, the sun was hanging low in the sky. Bo was chatting with Admiral Howell when Kathy appeared at his side. "Excuse me, gentlemen . . . But the bartender is running low on champagne, and I'm sending the general to get more."

"Your wish is my command," Bo said. After excusing himself, Bo circled around to the kitchen, entered through the back door, and made his way down a set of narrow stairs to the half basement below. The space was prone to flooding at times. But it was the perfect place for the old refrigerator that served as a wine cooler. Bo pulled the door open, reached inside, and heard what sounded like a clap of thunder.

Suddenly, most of the air was sucked out of the room, the ceiling caved in, and a two-by-four clipped the side of Bo's head. He fell to his knees. The possibility of a natural gas explosion was the first thing that entered his mind. But the house didn't use gas.

Then the awful truth dawned on him. *A bomb!* Dropped from a plane. No, that didn't make sense. Houston was a prime target, so it was surrounded by air-defense installations and protected by fighters. There would have been a warning had Northern planes headed south.

Bo placed the bottle of champagne on the floor and struggled to his feet. Plaster and other pieces of debris cascaded off his shoulders as he stepped over a shattered beam and was forced to crawl through a hole to reach the stairs. He had to find Kathy. She would be mad about the tux—and how dirty he was.

Bo battled his way up and into what amounted to a crater. The circular debris field was at least a hundred yards across, and with the exception of a single contrail, the sky was empty. There was no sign of bombers, fighters, or anything else for that matter. What then, Bo wondered? What would account for such devastation?

The answer was a missile. A fucking missile. Launched from a submarine off the coast and flying so low that none of the defensive radars had been able to detect it.

The attack was similar to those he had requested while serving in Afghanistan. Only instead of targeting the Taliban, the North had attempted to kill *him*. *And* the Joint Chiefs of Staff. It would be a coup . . . the sort of strike that would do incredible damage to the Confederate war effort. "Kathy!" Bo yelled. "Where are you?"

Sirens could be heard in the distance as Bo searched the rubble, looking for his wife. When Bo found her, he wished he hadn't. Kathy's body lay in a pool of blood. Her eyes stared sightlessly at the sky, and her right arm was missing. "Oh, God," Bo said as he fell to his knees beside her. "Please, no." Bo's tears landed on Kathy's face and cut tracks through the dust on her cheeks. He held her hand, the one with his ring on it, and sobbed. "I'm sorry, so sorry."

A fireman appeared. His voice was gentle. "There's nothing you can do for her, sir. Here . . . Let me give you a hand."

"Look at what the bastards did," Bo said, as the fireman helped him to stand. "I'm going to kill them. Not just a few . . . I'm going to kill *all* of them."

"Yes, sir," the fireman said soothingly. "You're bleeding. Come with me . . . We'll patch you up."

Bo had to step over Admiral Howell's decapitated body in order to leave the scene. Broken glass crunched underfoot, a helicopter clattered above, and sunlight glittered on the sea.

OFFUTT AIR FORCE BASE, NEBRASKA

When the helicopter touched down at Offutt, Sloan left the aircraft by himself. An air force officer was there to escort the president to Air Force One. Sloan paused at the top of the stairs, turned to wave at the cameras, and ducked inside.

Then, and only then, did Mac emerge from the helicopter. Yes, the press might grab a shot of her. But it wouldn't be the one they wanted so badly. Which was to say a shot that included Sloan. Not that it mattered much. Sloan had already heard from Press Secretary Besom. Footage of what the press was referring to as "the kiss" had aired and was getting lots of play.

A noncom was waiting for Mac. He saluted. "I'm Sergeant Lewis, ma'am. They sent me over to give you a lift." He gave her an envelope. "Your orders are inside. Here, let me give you a hand with that suitcase."

The drive took ten minutes. Mac chose to leave the envelope unopened until Lewis delivered her to the terminal, where the tubby C-17 sat waiting. "That's your bird," Lewis informed her as he removed the suitcase from the back. "It's scheduled to take off for NAS/JRB in thirty minutes. Have a good trip!"

Because of the time she'd spent down south, Mac knew the noncom was referring to Naval Air Station Joint Reserve Base New Orleans. So she was being sent back to Louisiana. But to do *what*?

Mac thanked Lewis and towed her suitcase up the ramp and into the equivalent of a flying bus. Her fellow passengers included a group of navy SEABEES, an army medical team, and a twenty-person detachment from the air force band. Mac noticed that the other passengers were staring at her and wondered why. Did they recognize her from TV? Had they seen footage of the kiss? The true nature of the attention became clear when a loadmaster approached her. "Yes, miss? Can I help you?"

That was when Mac remembered that she was wearing civilian clothing, and not just *any* civilian clothing but an outfit appropriate for a date. "Yes," Mac replied. "I'm Major Macintyre. Have you got a slot reserved for me?"

The noncom consulted a clipboard. "Yes, ma'am . . . We're expecting you. Please follow me."

Once her suitcase was secured, Mac found herself seated against the port bulkhead between an army chaplain and a navy supply officer. The swabbie was snoring and reeked of alcohol. The sky pilot was reading an e-book and humming to himself.

Mac strapped herself in and opened the envelope. There was the usual boilerplate to plow through. But the so-what of the orders was clear. Mac's Marauders were now part of the Joint Special Operations Command (JSOC). Meaning the same secretive organization that had sent her into Mexico after the POWs.

I'll bet it's a temporary gig, Mac thought, *like protecting a base or participating in a raid.* But that was pure conjecture, and there was no way to get real answers until she arrived in New Orleans.

The trip took forever. What should have been a five-hour flight took twice that given the need to avoid Confederate airspace and land at out-of-the-way airports. So it was dark by the time the C-17 landed in New Orleans, and Mac was able to drag her suitcase off the plane.

There was a swirl of activity, and Mac was searching the crowd for a friendly face when a sailor appeared out of the gloom. "I'm sorry about the delay, ma'am . . . My name is Givens. I didn't know you were wearing civvies . . . The loadmaster pointed you out. Have you got more gear? No? Please follow me."

Givens led Mac to a Humvee, placed her suitcase in back, and slid behind the wheel. "We're headed for the HQ building. The CO wants to see you right away."

Mac watched the headlights swing across the remains of a two-story building. The base had fallen to the rebs shortly after hostilities began. And, from what she could see, the North had bombed the shit out of the place before taking it back. "Can I stop at my quarters?" Mac inquired. "I'd like to change."

Givens glanced her way. "Permission to speak freely, ma'am?"

"Of course."

"When Commander Trenton says 'now,' she means 'yesterday.' If you know what I mean."

"Thanks for the heads-up," Mac replied, as the Humvee bumped through a pothole. It seemed that the CO was female—and a hard-ass. Ah, well . . . Mac had been there before.

"This used to be the base exchange," Givens told her, as the Humvee came to a stop. "But it serves as the unit's headquarters location now. I'll grab the suitcase."

Mac thanked him, followed a path toward double doors, and saw that the windows were blacked out. A man emerged from the shadows. He wore TAC gear and was carrying an HK MP7. That was one of the weapons SEALS favored for close-quarters work, and Mac wondered if he was one. "Hold on, ma'am. I need to see some ID."

Mac produced her ID card, the sentry aimed a flashlight at it, and made the comparison. "Thank you, Major . . . Please stand by while Compton checks your bag."

Another sailor appeared. This one was female and equipped with a headlamp, which she turned on. The rating had clearly searched bags before and knew how to do it quickly. Her report was clear and concise. "A Glock nine mil, two magazines, and a knife. That's all."

The male sentry nodded. "Zip it up. Okay, Major . . . You can enter."

Light spilled through the entryway as Mac opened the door and towed the suitcase inside. A reception desk faced her on the other side of the room, and wheels clicked as Mac made her way over to it. A petty officer first class sat behind the counter. He knew who she was. "Welcome to NAS/JRB, Major Macintyre. Commander Trenton is in her office—and would like to speak with you."

Mac glanced at her watch. It was a little after 2200, and Trenton was still at work. What had Givens told her? "'Now' means 'yesterday'"? Yes. Mac made her way over to the door and knocked three times. A female voice yelled, "Enter!" and Mac obeyed.

Trenton's hair was short, combed boy style, and parted on the right. The asexual look might have been weird on someone else but was consistent with Trenton's blue-eyed, hollow-cheeked face. Rather than a uniform, Trenton was wearing a navy tee shirt with a silver oak leaf pinned to the collar. A special operator? Yes. They weren't into uniforms. "Well, well," Trenton said. "What have we got here? A party girl? Or an army officer?"

"Ma'am, my name is . . ."

"Shut up," Trenton said as she rose from the chair and circled the desk. "I know who you are." By that time, Mac could see that the navy officer was wearing shorts. In a marked contrast with Trenton's left leg, which consisted of flesh and blood, the other had been fashioned from titanium and plastic. A pair of combat boots completed the look.

"*You* are Major Robin Macintyre," Trenton said, as if accusing her of a crime. "The officer who rescued the president from the mess in Richton, and went on to become his fuck buddy, which is why he pardoned your ass."

Even though Mac was wearing civilian clothes she found herself standing at attention. "That isn't true," she objected. "I'm not his . . ."

"I told you to shut up," Trenton said, as she circled Mac. "That was an order. But you don't like to follow orders, do you? That's why your fuck buddy had to intervene. And don't try to tell me that Sloan isn't your fuck buddy because I watched you trade spit with him earlier today. Everybody did. And that includes the slackers, thieves, and perverts in your so-called battalion."

Trenton stopped in front of her. "Well, guess what, *Major* . . . Your ass doesn't belong to Sloan. Your ass belongs to *me*. And I'm going to work it *hard*."

Trenton was nose to nose with Mac by then. So close that Mac could see the pores in the naval officer's skin. "Do you read me, bitch?"

"I read you, ma'am."

They stood that way, neither flinching, for a good fifteen seconds before Trenton took a step back. "Good. Now sit down and listen up. I want you to know what's going on."

Mac sat in one of two guest chairs while Trenton circled the desk. "You and your people have been selected to carry out an important mission. You participated in the battle for the Bayou Choctaw Strategic Petroleum Reserve. And, according to Colonel Walters, you're more than a pretty face. But then she chose the Marine Corps over the navy, which doesn't say much for her judgment.

"But regardless of that—this mission will be similar to the one at the Choctaw Reserve except that the West Hackberry Reserve is off to the west and well within Confederate-held territory."

Mac opened her mouth to speak, and Trenton raised a hand. "Hold that thought. I'll let you know when I'm done. A push is coming. A *big* push . . . And the rebs will be forced to retreat. Will they leave the Hackberry Reserve intact? Or will they destroy all of the infrastructure associated with it? We can't take that chance. So we're going to drop Mac's Marauders in there *before* the push begins. Your job will be to capture the base and hold it until you are relieved. Okay, you have questions. Ask them."

Mac locked eyes with Trenton. "What does the word 'drop' mean in this context?"

Trenton smiled thinly. "That's the correct question. Good for you. I mean we're going to attach parachutes to your Strykers, load them onto C-17s, and drop them onto the Hackberry Reserve. But don't freak out . . . I'm talking about a low-altitude auto-extraction from twenty feet in the air. So your vehicles aren't going to float all over the place and wind up in a swamp."

"With personnel aboard?"

"Yes. There are two reasons for that. First, we don't have the time to put you and your felons through jump school. Second, there's a strong possibility that you will find yourself in a hellacious firefight within minutes of putting down. There won't be time to round people up, dust them off, and have a cup of joe before engaging the enemy. Or, put another way, your ass will be surrounded."

"How long do I have to get ready?"

"Two weeks."

Mac stood. "Is there anything else?"

"There is *one* thing," Trenton said as she leaned back in the chair. "Your fuck buddy attempted to kill your father yesterday. Unfortunately, he failed. You have to give Sloan credit, though . . . It was your father's wedding day, so most of the Confederacy's Joint Chiefs were gathered at his house, sucking free beer. So it was a class-A juicy target. The cruise missile was spot-on. *Everyone* died. Everyone except your daddy, that is . . . Meanwhile, as that shit was going down, Sloan was tongue-fucking you up in Nebraska. Sweet, huh?"

It was meant to hurt, and it did. Mac did an about-face and left the office. The sound of Trenton's laughter followed her out into the reception area.

CHAPTER 9

In the midst of chaos, there is also opportunity.

—SUN TZU

FORT KNOX, KENTUCKY

Sloan's bedroom was furnished with odds and ends of furniture and generally messy. Some of that had to do with the clutter that covered the long, conference-room-style table that stood against one wall. It served as a place to stack his homework as well as a surface to work on. Sloan had both a laptop and a printer but had chosen to write the letter longhand. He read the most recent draft and swore. The shredder whirred as it consumed the letter. Then, determined to succeed, Sloan tried again.

Dear Robin,

By now you know about the attempt on your father's life and the fact that it failed. You, of all people, understand that it was necessary to try. And you know why I couldn't tell you that the attack was going to take place. You have proven yourself again and again. No one other than an idiot like Congressman Will would dare question your loyalty to our country. Yet there are rules, and I must obey them like everyone else. Plus it would have been cruel to tell you and thereby make you a coconspirator in the assassination attempt.

That said, there is something I wish to apologize for. In retrospect I realize that I should have broken our date when it became apparent that our time together was going to take place on the same day as the attack. But, because I'd been looking forward to spending time with you for so long, I managed to convince myself that it would be okay. After all, I reasoned, Robin's father put a price on her head. And he's an enemy combatant. So why would Robin care?

After giving the matter considerable thought, I realize how selfish, not to mention stupid, that was. And I hope you'll find it in your heart to forgive me.

Sincerely yours,
Sam

Sloan read it over, concluded that it was the best he could do, and signed it. The letter went into an envelope that already had an alter ego's name and return address on it. Mrs. Farrow would mail it in the morning. That was all he could do.

Sloan sighed, took a document off the top of a pile, and began to read. Bo Macintyre had spent time on Mexican President Salazar's vast ranch a week earlier and, according to a CIA agent who was also present, the two men had a private meeting. A great deal of encrypted radio traffic had been flying back and forth between Houston and Mexico City ever since.

Meanwhile, Confederate engineers were working to repair the B&M Bridge over the Rio Grande River. Even though *their* forces had destroyed it months earlier. *Why?* The question followed Sloan into his dreams.

NAVAL AIR STATION JOINT RESERVE BASE, NEW ORLEANS

Hangar 3 was barely large enough to accommodate all 250 members of Mac's Marauders. Mac entered through the enormous door, made her way over to the staging normally used to work on airplane engines, and climbed the stairs to the top. Company Sergeant Chris Bader's voice was loud enough to be heard outside. "Battalion! Atten-hut!"

Mac scanned the first rank of faces. Some were familiar, but they were the exception. There had been casualties during the months since the battalion had been commissioned. Lots of them. And, as the unit gained increased notoriety, there had been no shortage of volunteers. So many that two-thirds of the people assembled in the hangar had clean records. A fact that Commander Trenton seemed to be unaware of. When Mac said, "At ease," she was pleased to see her troops shift position in unison. Mac could thank Executive Officer Trey Munson for that . . . Along with Bader and the rest of the NCOs.

"We have a mission," Mac began. "A top secret mission the exact nature of which will become clear over the next couple of days. But I can tell you this . . . Mac's Marauders are going to operate behind enemy lines. That means we will be surrounded from the very beginning. And we won't be able to count on a whole lot of air support, either. Other than that, this is going to be a piece of cake." The words produced nervous laughter and scattered "Hooahs."

Mac smiled. "Simply put, our mission will be to take an objective and hold it until we are relieved. We were chosen for this task because our armor will give us an important edge—and because we are the best of the worst."

That produced a hearty cheer even though most of the battalion had never seen the inside of a jail cell. They liked the battalion's bad-boy rep as well as its edgy motto. Mac felt guilty about manipulating their emotions. But that was part of the job. "Now listen up," Mac told them. "Rather than drive into enemy territory, we're going to drop our Strykers from planes. *Why?* To scare the shit out of the rebs, that's why."

That *wasn't* why. But the line got a laugh. "We are going to spend the next two weeks learning all about parachutes and gravity," Mac told them. "During that time, there won't be any passes, there won't be any access to the Internet, and we'll be logging twelve-hour days.

"But, if you do well, I'll throw a party forty-eight hours prior to takeoff. And liquid refreshments *will* be served."

A predictable cheer went up, Mac waved, and Bader yelled, "Atten-hut!" There were tears in Mac's eyes as she left the hangar. A lot of her soldiers were going to die. And there wasn't a damned thing she could do about it.

MATAMOROS, MEXICO

The sun was little more than a buttery glow beyond the perpetual haze as General Bo Macintyre stood at the south end of the Brownsville & Matamoros Express Bridge and looked north. He felt guilty, and for good reason. Rather than being in Mexico, working on Operation Overlord, he should have been in Houston attending Kathy's funeral.

But Bo knew he couldn't get through it. And, after losing two generals and an admiral to a single missile, the last thing citizens needed to see was the Chairman of the Joint Chiefs sobbing on TV. Fortunately, Bo's job gave him an excuse to be at "an undisclosed location," "fulfilling his responsibilities," while Kathy's sister handled the funeral arrangements.

As for Kathy, well, she would understand. Would she approve of his new mission in life? Which was to avenge her death? No, she wouldn't. "That won't solve anything," she would say. But that's where Kathy was wrong. Killing Sloan, as well as the people who made him possible, would cleanse North America of a dangerous infection. Then, once he was dead, the North and South could reunite. In that way, something good would come out of Kathy's death.

Bo eyed the scene in front of him. Forces under Victoria's command had destroyed the B&M Bridge so that a Mexican drug lord couldn't use it. Now, ironically enough, Bo was in charge of the effort to repair it. Cranes had been brought up the Rio Grande on barges. And as Bo looked on, people from both sides of the border were working to drop a new support beam into place.

The Confederacy had delivered a ton of gold to Mexico City a few days earlier. And that meant all *three* of the bridges that crossed the river between Matamoros and Brownsville would be required as sixty thousand Mexican soldiers traveled north. By crossing at that point, the allied troops could enter Texas and pivot to the east without encountering the sort of resistance they would have confronted in New Mexico and Arizona.

Bo's train of thought was interrupted as a helicopter clattered overhead, circled the construction site, and came in for a landing. One of Bo's aides was a burly major named Ted Caskins. He arrived as the helo touched down. "The polo team has landed."

Bo made a face. Among other things, Major General Matias Ramos was one of Salazar's nephews, a graduate of the Citadel in South Carolina, and a well-known polo player. And, since Ramos liked to surround himself with *other* polo players, most of the people on his staff were better suited for a commission in a seventeenth-century cavalry regiment instead of a modern infantry division. "Here's hoping Ramos is on a sightseeing tour," Bo said darkly. "God help us if he wants to get involved." Caskins laughed.

Fortunately, Ramos didn't need to be competent in order to play his part in defeating the North. Bo planned to use the Mexican divisions as cannon fodder. If they fought well, then so much the better. And if they didn't? No problem. Bo saw Ramos and his peers as linemen in a football game. Meaning people the North would have to circumvent or run over in order to score. That would free Bo's forces to sack the quarterback, intercept passes, and do an end run on the enemy's defenses. So if Bo had to put up with the polo team, he would.

Ramos was still twenty feet away when Bo plastered a smile on his face and went forward to shake hands. "Matias! What an unexpected pleasure . . . I hope you have time for lunch."

"Of course, amigo," Ramos replied. "But first the bridge. I would like a tour."

It was going to be a long afternoon.

BASTROP, LOUISIANA

Tiny Morehouse Memorial Airport was located in Bastrop, Louisiana, and had been chosen for a number of reasons. It was well inside territory controlled by the North and, because the single runway had been employed by both sides, local citizens were used to all manner of military comings and goings. A fact that might put rebel agents to sleep. But, even if the rebs *were* watching the training exercises, it would be difficult to discern what the North was up to.

Mac was standing on the west side of the field, looking east, as the four-engined cargo plane dropped down to fly just fifty feet above the runway. Once the C-150 was lined up, an extraction parachute shot out through the rear hatch and jerked a Stryker out of the plane's hold. Cargo parachutes acted to slow the weighty package as it fell toward the ground.

Except that "slow" was a relative term. The platform the vic was strapped to hit hard. And having logged three such drops herself, Mac knew she would never forget the spine-jarring impact. As the platform skidded to a halt, six soldiers boiled up out of the cargo compartment. Then they jumped to the ground and hurried to release the tie-downs.

That was when Company Sergeant Bader popped up out of a firing position and opened fire on them with an LMG. The machine gun was loaded with blanks, and the soldiers knew that. But what they *didn't* know, or had forgotten, was what to do. Should they fire back? Or free the tie-downs?

Mac had a bullhorn, which she brought up to her lips. "Cease fire. Two of you are supposed to remain aboard and provide covering fire, while the others release the tie-downs. Remember . . . we're going to land on a two-lane highway. Once your vehicle is down, and freed from the pallet, you must clear the LZ quickly so that the next Herc can drop its load.

"*Twenty-seven Strykers*. Plus three trailers loaded with supplies. That's how much stuff we have to insert. We'll have the advantage of surprise at first . . . But that won't last long. Clear the runway."

They did it over and over again, day after day, until everyone was pissed. The long days were concluded with flights back to the Joint Reserve Base in New Orleans. Then, after a hurried meal, it was time to pack. Each container had to contain a little bit of everything. That way, if one box was lost, it wouldn't mean that *all* of their food, ammo, or medical supplies were gone.

Finally, after nearly two weeks of hard work, graduation day arrived—and Commander Trenton was on hand to witness the full run-through. The demonstration began with a series of successful drops. That meant all of Alpha Company's first platoon was on the ground when disaster struck.

The battalion had been able to carry out more than 135 drops without suffering anything more serious than a sprained ankle until then. But as the fifth Herc roared in, and the extraction chute popped, something went wrong. The Stryker and its platform slumped to the right and hit the runway hard. Sparks flew as the vic skidded on its side, screeched to a stop, and caught on fire.

Mac's RTO, Larry Duke, was standing next to her. Her voice was level. "Tell the ETV driver to push the wreckage off the runway. Clear the next C-130 to make its approach."

Part of the landing plan called for each company to drop a dozer-blade-equipped ETV first—so that it could clear wreckage. That hadn't been necessary before. Now it was, and the flaming vehicle was barely clear of the runway when the next Stryker landed.

A pre-positioned crash truck rushed in to put the flames out. It was a luxury the team wouldn't have at Hackberry. It soon became clear that while some of the soldiers in the damaged vic were okay, the rest hadn't been so fortunate. Air-evac helicopters were called in to take them out. *They're the lucky ones,* Mac thought to herself. *They'll come to realize that eventually.*

Mac glanced at Trenton. The navy officer's expression hadn't changed one iota. The demonstration continued. Finally, once it was over, Trenton turned to face Mac. "That was acceptable," Trenton said. "Carry on." And with that, the navy officer boarded a Black Hawk and left for New Orleans.

Mac felt a momentary sense of disappointment. Some sort of attagirl would have been nice. But, given Trenton's persona, perhaps "acceptable" qualified as high praise. *Besides, it doesn't matter what Trenton thinks of you,* Mac told herself. *What matters is whether the battalion is ready for combat. Or as ready as it can be under the circumstances.*

The battalion's vehicles had been kept at the Morehouse airstrip during the training period. Now it was time to transport them back to NAS/JRB for two days of maintenance and a final loadout prior to the attack on Hackberry. That necessitated dozens of flights during a six-hour period.

But finally, once the entire battalion was back in New Orleans, Mac threw the party she had promised. There was plenty of beer, endless buckets of crawfish, and plenty of side dishes. All of which were well received.

Once the party was going full blast, Mac filled a cooler with beer and loaded food into Styrofoam containers. Then a delegation that included Company Sergeant Bader left for the hospital. One of Mac's soldiers had suffered a severe head injury and was in a coma. But the rest were well enough to enjoy the visit—even if the nurses weren't that thrilled about it.

Secure in the knowledge that her XO would keep a lid on the party in Hangar 3, Mac allowed herself to go off duty. After returning to the BOQ, Mac entered her room to find that a letter had been slipped in under the door. From the notations on the envelope, she judged that it had been sent to three other locations prior to winding up at NRS/JRB.

The name in the upper-left-hand corner didn't mean anything to her, but Mac recognized the handwriting immediately and knew the letter was from Sloan. The bastard.

Mac ripped the envelope open, removed the letter, and scanned it. Then she read it again. Everything Sloan said was true. It would have been wrong for him to disclose the assassination plan in advance. And Mac knew that killing Bo Macintyre was the right thing to do in that it would set the Confederacy back and save Union lives. But those were intellectual arguments. And as her father's daughter, Mac found the whole thing to be repugnant.

As for Sloan's willingness to take her on a date, even as Union forces sought to murder her father, that was appalling. Fortunately, he had the stones to admit it. Could she forgive him? Yes, no, maybe. It didn't matter. When Mac tried to visualize the future, there was nothing to see. Everything beyond Hackberry was blank. Mac tore the letter into tiny pieces and dumped them into a wastepaper basket.

The next two days were spent getting ready. And there were multiple issues to resolve. A soldier named Harkin had gone AWOL. Would he wind up in reb hands? And would he spill his guts? If he did, the enemy could be waiting when the battalion landed. The MPs were looking for him. All Mac could do was hope.

Then there was the need for antiaircraft weapons. The battalion would have air cover on the way in. And Mac could call for more. But the air force was stretched thin and wouldn't be able to fly CAPs over Hackberry twenty-four/seven. That's why Mac had requested, and been granted, thirty FIM-92A man-portable launchers, with ten missiles each. But the weapons were sitting in a warehouse located fifteen miles away. Mac ordered Captain Munson to round up some trucks and go get them.

Finally, there was the issue of the Stryker that was generally referred to as the **HANGAR QUEEN**. It was a miserable piece of shit, which, no matter how much work the techs put into it, always broke down a few days later. No way in hell was Mac going to take the **QUEEN** into combat. And she needed to replace the vic that had been totaled on the final day of training as well.

Unfortunately, Supply Officer Wendy Wu hadn't been able to find any replacement vehicles. But after some hurried research, Mac discovered that two Marine Corps LAV-25s *were* available. And, having commanded some LAVs during the battle at the Choctaw Reserve, Mac knew how devastating the jarhead 25mm chain guns could be.

With support from Commander Trenton, Mac was able to requisition the vics and talk the Marine Corps out of a qualified wrench turner. And because the LAVs were very similar to Strykers, Mac's personnel would be able to crew them.

Finally, having done all that she could, Mac hit the sack. She didn't think sleep would come, but it did—and the alarm woke her four hours later.

Mac hadn't found the time to fill out a last will and testament, but it didn't matter. She had some money in the bank but no one to leave it to. As for packing her personal belongings, well, that would be the same as declaring herself dead. So she went to breakfast instead.

After finishing the meal, Mac went outside to peer up at the sky. She saw the usual high haze, but visibility was reasonably good, and that was critical.

Odds were that the rebs were watching from space, and Mac could imagine what they were thinking. Why were so many C-150s gathered in one place? What were the Yankees up to? But the possibilities were endless. And, now that Private Harkin was in custody, Mac felt better knowing that she would have the advantage of surprise.

Soldiers dashed from place to place as they ran last-minute errands, engines thundered as the Hercs taxied into position, and jet fighters circled high above.

Captain Munson had responsibility for the loadout—and he assured Mac that everything was proceeding smoothly. Mac thanked him and made a show of strolling over to the lead plane. Then, after surrendering her ceramic coffee cup to a member of the ground crew, Mac walked up the ramp. Duke held Mac's TAC vest up for her to inspect. "Good morning, ma'am. I took the liberty of adding four candy bars to your loadout."

Mac grinned as Duke lowered the vest into place. "Thanks, Corporal . . . That's the kind of ammo I need. Is everybody on board? Good. Pass the word to the cockpit. Let's roll."

The flight from New Orleans to the drop zone was scheduled to take thirty minutes. Rather than force everyone to remain inside their tightly packed vehicles, Mac's soldiers had been authorized to sit outside for the first half of the flight. Did Mac's claustrophobia have something to do with that? Hell yes, it did.

Mac was seated in front of the ESV called **LITTLE TOOT** with her back to the port-side bulkhead as the Herc rolled down the runway and lumbered into the air. Mac felt sleepy even though her adrenaline was pumping, and she knew that it was a reaction to her fear. Then her ears popped, and she wanted to pee.

It was important to *look* confident even if she wasn't. So Mac removed a fingernail file from one of her pockets and began to file her nails. Would that produce a story? Something that would burnish the legend? "There she was," one of the others might say, "doing her nails while we flew into enemy territory."

Or, would they notice that her hands were trembling? And tell their friends about that? At least she hadn't peed herself. Not yet, anyway.

Suddenly, it was time to release the seat belt and follow the rest of the team into the Stryker. Rather than a squad of infantry, the ESV was going in with Mac, her RTO, an air force JTAC (Joint Terminal Attack Controller), her assistant, a medic, a mechanic, two machine gunners, and the Stryker's two-person crew. Ten people in all. Captain Munson was on plane five. The hope was that at least one of them would survive the landing.

Even though Mac couldn't *see* what was taking place outside the plane, Duke had a headset on and delivered a stream of reports. "Our F-35s are keeping the reb fighters at bay," Duke announced. "There's no AA fire yet . . . We're a minute out . . . Stand by . . . Here we go!"

Mac felt a violent jerk as the extraction chute snatched the Stryker out of the cargo bay. One of the gunners swore as **LITTLE TOOT** entered a brief moment of free fall. The Stryker hit hard. The ESV's shock absorbers helped to cushion the blow, as did the foam squares that they were sitting on. *"Now, now, now!"* the TC yelled, and that was Mac's cue to release her harness.

The gunners surged up through the hatches first so they could provide covering fire should that be necessary. They were followed by Mac, the air force JTAC, her assistant, and the medic, each one of whom was expected to flip one of the quick-release latches that secured **LITTLE TOOT** to the platform it sat on.

As Mac scrambled up and out, she was painfully aware of the fact that the *next* Herc was lining up on the LZ by then. Highway 390 ran east and west. It was straight as an arrow, with nothing more than low scrub bordering it to the north and south.

Mac rolled off the vic, landed on her feet, and went straight to the red-colored release. A single jerk was enough to do the trick. Every soldier was wearing a boom mike and a TAC radio. "Hook one is clear," Mac announced. "Over." And so it went until all four had been released.

LITTLE TOOT's TC was a corporal named Olson, or Ollie to her friends, and she knew what to do next. Once her machine was free, Ollie gunned the engine and drove the ESV off the highway and into the neighboring field.

Once the vic cleared the road, it was time for the team to grab one side of the platform and lift it up. A set of built-in wheels allowed them to push it off the road.

What ensued could only be described as organized chaos. Engines roared as a succession of C-150s swooped in over the road. There was a loud bang as each platform hit, usually followed by a screech, and shouting.

In the meantime, air force JTAC Lieutenant Cassie Cassidy was standing atop the **LITTLE TOOT** talking into a boom mike. "You're too high, Bad Dog . . . That's better . . . Hit the gas, Surfer Girl . . . Bad Dog is right behind you." And so forth, as the Hercs made their runs.

Then something went wrong. Mac, who was standing next to Cassidy, heard the other officer's inflection change. "Roger the flameout, Backhauler. Break it off, I repeat break it off and return to base."

Mac could see the plane coming in from the east. It was flying on *three* engines, and that spelled trouble. Maybe three power plants would be enough, but maybe they wouldn't. The plan called for each C-150 to drop a Stryker and pull up *hard*. But Backhauler was determined to go for it, and in he came.

Mac saw the chute blossom behind the transport, saw the load appear, and saw the Herc falter as a *second* engine failed.

"Forget the pullout," Cassidy instructed. "Turn north and climb out gradually."

The pilot tried. But he was too low by then . . . And as the C-150's starboard wing dipped, it hit the ground, and part of it sheared off. That threw the transport into a loop. A propeller scythed through the air, the fuselage surfed on a wave of dirt, and Mac heard a dull thump. Flames appeared seconds later.

Mac turned to Duke. "Send the rescue truck."

The battalion didn't have a crash truck. But the third Stryker to land had been designated as the rescue vehicle—and was equipped with some fire extinguishers and extraction tools. It wasn't much, but it beat the hell out of nothing.

Mac turned back, and was about to tell Cassidy to carry on, when she realized that the JTAC was still doing her job. The next C-150 dropped an LAV and pulled up. Commander Trenton would approve.

Mac eyed her watch. The insertion was running five minutes slow . . . But that was pretty good given the nature of the situation. Now that she had ten vehicles on the ground, Mac had enough firepower to attack the rebel base. And the sooner the better. **LITTLE TOOT** was going to remain at the LZ, as were two "enemy-response trucks," and the rescue vehicle. The plan called for Mac to take the other Strykers with her. "Bravo-Six to Bravo-Five. Over."

"This is Five," Munson replied, from a position a thousand yards to the west. "Over."

"The LZ is yours. Keep me informed. Over."

"Roger that, over."

Six vics were lined up in the field behind Mac, with their engines running. The detachment was under the command of Tommy Whitehorse, Alpha Company's commanding officer. He tossed Mac a salute as she arrived. "Let's roll, Tommy . . . We wouldn't want to keep the rebs waiting."

"No, ma'am," Whitehorse agreed. "Perish the thought."

Mac climbed up on top of the **THUMPER** while Duke entered via the ramp. Whitehorse lowered himself through the front hatch—while Mac took the one to the rear. The Stryker belonged to him, after all. As did responsibility for the assault.

Had Mac taken command, not only would it make Whitehorse look bad, it would have diverted her attention away from the *big* picture, which included what was taking place back in the LZ. The vic jerked into motion.

Rather than use the local roads, which might be mined, Whitehorse ordered his drivers to cross open fields instead. What remained of the Herc lay to the left and continued to burn. A thick column of black smoke spiraled up into the sky.

It took less than five minutes to reach Black Lake Road and cross it. And that was when the platoon took fire. It came as no surprise. Mac and her officers had been studying high-altitude recon photos for weeks by then and knew that Hackberry was only lightly defended. What they estimated to be a single company of troops was stationed at the reserve, and that made sense, since the main battle front was located one hundred miles to the east. And the rebs weren't expecting trouble. Not at Hackberry, anyway.

Still, even though Black Lake offered some protection on the north, east, and west sides of the complex—the officer in charge had put his or her troops to work digging a network of trenches on the *south* side of the reserve. Some were wide enough to keep vehicles from crossing over them, while others were narrower and intended to connect defensive positions together.

Mac heard a series of thumps as mortar shells landed, followed by the rattle of machine guns. The incoming fire forced Mac to drop down into the cargo compartment. Bullets pinged against the **THUMPER**'s hull as the vic's gunner fired her 105mm gun, and the driver took evasive action.

Meanwhile as the **THUMPER** and a vic called **JERSEY GIRL** gave the rebs something to shoot at, the rest of Whitehorse's machines were circling around to attack the enemy's left flank. A large trench had been dug to prevent such a maneuver.

But the ditch was visible on recon photos, so the Marauders were prepared to deal with it. Two of Whitehorse's vics were carrying military-grade pierced-steel planks. And once they were thrown across the moat-like ditch, the Strykers could cross.

The reb commander sent a squad to stop the invaders, but it was no contest. The handful of defenders didn't stand a chance against the heavily armed vehicles. And Whitehorse's troops were able to take control so quickly that Mac found herself with more than sixty POWs to keep track of. Something she hadn't planned for.

All the Marauders could do was disarm the enemy troops, corral them in one of the wider trenches, and post guards. But what seemed like a simple situation wasn't. "Don't do it!" one of the rebs yelled. "Don't machine gun us!"

That was when Mac realized that the rebel troops had been fed a steady diet of propaganda—and believed that the Marauders were going to massacre them. Even though every second was precious, Mac did her best to assure the POWs that they wouldn't be harmed.

And it seemed that the effort was working until a reb removed a wanted picture from his pocket and held it aloft. "Look!" he said. "It's *her*! The officer who murdered her sister!"

At that point, Mac had to turn her attention elsewhere. Reports continued to flow in from Munson. All of the Strykers were down safely, all of the crew members on the Herc were dead, and a C-150 had been shot down while returning to base. There was no time in which to grieve. That would have to wait.

With the landings out of the way, Moody was about to bring the rest of the battalion onto the reserve. And not a moment too soon since word had arrived that a rebel relief column had departed Fort Polk and was coming their way. That meant the Marauders had only hours in which to prepare for a major counterattack.

Mac waved a noncom over. His name was Logan. "Keep the prisoners corralled until I send word to release them. We can't spare the personnel or the supplies required to cope with them."

Sergeant Logan nodded. "Yes, ma'am. No prob."

Thanks to the reconnaissance photos taken weeks earlier, Mac and her officers had been able to map the reserve and how their defenses would be laid out. As ESVs went to work scooping out revetments for the vehicles, teams of soldiers began to lay mines, while others took possession of the enemy's machine guns and mortars. Each weapon had to be checked, more ammo had to be brought forward in some cases, and more fighting positions had to be dug.

Meanwhile, Mac's supply officer, Captain Wendy Wu, had inventoried all of the equipment that had been captured from the enemy. Mac was watching a platoon leader position a Stryker when the diminutive officer arrived. Wu was one of the original marauders and a person Mac had come to rely on. "What's up, Wendy? Did you find some instant Starbucks for me?"

Wu's expression remained unchanged. "No, ma'am. But we are the proud owners of an uparmored Humvee, two trucks, a backhoe, some private vehicles, and an underground gas tank. There's an emergency generator, too . . . Plus a pallet of MREs."

"What about ammo?"

"There's a reserve supply, but it isn't especially large."

"Okay, good work. Let's put that backhoe to work digging more trenches. Eventually, we're going to need some fallback positions."

Duke spoke as Wu departed. "Lieutenant Cassidy reports that two attack helicopters are inbound from Fort Polk, with four Chinooks bringing up the rear. ETA, five minutes. She put out a call for air support."

Mac swore. The enemy had decided to send an airborne force *ahead* of the relief column, in the hope that they could recapture the facility quickly. And since each Chinook could carry up to thirty-three passengers, Mac could expect a 132-person assault team.

What was she up against? Mac wondered. A highly trained rapid-response force? Or a conglomeration of troops who happened to be available when the poop hit the fan? The first possibility was worse than the second, but both amounted to a threat. The battalion's Strykers didn't mount any AA weapons other than light machine guns and, once in their revetments, they couldn't maneuver. A ground attack would have been preferable from Mac's perspective, but the rebs didn't give a shit about her perspective.

Mac took the handset. "This is Bravo-Six actual. Even-numbered Stinger teams will prepare to engage *two* attack helicopters, ETA, four minutes. Odd-numbered Stinger teams will engage *four* Chinooks, in six minutes. The rest of the battalion will get ready to engage airborne troops. And remember . . . The enemy might try to land aircraft *inside* the compound, or they could fast rope down, so be ready for both.

"Don't forget . . . You are the best of the worst. Let's kick some ass. Over."

There were cheers all around. And then, as the sound died away, Mac heard the distinctive sound of helicopter engines, and the whup, whup, whup of rotors as the Apache gunships appeared from the north. Rockets flashed off stubby pylons and explosions marched across the compound. The battle had begun.

FORT KNOX, KENTUCKY

Samuel T. Sloan awoke in a good mood. And why not? The war was going well, or as well as any war can go, realizing that good people died every day. So he took a shower, got dressed, and ate a hearty breakfast. Then with Secret Service agents in tow, Sloan made his way through underground tunnels to the Situation Room for his daily briefing.

But, as Sloan entered the room, he could tell that something was wrong. Twice the usual number of briefers were present for one thing, and all of them had long faces. "Uh-oh," Sloan said as he paused to look around. "What happened?"

Director of National Intelligence Martha Kip cleared her throat. "Nothing good, Mr. President. Based on orbital imagery, plus photos taken during high altitude flyovers, it's clear that *thousands* of Mexican troops are streaming into Texas! The lead element passed through Brownsville last night. And if you look at the main screen, you'll see a montage of pictures taken an hour ago."

Sloan looked. What he saw was a bird's-eye view of American Humvees, French Jaguars, German personnel carriers—and what might have been Kenworth trucks hauling tank carriers behind them. All of which was consistent with Kip's report since the Mexicans had a tendency to buy military equipment from everyone. He dropped into his chair. "Please tell me that the Mexicans are attacking the Confederacy."

"There are no signs of resistance," Secretary of Defense Garrison said tactfully. "So we aren't looking at an invasion."

Sloan's mind flashed back to the report he'd read. The one that mentioned a meeting between General Macintyre and President Salazar. And a lot of encrypted radio traffic flying back and forth between the Confederacy and Mexico. Shit, shit, and more shit.

Various theories had occurred to him at the time, including the possibility of a drug deal, but an alliance? That never crossed his mind. Sloan's previously high spirits plummeted. "Okay, lay it out for me. What are we looking at?"

"That depends," General Jones said cautiously. "President Stickley cut some sort of deal with President Salazar. That much is clear. But, as with most things, the devil will be in the details. How *many* Mexican troops are coming our way? What role will they play? None of their units have combat experience . . . Yet a lot of their officers were trained in the U.S. And, based on our experiences fighting Mexican mercenaries, we know they can be effective.

"But one thing is for sure," Jones continued. "Assuming the Mexicans plan to fight, the strategic situation will change."

"In what way?" Sloan inquired. "What does that mean in practical terms?"

"It means that the advantage will shift to the Confederacy," National Security Advisor Toby Hall said. "It means the big push will stall."

"Or the big push will turn into a big retreat," Garrison added gloomily.

Press Secretary Besom broke the ensuing silence. "There's another problem as well. Once news of this gets out, it will reenergize our critics, scare the crap out of our citizens, and have a negative impact on military morale."

Sloan scowled as he scanned the faces around him. "Okay," he demanded. "Would anyone else like to chime in?"

Lora Michaels, the Secretary of the Treasury, raised a hesitant hand. "Yes, Mr. President. Once the news comes out, the Dow Jones Industrial Average is likely to drop by three or four hundred points."

Sloan winced. "All right. We have a lot to do. Let's get to work."

WEST HACKBERRY STRATEGIC PETROLEUM RESERVE, HACKBERRY, LOUISIANA

Mac jumped down into a trench as the Apache helicopters fired their rockets. Duke was right behind her. An engine roared, and Mac could feel the wash from the gunship's rotors as it passed over her head. Rather than leave the Stinger teams in their respective companies, Mac had chosen to consolidate them into a single platoon, led by Lieutenant Burns. He had orders to coordinate their efforts. And that plan paid off as Burns called the shots from his position near the center of the complex. "Stand by, six. Stand by, two. Fire!"

The FIM-92A Stingers were infrared-seeking, fire-and-forget weapons specifically designed for use against low-flying aircraft. And when two missiles struck a single Apache, the results were spectacular. A loud BOOM sounded as the gunship exploded, sending pieces of fiery debris whirling in every direction. Wreckage continued to rain down as Burns spoke again. "Nice job . . . Now let's . . ."

Burns never got to finish his sentence because a Union A-10 swooped down out of the sky. Rockets flashed off the Warthog's wings and barely missed the remaining Apache as it turned to race away. "Bravo-One-One to Warhorse-Three," Cassidy said over the air-ground frequency. "Thank you, and good hunting. Over."

So far so good. But as Mac climbed up out of the trench, she was painfully aware of how little she'd been able to see from down in the ground. And that would be an even greater problem once the rebel soldiers arrived.

"Come on!" Mac said, and began to run. Duke had little choice but to follow. They ran toward a white storage tank that loomed to the north and would offer a good vantage point. The distant drone of helicopter engines was getting louder as Mac reached the tank, made her way to a maintenance ladder, and started to climb.

Mac was short of breath by the time she stepped off the ladder onto the top of the tank. And sure enough . . . the lead Chinook was halfway across Black Lake and coming straight at her! Closer in, at the edge of the lake, Mac could see a dock and the barges that were moored just offshore.

"We're kind of exposed up here," Duke observed. "And what's *in* this tank anyway? Something flammable?"

Mac's mind was elsewhere. "Give me the handset. This is Bravo-Six actual. I have eyes on four Chinooks coming in from the north. Odd-numbered AA teams will stand by. Over."

"There's no cover up here," Duke said wistfully. "Maybe we should find a place to hide."

Mac's attention was focused on the lead Chinook. It was turning west. Why? *They're going to put down south of the complex,* Mac concluded. *And that works for me . . . The rebel troops will be forced to cross the minefield and face the Strykers to enter the compound.*

The second helicopter followed the first. But just as Mac was starting to feel good about her chances—the *third* ship began to bore straight in! Closely followed by the fourth. *They're going to fast rope down on the north side of the complex,* Mac decided. *And crush us in a vise.*

"This is Bravo-Six actual . . . It looks like choppers three and four are going to drop troops on the north side of the reserve. Wait for the Chinooks to hover, then hit them hard.

"Bravo-Six-One, do you read me? Over."

Six-One was a second lieutenant named Taylor Forbes. She was in charge of the six-Stryker fast-response team that was hiding in a metal building at the center of the reserve. "This is Six-One," Forbes responded. "I read you five by five. Over."

"Wait for it, Six-One . . . Then make your move. Over."

The lead Chinook had swung into position by that time. Ropes fell, soldiers slid down them like beads on a string, and the Chinook was firing flares that were intended to pull Stingers away from them. Burns ordered one of his team to fire, but the ruse was successful, and the Stinger missed.

The second missile wasn't to be denied, however . . . It slammed into the Chinook as the last soldiers touched down. The resulting explosion blew the big ship in half. As a rotor blade whirled away, Mac saw a stick figure drop out of the aft section of the fuselage and fall free.

The forward half of the ship slammed into the ground, quickly followed by the other section. There was a loud whump as the wreckage burst into flames. One down, and one to go.

But as Mac turned her attention to Chinook Four, she saw that the helicopter was flying north and racing away! Was it running? Yes, but only after dropping its load of thirty-plus soldiers into the water. As they waded ashore, the troops from Chinook Three were there to greet them.

Forbes was ready. Her vics began to fire seconds after they emerged from hiding. Rebel soldiers fell like tenpins as the Strykers fired their .50 caliber machine guns and 40mm grenade launchers. "We have a problem," Duke told her. "Chinooks One and Two put down half a mile south of the reserve and sent troops north. But that isn't the worst of it . . . The POWs were able to overwhelm our guards and are holding them hostage."

Mac felt a terrible sinking sensation. She'd forgotten to turn the POWs loose. And, as a result, the battalion had something like sixty enemy soldiers inside the compound—while more attacked from the south. Mac remembered her conversation with Sergeant Logan. "Yes, ma'am. No prob." That's what he'd said. But Mac had let Logan and his fire team down. Now it was her responsibility to free them, but *how*?

Mac turned to the south and raised her binoculars. Thanks to the height of the storage tank, and the angle involved, Mac could see into the trench. And sure enough . . . four of her soldiers were seated on the south side of the ditch, with their hands clasped behind their heads. Five of the rebs had weapons. Four assault rifles plus Logan's handgun.

Mac held the glasses with one hand and motioned for the handset with the other. Negotiations were out of the question under the circumstances. Was there a bloodless, risk-free way to resolve the situation? If so, she couldn't think of it. "Bravo-Six actual to Bravo-Five. Pull a rescue team together. Tell them to put night-vision gear on and drop smoke into the trench. The rest of it is obvious. Over."

"Roger that," Munson replied. "Over."

A full-fledged firefight was under way by then as the rebs on the south side of the complex attempted to advance and were systematically driven back by the wall of fire from the Strykers and two LAVs. Had things gone as planned, the Confederates attacking from the south would have faced half of the Marauders—while the rest were forced to turn north. But things *hadn't* gone as planned, and the rebs were getting their asses kicked.

"This is Six," Mac said. "Put some mortar fire on those bastards . . .

Push them at least a thousand yards back. We need to regroup before the rest of our guests arrive."

The mortars began to thump even as gray smoke billowed up out of the trench where the POWs were corralled. Mac heard the sharp crack of pistol fire, followed by the rattle of an assault rifle on full auto, and knew there would be casualties. She was correct.

"This is Five," Munson said. "We lost a hostage but rescued the others. Three POWs are down. Over."

Mac felt a terrible mix of sorrow and self-recrimination. There was nothing she could say except, "Well done. Carry on."

A strange silence settled over the scene. As Mac turned to the north, she saw the scattering of bodies marking the area where a quick, decisive battle had been fought by the response team. A column of reb prisoners was being marched south to join the rest. Mac wouldn't make the same mistake twice. Something had to be done regarding the POWs.

Mac closed her eyes and opened them again. Everything looked the same. West Hackberry was hers for the moment. But more enemy troops were on their way—and she was supposed to hold the facility for *what*? A few days? A week? *When will the big push arrive?* Mac wondered. *And who will own this chunk of land when it does?* There was no answer other than the crackle of static from Duke's radio, the intermittent pop, pop, pop of rounds cooking off inside the burning Chinook, and the raucous caw of a crow.

CHAPTER 10

They've got us surrounded again, the poor bastards.

—GENERAL CREIGHTON WILLIAMS ABRAMS JR.

EAST OF HOUSTON, TEXAS

It was a surreal moment. Bo was sitting next to Major General Matias Ramos in that officer's restored Cadillac convertible as they rolled through the town of El Toro, Texas. Locals lined both sides of the highway, and many of them were waving Mexican flags. Never mind the dislike that many citizens of Texas had felt for Mexico prior to the war.

Now, based on the carefully managed news reports they'd seen, Texans were ready to welcome the Mexican Army with open arms if it could defend them from Yankee aggression. "God bless you!" a man in a Stetson shouted, and Ramos waved at him.

The whole thing was a shit show. As the convoy traveled east, at least a hundred disabled vehicles had been left in its wake. Ramos expected the Confederates to recover, repair, and deliver them to the front. And that was the least of it. Bo's supply people were struggling to obtain the fuel required to fill hundreds of Mexican gas tanks and keep them filled.

Meanwhile, thanks to iffy communications, the Mexicans had fired on and done damage to a Confederate supply column that was traveling in the other direction. And that would happen again if steps weren't taken to stop it. And on and on. So it wasn't surprising that most of Bo's staff were in favor of a four-or-five-day pause. Time that could be used to address some if not all of the problems associated with the sudden influx of soldiers.

But Bo was adamantly opposed to the idea. "We will deliver at least a third of this traveling circus to the front and do so within three days," Bo had insisted. "Because if we don't, the Yankees will take more ground. Once the Mexicans are in place, you can work on the logistical problems."

Meanwhile, Sloan and his lapdog General Jones had been trying to hit the column from the air. But, thanks to the brave pilots of the Confederate Air Force, only a handful of Northern bombers had been able to break through. That situation wouldn't last forever, however. And when push came to shove, the Mexicans would have to earn their ton of gold.

In the meantime, a cruise missile launched by a Union submarine *had* struck the expeditionary force. But since each cruise missile cost 1.4 million prewar dollars, they were poorly suited for that type of mission. Four of the weapons had been fired the previous night. And, even though all of them were on target, the damage had been negligible. Five-point-six million was a lot to pay for the privilege of killing twelve soldiers and destroying three trucks. And that, Bo felt sure, was why there hadn't been any missile attacks since.

Bo spotted an overpass up ahead. A banner was draped along the front of it. ¡VIVA MÉXICO! it proclaimed. People waved and cheered as a Humvee passed beneath the span.

Bo looked up, saw what looked like a black dot start to fall, and shouted: "Grenade!" He tried to catch the object but fumbled it. There was a thump as it hit the floor. Ramos picked it up. "Look, General, a beer! And a Pacifico at that . . . Do you have an opener?"

Bo felt stupid as he passed a pocketknife over. No, there was more to it than that. He was old, tired, *and* stupid. Kathy . . . Kathy was gone. The Union would pay for that.

A news chopper clattered overhead. "Pink Cadillac," by Bruce Springsteen, was playing on the sound system, and General Ramos was sipping beer. The world had gone crazy.

WEST HACKBERRY STRATEGIC PETROLEUM RESERVE, HACKBERRY, LOUISIANA

The attack on the West Hackberry Petroleum Reserve had failed. But, according to the satellite imagery available via the people in New Orleans, a battalion-strength convoy of Confederate soldiers was southbound from Fort Polk. Mac expected them to arrive in the evening or just after dark.

With that in mind, she drove her people hard. There were *more* revetments to scoop out of the rich soil, *more* trenches to dig, and *more* bunkers to construct. Not the least of which was an underground command post.

But for reasons known only to them, the Confederates had chosen to stop short of Hackberry and spend the night. Or so it appeared. But what if the bivouac was fake? What if enemy troops were going to attack under the cover of darkness? Mac had to consider every possibility.

That meant that the Marauders had to work through the night. But Mac knew her soldiers had to get some rest as well. So she ordered Munson and roughly half of the battalion to grab four hours of sleep. Then it would be time for the rest of them to get some shut-eye.

A building at the center of the compound had been chosen for use as a communal sleeping hall. The metal roof and siding might stop a .22 caliber bullet but nothing larger.

So even as some of the battalion's troops slept, others were busy reinforcing the roof and walls with whatever they could lay their hands on. That included pieces of metal taken from neighboring buildings and sheets of plywood "liberated" from a construction site.

Later, Mac hoped to construct underground quarters that could withstand a direct hit from a five-hundred-pound bomb. For the moment, however, most of the battalion's resources had to go into military fortifications. And Mac was supervising the construction of what she called a "pop-up" ramp when Lieutenant Forbes approached her.

Forbes had a bowl haircut and was sporting a pair of army-issue "birth control glasses." She delivered a smart salute, which Mac returned. "You did a nice job today, Lieutenant. Thank you."

Forbes was visibly pleased. "I'll pass that on to my soldiers, ma'am. I know you're busy, but there's something that worries me. I took it to my CO, and he sent me to see you."

Mac was running on empty at that point . . . And the last thing she needed was another problem. But she'd been a lieutenant not that long ago and knew it was important to hear junior officers out, even if it was a drain on her energy. "Shoot . . . What's on your mind?"

"It's the lake, ma'am . . . What's to stop the rebs from sending boatloads of soldiers across the lake? It surrounds us on three sides."

The question fell on Mac like a thunderbolt from the sky. Mac should have addressed the threat but hadn't done so. Because she was stupid? Or because she was exhausted? No. If others weren't allowed to offer excuses, then neither could she.

Then a scary possibility entered her mind. Was that why the rebs were taking the night off? So that a *second* force could make preparations for an amphibious assault? One which, like the airborne attack, would try to put the battalion in a vise?

Maybe, and maybe not. But one thing was for sure . . . The hole had to be plugged. And that realization was enough to get the wheels turning. Mac smiled. "That is a very important question, Lieutenant. Thank you for asking it. Let's put our heads together and come up with an answer."

Mac spent the next fifteen minutes with Forbes, gave the platoon leader some additional resources, *and* responsibility for defending the battalion's north flank. It was nearly midnight by then, and Forbes delivered another textbook salute before disappearing into the night. *That one has promise,* Mac thought to herself. *And her company commander gated her through. I won't forget either one of them.*

Munson returned to duty shortly thereafter. That gave Mac the chance to get her pack out of the **LITTLE TOOT**'s cargo bay, eat half of an MRE, and stretch out on one of the cots the rebs had been forced to vacate. *The POWs,* Mac thought, as sleep pulled her down. *I need to deal with the POWs.*

"Major? I'm sorry to bother you . . . But the rebs are closing in. Captain Munson sent me to wake you."

Mac opened her eyes. RTO Larry Duke was standing next to her cot. What had it been? Five minutes since she'd gone to sleep?

No. According to her watch, four and a half hours had elapsed since then.

Mac yawned, swung her boots over onto the concrete floor, and stood. The soldiers around her were getting up as well. Most were bitching and griping. "Thanks, I think," Mac said. "Are they shooting at us?"

Duke shook his head. "No, ma'am . . . Not yet. But we have a drone up, and Sergeant Evans says they're no more than thirty minutes out."

"Okay. That means I can pee before they kill me. Is there something else?"

"Yes, ma'am. Captain Munson told me to tell you that they have tanks. Two of them."

Mac swore. "All right, thanks. I'll meet you in the command bunker."

Duke looked what he was, a scared nineteen-year-old kid. "Your coffee will be ready, ma'am. And an MRE, too."

Mac smiled. "Keep it up, soldier, you'll be a sergeant major by Friday."

Mac arrived in the command post fifteen minutes later. It was located on the south side of the oil reserve, which was where Mac expected most of the fighting would take place.

The bunker had been dug just off one of the larger trenches. By placing sheets of metal siding over a hole and dumping two feet of soil on top, the Marauders had been able to create a serviceable bunker. A table occupied the center of the room. That's where the controls and monitor for the RQ-11 drone were located. "Good morning," Sergeant Evans said. "Check *this* out. It looks like the rebs want to parley."

Mac accepted a hot mug of coffee from Duke before circling around to look over the drone operator's shoulder. And sure enough, four rebel soldiers were crossing the open area where two dozen of their comrades had been killed the previous day, and where their bodies still lay.

Two of the enemy soldiers were carrying flags. One was white, and the other bore the iconic blue X, on a field of red. Mac assumed that the others were officers. Once the party arrived at the edge of the bloodied ground, they came to a stop. "I have a reb on the horn," Duke said. "They want a meeting."

Mac was surprised. Very surprised. She'd been expecting an assault rather than a chat. But if the rebs wanted to talk, she was happy to accommodate them. The longer Mac could run the clock, the better. She turned to Duke. "Tell them that I'm on my way. Where's Sergeant Bader? We need flags. A Union flag *and* Old Glory."

It took five minutes to round up the flags and depart. Bader carried one of the flags and Duke had the other. Mac couldn't ask Munson to accompany her on the off chance that the rebs planned to kill her, so she asked Bravo Company's commander to go instead. His name was Bruce Holly, and he was the officer that Forbes reported to. None of them were armed with anything other than pistols.

In order to reach the meeting point, the Union soldiers had to pass through their own minefield. And as they did so, Mac knew there was the distinct possibility that the enemy was watching via a drone and mapping their route. There was no way to fully counter such an effort. But Mac was careful to pursue the most complicated path possible, hoping to make things difficult for the enemy.

It felt strange to cross a battlefield in order to attend the sort of meeting that had been a common occurrence during the first civil war. A lot of things had changed since then, yet in many ways, war remained the same. Especially the dying part.

As the parties came together, Mac saw that two officers were waiting for her, a colonel and a major. She saluted the colonel. "Major Macintyre, sir . . . And Captain Holly."

The colonel appeared to be fortysomething. He had the long, lean body of a runner. "I'm Colonel Oxley, and this is Major Boyington. Macintyre you say . . . Not *the* Major Macintyre by any chance? Meaning the officer who rescued President Sloan from Richton?"

There was no point in denying it. "Yes, sir."

"Well, well," Oxley said. "I worked for your father until recently, and it might interest you to know that your sister reported to me prior to her death. She was an excellent officer. It's too bad that you chose to murder her."

"I didn't murder Victoria," Mac replied stiffly. "She was killed by a rebel deserter, not that it matters, since dead is dead. Is there something you wish to discuss, Colonel? I hope so, because I have better things to do than stand around and shoot the shit."

Oxley's anger was plain to see. "We want to recover our dead."

Mac nodded. "That's a good idea. I like a tidy battlefield. How much time do you need?"

"An hour."

"Perfect . . . That'll give me time to eat breakfast. Is there anything else?"

"You are holding Confederate prisoners."

"That's correct, I am," Mac conceded. "I'll tell you what . . . Once you're done hauling bodies away—I'll send the POWs out ten at a time, every hour on the hour, until all of them have been released."

Oxley squinted. "You're stalling for time."

Mac smiled. "Yup."

"It won't help you," Oxley told her. "The Mexicans will roll over this area soon. Then they'll push farther east, throw your forces back into New Orleans, and establish a new front. So you can surrender to me or die. Which would you prefer?"

Mac was floored. Mexicans? *What* Mexicans? And her astonishment must have been visible on her face because Oxley laughed. "Oh, my! You didn't know, did you? Our government cut a deal with Mexico—and they're sending sixty thousand soldiers to fight alongside us! I wonder why your commanding officer failed to mention it. Will your superiors leave you here to die? That's how it appears to me. I will restate my offer. Surrender now or die here. I have a battalion of troops waiting ten minutes away—plus two Abrams tanks. You know what that means. Your Strykers won't stand a chance."

Mac looked him in the eye. "Fuck you, sir . . . *And* your tanks. This meeting is over."

And with that, Mac turned and walked away. The rest of her party hurried to catch up. "I think he's pissed," Holly said. "*Real* pissed."

"I hope so," Mac replied. "Angry people make mistakes."

"It's going to be battalion on battalion," Holly observed. "But *they* have the edge."

"That's what Oxley believes," Mac allowed. "But we'll see."

They had to wind their way between the dead bodies on the way back. Crows had been feasting on them. They lumbered into the air.

Mac felt guilty about leaving the corpses to rot. But Oxley had left her with no other option. If Mac gave Oxley the bodies, *and* the POWs, he would win a psychological victory. And that was a piss-poor way to start a battle. No, it was better to make Oxley's troops advance through an obstacle course comprised of their own dead as they attacked the compound.

Something *was* eating away at Mac, however . . . And that was the fact that Trenton had chosen to leave her in the dark. Was Oxley correct? *Had* JSOC written the battalion off? Doing so might be advantageous. Mac could imagine Sloan's press secretary putting some top spin on it. "We're sorry to announce that Major Robin Macintyre, and her entire battalion, were lost in a desperate battle to control the strategic oil reserve located in Hackberry, Louisiana. This was a particular blow to the president, who has made no secret of his admiration for Major Macintyre and commissioned the battalion that bore her name."

Would Sloan allow the battalion to die? Mac didn't think so. But did Sam *know*? He'd gone to considerable lengths to stay clear of operational matters, both as a matter of policy and good politics. Holly must have been harboring similar thoughts. "What do you think, ma'am?" he inquired, as they jumped a trench. "*Did* the rebs cut a deal with Mexico?"

"They must have," Mac allowed. "That shit is too weird to make up."

"So why haven't we heard anything from JSOC?"

Mac glanced at him. "I don't know. But we have our orders—and people to shoot at. What more does a soldier need?"

Holly grinned. Mac knew he would pass the comment on. "Nothing, ma'am. Nothing at all. You can count on Bravo Company."

"I will," Mac replied. "I certainly will."

Captain Cassidy was waiting for Mac in the command bunker. She looked tired. "I requested two A-10s," the air force JTAC said. "But it doesn't look good. It sounds like something big is in the works—and everything that can fly has been assigned to that."

Mac took the news in. *Something big?* Like the arrival of sixty thousand Mexican soldiers? Yeah, that made sense. "No problem,"

Mac lied. "We'll take care of the M-1s ourselves. Duke, find out where Lieutenant Burns is. I want to speak with him."

"Here they come," Sergeant Evans warned, as his drone circled to the south. "They're sending the tanks in first."

No sooner had the words left the noncom's mouth, than Mac heard a dull thump and knew that a 105mm round had exploded nearby. "All right," Mac said, as she turned to face Captain Holly. "Get in touch with the truck commanders on the Stryker 1128s. Tell them to start their engines and prepare for Operation Pop-Up. I'm going to rely on you to direct their fire."

Mac heard a thump followed by a dozen more in quick succession. She frowned. "What was *that*?"

"The rebs are using cannon fire to clear a path through the minefield," Evans replied.

Mac's estimate of Oxley's abilities went up a notch. He wasn't the first officer to use the strategy. And it made sense to clear a path *before* shelling Mac's defensive positions. Once Oxley accomplished that, he could send his infantry forward even if his tanks had been destroyed.

Just as Mac couldn't stand being cooped inside a Stryker, she didn't like being stuck in the bunker. Plus, she needed to talk to Lieutenant Burns, who, according to Duke, was on the front line just east of the **HONEST ABE**.

Mac left the bunker, with the RTO following close behind. She led him through the main trench to a smaller ditch that provided access to a four-man fighting position. Burns was present, along with a two-man AA team, and their launcher. "Good morning," Mac said cheerfully. "I like what you've done with the place."

Burns had dark skin, wide-set eyes, and a friendly grin. "Thanks, ma'am . . . We aim to please."

Mac brought her glasses up and swept them from left to right.

The tanks were out in the open but partially obscured by the smoke that was pouring from their onboard generators. Both M-1s fired, and high-explosive shells landed in the minefield. Each impact triggered secondary explosions that launched geysers of black soil up into the air. Mac turned to Burns. "Divide your fire between the tanks. Both groups will launch on my command. Understood?"

Burns looked concerned. "Permission to speak freely?"

Mac nodded. "Of course."

"Aircraft are one thing," Burns said. "They're relatively fragile. But a Stinger doesn't pack enough punch to stop a tank."

"That's true," Mac agreed. "But we're going to fire *fifteen* Stingers at each one of those bastards, and our Stryker 1128s are going to hit them, too."

Burns's eyebrows rose. "Holy shit, that might work."

Mac smiled grimly. "Here's hoping it does. Get your people ready. Let me know when they are."

Burns spoke into his TAC radio, answered a couple of questions, and turned back. "We're ready, ma'am."

Mac took the handset from Duke. "This is Six actual. The 1128s and the AA teams will fire on my command. Ready, aim, *fire*!"

A lot of things happened at once. Four Strykers, all equipped with 105mm cannons, rolled to the top of specially graded pathways and paused. Because of the way the vehicles were designed, they couldn't depress their guns very far. That meant the "pop-up" ramps had to be just right in order for the vics to target the tanks.

Four seconds passed while their gunners used the heat generated by the M-1s to target them. Then they fired. Not in perfect unison, so the reports overlapped each other, to create a sound like rolling thunder. Six seconds were required to reload and fire *again*. Then, after ten seconds in the open, the Strykers backed down and out of sight.

Mac's binoculars were focused on the tanks. She caught glimpses of them through the drifting smoke. M-1s were equipped with composite armor. It offered superior protection against the sort of high-explosive, antitank rounds the Strykers were firing at them.

Mac saw that five out of the eight shells fired at the tanks had been on target. And having been through the armor school at Fort Benning, Mac knew the pounding would take a toll.

Meanwhile, fifteen Stinger missiles had been fired at each tank. Each launch resulted in a loud bang. So as thirty of them sped downrange, it sounded as if a string of giant firecrackers was going off. Smoke trailed behind each missile. And there were so many of them that most of the battlefield was obscured as the Stingers found their targets.

Mac saw bright flashes through the haze. But she couldn't assess how much damage had been done until a light breeze blew some of the smoke away. There was a loud boom as the tank on the left fired its gun, but the machine on the right had been holed, and the crew was bailing out. "This is Six actual," Mac said. "*Don't* fire on the tank crew . . . Let them go. Over." The Marauders watched the rebs sprint to safety.

"All right," Mac said. "Let's finish this. Ready, aim, fire!"

The pop-up Strykers loosed another salvo. But, because all of them were aiming at the *same* target, the results were even better. After taking seven hits, the remaining M-1 exploded. Flames shot up through the top hatch, and the tank shuddered as shells cooked off inside the hull. That was followed by a loud BOOM as the hull disintegrated, and chunks of metal flew every which way. "It worked," Burns said. "It actually worked!"

"Of course it worked," Mac replied with a confidence she didn't feel. "But this is far from over. The tanks plowed a passageway through our minefield, and now their infantry will try to use it."

Duke interrupted them. "Lieutenant Forbes is on the horn, ma'am. She says that three self-propelled barges are crossing Black Lake—and all of them are loaded with troops. ETA, fifteen minutes."

Even though the move wasn't unexpected, Mac felt a sudden stab of fear. Could the Marauders fight on *two* fronts and win? They were about to find out.

Jet engines screamed as two enemy fighters swooped in, dropped two-thousand-pound bombs on the complex, and accelerated away. Powerful explosions shook the ground as three Strykers were destroyed, and a dozen soldiers were killed. The *real* battle had begun.

NEW ORLEANS, LOUISIANA

Sloan had been in New Orleans for a day by then. The purpose of the visit was to convince critics that he wasn't asleep at the wheel, as some of them claimed, and to boost sagging morale. Even though the Mexican advance wasn't pretty from a military perspective, the sudden influx of enemy troops had been devastating. Because contrary to what some people expected, the Mexican troops had come to fight. The reason for their fervor wasn't entirely clear and was the subject of considerable conjecture.

Fortunately, Union forces had been able to stop the advance west of Baton Rouge. But a lot of hard-won ground had been lost. And now, rather than the big push that Sloan had been planning, he faced another stalemate.

That was what he'd been told the previous afternoon. And now, as Sloan sat through still another briefing, everything he heard amounted to more bad news. The latest tidbit was that a battalion of troops had been sent deep into enemy territory in order to capture and hold the West Hackberry Strategic Oil Reserve. Now they were trapped and fighting for their lives.

That would have captured Sloan's attention no matter what. But the fact that he'd been to the Hackberry site as Secretary of Energy and survived the ill-fated attempt to capture the reserve in Richton, Mississippi, meant that he could imagine the battle that was taking place. He raised a hand. "Excuse me, Admiral . . . Let's back up. I'd like to know more about that battalion and our plans to extract it. There *are* plans, right?"

Three generals, two admirals, and a dozen lesser officers were present in the meeting room. The admiral gestured toward one of them. "The battalion in question is part of JSOC—and that's Commander Trenton's area of expertise. Commander? What can you tell us?"

Trenton stood. Sloan saw that the woman had a hard face and was dressed in camos, rather than the khaki uniforms that the other naval officers had chosen to wear. Was that intended to set her apart? To emphasize her membership in the special forces community? Perhaps.

"Yes, sir," Trenton said. "The unit you referred to is Mac's Marauders under the command of Major Robin Macintyre. The original plan was to take control of the facility in advance of the big push—and prevent the rebs from destroying it when they were forced to pull back. But the strategic situation has changed."

Her eyes were locked with his, and Sloan could see the challenge in them. It seemed safe to assume that Trenton knew the battalion was *his* idea—and that she was cognizant of his relationship with Robin. And Sloan knew the people in the room were waiting to see how he would respond. He chose his words with care. "Yes, the situation has changed. So, since you're in command, how are *you* going to get our people out?"

The emphasis on "you" was intentional—and Sloan watched Trenton's shoulders stiffen slightly. She couldn't pass the buck the way the admiral had and made no attempt to do so. "We have teams both large and small trapped inside enemy territory," she answered. "Mac's Marauders is in queue behind a platoon of Rangers and a couple of downed pilots.

"As you can imagine, combat search and rescue teams are in short supply right now. Would you like me to move the Marauders up to the top of the list?" It was said sweetly and with a sardonic smile.

Hell yes, Sloan wanted to move the battalion up, but it wouldn't be right to do so. More than that, it would be political suicide to show any hint of favoritism. Something which, judging from the look on her face, Trenton was well aware of.

"No," Sloan said. "I never interfere with operational matters. But I'm worried about *all* of the people on your list. For that reason, I'm going to ask my attaché, Lieutenant Colonel McKinney, to track the situation. Please keep him informed."

"I will," Trenton replied tightly. "Is there anything else?"

"Just this," Sloan said flatly. "Thank you for your service to our country."

Some of those in the room took the comment at face value. Others thought the sentence had an ominous ring to it. As if Trenton's military career might be coming to an end. McKinney, who was seated behind Sloan, smiled.

WEST HACKBERRY STRATEGIC PETROLEUM RESERVE, HACKBERRY, LOUISIANA

Mac had returned to the command bunker. The good news, such as it was, lay in the fact that the air attack had taken place *after* the tanks had been neutralized. Mac knew it would have been nearly impossible to stop the behemoths while being bombed at the same time. "This is Six actual," Mac said over the radio. "Get ready . . . They'll be back."

At that point, Mac left Lieutenant Burns to handle the AA effort while she focused on the ground war. "Here they come," Evans said. And, as Mac eyed his monitor, she could see that at least two companies of enemy troops were moving forward. "Six here," Mac said, as she watched a group of rebs bunch up behind the burned-out tanks. "Put mortar fire on *both* tanks. Then, when they break cover, take them down. Over."

"Show me the lake," Mac said, as the outgoing mortar fire began. "I want to see those barges."

The drone circled out over Black Lake. "There they are," Evans said. "It looks like there are about ten people on each one of them. That adds up to a platoon."

Mac knew what the noncom was thinking. Once the platoon landed, Mac would be forced to shift resources to the lakeshore, thereby weakening the battalion's southern defenses.

But, before the rebs could land, they'd have to deal with Lieutenant Forbes and her tiny command. "Six actual to Bravo-One-Six. They're coming in. You know what to do." Mac heard three clicks by way of a response.

Captain Cassidy was there along with her radio operator. "I put out a call for help," the air force JTAC said. "Nothing so far."

"This is Charlie-Two," Burns said over the tactical frequency. "Two northbound aircraft at six o'clock. Ready, aim, fire!"

Even though Mac was in the command bunker, she could hear the now-familiar bang, bang, bang sound as Stingers took to the air. "The rebs are popping flares," Burns added. "They're trying to pull the Stingers away. Damn . . . No hits."

Mac swore, and was about to reply, when a precision-guided 250-lb glide bomb hit the roof. It exploded, and half of the ceiling caved in. A sudden avalanche of dirt knocked Mac to the floor. *They've been watching,* Mac thought. *They know where the command post is.*

Duke was untouched. He bent over to give Mac a hand. Dirt fell away from Mac's shoulders as she stood. Cassidy was okay, as was Evans, but a runner named Minsky was down. The reason was obvious. A beam had fallen on the private's unprotected head. Cassidy's RTO knelt next to the body. She looked up and shook her head. "He's gone."

Mac made a face and turned to Duke. "Help her haul Minsky out of here . . . Evans, it's time to move. Follow me."

With Evans right behind her, Mac exited the bunker, followed the main trench to the back end of a Stryker, and made her way inside. The vehicle was empty except for the truck commander and his gunner. Duke followed Evans up the ramp. "Forbes is about to engage the rebs," he said. "They're a thousand yards offshore."

"Show me the drone feed," Mac said, as Evans hurried to get his gear up and running again. The process ate fifteen long seconds, and by the time video appeared, the battle was under way. Mac had been forced to place most of Forbes's vics elsewhere. But the platoon leader had one Stryker, and more importantly, both of the Marine Corps' LAVs. Three vehicles in all.

When Forbes gave the command, the Stryker emerged from hiding, sped down to the lakefront, and opened fire. The rebs returned fire as geysers of water shot up all around the lead barge. They had an AT4 launcher, but the rocket went wide and struck a shed. There must have been something flammable inside it because the structure exploded. And that was fine with Mac since it was a good diversion.

The LAV-25s had been launched during the hours of darkness. Then they had been moored in between two-hundred-foot-long barges and covered with tarps. Now both of the amphibious vehicles were under way and about to attack the rebs from the east.

The LAVs weren't fast, but they were steady, and Mac could see their wakes as the drone circled above them. The moment they came within effective range, both vehicles fired their 25mm chain guns.

That, combined with the .50 caliber fire from the Stryker, was devastating. The rebel soldiers had no protection—and were swept away by the hail of lead. One of the barges started to sink. And as the drone flew low, Mac could see the bodies heaped on the others, and the rivulets of blood that ran down into the lake. She felt sick to her stomach. It was *her* doing. But what choice did she have? It was either their people or her people. The choice warriors had been forced to make for thousands of years.

"Four navy F-14s are inbound," Cassidy said, as a reb fighter roared overhead. "Maybe they can chase the bad guys away."

Mac heard the now-familiar bang, bang, bang as Stingers were fired, followed by a whoop of joy from Burns. "A hit! We got a hit! He's trailing smoke and losing altitude."

That was good news indeed. But they weren't out of the woods yet. The Stryker shook as the top-mounted fifty fired a burst. Listening to the TAC frequency was like checking the battalion's pulse. "Put a rocket on that Bradley, One-One-Alpha . . . Kill that bastard. Over."

"This is Two-Two-Delta . . . We need some ammo, and we need it *now.* Over."

"Three-Three-Charlie here . . . The lieutenant is down. Send a medic! Over."

Platoon leaders, and in some cases platoon sergeants, responded to the calls. But there was only so much they could do. The battalion was starting to bleed out. Mac turned to Duke. The RTO *heard* everything, which meant that he *knew* everything. "Where do we stand, Larry? How many wounded? How many killed?"

Duke flipped a page on his notebook. "Fifty-six wounded, eighteen dead," he said. "Company Sergeant Bader was killed ten minutes ago."

Mac felt something cold trickle into her veins. The situation was even worse than she had feared. "Put a call in to Kingpin. Tell them we have five-six WIAs to get out of here, plus at least one-eight bodies. And tell them we are prepping for Final Protective Fire."

Duke's eyes were huge. "'Final Protective Fire'? What's that mean?"

"It means this is the fucking Alamo," Evans answered from a few feet away. "And you are Davy Crockett. Get on the horn. Maybe we can get some people out of here."

Duke swallowed, keyed the handset, and went to work. "This is Reacher-Four-Six, calling Kingpin-Two-Two-One . . ."

Mac didn't have time to hang around and see what Trenton would say. She grabbed an M4 carbine, and as she made her way down the ramp, Mac heard bullets snap overhead. The combination of Burns's AA fire and the incoming F-14s had been enough to clear the sky for a moment. And that was a good thing.

The rebs were so close that Mac couldn't separate the sound of outgoing fire from the sound of incoming fire. She was careful to keep her head down while she dashed from position to position. Mac wasn't there to give orders. Lieutenants and sergeants could handle that.

No, Mac's purpose was to be seen and to give her soldiers hope. Little things could make a difference. Like when she called a soldier by her name, helped to shift a machine gun from one location to another, or held a dying soldier's hand. She'd done it before but never so many times. Tears cut trails through the grime on her cheeks as Mac trudged from place to place.

But the worst, the *very* worst, was the battalion aid station—where PA Lieutenant Tom Brody and his medics were sorting the Marauders into three groups: those they could help, those they *couldn't* help, and those who were dead. The blood-covered medics looked more like ghouls than angels as they made their rounds. When Brody saw Mac, he came over. The PA accidentally wiped some blood onto his forehead. "How bad is it?"

Mac forced a smile. "I put in a call . . . Help will arrive soon."

Brody nodded. "Thanks, I'll try to believe that."

Then they heard a burp of static from Mac's radio followed by the sound of Duke's voice. "This is Bravo-One-Zero to all personnel. We have two, repeat *two* friendly aircraft inbound from the east, ETA one minute. Put your heads down—and *don't* fire on them. Over."

"See?" Mac said. "I told you so."

Brody grinned. "No offense, Major . . . But you're full of shit."

"And none taken," Mac responded. "I'm not sure if this is the close air support that we asked for or the prelude to an extraction. Let's hope for the latter. Prep your patients for the trip out. I'll send a squad to help you with the KIAs."

Brody was giving orders as Mac left. Once she was outside, Mac made her way forward, entered a fighting position, and was staring at the eastern horizon when the A-10s appeared. Rockets flashed off their wings as they came in low, 500-lb laser-guided GBU-12 bombs fell free, and the results were nothing short of spectacular. A Bradley took a direct hit and blew up. All of the enemy troops had to go facedown in the dirt, and the volume of incoming fire dropped accordingly.

Mac looked past the circling Hogs and up into the sky beyond. Yes! The navy F-14s were still there, keeping the reb fighters at bay. And that was crucial since the A-10s were especially vulnerable while operating that close to the ground.

A .50 caliber machine gun was sited just forward of the hole. "Uh-oh," the loader said. "Here they come!" As the gunner opened fire, Mac saw that the soldier was correct and made a grab for her M4. The Confederates were on their feet and charging forward.

Were they brave? Hell yes, they were brave. And they were smart, too. *If* the rebs could reach the battalion's front line, and *if* they could break through it, they'd be safe from the Warthogs. Because once the two sides were intermingled, the planes wouldn't be able to attack. "Stop them!" Mac yelled into her boom mike. "Stop them *now*!"

Every Stryker was firing, and all of the troops were, too. The first rank of enemy soldiers appeared to wilt as the defensive fire swept across them. But there were more, at least a hundred of them, and they were only two hundred yards away when the A-10s returned.

Each A-10 was armed with a GAU-8/A Avenger 30mm Gatling-style auto cannon. And the fearsome weapons roared as the Hogs came in. Mac saw puffs of dirty gray smoke blow back from the nose of each plane and trail away.

Mac stopped firing as the armor-piercing shells plowed bloody paths through the rebel ranks and brought their charge to a halt. A noncom managed to plant a Confederate flag in his native soil before falling forward next to it. His body marked what amounted to the attack's high-tide mark. Mac couldn't help but admire the man's courage.

There were very few survivors, and most of them were wounded. Those who could waved scraps of white cloth. Mac keyed her radio.

"This is Six actual . . . Cease firing. Allow the rebs to pull back." Then, to Cassidy, "Notify the A-10s. Tell them to lay off. Over."

Once the firing stopped, voices could be heard. Some were calling for medics. One soldier wanted his mother. And another was singing. He had a beautiful voice, and the lyrics seemed to float over the battlefield.

Mine eyes have seen the glory of the coming of the Lord;
He is trampling out the vintage where the grapes of wrath
are stored;
He hath loosed the fateful lightning of His terrible swift
sword,
His truth is marching on.

Then Duke arrived, and the moment was over. "There you are," the RTO said crossly, as if Mac had been hiding from him. "I just got off the horn with Kingpin. They're going to pull us out. We have one hour in which to destroy all the pumping infrastructure we can, prep the wounded for the dust-off, and collect the dead. The F-14s and the A-10s will remain on station."

"Thank God for that," Mac said. "Let's get to work."

There was a lot to do. And as the minutes ticked away, Mac dashed from place to place. Were the truck commanders ready to destroy their vehicles? Check. Had the LZs been cleared and marked? Check. Had the Confederate POWs been loaded onto one of the barges? And set adrift? Check. And so on as Mac ran through a mental checklist of all the things that needed to be done.

And while all of that was taking place, *more* rebs were closing in. Except that the newcomers weren't Confederate soldiers, they were Mexicans, at least a thousand of them according to Sergeant Evans.

But *why*? It was clear that the Marauders were getting ready to pull out by then. So all Oxley, or whoever was in charge, had to do was sit back and wait. Maybe the counterattack was a matter of honor. Or, and this seemed more likely, the Confederates were out for revenge. Whatever the reason, the Mexicans were coming in hard. So hard, and from so many directions, that it was difficult for the A-10s to hold them off.

That forced Mac to roll a dozen Strykers and position them around the LZ facing out. And not a moment too soon. Six Jaguar armored cars appeared from the south and opened fire. The Marauders responded in kind, and with Stingers, too, in hopes of scaring the shit out of the foreign troops.

Cassidy summoned the Warthogs again. But even though the A-10s destroyed six Jaguars, the rest remained operational. A wave of Mexican soldiers surged forward as the first Chinook landed. Mac was there, firing her M4, when Trenton jumped to the ground. The navy officer was wearing a ball cap, a TAC vest, and shorts. A red, white, and blue artificial leg completed the look. Trenton was armed with a Belgian FN SCAR-H. She nodded. "Good afternoon, Major . . . This is quite a shit show. But I've seen worse."

And with that, Trenton knelt next to the **LITTLE TOOT**, raised the SCAR, and began to fire single shots. Mac was firing, too, but not as accurately. Each time Trenton squeezed the trigger, an enemy soldier died.

What ensued was a hellish symphony of roaring engines, machine-gun fire, and shouted orders. The Mexicans attacked, went to ground, and attacked again. Cassidy called for the Strykers to drop red smoke, waited for it to billow upwards, and put out the call.

Some of the Mexicans were belly-crawling toward the LZ. Mac was so focused on killing them that she barely noticed the roar of jet engines as the Hogs made another gun run. Thirty mike-mike rounds tore the enemy infantry to shreds.

Then the ground shook, and Mac thought the planes were dropping bombs, until someone shouted, "Incoming!" That was when Mac realized the truth. The rebs had brought artillery to bear and were determined to kill the Chinooks.

Mac shoved a fresh magazine into the M4 while Cassidy's RTO spoke with one of the F-14 pilots. There was no way for them to know what the zoomie did, but the shelling stopped two minutes later. Mac's ears were ringing, and she felt dizzy.

"Major," a male voice said. "Shall we blow the charges?"

Mac turned to find that Captain Munson was standing behind her. He was alive! She wasn't sure of anything by that point. "Yes, blow the charges," she said. "And get your people on that Chinook."

The ground shook as charge after charge went off, destroying all of the reserve's infrastructure, the battalion's supply dump, and the Strykers that remained in their revetments.

With only one helicopter remaining, Trenton approached her. The navy officer extended her right hand, and Mac shook it. "I apologize," Trenton said. "You *are* the real deal. Come on . . . Let's go home. There's plenty of booze in the O club, and I'm buying."

They walked side by side to the waiting helo and climbed on board. The twin engines spooled up, the ground fell away, and the battlefield appeared. Hundreds of people lay dead. *For what?* Mac asked herself. *A failed plan? Yes.* But there was no point in dwelling on that. Such things were outside the sphere of her control. *We had orders,* Mac concluded. *And we followed them. And that is all that a soldier can do.*

CHAPTER 11

> The battlefield is a scene of constant chaos. The winner will be the one who controls that chaos, both his own and the enemies'.
>
> –NAPOLEON BONAPARTE

NEAR CALUMET, LOUISIANA

The small group of officers were standing on the west side of the channel looking east as they sipped coffee and nibbled on the cinnamon rolls that had been brought forward from the town of Centerville. A layer of mist floated just above the land on the other side of the divide and eddied gently as a breeze slid in from the south.

The Yankees had been pushed east to Calumet, Louisiana. And that was a natural place for them to make a stand. The Atchafalaya Spillway formed a barrier that ran straight as an arrow all the way to the Gulf of Mexico, and the only bridge was in Calumet. Or *had* been in Calumet, until the Confederate Army had been forced to destroy it thirty days earlier, when it appeared as though the enemy was going to chase them all the way to Houston. So, with swamps protecting both its north and south flanks, the Union Army was in a strong position.

And if it could hold the Mexicans off long enough, the Union might be able to force a stalemate and use it to buy some much-needed time. That scenario was one that Bo was determined to prevent by pushing through what he thought of as "the squeeze" at Calumet and recapturing the city of New Orleans, which lay to the east.

Unfortunately, Bo had more than the Union Army to worry about. His new allies were both a blessing and a curse. Major General Matias Ramos emptied his coffee mug and held it out. An orderly wearing a white jacket stepped forward to fill it up. "A nice day for it," the Mexican general remarked, as a 155mm howitzer shell rumbled overhead and exploded somewhere behind them.

Much to Bo's amazement, Ramos looked none the worse for wear despite the party he'd thrown the night before. "*Every* day is a good day for killing Yankees," Bo observed. "It's my pleasure to inform you that our engineers are ready to put an Improved Ribbon Bridge (IRB) in place, so that your forces can cross the spillway. Shall I give the order?"

Bo held his breath while Ramos dabbed at the corners of his mouth with a linen napkin. Would the son of a bitch agree to move forward? Or would he spend half the morning getting a hot shave? "Excellent," Ramos replied. "Please proceed. I would like to send a brigade across before nightfall. However, it's quite likely that our northern friends will object and send planes to destroy the bridge. Will we have air cover?"

"Of course," Bo replied, hoping that the wish would come true. Based on previous experience, he knew that Ramos wouldn't move even a foot without jet fighters circling above. "Now, if you'll excuse me, I'll make the necessary arrangements."

Work began immediately. In order to deploy the IRB, it was necessary to bring the sections in on Common Bridge Transporter trucks, dump the prefab elements into the channel, and hook them together. And as the Confederate engineers worked, Union gunners shelled the spillway, sinking two work boats. Shortly after that, a surface-to-surface missile severed the span, and a brace of the enemy A-10s attempted to sneak in under the fighters circling above. The span was repaired, and the intruders were shot down.

Still, by the time the sun set, the bridge was operational, and Ramos kept his word. A brigade of troops crossed the IRB, secured a bridgehead, and dug in. Bo wanted to push on and take more ground. But Ramos and his polo-playing buddies had other ideas.

They were quartered in the picturesque town of Franklin, which was located twelve miles to the rear, and they liked their comforts. So Bo had to accompany them there *and* sit through an evening of revelry or run the risk that a staff officer would take the opportunity to fill Ramos's head with bullshit.

Ramos, Bo, and the other officers were staying at the Quality Inn. One of the hotel's meeting rooms had been transformed into a lounge, complete with a buffet table and a makeshift bar. Plus, each night local beauties were on hand to offer the foreigners some Southern comfort. And if Ramos had a weakness, that was it. The man seemed to have an insatiable libido and typically took a different woman to bed every night, an indulgence that Bo saw as a weakness.

But finally, after Ramos and his entourage spent hours eating, drinking, and groping their female companions, they went to bed. Then, and only then, could Bo and *his* staff turn in. Once in his room, Bo lay on the bed, stared at the ceiling for a while, and closed his eyes.

Where were the dreams? The hopes? The plans? Nearly all of

them were dead. Like his wife. Like his daughter. The exception, the thing Bo lived for, was the chance to kill Samuel T. Sloan. The man directly responsible for Kathy's death . . . And the man who, according to various news stories, was screwing the daughter he no longer acknowledged. Why did he care then? Because Robin was *his* . . . That's why.

Sleep pulled Bo down. Various people were waiting to speak with him. And all of them were dead.

NEW ORLEANS, LOUISIANA

As Union troops were forced to retreat to the east, and reinforcements arrived from the north, the city of New Orleans struggled to absorb the sudden influx of people. Mac returned to NAS/JRB to find that another female officer was sharing her room, and there were long lines for almost everything.

And, when it came to locating the soldiers who had been wounded in Hackberry, Mac discovered that they were in three different hospitals. She went to visit each one of them nevertheless—and usually arrived with much-sought-after gifts like candy, spicy food, and magazines.

Meanwhile, it seemed as if her battalion had been relegated to a military never-never land. Though still part of JSOC, it wasn't clear if the unit was going to remain there. Did JSOC *need* a battalion of Strykers? Some people said, "yes," and others said, "no."

Plus, as Trenton pointed out to Mac, "All of your Strykers were destroyed. And replacements aren't available. Don't worry, though . . . We'll find something for you to do."

The "something," as it turned out, was a slot as the "Recreation Officer," in a war zone where no one had time to recreate. So Mac was sitting around drinking coffee when a request came down for her to, "coordinate recreational activities in conjunction with the upcoming Southern Command Conference to be held at the New Orleans Hilton Hotel." And, with nothing else to do, Mac found herself looking forward to the event.

As with all such functions, a committee had been formed to organize the gathering, and the first meeting was to be held in a conference room at the Louis Armstrong International Airport. But when Mac arrived, there was only one person there to greet her. "Hello, Mac," Sloan said as he rose from a chair. "You look wonderful! I apologize for the misleading invitation . . . But I know you understand."

Mac stood and stared. In marked contrast to the last time she'd seen Sloan, his face was drawn and tired. Not only that, but his clothes were loose, as if he'd lost some weight. Mac felt a surge of concern. The war was taking a heavy toll. Sloan offered a smile. "Did you get my letter?"

"Yes," Mac replied.

"And? Is there any chance that you'll accept my apology?"

Mac knew the answer should be "no" since Sloan's actions should have been unforgivable. But the anger she'd felt earlier had dissipated. Because of the passage of time? Because she still felt drawn to him? It didn't matter. "Yes," Mac answered. "There's a chance."

Sloan's expression brightened. "Thank you. Although, should I get another chance to kill your father, I'll be forced to take it."

The line was delivered with a smile, and dark though the humor was, Mac had to laugh. "Understood. But not while we're on a date."

Sloan came forward to place his hands on her shoulders. "You're alive. Thank God for that. This is like a dream."

He raised his hands to cup her face. "Can I kiss you? To make sure that you're real?"

Mac closed her eyes as their lips met, felt his arms take her in, and wanted to cry. She was happy there. But conscious of how fragile life was—and the uncertainties that lay ahead. "Thank you," Sloan said, as the kiss came to an end.

"For what?" Mac inquired as she looked up at him.

"For being you, for giving me a second chance, and for the kiss."

"Consider it a down payment," Mac said. "On the future."

"Yes," Sloan replied. "I need something to hope for."

"The situation is that bad?"

Sloan looked away and back again. "I'm afraid so. The Confederates put a ribbon bridge across the Atchafalaya Spillway yesterday. Then the Mexicans sent a brigade across to protect the bridgehead. We tried to stop them and failed. *I* failed."

"That's bullshit," Mac replied.

Sloan forced a grin. "Thanks. But, for better or worse, I'm the commander in chief."

"And a good one," Mac put in. "Remember where you are, which is deep inside what used to be enemy territory, only 350 miles from Houston."

Mac saw a flicker of hope in his eyes. "You're a good cheerleader. Were you one?"

Mac nodded. "Yes."

"I wish I could have seen that," Sloan said wistfully. A side door opened, and a man appeared. And, when Sloan raised a hand by way of an acknowledgment, the man disappeared.

"Take care of yourself," Sloan said. "I'll be in touch."

Mac took the initiative, kissed him hard, and turned away. Tears were running down her cheeks as she left. Tears she needed to hide.

IIIIIIIIIIII

With the exception of the Marauders who were in hospitals, the rest had been given five days of leave and sent off to Biloxi, Mississippi, for some R&R. And now, as they returned to duty, Mac had a problem. What should the battalion be focused on? Training seemed like the obvious answer, and Mac was ready to make some specific recommendations, as she went to see Commander Trenton.

But as Mac entered Trenton's office, everything changed. Because there, seated in one of the guest chairs, was Lieutenant Thomas Lyle! Mac had worked with the young Green Beret on two occasions in the past. The most recent occasion was the mission to grab Confederate Secretary of Energy Oliver Sanders down in Odessa, Texas, and take him north for interrogation.

There was a big grin on Lyle's face as he came forward to collect a hug. "Good morning, Robin . . . I heard about Hackberry. I'm glad you're safe."

Trenton cleared her throat. "This is sweet. But I have better things to do than watch the two of you play kissy face. Have a seat, Major . . . We have work to do."

Mac sat next to Lyle, and Trenton nodded. "Okay, that's better. Two things . . . The first concerns Mac's Marauders. I have some bad news to share. JSOC *doesn't* need a Stryker battalion. Especially one that doesn't have any Strykers. And the army wants its soldiers back. So your unit is being transferred to the 32nd Infantry Brigade. Captain Munson will assume command during your absence."

The announcement didn't come as a complete surprise since Mac had been aware of the battalion's uncertain status, but she still felt a sense of shock. She was a cavalry officer, and that meant something. To her at least. Even if the difference between being an infantry officer and a cavalry officer wasn't that great. And given the army's pressing need for troops, Mac knew it made sense to put her people back in the fight.

But Mac could tell that something else was brewing as well. Trenton's comment had an ominous quality. "During your absence." *What* absence? And what about Lyle? Why was the Green Beret present?

Trenton had been watching. She nodded. "I'm sorry. I know how much you enjoy driving around and shooting people. But, if all goes well, some new Strykers will become available in the near future. In the meantime, we need to beat the Mexicans back.

"And that raises a very important question: Why are those bastards fighting for the Confederacy anyway? The easy answer is that the rebs are *paying* them to fight. According to a top secret report, one ton of gold was shipped from the Texas Gold Depository near Austin to the airport in Mexico City.

"That's a lot of gold," Trenton added. "And it's worth a lot of money. Especially these days. But is it enough for Mexico to field *four* divisions of troops? And run the risk of winding up on the wrong side of our civil war? There are a whole lot of eggheads who don't think so. They think the gold is part of a larger, more significant transaction of some sort. One that we need to know about and understand. And that's where you two come in."

Trenton looked from face to face. "Your job will be to slip in behind Mexican lines, snatch Major General Matias Ramos, and bring him back for questioning. If you succeed, maybe we can convince Ramos to tell us why his country was willing to do such a risky deal with the Confederacy."

Trenton turned to Lyle. "The major will be in overall command. But you'll be in charge of the snatch itself." Trenton pushed two sealed envelopes over to them. "Study this stuff and return here at 1400. You will be leaving at 1700 tomorrow."

Mac frowned. "Why so soon?"

"Because we know where Ramos will be tomorrow night," Trenton replied, "unless the Mexicans break through our lines before then."

Mac had all sorts of questions, not to mention objections, but could tell that Trenton didn't want to hear them. Not yet, anyway. So she stood and tossed a salute. "Yes, ma'am."

Lyle did the same, and they left together. "Holy shit," the Green Beret said, once they were outside. "*Tomorrow?* That's tight."

"It sucks," Mac agreed. "Come on . . . We'll get some coffee and do our homework. Then, assuming this mission is as fucked up as it sounds, we'll go AWOL."

Lyle laughed. "Done and done. I'm in."

After a visit to the chow hall, the officers sought refuge in the tiny R&R office that Mac had been using. As the officers read the operation plan and studied the accompanying maps, it was clear that a lot of forethought had gone into the documents.

The team was to consist of ten people—two of whom would be navy Riverines. Their job was to take the team up the Atchafalaya Spillway to a rendezvous with a CIA agent. He would provide the operatives with the transportation required to reach the town of Franklin. That's where Lyle and three Green Berets would carry out the snatch.

Maybe the vehicle the CIA agent furnished to them would be sufficient to get them home, or, as the operation plan stated, "it might become necessary to source additional transportation locally."

"What," Mac wanted to know, "is this 'transportation will be sourced locally' shit?"

"It means we might have to steal it." Lyle replied. "That's more common than you might think."

Mac frowned. "But what if we can't?"

"Then we're SOL," the Green Beret replied. "But we will," he added confidently.

Mac made a note. When it came to recruiting some "volunteers," she would need an extremely competent driver, and the best "wrench" available. Meaning a tech who could break into vehicles if necessary, hot-wire them, and carry out minor repairs while on the move. No problem there . . . Her battalion was home to some very skilled ex-criminals.

As for the proposed exfil route, that sucked big-time. They couldn't, in the judgment of the people who had authored the plan, go east after the snatch. That's what the rebs would expect them to do.

So the answer was to head west, turn north toward Lafayette, and flee east on I-10. The freeway would take them over the Atchafalaya National Wildlife Refuge to the outskirts of Baton Rouge, where a team of CIA spooks would be waiting. According to Mac's calculations, the exfil would take roughly four hours. Assuming no one attempted to stop them. And how likely was *that*?

But what was, was. Both officers drew up wish lists, which they took to the meeting with Trenton. All of their requests were approved. And the whole thing was very matter-of-fact until the officers stood to leave. That was when Trenton circled her desk in order to shake hands with them. "I want you back," she told them sternly. "Don't disappoint me."

Lyle grinned. "No, ma'am . . . We wouldn't dream of it." The meeting was over.

The rest of that day, and half of the next, were spent prepping for the mission. That included choosing people for the team, meeting with them, and drawing their gear.

Unfortunately, that left very little time for Mac to meet with Captain Munson. Mac wasn't free to disclose anything about the mission, other than there was one, and it wouldn't take long. "Assuming that things go well, I'll be back within forty-eight hours," she promised him. "And if they don't go well, put in a requisition for a new major. I don't know anything about the 32nd Infantry Brigade. Report in, find out what you can, and kiss some butt. I want the CO to be in a good mood when I request some Strykers."

Munson chuckled. "Yes, ma'am. Take care out there. I'll see you in forty-eight."

In order to cut the travel time down, the decision had been made to depart from Port Fourchon, which was located southwest of New Orleans. Mac had been too busy to worry right up to the moment when the team boarded the thirty-six-foot Chris Craft that Chief Petty Officer Myron had chosen for the infil. Now Mac felt the first stirrings of fear. Because even though she had participated in *three* special ops missions, all of them had been large-scale endeavors like the attack on the Hackberry Reserve. And there was a certain amount of comfort to be derived from having a lot of people around even when outnumbered by the enemy.

But this felt different to her, even if Lyle took it in stride. "In and out," the Green Beret said. "A piece of cake." *Maybe,* Mac thought. *And maybe not.*

Like the rest of the team, Mac was dressed for a boat ride. Her outfit consisted of a cotton blouse and white shorts. Meanwhile, navy petty officer Casey Hunt had chosen to wear a two-piece bathing suit and a pair of slip-on tennis shoes. And, because Hunt had a nice figure, there were no complaints from the men. They were dressed in garish Hawaiian shirts, board shorts, and flip-flops. A disreputable group for sure, but members of a special ops team? No. Spies, if any, were unlikely to suspect the group of anything more than bad taste.

"Make yourselves at home," Chief Myron said. "Hunt and I will handle all of the boatey stuff." Mac knew that Myron was a very experienced member of the navy's Riverine Squadrons. An organization that specialized in small-boat operations, often in conjunction with Navy SEALS. Myron had dark skin, a long, tall body, and the confident swagger typical of professional noncoms everywhere. There was a roar as the twin Volvo engines came to life, followed by the throaty burble that Chris Craft boats are famous for and a wave from Myron. He was playing his part and enjoying it. "Feel free to cast off, hon."

"Fuck you," Hunt replied sweetly, as the rest of the team laughed.

Once both lines were aboard, Myron pushed the throttles forward, and the boat pulled away from the dock. That was when "Kokomo," by the Beach Boys, began to blare over the sound system, and the people on a sailboat waved. "Here you go," Lyle said as he offered Mac a beer. "It's your duty to drink this. Spies are everywhere."

Thus began a wonderfully boring trip, past the point where the Atchafalaya River joined the Gulf, and into the maze of channels associated with the Atchafalaya Delta Wildlife Management area. Thanks to the boat's three-foot draft, Myron was able to navigate the shallows without running aground, something they couldn't afford to do, lest they be late for the rendezvous.

The sun was low in the sky by then, and based on aerial surveillance conducted the previous day, the team had been told to expect some sort of interdiction. It came in the form of a twenty-five-foot rebel patrol boat, which, given the gray-over-red paint job, had been the property of the United States Coast Guard before the war. It was armed with machine guns fore and aft, plus a police-style light bar on top of the cabin. Myron cut power the moment it began to flash. "No need to get up off your army asses," the chief advised. "The navy will take care of this."

Hunt had dropped her jacket by then and was standing by the rail, waving to the men on the patrol boat. "Hey there!" Hunt said loudly, as she raised a can. "Would you guys like a beer?"

The man at the wheel put it over, and all of the rebs were staring at the half-naked petty officer, when she tossed the incendiary grenade into the patrol boat's cockpit. Myron applied power and was veering away when the device went off.

Mac saw a bright flash, followed by a BOOM, as the fire found both gas tanks. Part of the cabin soared up into the air—then fell like a rock. There was a splash as it hit dead center in among bits of still-flaming debris. The whole thing was over in a matter of seconds.

Mac had witnessed hundreds of deaths, but the casual, almost offhand, way in which Hunt destroyed the patrol boat *and* killed its three-man crew came as a shock. This was a different kind of war than what Mac was used to. One that relied on surprise, subterfuge, and sudden violence to get the job done.

What remained of the patrol boat slid below the surface of the water as the Chris Craft sped upstream. Would it be missed? Certainly. But it would take at least a day to find the wreckage and figure out what had transpired.

"It's time to gear up," Lyle said. "Orney, Timms, Wynn, and Yang will go below first. Our female personnel will follow."

The Green Berets were back on deck fifteen minutes later. The casual wear had been replaced by camos, heavily loaded TAC vests, and hydration packs. Three of the four were armed with Heckler & Koch MP7 submachine guns, all equipped with suppressors and laser sights. Yang was carrying a Remington Model 700 sniper's rifle with a suppressor attached.

The armament had been chosen by Lyle. "We need to standardize our weapons," he'd said. "So we can trade stuff around as necessary."

Mac knew that was a nice way of saying that common weaponry would allow the living to scavenge supplies from the dead. It was a logical if somewhat off-putting thought.

As for handguns, the Green Berets were carrying Ruger Mark III .22LR pistols equipped with suppressors and laser sights. They were too damned long in Mac's opinion. But Lyle insisted. "You'll see," he told her. "Stealth will be extremely important. And the Rugers are very quiet."

Mac followed Hunt below, located her bag, and went about the process of gearing up. Despite the decision to prioritize mobility over everything else, Mac knew she would be carrying fifty pounds of armor, grenades, and ammo. Not to mention a chocolate bar or two. And that didn't include the weight of the MP7 and the Ruger.

Hunt was carrying everything that Mac was, *plus* a field radio, because she was the navy equivalent of an RTO. And the team's link with Trenton. Mac followed her up on deck. Hunt took the wheel, so Myron and Lyle could go below. "Don't worry, ma'am," Hunt said. "I'm qualified to do everything the chief does except pee standing up."

Mac laughed. "Men have us there . . . How are we going to navigate? The moon is up . . . But the haze doesn't let much light get through."

"See the laptop? That's us," Hunt replied. "All we have to do is stay in the groove."

The computer was positioned in front of the wheel. The display showed a representation of the spillway with the boat icon centered in the middle of it. "That's slick," Mac said. "Stop if you see a Starbucks."

Lieutenant Lyle and Chief Myron returned shortly thereafter. They were carrying a cooler loaded with thick, deli-style sandwiches and a selection of cold drinks. No beer though . . . Not at that point. Mac selected a Coke and what turned out to be a turkey sandwich. She ate sitting in the stern, with the TAC vest and the MP7 beside her.

There was no commercial traffic on the river. And that made sense given the fighting. Mac saw lights every now and then. Some were associated with boats that were moored along both sides of the spillway.

Others were deeper in the swamp and only visible for a split second before they disappeared. Houseboats? Probably. If so, Mac envied the people who lived on them. They could spend weeks or even months safe from the war.

After forty-five minutes of travel, Myron issued a warning. "We're coming up on a turn to port . . . Then a straight channel will take us west, to the point where Highway 317 crosses the canal. And that's where Victor-Romeo should be waiting for us."

"You heard the man," Mac said as she put her vest on. "Gear up, turn your night-vision gear on, and give me a radio check. Over."

Because the team was small, and their transmissions were encrypted, the operators could use their names. "Lyle," "Yang," "Hunt," and so forth.

The bow fell as the boat slowed, and a spotlight came on. It speared the left bank and coasted along until a gap appeared. The light disappeared as Myron put the wheel over, and the bow swerved. Thanks to the spill from the map light in the cockpit, Mac saw that a team member was stretched out on the seat across from her. Private Ryson? Of course. The ex-thief and ace mechanic had been written up for sneaking naps on numerous occasions.

Mac turned to Corporal Marci Carter. The truck commander was chewing gum. "Roust Private Ryson, Corporal. The method is up to you."

An evil smile appeared on Carter's face. "Say no more, Major . . . I'm on it."

Ryson spluttered as the TC poured half a bottle of water on his face. He sat up. "What the hell?"

"Get your shit together," Mac told him. "We're counting on you."

Carter took a sip of water. "Yeah, shithead. We're counting on you."

Ryson gave her the finger, and one of the Green Berets laughed. "Cut the crap," Lyle said. "And stand by. The rebs might be waiting for us. Lock and load."

Five long minutes passed as the engines burbled, and Mac stared into the darkness. Then she saw it. Three long flashes, followed by a couple of blips. That was the recognition signal. Hunt answered with three blips from the spotlight. So far, so good. Assuming that Victor-Romeo was the one who was holding the flashlight.

Myron couldn't turn the engines off without compromising their ability to make a speedy departure. But he could shift into neutral, and he did. Lyle and Wynn jumped off the boat as it coasted to a stop. They were about four feet out and had to wade ashore. Mac was relieved to see a single figure standing on the beach.

Mac went next, felt the water come up to midthigh, and made her way up out of the canal. Green Berets rushed past her and immediately spread out into a skirmish line. Lyle was talking to

Victor-Romeo when Mac arrived. They were using a penlight to examine a map. The spill was sufficient to reveal that the agent was a woman. More than that, a pretty woman. "This is Bravo-Six," Lyle said, as Mac arrived.

The CIA agent smiled. "Nice try, but Major Macintyre is pretty well-known north *and* south of the New Mason-Dixon Line. Now, here's where we are. I brought a van. Follow 317 north to the intersection with 90. Take that west to Franklin. Ramos and most of his officers are staying at the Quality Inn.

"He doesn't trust the Confederates to protect him. So soldiers drawn from his division have been assigned to provide security. Don't let that fool you . . . They are quite competent and extremely loyal. Chances are that Ramos will be in bed with a noncombatant when you enter his suite. There's no reason to kill her."

Mac looked into the other woman's eyes. "How do you know all this?"

The answer was unapologetic. "I know because I slept with him two days ago."

Mac thought about that. Here was still another aspect of warfare. Was it something she would be willing to do? Mac wasn't sure. "Okay, thank you."

"All right," Lyle said. "Is there anything else?"

"Yes," Victor-Romeo replied. "The major will be interested to know that her father, *General* Macintyre, has been spending a great deal of time with Ramos. And he's at the Quality Inn, too. I'll take the boat down the slipway and hide it. Good hunting."

Victor-Romeo faded into the darkness, leaving Mac to think about her father. Would she see him? And what should she do if that happened?

The noise generated by the Chris Craft's twin Volvo engines increased, and Mac saw the boat turn. Myron and Hunt appeared as it sped away. "Victor-Romeo knows her way around boats," Myron commented. "We could use her in the canoe club."

"This is Carter," the TC said over the radio. "I located the van. The key is in the ignition. Over."

"Okay," Mac said. "Let's hit the road." A path led up to a graveled parking area normally used by fishermen and kayakers. The Chevy was HUGE, with seating for twelve. The team piled in. Carter slid behind the wheel—and Timms was going to ride shotgun. The rest of them were seated in back. It was nearly midnight by then, which meant there was very little traffic on Highway 317, and that was good.

But conditions changed as they turned onto westbound 90. A Mexican convoy was traveling eastbound in the lane next to them. None of the team members said anything. But Mac figured that their thoughts were similar to hers. How long could Union troops hold the line? Mac pushed the question away. *Stay focused,* she told herself. *Do what you can do. Sam will find a way.*

It was a short drive to Franklin, and with Victor-Romeo's map to guide him, Timms gave directions. Would someone attempt to stop the van? If they did, the mission would be blown. That was Mac's greatest fear. So she felt a profound sense of relief when the hotel appeared. It was a block away, and a Jaguar armored car was blocking the street that led to it. Carter turned without being told to, followed an alley into the parking lot located behind a restaurant, and parked.

"Okay," Lyle said. "Let's go over this again. Carter, Ryson, Myron, Hunt, and Yang will remain here. Find cover away from the van. If the cops stop to look at it, or the Mexicans come by, let them scope it out. What we *don't* need is for you to start a firefight while we're in the hotel.

"The rest of the team will follow me. The major will be in the six slot. She will assume command if I go down. And remember . . . No noise! And if you have to off somebody, hide the body. Are there any questions? No? Let's do this thing."

Lyle departed at a jog. The rest of them followed. And, thanks to the well-lit sign on the front of the hotel, they knew where they were going. *The Mexicans have arrived, and the locals feel safe,* Mac mused. *But not for long.*

According to the military intelligence, only 20 percent of the Mexican troops were equipped with night-vision gear. But it seemed safe to assume that the individuals assigned to protect Ramos would have the latest goodies. So concealment was important.

Lyle made good use of what cover there was as he led the team out and around the roadblock, as well as the troops stationed at it. Then he followed the edge of the parking lot past parked cars, islands of shrubbery, and a Dumpster to the east side of the hotel. A door was located there, but it was locked.

As the last person in the file, Mac had responsibility for the team's six, and she was looking back, when Lyle spoke. "Down!" It was a whisper but emphatic nonetheless.

Mac dropped into a crouch. And, when she swiveled, the threat was obvious. A sentry had rounded the corner of the building and was walking toward them. He was using a flashlight to probe the surrounding shadows, and he had a dog on leash.

Mac knew that while the soldier might miss them, the animal wouldn't. So she wasn't surprised when Lyle rose from his hiding place and fired his pistol four times. Two for the dog and two for the sentry. Both died without uttering a sound.

"Timms and Wynn on me," Lyle said. That left Orney and Mac to provide security, while the others went forward to grab the bodies and drag them behind a knee-high hedge.

So far, so good. But the clock was running. A noncom would

go looking for the sentry eventually, find the bodies, and sound the alarm. In the meantime, every second was precious, and the team would have to rely on brute force rather than stealth to enter the hotel.

Lyle peeked around the corner. "Five soldiers are standing around the front door shooting the shit," he whispered. "We're going to approach them like Confederates on a patrol. Then, when we get close, we'll put them down. Be ready, Timms . . . Use your HK."

It went down exactly the way Lyle said that it would. The Mexicans had seen plenty of Confederate soldiers by that time—and had no reason to expect an attack. They turned as the team walked towards them, but showed no signs of alarm. *"Buenas noches, amigos,"* Lyle said. *"¿Cómo va todo?"* (Good evening, friends . . . How's it going?)

The Mexicans never got an opportunity to answer as Timms opened fire with his MP7. It made a soft clacking sound as the Green Beret emptied a thirty-round magazine into the group. They jerked spastically. Some twirled, two collapsed, and one fell over backwards. Mac had seen a lot of killing, and killed people herself, but was shocked by the sudden brutality of it.

But there was no time for reflection as Lyle gave orders. "Drag the bodies over to that pickup truck . . . Throw them in back. Mac will provide security."

That was Mac's cue to turn her back on the carnage and scan the surrounding area for threats. None had appeared as the men completed their task.

As Lyle led the way into the lobby, Mac paused to pull a piece of indoor-outdoor carpeting over the bloodstains before entering the hotel herself.

The lobby was empty except for the night clerk. She took one look at the warlike intruders and raised her hands. Timms circled the counter and ordered her down onto the floor.

"Be sure to gag her," Lyle instructed. Then he turned to Mac. "Take over the desk, Mac. Shed the vest and the shirt—but keep the headset. If someone enters, they'll assume it's for answering the phone. Your job will be to make things look normal. Are you up for that?" Mac had no choice but to nod.

Lyle smiled. "Good. Let me know if things go south." Then he left, and the others followed along behind.

Mac circled around the counter to the point where the *real* receptionist lay hog-tied on the floor. The woman's eyes were huge, and Mac felt sorry for her as she placed the MP7 on a shelf under the counter. Then she removed the vest and her shirt. The reception desk would conceal her clothing from the waist down.

The phone rang and rang again. Mac answered it. "Hello, this is the front desk."

"Yeah," a female voice said. "I need a six A.M. wake-up call."

"No problem," Mac told her. "Have a good night."

The woman said, "Thanks," and hung up.

Lyle and the others were up on the top floor by then. And Mac could listen in as Lyle gave orders. "Drag him into the linen closet. Okay . . . Wynn will blow the door. We'll go in fast. Is the injector ready? Good. Place the charge."

That was when a Mexican soldier dashed in through the front door, and looked around. He was an officer, judging from the railroad tracks on his epaulets, and his English was good. "I'm looking for my men . . . They were stationed out front."

Mac brought the .22 up, waited for the red dot to center itself on the officer's chest, and fired two shots. The soldier staggered, but he didn't fall!

Because he's wearing armor, Mac told herself, as the Mexican went for his sidearm. The pistol was halfway out of its holster when Mac put three bullets into the man's head. There was a thump as the body hit the floor. "Mexican officer down," Mac said into the boom mike. "I'm going to drag him out of sight."

"Roger that," Lyle replied. "We have the package, and we're on the way."

Mac hurried to tow the officer around to the other side of the counter. There were three entry wounds, but no blood. The receptionist saw the body and attempted to scoot away from it. The phone rang. "Front desk."

"Yes," a male voice said. "I heard a noise . . . Like a firecracker going off in the next room. Is everything all right?"

That was when Mac felt a sense of shock. The man on the phone was her father! Should she hang up? Or try to bullshit him? The answer was obvious. Mac had never been able to bullshit her father. Mac put the receiver down.

Now Mac faced a difficult decision. Bo Macintyre was an important target. Should she order the team to abduct him? Or failing that, to kill him? The possibility was tempting, in spite of the emotions involved. But, Mac concluded, going after her father would threaten the Ramos abduction. How long would it be before someone discovered the bodies in the pickup or behind the hedge? When that occurred, all hell would break loose. Her decision was made.

||||||||||||

Bo was sitting on the edge of his bed, staring at the handset. The bitch had hung up on him! First the muffled thud from the room next door, then this. What did it mean? Nothing, most likely. And he wanted to sleep. But *could* he sleep? Or would he lie there, wondering about the noise?

Bo stood and crossed the room to where his pants were draped over a chair. After pulling them on, he grabbed his keycard and a SIG SAUER P226 off the dresser. With the pistol in his hand, Bo opened the door and stepped out into the hall. The first thing Bo noticed was that the soldier who had been stationed outside of Ramos's suite had disappeared. And general's door was ajar. The reason for that was obvious. The lock had been blown!

Bo raised the SIG, held it in the approved two-handed grip, and pushed his way in. The bathroom was empty. A light was on in the room beyond. And the only person present was the brunette that General Ramos had been sleeping with. She'd been gagged and bound with zip ties. Her big brown eyes looked at him beseechingly, and she made moaning sounds.

Bo had no interest in freeing the woman. Someone else could handle that. His mind was on the snatch. Had it been carried out by Union forces? Hell yes, it had . . . Hence the blown lock and the zip ties. But *why*? Because Ramos was a high-ranking officer, that's why.

But unbeknownst to them, the Mexican was something else as well . . . Ramos was one of the few people who knew about the plan to give a chunk of the United States to Mexico in return for that country's help.

Would Ramos tell them? Hell yes, the weak-kneed, polo-playing son of a bitch would spill his guts in return for a martini. And if Sloan made the news public, it would serve to rally the North and raise doubts in the South. The Confederacy had no intention of honoring the deal with President Salazar. But Stickley couldn't say that, nor could she talk about the plan to conquer Mexico and Central America. What she could do, however, was come after the plan's author . . . And that meant *him*.

Bo swore and hurried out of the room. It wasn't over yet . . .

The Union's special ops team couldn't get out by helicopter. Not with the Confederate Air Force protecting the Mexican troops. That meant the bastards would be forced to use surface transportation. Bo entered his room, grabbed his cell phone, and thumbed a contact.

The phone rang four times before Colonel Hiram Roston picked it up. And no wonder given how early in the morning it was. "I don't know who you are," Roston growled. "But you'd better have one helluva good reason for waking me up."

"I do," Bo assured him. "We have a problem. A BIG problem, and you're going to solve it."

CHAPTER 12

> We sleep safe in our beds because rough men stand ready in the night to visit violence on those who would do us harm.
>
> —RICHARD GRENIER

FRANKLIN, LOUISIANA

After leaving the hotel, the Green Berets took turns carrying Ramos and followed the edge of the parking lot, back to the point where the van was parked. After being injected with a powerful sedative, Ramos had gone out like a light.

The van was running when the team arrived, and there were plenty of hands to help. Once Ramos was stashed in the back, the team piled in. "Okay," Mac said as she slid in next to Carter. "Take 90 west toward Lafayette. And don't speed . . . The last thing we need is to get crosswise with the police. Hunt . . . get on the horn. Tell Kingpin that we have the package, and we're headed home."

They were on Highway 90 by then. Mac could see a backup ahead and flashing lights in the distance. Had there been an accident? Was roadwork under way? Or was she looking at a military checkpoint? There was no way to be sure, and they couldn't afford to take any chances. "Get us off the highway," Mac said. "And I mean *now*."

"There isn't any exit," Carter replied.

"Then *make* one," Mac said. Carter looked to the right. Because she was wearing night-vision gear, Carter could see the ditch next to the highway, the field beyond, and the transmission tower in the distance. "I'll have to jump the ditch," Carter said. "Or *try* to. Get ready."

By letting the car in front of her pull ahead, Carter was able to create some running room. Tires screeched as she stomped on the accelerator, the Chevy took off, and landed hard.

But the rear wheels were in the ditch. And all they did was spin. "Everybody out!" Lyle ordered. "Timms . . . Wynn . . . Grab the general. We need to haul ass."

Mac felt a sense of foreboding as she jumped to the ground. Everything had gone reasonably well up to the point where the exfil began. Now it was as if something had changed. But *what*?

They were jogging across the field when Mac heard the roar of helicopter engines and saw geysers of dirt leap up all around, as an Apache helicopter passed over them. Sergeant Orney went down and stayed down. Mac rushed to his side, and Hunt arrived seconds later. A huge chunk of meat was missing from Orney's left thigh, blood was spurting, and she could see bone. Mac felt a sinking sensation as Hunt produced a tourniquet and went to work. Could the team carry *two* men? And still escape?

The Green Beret attempted to smile but produced a grimace instead. "No worries . . . I have this." The .22 was in his hand, and Mac was just starting to react as Orney brought the barrel up under his chin. There was a pop, and his head fell to one side. Lyle had arrived by then. He winced. "Follow me . . . They're coming back!"

The three of them began to run. The others were up ahead. Trying to escape was pointless, or that's how it seemed, as the gunship began its second run. Then something unexpected occurred. In order to get a better angle on the fugitives, the pilot attempted to fly *under* the power lines that ran across the field but failed to give himself enough room. A rotor clipped a wire. The results were spectacular.

As the Apache started to tilt, its blades cut *three* lines, and caused electricity to arc, even as the ship hit the ground. The impact was followed by a muffled explosion, and the equivalent of a funeral pyre, as flames shot up into the air. There was no time in which to stop and stare.

"Run!" Mac shouted. And they were off. Timms and Wynn were lugging Ramos. A farmhouse was visible ahead. And there, parked next to an old barn, was a tractor-trailer rig!

"Ryson!" Mac said. "Head for the truck . . . Get it started. Carter will drive, and I'll ride in the sleeper. I want everyone else in the trailer."

Flashing blue lights could be seen on Highway 90 as both the police and the local fire department responded to the helicopter crash. What would they make of the van? And of Orney's body? Mac hoped the locals would spend a lot of time sorting things out.

The house was dark. Thanks to the power outage? Or because no one was at home? The answer became clear as Ryson started the truck, and a man with a shotgun came dashing out of the house. Then he ran into Wynn and wound up flat on his back. "I'll take that," Wynn said as he appropriated the scattergun. "Stay where you are, and everything will be fine."

"Come on!" Mac said. "Get aboard."

Carter could drive anything, big rigs included. And it took only a minute to clear the farm and turn onto a country road. The owner chased them but was forced to give up as his property pulled away. "We'll take Highway 182 instead of 90," Mac said, from her perch in the sleeper. "Maybe we'll have better luck with that."

Then Mac's thoughts turned to Sergeant Orney. The rule was, "No man left behind." But Orney had been. And the thought of it made Mac feel sick to her stomach.

Orney's last words had been, "No worries, I have this."

Mac fought to prevent the tears from flowing. *Not here,* she thought. *Not now.* She forced herself to focus. Had the semi departed the farm unnoticed? That was possible since local authorities had a van, a burning helicopter, and a body to puzzle over. But a clean getaway was by no means certain.

So it wasn't until they'd been under way for fifteen minutes that Mac allowed herself to relax a little. But something was bothering her . . . Something important. But *what*? Now, in the wake of the gunship attack, Mac felt increasingly certain that the traffic jam had been the result of a roadblock rather than a car accident.

And come to think of it, why send an Apache rather than the Black Hawk loaded with troops? Then it struck her. The rebs were trying to *kill* Ramos! But that didn't make sense. Or did it? Maybe Ramos was even *more* valuable than JSOC thought he was.

But *how*? How had the rebs been able to locate the team so quickly? The answer came in a flash. Ramos was carrying a GPS tracker! Mac keyed her mike. "Thomas . . . I think Ramos is carrying a tracker. Search him. Check everything he has. Over."

"We're on it," Lyle responded. "Stand by. Over."

Mac saw a sign flash by. The semi had passed the turnoff for

New Iberia, which meant Cade was up ahead. Lyle broke into her train of thought. "All Ramos has on is a pair of boxer shorts, a wedding ring, and a Rolex. The back is engraved with a Confederate flag, and the words '*Amigos Para Siempre*,' or 'Friends Forever.' How much do you want to bet the rebs gave Ramos more than a watch? They want to keep track of him."

"Damn it," Mac said. "You can throw the Rolex out the back if you want to . . . But it won't make much difference. The bastards have a drone following us by now."

"Then why are they allowing us to run?" Lyle demanded. "A Predator could take us out with a Hellfire missile."

Mac saw the Cade exit pass by. The town of Broussard was next. As for the "why," that wasn't clear. "I'm not sure," Mac answered. "But I think they'll be waiting for us somewhere."

"So what's the plan?" Lyle wanted to know.

There was no plan. But Mac couldn't say that. So she said the only thing that she could. "We'll take the semi as far as we can, fight when we have to, and complete the mission."

"Roger that," Lyle said flatly. "We'll be ready."

"Hunt," Mac said. "Do you read me?"

"Five by five," the petty officer answered. "Over."

"Get Kingpin on the horn. Explain our situation. Tell them we need air cover. Who knows? Maybe we'll get lucky."

"I'm on it," Hunt replied. "Over."

At that point, all Mac could do was wait. The town of Broussard marked the point where Carter had to switch from Highway 182 back to 90. Mac half expected to encounter a roadblock at the crossover point. But for reasons known only to them, the rebs had chosen to let the tractor-trailer rig pass. Maybe the shit would hit the fan in Walroy then. Or when they arrived in Lafayette. "Hunt here," the sailor said. "Kingpin says that most of their assets are up and trying to defend New Orleans from enemy bombers. They'll see what they can do. Over."

That wasn't much but gave the team something to hope for. After they passed Walroy, Highway 90 turned into Highway 167. That suggested that the enemy would try to stop the semi in Lafayette. Mac spoke to Carter. "I think they're waiting for us up ahead. If so, there won't be time for me to give orders. Do what you think is best. But remember this . . . Our immediate goal is to reach I-10 east. If we get that far, there's a good chance we can make it the rest of the way."

"Uh-oh," Wynn said. "Look at that. The road is empty."

Mac saw that he was correct and knew what that meant. The rebs had been busy clearing a path and setting their trap.

Mac's thoughts turned to Sloan. What would the outcome be? A paragraph in his morning briefing? Mac felt a moment of regret for what was . . . And for what could have been. Lights flashed ahead of and behind them. The trap snapped closed.

NEW ORLEANS, LOUISIANA

During the period when they ran New Orleans, the Confederacy's military commanders had chosen to meet on the ninth floor of city hall because that was where the city's Emergency Operations Center was located. But then the North attacked. So to avoid the possibility of being killed during a bombing raid, or by a Predator drone, the military brass moved their meetings to an underground data-storage facility located just outside New Orleans. Now Union officers were in control, and the subsurface command and control center was theirs.

As a result, Sloan was spending a great deal of his time 650 feet below sea level, behind four-hundred-foot-thick limestone walls, living in what amounted to a series of interconnected caverns. But nice caverns to be sure . . . Complete with polished floors and excellent lighting.

So when Sloan and his bodyguards stepped off the freight elevator, two green golf carts were waiting. Motors whirred as Sloan and the members of his security detail were whisked away to what staff referred to as "the Situation Room South." It consisted of a large oval table, surrounded by two dozen chairs, and banks of video screens.

A number of Sloan's advisors were present, and all of them stood as he stepped off the cart and walked over to the table. "Take a load off," Sloan said. "I'm sorry about the late hour, but I had to address a joint meeting of Congress this morning. Even our most ardent supporters are feeling a bit antsy. And for good reason. The rebs are, as the saying goes, knocking on the door."

Sloan grinned. "I assured them that we have a plan and that there's no reason to worry. Please tell me that I was correct."

Chairman of the Joint Chiefs General Jones made a face. "We have a plan," he agreed. "That's true. But we aren't ready to act on it yet."

"*Why?*" Sloan demanded.

"Simply put, we're twenty thousand soldiers short of what we require to push the Mexicans back," Jones replied. "But even if the additional troops were *here*, ready to fight, we would need more of everything before launching a counterattack. Don't get me wrong," he added. "Most of the resources are in the pipeline. But it will take a week to get all of it here and spread it around."

Sloan eyed the faces around him. "A week . . . Do we have a week?"

"That depends," National Security Advisor Toby Hall replied. "According to the most recent intel reports, Confederate General Bo Macintyre is spending every waking moment with Division Commander Matias Ramos and wants him to launch an all-out attack.

"Fortunately for us, Ramos continues to drag his feet. Sources indicate that while Ramos is perfectly willing to fight—he doesn't like to advance unless he has half of the Confederate Air Force circling overhead."

"Meanwhile," Secretary of Defense Garrison added, "Mother Nature is about to weigh in."

Sloan frowned. "Meaning?"

"According to the National Hurricane Center, a powerful storm is headed our way. Assuming it maintains its present course, the hurricane will cross the coast somewhere between Biloxi and Port Arthur. And that might help *or* hurt us. It's too early to say which."

"It would keep *all* aircraft on the ground," Director of National Intelligence Kip said. "Confederate planes included. And Ramos won't advance without them."

"That's true," Jones agreed. "But, while a serious storm might prevent Ramos from taking more ground, it would hinder our ability to help civilians as well."

Sloan tried to imagine it. A meteor fall, followed by a war, followed by a hurricane. If there was a worse scenario, he couldn't imagine it. "All right, keep me informed. In the meantime, I expect FEMA to keep the public informed and to coordinate with the usual NGOs."

Sloan eyed the faces around him. "Cheer up, people . . . It's like someone said to me a few days ago. We're deep inside what used to be enemy territory—and only 350 miles from Houston. We have the bastards where we want 'em."

LAFAYETTE, LOUISIANA

"Hang on!" Carter shouted as she shifted into a higher gear and put her foot down. "We're going through!"

Mac was forced to hang on as the truck accelerated. Lafayette's streetlights were on. A flare popped high above the truck and began to float down. The roadblock consisted of three cop cars and two city buses, which were parked nose to nose.

That would have been sufficient to stop most vehicles. But the weight of the semi, plus the half-loaded trailer, totaled to something like seventy thousand pounds. And the combo tossed the police cars aside as if they were toys.

Then, with plenty of inertia left, the big rig smashed into the barricade that lay beyond. Tires screeched, and safety glass shattered, as the buses were forced to part. Mac was thrown into the sleeper, where thick padding kept her from being hurt. "The engine's on fire!" Carter exclaimed. "Everyone out."

The sleeper had a door. Mac pushed it open, jumped to the ground, and found herself surrounded by swirling smoke. But, thanks to her night-vision gear, she could see.

The team was surrounded. Rebs, Mexicans, and police officers were shooting at them from every direction. Bullets snapped past, pinged the truck, and buzzed like bees.

Mac saw Timms stagger as a burst of automatic fire took him down. Wynn ran forward to provide first aid but stood a moment later and began to return fire.

Myron bellowed a war cry and was firing his MP7 at a police officer when a bullet struck his head. Mac ran to check on him, but the chief petty officer was dead.

"Follow me!" Lyle shouted. "Get to the Hummers!"

Mac could see the vehicles through the drifting smoke. Mexican soldiers were using them for cover, and the Humvee on the right had a top-mounted fifty. It began to chug.

Lyle ran straight at the vehicles, pushing the half-naked Ramos in front of him. The general was wearing a Union TAC vest and a pair of striped boxer shorts. That was when Mac realized that Lyle had given *his* body armor to Ramos! In an effort to protect the prisoner. Mac shouted, "No!" But it came too late. A bullet knocked Lyle down.

Ramos stopped and raised his hands. *"¡Dejar de disparer! ¡Soy yo! ¡General Ramos!"* (Stop firing! It's me! General Ramos!)

The fifty stopped firing as the rest of the team caught up. Then *all* of the Mexicans stopped firing, and one of them ordered the Confederates to do likewise. And they obeyed.

It seemed that even though the rebs wanted to kill Ramos, they couldn't do so with the Mexicans looking on because the alliance would come apart. That meant Ramos was their ticket out. But only so long as he was alive. What if a gung ho reb took him out?

"Surround the general!" Mac ordered. "So they can't shoot him. Grab Lyle . . . And take control of those vehicles."

Mac looked back at Timms and Myron. She wanted to recover their bodies. But at what cost? Could the team retrieve and load the bodies without losing the initiative? And sacrificing the mission? Mac couldn't take that chance.

Hunt and Wynn got Lyle up and on his feet as Ryson and Yang advanced on the Mexican soldiers. The Mexicans had no choice but to fall back. That cleared the way for Yang to scramble up onto the armed Humvee and aim the fifty at them. "Don't fire," Mac told him. "Not unless they try to stop us. We're here to snatch Ramos . . . Not mow people down."

Thanks to their hostage, plus Yang's fifty, the rest of the team were able get in the vehicles and depart. No shots were fired at the

Humvees as they pulled away. Ryson was driving the vehicle with the fifty and was in the lead.

But Mac, who was riding shotgun in the second Humvee, ordered him to fall back. "They're going to tail us," she told him. "And if the Confederates can get rid of the Mexicans, they'll attack. That's when the fifty will come into play."

That prophecy was borne out five minutes later. The team was eastbound on I-10 when the Apache helicopter caught up with them. Yang's fifty was the only defense they had, but it was a potent weapon and sufficient to draw the pilot's attention. He or she fired a brace of unguided rockets at the Hummer and missed.

Mac turned to Hunt. The sailor was seated in the backseat with Wynn and Ramos. "Get Kingpin on the radio. Tell them we're eastbound on I-10 in two Humvees—and that a Confederate helicopter is trying to take us out."

"Should I request air support?" Hunt inquired.

"I think that's implied," Mac said dryly.

"You won't make it," Ramos predicted.

"You'd better hope that we do," Mac countered. "Because if we go down, you'll go with us. I guarantee it."

Ramos shrugged. "So be it. You're quite pretty for a commando."

Carter produced a snorting sound. "Holy shit! He's hitting on you!" Wynn laughed.

Hunt had finished speaking with Kingpin by then. She leaned forward. "They say help is on the way. ETA ten minutes."

"Did they say what kind of help?" Mac inquired.

"No, ma'am."

Mac considered it. *Ten fucking minutes?* That was a lifetime. And what could be a short one. She opened her mike. "Hey, Yang . . . Quit screwing around and grease that bastard."

"I'd like to try something," Yang responded. "I'm going to spin the fifty around. When I give the word, I want both Humvees to stop. Over."

Mac understood the plan. The Apache would pass overhead. And, once Yang's vehicle came to a stop, he would be able to fire at it from a stable platform. Could he shoot the reb helo in the ass? Possibly. It was worth a try. "Go for it," Mac told him. "Ryson, Carter, stop when Yang gives the word. Over."

"Here it comes," Yang said. "Wait for it . . . *Now!*"

Both drivers stood on the brakes. And that ruined the copilot's aim. At least a hundred rounds of 30mm shells plowed a furrow in the concrete up ahead.

Meanwhile, Yang was aiming forward, waiting for the Apache to appear in his sights. Once it did, Yang sent a long, uninterrupted flow of .50 caliber shells after it. Mac heard a celebratory whoop of joy as the helicopter's port engine belched fire. The pilot banked out over the surrounding swamp before scooting away. One engine was sufficient to get him home . . . But his part of the fight was over.

Mac had just started to relax when Yang spoke. "Uh-oh . . . A couple of vehicles are coming up fast. They look like Strykers. Over."

Mac felt a rising sense of hopelessness. Strykers. They could, and they would, grease the Humvees in a matter of minutes. She glanced at her watch. Help was supposed to arrive in ten minutes—which meant it was five away. Could the Humvees outrun their pursuers? No. The Strykers were faster. Okay, so maybe . . .

That was when Mac heard a loud explosion. She couldn't see out the back, but Carter confirmed her worst fears. "It's gone," the TC said, as a fireball appeared in both outside mirrors. "I'll take evasive action."

Mac struggled to absorb it. Ryson, Lyle, and Yang. All of them were dead. And the rest of the team was going to wind up KIA, too, if help didn't arrive soon. "The first Stryker is catching up with us," Carter announced as she swerved to the right. "And my foot is all the way to the floor."

"I don't understand," Ramos put in. "Don't they realize that I'm in the vehicle?"

"Oh, they realize it all right," Mac replied. "The rebs would rather kill you than allow you to be questioned. But they can't murder you in front of your troops. Think about that if you're still alive at this time tomorrow."

"*General* Macintyre," Ramos responded. "That sounds like something he would do."

"It sure as hell does," Mac agreed.

There was a burst of static from Hunt's radio. "This is Super-Spooky-Three to Bravo-Six. We are on station and ready to perform some pest control. I see three vehicles. I want all friendlies to turn their lights off and on. Over."

Mac understood. The AC-130 pilot needed to confirm which vehicles he was supposed to protect. Carter said, "Done." And the pilot confirmed it.

"One vehicle, and it's in the lead. Stand by. Over."

Mac couldn't see it but knew that the Lockheed AC-130 fixed-wing, propeller-driven transport was a flying weapons platform. There were a lot of different versions, but even the oldest planes mounted a fearsome array of miniguns. Four of each in some cases. "Come on!" Carter demanded. "What are you waiting for?"

The lead Stryker fired. The 105mm shell screamed past, and a bright flash lit the road up ahead. Then, as if in answer to Carter's request, the AC-130 opened fire. Four streams of tracer fire poured out of the pitch-black sky, converged on the lead Stryker, and tore into it. Mac couldn't see the action . . . But she heard the thunderous explosion as the vehicle behind them exploded.

"One down," Super-Spooky said, "and one to go. Over."

Strykers had no effective means to defend themselves against aircraft. Something Mac knew from personal experience. So it took the AC-130 less than a minute to score the second kill. "Your six is clean," Super-Spooky announced. "We'll escort you in. Over."

It took fifteen minutes to finish crossing the Atchafalaya Basin Bridge and pass through the Union checkpoint located just west of Ramah. It was defended with troops and tanks. But because they had been ordered to clear the way for the Humvee, the concrete barriers had been pushed over to one side of the road.

Pole-mounted lamps threw an eerie glow over the scene. As the Humvee rolled through the checkpoint, Mac saw that clusters of soldiers were standing at attention while their officers saluted. All of them knew. Ten soldiers and sailors had gone out. Four had returned.

From there it was a short drive to the Tiger Truck Stop, where a Black Hawk helicopter and three black-clad men were waiting in the otherwise empty parking lot. One of the operatives gave Lyle's TAC vest to Mac. "The general won't need this where he's going. I'm sorry you lost so many people." Then the agents took Ramos away. The helicopter departed three minutes later. The team watched it go.

"What now?" Carter inquired, as the noise died away.

Mac looked across the parking lot to the truck stop's brightly lit façade. "Now we go in and eat breakfast. Does beer go with pancakes?"

"Beer goes with everything," Wynn assured her.

"Good," Mac replied. "Then we'll have a beer for every person we left behind."

"They'd like that," Carter said.

"Kingpin is calling," Hunt said as she pressed a headphone to her ear.

"Turn the radio off," Mac said. "This mission is over."

NEW ORLEANS, LOUISIANA

The sun was rising in the east. But there was no way to see that from hundreds of feet underground in the Situation Room South. Sloan had just returned from a two-hour nap . . . It was the only sleep he'd had in more than a day. As Sloan scanned the faces around him, he could tell that things had gone from bad to worse.

"Give it to me straight," Sloan said, as Doyle Besom poured him a cup of coffee. "What kind of condition is our condition in?"

"Hurricane Whitney is packing winds of up to 145 miles per hour," FEMA Administrator Nathan Freely said. "That makes it a class four storm. The eye is 130 miles out, and it's going to hit New Orleans hard."

Sloan took a sip of coffee. "Will the gates and levees hold?"

"We hope so," Freely replied. "A lot of improvements have been made since Katrina. But there's bound to be some flooding. And the locals are going to suffer."

Sloan was under no illusions where the locals were concerned. A lot of them were Confederate sympathizers if not outright insurrectionists. And their activities were a continual drain on Union resources. But they were, like it or not, American citizens. And it was Sloan's duty to assist them to the extent he could. Even if they were unlikely to thank him for it.

On the other hand, Sloan reflected, Hurricane Whitney would buy him some time. The enemy wasn't likely to attack during a major storm. The thought prompted a memory. Something he'd read about. A war in Korea? Or was it Japan?

Sloan put the coffee mug down. "I need to borrow a computer. One with Internet access." It didn't take long to find what he was looking for. All Sloan had to do was enter the words "Divine Wind" in the search bar. What he found was inspiring.

The First Mongol Invasion of Japan took place in the autumn of 1274, when approximately six hundred vessels, loaded with forty thousand Chinese and Korean warriors, arrived on the shores of Hakata Bay. The Mongols attacked, and the Japanese had to pull back.

Fearing that the Japanese would return with reinforcements, the Mongols retreated to their ships. A typhoon struck that night, destroying most of the ships and killing thousands of Mongol warriors. That battle was over, but the Mongols were still determined to conquer Japan.

During the next seven years, the Japanese built high walls to protect themselves from future attacks. And a good thing, too. Because when the Mongols returned, they had forty-four hundred ships and as many as 140,000 soldiers.

But thanks to the recently constructed walls, the Mongols couldn't land where they wanted to and spent months on their ships—before deciding to go ashore. But on August 15, as the Mongols prepared to attack, a powerful typhoon struck, saving the Japanese yet again! A divine wind indeed.

Sloan stood and took another look around. General Jones was nowhere to be seen. Major McKinney was present, however. "Sam, find General Jones. Tell him to get ready. The moment the storm hits, we're going to attack."

McKinney's eyebrows shot upwards. "You're joking."

"No," Sloan replied. "I'm serious. The Mexicans won't expect it, and neither will the rebs. Mother Nature can be a bitch, but she'll be on *our* side, and we're going to win." McKinney reached for a phone.

Sloan looked up at the main monitor. A computer-generated image of Whitney filled most of it. *Come on honey,* Sloan thought. *We need you.*

HOUSTON, TEXAS

Bo had been taken to Houston in a Learjet, transported to the command and control center in a helicopter, and escorted to the room that Stickley was using as an office. And now, as Bo looked across the table at her, he could see the anger in the president's eyes. "So let me see if I understand," Stickley said. "You tucked General Ramos into bed with some slut, went beddy-bye next door, and awoke to discover that the stupid bastard had been abducted."

Bo didn't like the sarcastic tone or the implied criticism. But the account was essentially correct. "Yes, ma'am."

"Then you issued the order to have Ramos killed."

"Yes, ma'am."

"But he wasn't killed."

"No, ma'am."

"And the Union is draining him dry."

"Probably," Bo allowed. "We don't know for sure."

"I think we can assume that they are," Stickley replied. "Just as we can be sure that Ramos will trade what he knows for better treatment."

"If you say so," Bo agreed reluctantly.

"I do," Stickley said. "And the information he gives them will result in a fucking disaster. You are relieved of your duties, General.

And you are hereby restricted to the city of Houston. In order to go anywhere else, you will need permission from *me*. Do you understand?"

Bo knew his face was flushed, and he could barely contain his rage. Victoria and Kathy had been sacrificed to the cause. And now it was *his* turn. All because of Robin and Samuel T. Sloan. "Yes, I understand."

And with that, Bo left. He had no office, no home, and no place to stay. And once his situation was made public, he would be a pariah. What could he do? Who could he turn to? The answer, when it occurred to him, made Bo smile.

NEW ORLEANS, LOUISIANA

The wind was blowing, and sheets of rain were falling by the time the team left the truck stop and made their way over to the Humvee. All of them were wasted, including Carter. *The woman shouldn't be allowed to drive,* Mac thought to herself. And then she passed out.

When Mac awoke, it was to find that it was light outside, and Carter was touching her shoulder. "Wake up, Major . . . We're at NAS/JRB."

Mac could hear a continuous rattle as rain hit the Humvee's roof. She sat up straight. "Thanks for getting us here, Carter. I'm going to put you in for the army's drunk-driving medal."

"I'll wear it with pride," Carter replied. "Are you okay? Can you make it inside?"

Mac looked out through rain-streaked glass. The wind was tearing at a trio of oak trees. They swayed alarmingly. A piece of aluminum siding sailed past. "Yes, thanks."

Mac turned to look at the others. Hunt was asleep, with her head on Wynn's shoulder. "Don't worry," Carter told her. "I'll get them home."

Mac thanked the TC, battled to push the door open, and got out. The wind tried to bowl her over—and Mac was soaked by the time she entered the BOQ. Her room was on the second floor. And when Mac opened the door, it was to discover that her roommate wasn't there. Was she on duty? Probably.

Mac put the HK on the floor, shrugged her vest off, and went facedown on the bed. Rain tapped against the window, and sleep took her down.

When Mac woke four hours later, it was in response to someone pounding on the door. "Major Macintyre? Are you in there?"

Mac swore, rolled off the bed, and clumped over to the door. *I went to bed with my boots on,* Mac observed. *And I need a shower.* She opened the door. A corporal was standing there with a fist raised, ready to knock again. "Yes?"

Mac saw the soldier's eyes widen—and knew she looked like hell. "Spit it out," Mac said. "What do you want?"

"Lieutenant Colonel Prevus wants to speak with you, ma'am. He's on the phone."

Mac didn't bother to ask who Prevus was because she felt sure that the corporal didn't know. "Okay, thanks."

Mac followed the soldier down to the reception desk and was surprised to see how dark it was outside. She lifted the phone. "This is Major Macintyre."

"My name is Prevus," a male voice replied. "I'm the division's supply officer. Most of the 32nd pulled out at 0600 this morning, and that includes *your* battalion, under Captain Munson's command. So the CO handed you off to me. And I have a job for you."

Mac was mystified. "The 32nd *left*? To go where?"

"Where the hell have you been?" Prevus demanded crossly. "Some idiot decided to launch a full-on counterattack in the middle of the goddamned storm! And I have supplies to move. So get your butt down here."

"Sir, yes, sir. Where are you?"

"Jesus H. Christ, don't you know *anything*?"

Mac scribbled as Prevus gave her the address. "Got it."

"Good," Prevus said, before slamming the phone down.

Mac returned to her room and took a hot shower. And just in time, too . . . Because the power went down ten minutes later.

After donning a fresh uniform and shoving some personals into an AWOL bag, Mac put her combat gear on. Then, with the MP7 in hand, she made her way down to the empty lobby. What she needed was some transportation—and the corporal didn't know where to get any. "*Everyone* left," he said forlornly. "Some of the officers drove their own cars."

For some reason *that*, more than anything Prevus had told her, served to communicate the true scope of the effort that was under way. It looked as if Sloan was risking everything he had on what Kipling would have called "one turn of pitch-and-toss."

Would the strategy work better than the disastrous airborne attack on the Richton Oil Reserve had? Mac hoped so. And, in order to do her part, Mac needed to join Prevus. She made her way over to the window. Heavy rain lashed the parking lot beyond. And there, parked all by itself, was a navy-gray bus.

Mac turned to the corporal. "Who has the keys to the bus?"

"I do," he admitted. "But you can't . . ."

"Oh yes, I can," Mac replied. "Give."

Ten minutes later, Mac was behind the wheel of the bus and leaving the base. The address Prevus had given her was for a freight terminal located near the river. Rain thundered on the roof, and no matter how hard the wipers tried, they couldn't keep up with the deluge. Each time there was a gust of wind, it felt as if the bus was going to tip over. The whale had one advantage, though . . . And that was lots of ground clearance.

Even so, Mac had to traverse intersections where the water was so deep she feared that it would rise high enough to kill the engine. The traffic lights weren't working, columns of miserable-looking civilians were trudging toward higher ground, and at one point a man with a pistol banged on the door. Mac pointed the HK at him, and he backed away.

A Humvee and a squad of soldiers were guarding the gate to the terminal. And once Mac was inside the compound, she saw *more* soldiers, plus some civilians, all loading trucks.

Mac parked the bus and left the keys in the ignition, knowing that somebody could and would use it. Then she went looking for Prevus. When Mac found the colonel, he was standing in the door of a warehouse, shouting at a civilian on a forklift. "Jesus H. Christ! No, you can't put all of the food on one truck . . . What if it's destroyed? I'm surrounded by idiots."

It wasn't the lead-in that Mac would have preferred. She popped a salute. "Major Macintyre, sir. Reporting as ordered."

Prevus was short, built like a fireplug, and too old for his rank. A reservist then? Pulled in to help with the war? Mac thought so. The supply officer had a round face and beady eyes. They looked her up and down. "You're a cavalry officer," he said accusingly.

"Yes, sir. Sorry, sir."

"Well, something is better than nothing," Prevus allowed. "Now listen up . . . Because I'm too busy to tell you twice. The 32nd had to leave on only a few hours' notice. That meant they couldn't take much with them. Your job is to lead a convoy loaded with supplies west and find them. Follow me," Prevus said as he gave Mac an umbrella. "Your vehicles are lined up and ready to roll." The wind threatened to grab Mac's umbrella, and whip it away as they walked out into the storm. She battled to keep it under control.

"It's going to get worse," Prevus predicted. "The eyewall will pass over New Orleans during the night. That's one of the reasons why we need to get you out of the city as soon as we can."

There were ten vehicles in the convoy. The first was an up-armored Humvee with a fifty mounted on top. Immediately behind that was a hulking, mine-resistant, ambush-protected vehicle. They were commonly referred to as MRAPs, or Cougars. The trucks came in all sorts of configurations. This one boasted a remote-controlled fifty, firing ports along both flanks, and was sitting on six wheels rather than four.

Seven thin-skinned civilian tractor-trailer rigs were lined up behind the Coug. They were old, new, and everything in between. Most of the semis had colorful paint jobs. *And why not?* Mac mused. *We wouldn't want the reb pilots to miss them.*

"Your drivers are civilian contractors," Prevus informed her. "But don't worry . . . A soldier will ride shotgun next to each one of them."

"Why would I worry?" Mac wanted to know.

Prevus looked at her as if she was stupid. "Jesus H. Christ, Major . . . Any one of those bastards could be a rebel agent or a resistance fighter! So keep a close eye on them."

It keeps getting better, Mac thought. "So, what about the soldiers? What outfit are they from?"

"What outfit *aren't* they from?" Prevus replied. "I pulled them out of a transit barracks. You have a little bit of everything."

The last vehicle was a Stryker M1128 MGS, complete with a 105mm tank gun. That, at least, was a source of comfort.

"Okay," Prevus said. "Lieutenant Carey is your XO. She graduated from West Point two weeks ago—and believes all of the crap they taught her. Here are your orders, plus a map. *Vaya con dios.*"

Mac took the envelope. "That's it?"

Prevus frowned. "Of course that's it . . . What did you expect? A going-away party? Your call sign is Road-Runner-Three."

A gust of wind found his umbrella as Prevus turned away and tried to turn it inside out. Mac looked up at the gray, forbidding sky. Cold raindrops hit her face. Whitney was coming.

CHAPTER 13

> My logisticians are a humorless lot . . . they know if my campaign fails, they are the first ones I will slay.
>
> –ALEXANDER THE GREAT

NEW ORLEANS, LOUISIANA

As the rain swept across the huge parking lot, and Mac made her way toward the front of the column, a small figure hurried toward her. Once the woman was closer, Mac realized that she was a second lieutenant. The officer came to a stop and delivered a crisp salute. "Second Lieutenant Lisa Carey, reporting for duty, ma'am!" Then, as an afterthought, "I'm your XO."

Mac returned the salute. "It's a pleasure to meet you, Lieutenant, and welcome to the war. Please don't salute me unless we are in a secured area. And don't let the troops salute you either. Snipers look for things like that."

Carey had a small, finely boned face. And Mac saw her eyes widen as she took the advice in. "Oh," Carey said. "I'm sorry."

"Don't be," Mac said. "There's a lot to learn. I see you have a radio. Can you get one for me?"

"Yes, ma'am," Carey said eagerly. "Is there anything else?"

"Yes," Mac replied. "Tell our soldiers to meet us in the warehouse. And instruct the civilians to gather separately. I'll speak to them after I talk to the troops. Oh, and tell the drivers to make sure that their fuel tanks are full and that they have a full day's worth of food and water aboard. And that's for *two* people. Got it?"

"Yes, ma'am," Carey said, and took off at a jog. *Ring knockers,* Mac mused. *They're so cute.*

It took fifteen minutes for Carey to pull the soldiers together and herd them into two ranks. That was unnecessary, but Mac couldn't say that without undermining the officer's fragile authority. So Mac had to wait until the process was complete before starting her impromptu speech. "Welcome to whatever this is."

That produced some laughs, and Mac nodded. "My name is Major Macintyre. Lieutenant Carey is my XO. I know you represent a lot of different units. But for the moment, you are part of *this* one . . . And our mission is to deliver critical supplies to the 32nd Infantry Brigade, which is fighting somewhere west of here. It's an important task, and it won't be easy. Chances are that we'll have to defend ourselves *and* the convoy.

"Those of you assigned to ride shotgun in one of the civilian trucks will have an additional responsibility as well. No one had time to vet our civilian drivers. That means one or more of them could be working for the enemy. I want you to support them, and help in any way that you can, but remain vigilant. If you notice something suspicious, report it to Lieutenant Carey or me immediately. And if you're unsure of whether you should report, then report it. We'll sort it out from there.

"Remember, you aren't here to make friends. So just to stir things up, I'm going to rotate you from truck to truck on a daily basis. Do you have any questions?"

There weren't any. None the soldiers dared ask, anyway.

"Okay," Mac said. "We have radios. Please use your headsets so I can communicate with you privately if needed. And one more thing . . . As soon as you have time, write your name and MOS (military occupational specialty) on a slip of paper and hand it to Lieutenant Carey. We may have need of your expertise during the days ahead.

"Take a bio break and report to your assigned vehicle. The convoy will roll in fifteen minutes. Dismissed."

As the soldiers dispersed, Mac made her way over to where the civilians were gathered. There were seven of them. Six men and a woman. Mac counted one pair of bib overalls, two cowboy hats, and three potbellies—one of which belonged to the female driver.

"Hello," Mac said, as they turned to look at her. "I'm Major Macintyre. I look forward to getting to know you during the days ahead. A soldier has been assigned to ride with you. If we come under attack, he or she will try to protect you."

"She-it," a man wearing a do-rag said. "If we come under attack, I will sure as hell protect myself!" So saying, he hauled a .44 out of a shoulder holster and waved it around. "Anybody who shoots at my truck is gonna die."

Mac decided to ignore the bravado. "And your name is?"

"Ollie Eason. My handle is 'Road Warrior.'"

"Okay," Mac said. "Here's hoping you won't have to shoot anyone with that hog leg. Now, one more thing . . . If you take exception to something a soldier says or does, try to work it out with them. Failing that, take the matter to Lieutenant Carey. I will get involved if necessary. Are there any questions?"

"Yeah," the man in the bib overalls said. "What about hazardous duty pay?"

"Was that mentioned in your contract?"

"No."

"Then there isn't any," Mac replied. "All right . . . We're leaving in ten minutes. Be ready." And with that, she made her way over to the enormous doorway. The sky had an ominous look, the rain was falling in sheets, and large puddles were forming on the concrete parking lot. How was the counterattack going? Mac wondered. Did Sloan have reason to be happy? She was about to find out.

FORT HOOD, TEXAS

Four-Star General Bo Macintyre was AWOL as Hurricane Whitney closed in on the Gulf Coast. And he didn't give a shit what President Stickley thought. It had been a three-hour drive from Houston to Fort Hood, a normally bustling city that looked like a ghost town. *Why?* Because the army was the engine that made Fort Hood go, and most of it was in the field fighting, and all too often dying.

One of the people who had given their lives for the Confederacy was Bo's daughter, Major Victoria Macintyre. All of her possessions had been left to him, and that included the sleek, modernistic condo that was located a few miles from the base.

Did the military know that he owned it? Bo didn't think so, although he knew they would figure it out once they got around to looking for him. But that would take a while. And Bo would be gone by then. In the meantime, the condo represented a link between Bo's past and his future. Bo put the key in the lock, turned it, and pushed the door open.

It was the first time Bo had been inside the condo since Victoria's death. And that had been what? Three months earlier? Something like that. He should have come sooner, like Kathy urged him to do, but he'd been busy.

No, that was a lie. He *could* have visited the condo, in order to pack things up, but that would have required him to accept Victoria's death. Something he hadn't been ready to do. So as Bo closed the door behind him, he expected to feel a surge of raw emotion. There wasn't any.

What was the saying? "The passage of time heals all wounds?" Yes. And that's why the tears weren't flowing.

The kitchen was just the way his daughter had left it, which was to say neat as a pin. And that was very different from the fifteen-year-old who hated washing dishes, taking out the trash, and cleaning the house. That was one way in which the army had left its stamp on her.

The living room was nicely furnished but reminiscent of an upscale hotel suite. The guest room was equipped with a treadmill, free weights, and a yoga mat. The only thing that resembled a personal touch was the photo montage on the wall next to the treadmill.

All of the pictures had a common theme: Victoria crossing the finish line. Victoria running an obstacle course. And Victoria jumping out of a plane. Bo smiled. The girl was an asskicker . . . That was for sure.

But the master bedroom, well, that was different. It had a feminine flair . . . And like an echo of Victoria's younger persona, the bed was unmade.

A single photo sat on the dresser. A photo of a much younger *him*. And he was in uniform. Was that important somehow? Bo figured it was. And the realization produced a twinge of regret.

What if he'd been an accountant? Or a teacher? Maybe Victoria would still be alive.

As for the big walk-in closet, that was the way Bo expected it to be, which was filled with uniforms. But there was something else as well. Something most young women *didn't* have. And that was a refrigerator-sized gun safe.

Most fathers would have been surprised to make such a discovery, but Bo wasn't one of them. Victoria had been part of an elite special operations organization. Although it was classified as a counterterrorism team, and functioned as such, the supersecret cell had been called upon to carry out "special sanctions" when they were deemed necessary. Were the assassinations legal? No. Were they necessary? *Yes*. And that was why Victoria needed to keep an array of "clean," untraceable weapons in her home.

Bo entered Victoria's birthday into the combination lock and heard a click. The door swung open. And there, racked side by side, were three assault rifles and two submachine guns. Pistols were kept in separate drawers. But the *real* prize was a .50 caliber ammo box filled with American Eagle gold coins! Each eagle would fetch something on the order of three thousand dollars on the wartime black market. And, after twenty-seven years of service, Bo figured that he was entitled to something. Especially since he wasn't going to get any retirement checks. Bo sat on the floor, leaned back against the safe, and began to sob.

NEW ORLEANS, LOUISIANA

As Mac left the building, she saw that teams of soldiers were placing magnetic stickers on the vehicles in her convoy. The graphics consisted of a huge red ball without text. Lieutenant Carey was supervising the process. "What's going on?" Mac inquired, as rain rattled on her slicker.

"This is a high-priority convoy," Carey explained, "and the red balls signify that. Other vehicles are supposed to get out of the way."

It was an echo of the famous Red Ball Express of WWII, when trucks emblazoned with the iconic red balls rushed desperately needed supplies from the beaches of Normandy up to the front. Most of the big six-by-six trucks had been driven by African-Americans, who were prime targets for German planes. Now someone up the chain of command was bringing the concept back. "Good," Mac said. "When you're finished, report to the Stryker. I will ride at the head of the column. If I get killed, you'll be in command. So conduct yourself accordingly. The way the troops perceive you *now* is how they will perceive you then."

Judging from the expression on Carey's face, the possibility of being in command hadn't occurred to her. And no wonder . . . Like most butter bars, she hadn't led anything more than a play-pretend platoon. She swallowed. "Yes, ma'am."

Then Carey started to salute, stopped, and brought her arm down. Mac grinned. "Well done. Learn everything you can about Strykers . . . The knowledge might come in handy sometime. Who knows? Maybe we can turn you into a cavalry officer."

Mac made her way up along the column of trucks to the Humvee, checked to make sure the front passenger seat was available, and opened the door. The wind tried to snatch it away, but Mac held on, and pulled it closed.

A corporal was seated behind the wheel. He smiled. "Welcome aboard, Major. I'm Corporal Ito. Private Ann Green is your RTO, and Private Duncan Hemmings is our gunner."

The other soldiers were seated in the back. Mac greeted both of them before turning to Green. The RTO had black hair, brown skin, and a serious demeanor. "Who is supposed to track our progress?"

"That would be Pushback-One-Two."

"Call 'em," Mac said. "Get a weather report if you can—and tell them that we are about to depart."

As Green made the call, Mac made use of the tactical frequency to hold a roll call. All of her personnel were ready to roll. An MP waved as the Humvee passed by him. And that, Mac knew, was the only fanfare they were going to receive.

"Pushback says the storm will get steadily worse," Green said.

Mac thanked Green and opened the map that Colonel Prevus had given her. The plan was to drive west on Highway 90. A route that, ironically enough, would take her back to the same spillway that she, Lyle, and the rest of them had used what? Two days earlier?

The thought of Lyle and the others caused a lump to form in Mac's throat. She turned to look out of the side window. There was so much grieving left to do. When would it end? Mac pushed the thought aside—and forced her eyes onto the map.

This time, instead of speeding up the spillway in a boat, they would have to cross it. According to the colonel's handwritten notes, the rebs had thrown a ribbon bridge across the waterway. But after crossing it, and having secured a bridgehead, the Mexicans had chosen to retreat to Franklin, the town where Ramos had been staying.

Was the retreat the result of Sloan's surprise attack? The effects of the storm? The sudden loss of General Ramos's leadership? Or a combination of those factors? It didn't matter. What mattered was whether the bridge was intact. Mac hoped it was as Ito led the convoy through partially flooded streets and out of the city.

Under normal circumstances, the ninety-five-mile trip would have taken an hour and a half. But current conditions were anything but normal. The winds were getting stronger, and that forced the high-profile trucks to move slowly or run the risk of tipping over.

There were very few civilian vehicles to deal with, thank God . . . Most refugees were smart enough to flee north, or east, rather than enter the war zone.

But although Union forces were using three lanes of the four-lane highway to push people and equipment west, there were lots of slowdowns. Some were the result of storm-related accidents, others were caused by human error, and the rest could be attributed to the enemy. Dozens of reb mines and IEDs had been left behind to delay Union forces, and they were taking a toll.

When the column was forced to stop, so that a Cat could push a burned-out Bradley off the road, Mac took the opportunity to move the mine-resistant Cougar up into the one slot. That meant Mac and her RTO had to transfer because it was important to take the same chances the MRAP crew did and to see what lay ahead.

The Red Ball designation was helpful because it allowed the convoy to use the so-called express lane, which normally served eastbound traffic. That was good but only in relative terms. Rather than traveling at 5 mph, they were doing 10, with occasional spurts of 15.

It took four hours to reach the checkpoint located east of Calumet. That's where a team of MPs had the unenviable task of deciding who, if anyone, would be allowed to cross the increasingly dangerous ribbon bridge.

Mac opened the passenger-side door and jumped to the ground as a lieutenant approached. The officer's face was haggard, and he needed a shave. He had to yell in order to make himself heard over the storm. "I won't say 'good afternoon,' Major . . . That would be absurd."

"Agreed," Mac replied. "We need to cross the spillway. Is the bridge intact?"

The lieutenant made a face. "Yes, ma'am. But it won't be for long. The wind is playing hell with the floats, and the water continues to rise. Once all of the slack comes out of the cables, they're going to jerk the anchors up off the bottom, and the bridge will swing sideways. So you might want to turn around and head back."

Mac shook her head. "No, way. The 32nd Infantry Brigade needs the food and ammo in those trucks."

"Roger that," the lieutenant replied. "Follow my Hummer. I'll lead you to the ramp. Good luck."

The MP's Humvee was equipped with yellow lights. So all Private Brown had to do was follow the strobing lights off Highway 90 and into a neighboring field. In order to make sure that the Mexican vehicles could get plenty of traction, Confederate engineers had laid pierced-steel planking down for them. And a good thing, too, because it would have been impossible for the big rigs to proceed without it. The war-torn landscape was turning to mud as the rain continued to sleet in from the south. Everywhere Mac looked, she saw water-filled bomb craters, trash-strewn trenches, and burned-out wrecks. And no wonder . . . The fields had been fought over *three* times: When the Confederates were forced to retreat, when the Mexicans fought their way forward, and when they, too, were driven back across the Atchafalaya Spillway.

Would Sloan manage to follow up? Or would his decision to attack in the midst of a hurricane turn out to be a disastrous mistake? Mac didn't know. But she was determined to do her part. The moment the spillway came into sight, the MP turned his Humvee around and waved to them as he drove by.

"Pull up here," Mac instructed. "I want to look around."

Brown braked to a stop, and Mac got out. The wind attempted to knock her down but failed. Mac followed the slope down to a spot just above the raging flood. The spillway was doing its job, which was to transport runoff down to the Gulf of Mexico, and do so quickly.

A hard rain whipped the gray-brown flood into a froth as the water ripped past and took all sorts of flotsam with it. Mac heard a series of booming sounds as uprooted trees struck the bridge before being trapped along the side of it. The weight of that, plus the force of the current, had caused the span to bow.

Mac knew the span consisted of large floats. But how were they connected? And how much stress could those connections endure? Plus there was the possibility that the anchors would be jerked up off the bottom. An engineer would know, but Mac didn't. One thing was for sure though . . . The longer she stood there, the worse things would get.

Mac made her way to the MRAP and climbed up into the cab before keying her mike. "Listen up . . . We're going to cross the bridge one vehicle at a time. I want those of you who are riding shotgun to share the following with your drivers: Keep the speed down but don't stop.

"And one more thing . . . We don't have any personal flotation devices. So shed those TAC vests before you cross. If you wind up in the water, keep your feet downstream, work your way over to one side of the channel, and look for a place to eddy out. All right . . . Stand by. Private Brown will show us how it's done. Over."

Mac turned to Sergeant Buck Percy and the squad of soldiers riding in the back. "I don't know if you and your people should cross on foot or remain in the vehicle."

Percy took a look around. “How ’bout it?” he inquired. “Walk or ride?”

“Let’s stay in the Cougar,” Private Hernandez said. “The wind might mess my hair.”

Apparently, Hernandez was known for his hair because the rest of them laughed.

“Okay,” Mac said. “That’s a risk we can’t afford to take. Let’s do this thing.”

Brown took his foot off the brake, allowed the sixteen-ton MRAP to roll down to the bottom of the slope, and powered up onto the bridge deck. Mac felt the span heave and shudder and wondered if she was going to be sorry. The rain, combined with the spray breaking over the north side of the span, made it impossible to see more than a few yards.

So Mac opened the door, got out, and lurched forward. The wind was hitting her from the south, and it was all Mac could do to stand up straight, as she made her way out to stand facing the Cougar. Then it was a matter of using the radio and hand signals to keep Brown on course while she backed away. Foot by foot, yard by yard, the MRAP crept across the bucking bridge until it was fifty feet from the western shore.

That was when Mac stepped out of the way, and ordered Brown to “Hit it.” He did. The engine roared as the Cougar’s all-wheel drive powered the boxy vehicle up the slope and onto the metal planking beyond.

The Humvee went next, followed by the first semi, with a driver named Austin at the wheel. There was a bad moment when a sudden gust of wind hit Austin’s rig and lifted all of the tires on the left side up off the deck. But disaster was averted when the wind shifted, and the Peterbilt landed.

Then a different sort of problem arose. Carey was on the east side of the spillway managing things there. And Mac could hear the stress in her voice as she spoke. "We have a problem, Major . . . Mr. Bowers is refusing to cross. He says it's too dangerous."

Mac was standing midspan at that point—waiting for truck four to complete the crossing. She swore under her breath. "I believe that one of our soldiers is a qualified motor transport operator."

"Yes," Carey replied. "That would be Private Rigg."

"Is he with *you*? Or on the west side?"

"He's over here," Carey answered.

"Perfect. Tell him to drive Mr. Bowers's vehicle. And tell Mr. Bowers to walk home. Someone will notify him to come get his truck eventually. Oh, and don't sign anything."

All of the soldiers had been privy to the interchange, and Mac figured that most of them would share it with their respective drivers. Maybe that would prevent further defections. She hoped so. Mac's thoughts were interrupted by an unfamiliar voice. "Look upstream! It's going to hit the bridge!"

Mac turned to the left. "It" was a full-sized houseboat! Complete with a satellite dish mounted on the roof. And all Mac could do was watch as the barge-like vessel crashed into the bridge and sent an earthquake-like tremor in both directions.

Mac lost her footing and fell. Her arms were wrapped around a bollard when the current sucked the front end of the houseboat *under* the span. That caused the stern to rise into the air! Then it toppled over onto the semi owned by a man named Raskin.

The soldier assigned to Raskin's truck was out on the bridge, giving directions at that point. And he remained untouched as the force of the blow knocked the Kenworth and its trailer off the bridge and into the churning water.

There was nothing to be done, as Raskin and tons of desperately needed supplies were swept downstream. Meanwhile, what remained of the shattered houseboat was sucked *under* the span to surface farther down the spillway.

The truck and its driver were a terrible loss. But what about the bridge? It was intact. But for how long? Mac staggered forward to the point where the private still stood. "Check the downstream side for damage!" Mac yelled. "I'll take the upstream side."

Mac expected to find damage and did. A huge dent was visible where the houseboat's bow had hit. But the float remained airtight as far as Mac could tell. And, when the soldier gave her a thumbs-up, Mac made the call. "Send the next truck. We have three vehicles left to go."

Finally, with six of the original seven semis safely across, it was time to bring the Stryker over. Mac held her breath as Truck Commander Larry Washington guided the **BUFFALO BOB** over the bridge. The span was shaking as if palsied at that point, and Mac feared that it would disintegrate at any moment. So she felt a tremendous sense of relief when the vic rolled up the slope to join the rest of the trucks.

Then something unexpected happened. "Look!" a soldier exclaimed, as she pointed to the east. And there, rolling down the slope and onto the bridge, was an M984A4 Wrecker! Mac turned to Green. "Contact the driver . . . Tell him we think the bridge is about to go."

But before Green could respond, another soldier said, "Oh, shit! There it goes!"

And he was correct. The group watched as the bridge snapped in the middle. The force of the current pushed both halves over to their respective banks, where it caused them to wiggle from side to side.

Mac watched as two tiny figures fled the wrecker, made their way to the shore side of the bridge, and took the jump. Mac felt a sense of relief as they landed safely. "What now?" Carey inquired.

"We have supplies to deliver," Mac said. "Let's saddle up."

The east half of the bridge broke free and was carried away.

NEW ORLEANS, LOUISIANA

Gusts of wind as high as 135 mph had been recorded over the previous six hours. Now, as the eye of the storm crossed the coast west of New Orleans, conditions had begun to moderate. Sloan had opened the underground command center to the public early that morning. Except for Doyle Besom, the rest of Sloan's aides were against that, citing security concerns.

But Besom saw everything in terms of good or bad publicity. And he knew that video of the president welcoming refugees into *his* sanctuary would play well both north *and* south of the New Mason Dixon Line. Plus, the old mine was *huge*. So it wasn't all that difficult to isolate the area being used for command purposes.

Sloan took his role as host seriously and had spent two hours passing out blankets and trying to comfort people. When he arrived in the Situation Room South, it was to find that a new executive summary was sitting on the table waiting for him. And there was some good news for a change. "The storm has lost some of its strength," FEMA Administrator Freely said. "We think the worst is over."

"That's what I want to hear." Sloan said as he turned to General Jones. "How is Operation Pushback going?"

"Pretty well, all things considered," Jones answered. "The army has been able to force the Mexicans west to the town of New Iberia. The enemy is holding for the moment. But a brigade of Marines will land to the south of them the moment weather conditions allow. And once the jarheads arrive, we'll be able to push them back."

"There is *one* problem, however," McKinney added. "And that's supplies. In order to move quickly, our people took off with only five days' worth of food, ammo, and fuel. Normally, we could fly supplies in. But Whitney has kept our aircraft on the ground."

Sloan frowned. "So we can't use the roads?"

"The rebs dropped the Highway 90 bridge at Calumet when they retreated the first time," Jones explained. "Then, when the tide turned, they threw a ribbon bridge across the Atchafalaya Spillway for the Mexicans to use.

"But, based on the most recent report from a convoy with the call sign Road-Runner-Three, Whitney took the ribbon bridge out. That leaves I-10 to the north—and we're advancing on Lafayette."

Sloan nodded. "Good. Is there anything else?"

"I have *two* things to report," Director of National Intelligence Kip said. "The first is a special operations coup! A team led by Major Robin Macintyre snatched Mexican Major General Matias Ramos out of his bed in Franklin and brought him out. Ten soldiers and sailors went in. Four of them survived."

Sloan felt his heart sink. His staff knew about the rumors—so he couldn't ask about Mac. McKinney came to Sloan's rescue. And he did so in a very skillful manner. "We lost some good people. By way of a side note, it's worth mentioning that Major Macintyre is in charge of Road-Runner-Three, and her convoy crossed the bridge just before half of it went downstream."

Sloan managed to conceal the surge of relief that he felt. *Mac was alive!* He cleared his throat. "Please give me some background on each person who died. I will write letters to their families."

McKinney nodded. "Yes, sir. That will mean a lot."

Sloan turned to Kip. "So where did you stash the general? And how is the interrogation going?"

"He's at Fort Knox," Kip replied. "And he wants to cut a deal. Negotiations are under way. But, regardless of how that turns out, we know that the abduction was a blow to Mexican morale. In fact, it looks as if the snatch, plus the impact of the storm, were largely responsible for the pullback."

"Sweet," Sloan said. "That makes sense. If you're a foot soldier, and the enemy can snatch a general, what does that say about *your* chances? What's the second item you have for me?"

"It's related to the first," Kip replied. "President Stickley relieved Confederate General Bo Macintyre of his duties and named an admiral to replace him. The announcement was made immediately after the Ramos abduction, so the two events could be related. Macintyre was at the front. So, when the pullback began, it's possible that he made a convenient scapegoat.

"But," Kip continued, "regardless of the reason, imagine the fallout! A replacement was named, the command structure was severely disrupted, and all of Macintyre's standing orders had to be reviewed. All while running a war.

"The whole episode is extraordinary," Kip added. "So much so that our analysts wonder if there was another reason for Macintyre's dismissal. Did he have one hand in the till? Was he having sex with an underage girl? Time will tell."

"That's amazing," Sloan said. And it *was* amazing. Especially given the roles that Mac and her father had played in the campaign. But there were more important things to focus on.

"Supplies," Sloan said. "Let's talk about supplies. Can the navy help us? How strong are the rebel defenses at Port Arthur? Could we capture it? And bring supplies in by sea?" The discussion began.

NEAR CENTERVILLE, LOUISIANA

The rain was falling, and the MRAP shuddered each time a gust of wind hit it. But as the eye of the storm passed over, conditions had improved.

It was getting late by the time the convoy cleared the spillway and made its way onto Highway 90. Thanks to the combined effects of the storm *and* the war, they had the much-abused road to themselves. The convoy couldn't travel at night, however. Both the civilians and Mac's soldiers were bone tired.

So as Mac spread the map out in front of her, she was looking for a place to laager up. And the logical choice was the town of Centerville, which lay near the intersection of Highways 317 and 90. "Take the next right," she ordered. Then Mac turned to Green. "Warn the other drivers."

Brown made the turn, and it wasn't long before a school appeared on the left. "Turn into the parking lot," Mac ordered.

Brown did as he was told, and the rest of the vehicles followed. The parking lot was large enough to accommodate *two* convoys. As soon as all of the trucks were in off the highway, Mac put Road-Runner-Three on standby while she got out to look around.

Normally, with a company of Strykers, Mac would have put some space in between them. A measure calculated to reduce the amount of damage that an exploding truck could cause to neighboring vehicles. But with no enemy aircraft to worry about, and only twenty soldiers available to guard the perimeter, Mac decided to keep the convoy's footprint as small as possible. So she ordered the drivers to park their vehicles side by side in two columns of three.

Because the school buildings were located on the north side of the lot, Mac used the Cougar to protect the convoy's east flank and placed the Stryker to the west. That left the Humvee to guard the driveway. Then it was time to set the watch schedules, listen to the drivers bitch about it, and let the Operation Pushback staff know where the convoy was.

The night passed uneventfully—for which Mac was grateful. As for the weather, that was a little worse but still better than it had been twenty-four hours earlier.

The convoy was ready to pull out when Lieutenant Carey's voice was heard on the TAC frequency. "Hold on . . . All vehicles will remain where they are. Major? Please join me at the Humvee."

Mac was struck by the junior officer's tone. Carey sounded much more confident than she had back in New Orleans, and that was a good thing. "What's up?" Mac inquired as she arrived at the Humvee.

"Follow me," Carey said, and led Mac out to the point where the driveway met the road. Some traffic cones were located there . . . And, judging from the presence of a backhoe, a drainage project was under way. But what immediately caught Mac's attention were the footprints in the mud—and the flat spot located at the center of them. A flat spot with gravel sprinkled on top. That suggested the presence of a mine! Or an IED. Mac produced a low whistle. "Wow. Nice work, Lieutenant."

"The credit goes to Corporal Ito," Carey replied. "He brought it to my attention."

Mac was impressed. Ito wasn't present, and it would have been easy for Carey to take credit for the discovery. "I'll thank him," Mac said. "But you took his input seriously. Keep it up, Lieutenant. I'm impressed." Carey beamed.

Mac took a look around. She didn't want to deal with the explosives; nor did she need to. There was plenty of room to drive around the spot. *We'll swing wide,* Mac concluded. *In case the actual charges are to the right or left of the suspicious area.*

Problem solved. But the episode raised a question: Had local resistance fighters spotted the convoy? And planted the explosives? Or had they been *invited* to do so? Mac remembered what Colonel Prevus had told her regarding the civilian drivers. "Any one of those bastards could be a rebel agent or a resistance fighter! So keep a close eye on them."

"Make a warning sign," Mac ordered. "And place it in front of the mine."

The convoy departed fifteen minutes later by driving across a section of lawn onto the road that led to Highway 90. Franklin was only a fifteen-minute drive to the west. Mac wasn't surprised to see that a major battle had taken place on and around the highway. Shell craters and wrecks forced the MRAP to snake in and out. Had mines been planted there, too? If so, the Cougar would set them off and clear a path for the big rigs. Or so Mac hoped.

As Brown guided the Cougar through the maze, Mac saw lots of burned-out vehicles, most of which were Mexican. And that made sense. Because without air assets to protect them, the Mexican tanks and armored cars had been severely outgunned.

It hadn't been a completely one-sided affair, however, since one Abrams continued to burn as they passed by it, and the enemy had been able to take out some Bradleys and Strykers as well. So where *were* the combatants? There was nobody to be seen as the convoy passed Franklin. Perhaps the Mexicans had been forced to fall back during the night.

Mac liked that from a strategic point of view. But her job was to link up with the 32nd. And to do so *before* the outfit ran out of supplies. That was going to be difficult so long as the unit continued to push west.

Half an hour later, the convoy arrived at the cutoff for Jeanerette and the checkpoint that had been established there. It consisted of a Bradley and a squad of infantry. A sergeant was in charge. He claimed that the *new* front was located approximately twenty-five miles ahead, just short of New Iberia. "That's where the tacos are making their stand," the noncom said with a grin and waited for Mac to laugh. She didn't. There was nothing funny about what the Mexicans had been able to accomplish.

A trail of carnage led to New Iberia. The highway was littered with shot-up vehicles, the countryside was pockmarked with shell craters, and it was deeply scarred wherever the main battle tanks had been.

The convoy was about ten miles from New Iberia when it came upon an increasing amount of traffic and the rear-echelon support units that were camped along both sides of the highway. Mac saw a variety of spray-painted signs, including one that pointed north to Chicago.

It wasn't long before the convoy had to stop so that a couple of heavily laden tank carriers could enter the highway. Mac took advantage of the opportunity to jump down and chat with an MP. The rain had stopped, the distant thump of artillery could be heard, and rotors clattered as a Black Hawk helicopter passed overhead. "I'm looking for the 32nd Infantry Brigade," Mac said. "Do you know where it is?"

"I don't," the MP replied. "But the folks at HQ would. Take the Damall Road exit and turn right. You'll see the HQ compound right away."

Mac thanked the soldier, climbed up into the MRAP, and passed the directions to Brown. And sure enough, the collection of vehicles, tents, and antiaircraft-missile launchers was right where the MP said it would be.

Rather than take the convoy into the already crowded encampment, Mac ordered her drivers to park along the edge of Damall

Road. Then, with Green at her side, Mac made her way back to the compound. Both women were required to show ID before being allowed to enter the area.

A captain stood in front of a large tent performing organizational triage. As Mac joined the queue she noticed that very few people were getting through. It took fifteen minutes to reach the head of the line. "TGIF," the captain said cheerfully. "And what, pray tell, can I do for *you*?"

The captain took notes as Mac explained her situation. "Got it," he said, once she was finished. "I have good news, and I have bad news. The good news is that you came to the right place. The bad news is that the general and his staff are busy fighting the Mexicans. That means it might be tomorrow before we get this sorted out.

"But we need all the supplies we can get, so if you'd like to sign everything over to the Division's supply officer, I can make that happen. And why not? The 32nd is part of the division."

"Thanks but no thanks," Mac replied. "I don't think my CO would appreciate that."

The captain smiled. "You may be correct. Feel free to pick a spot down the road and laager up. I'll let you know if I hear anything. Otherwise, please check with me in the morning."

It was an anticlimactic ending to a difficult trip, and Mac was disappointed. But there was nothing she could do other than thank the officer, return to the convoy, and give the necessary orders.

After days of torrential rain, the surrounding fields were far too soft for the semis to negotiate. As a result, Mac had to settle for a side road bordered by rows of badly shot-up manufactured houses. There was no parking lot. So Mac ordered the vehicles to park in a line, with lots of space between them. Then, after blocking both ends of the street, Mac felt reasonably secure. The problem was that she didn't have enough troops to clear the houses and push a perimeter out beyond them.

That was one of the issues Mac discussed with her soldiers when she pulled them together. The other was the mine that had been planted the night before. "How about it?" Mac inquired. "Do any of you have a reason to believe that one of our drivers was involved?"

None of them did. So all Mac could do was to urge caution, set up shifts, and stress the need to perform routine maintenance on the military vehicles. The rumble of cannon fire could be heard in the distance—and an A-10 passed over at around 1500. But everything was peaceful other than that.

As afternoon gave way to night, Mac and Carey flipped a Confederate coin to see which one of them would take the first watch. Mac won, and that meant she got to sleep first. And rather than crash in a semi, Mac chose to stretch out in the back of the Stryker. And that's where she was when the attack began. A rocket hit one of the big rigs, machine-gun fire raked another, and a flare went off high above. Road-Runner-Three was under attack.

CHAPTER 14

The darkest hour is just before dawn.

—PROVERB

"Crank her up!" Mac yelled as she rolled off the seat and came to her feet. Corporal Larry Washington started the engine, while gunner Trish Vesey hurried to claim her seat and bring the truck's weapons systems online.

Mac pulled the TAC vest over her head, put her brain bucket on, and stuck her head up through the forward air-guard hatch. A tractor-trailer rig was on fire, and the flames lit the area. Shadows flickered as soldiers fought the blaze with fire extinguishers. One of the firefighters staggered and fell as a Confederate resistance fighter shot him from a house on the north side of the street. "Use the fifties!" Mac ordered. "Suppress their fire."

The volume of incoming fire lessened as the big machine guns began to chug. Mac opened the intercom. "Take us around the west end of the housing complex," she ordered. "We'll attack those bastards from behind."

Then, on the tactical frequency, "Heads up in the MRAP . . . We're going to cross in front of you."

The Stryker produced a sound reminiscent of a city bus pulling away from a stop as it came up to speed. It took less than a minute to reach the end of the street and take a hard right. The vic crashed through a fence, sideswiped a storage shed, and demolished a play-set before rolling into the field beyond. And that was when the insurgents were forced to back out of the shot-up houses and run. But Vesey could see them thanks to her thermal-imaging gear, and she fired a round.

The Stryker lurched, and Mac wished that she was wearing ear protection, as the 105mm cannon went off. Where the shell struck, Mac saw three bodies cartwheel through the air before landing hard. Vesey fired again—and with similar results.

"Give the fifties a rest," Carey ordered, "and clear those houses. But be careful . . . Dead bodies could be booby-trapped."

Good girl, Mac thought, before ducking below. Both crew members turned to look at her. "Watch the field," she told them. "A follow-up seems unlikely, but you never know. Holler if you need me."

Washington lowered the ramp as Mac paused to grab her HK submachine gun. "Don't shoot me," Mac said over the tactical frequency. "I'm about to appear at the west end of the street."

She kept the HK ready as she passed between a couple of houses and made her way down a driveway. The truck fire had been extinguished, and a good thing, too, since all of the tractor-trailer rigs were carrying some of the ammunition. Sergeant Percy was speaking. "House two is clear, one body. Over."

And so it went as Mac headed east. "Major?" Carey said. "I'm near the Humvee. There's something I want you to see."

A cluster of headlamps marked the spot where Carey was standing. A small crowd was gathered by the body of a driver named Jessie Jameson when Mac arrived. "The bastard had a radio," the driver named Eason said bitterly as he toed the device with a boot. "He called them in."

Mac looked at Carey. "How 'bout that, Lieutenant? Is Mr. Eason correct?"

"Yes, ma'am," Carey replied. "I saw Jameson shoot Private Potter in the back. His body is over there." Carey pointed.

"God damn him," Mac said bitterly. "What happened then?"

"I shot him," Carey said. Her voice was strained, and her face was pale.

"Well done," Mac said. "How much you wanna bet that Jameson called the rebs in last night, too. Check on Sergeant Percy's progress, Lieutenant. I'll handle things here."

Percy didn't need checking on. But Mac figured Carey could use a couple of minutes in which to regroup emotionally. As she left, two Humvees arrived. The lead vehicle screeched to a halt and a sergeant jumped out. His maroon beret was worn at a rakish angle, and he was cradling an LMG. "Sergeant Colby, ma'am . . . We're part of the division's quick-response platoon. What's the situation?"

Mac gave Colby a briefing and assured him that everything was under control. "The 32nd?" he said. "I know where it is. Or where it was as of yesterday."

Mac pulled the map out of a cargo pocket. "Can you show me?"

He could and did. The 32nd was west of the convoy's present position and south of Highway 90. "Take a left on Week's Island Road," Colby told her. "But you'd better coordinate your movements through HQ, or you could come under fire."

Mac thanked Colby and cut him loose. Then she said, "Where's Green?" only to discover that the RTO was standing right next to her. "See if you can find an MA (Mortuary Affairs) team."

"I did," Green replied. "They'll be here as soon as they can. But it'll be a while."

"You're amazing," Mac said. "So tell me . . . What do I want now?"

"A mug of Starbucks. But you can't have it."

Mac laughed. "No, I can't. Come on. We have a damage assessment to do."

NEW ORLEANS, LOUISIANA

Sloan had spent four hours touring the city of New Orleans with the mayor, who, like most of his subordinates, had been installed by the New Confederacy. But rather than throw him out, Sloan was mindful of President Lyndon B. Johnson's comment regarding FBI Director J. Edgar Hoover: "It's probably better to have him inside the tent pissing out, than outside the tent pissing in." And as far as Sloan could tell, the strategy was working. The mayor was happy to take credit for the supplies pouring in from the North and had moderated his public stance accordingly.

Now, as Sloan got off the freight elevator, a group of citizens was waiting to get on. The storm was over, and they were eager to assess the damage to their homes. At least some members of the group recognized Sloan, and one woman shouted, "We love you, Mr. President! Thank you!" Sloan paused to shake hands and wish the refugees well.

"You were right," Secretary of Defense Garrison said, once the group was on the elevator. "Inviting people to stay down here was good PR."

"It was also the right thing to do," Sloan added. He knew the comment made him sound like a self-righteous jerk, but he didn't want to run a government that was based on appearances. And if that meant coming across as a sanctimonious jerk, then that was a price he'd have to pay. "So what gives?" Sloan inquired. "I got your message and came back early. This isn't bad news I hope."

"No," Garrison assured him. "It isn't bad news. Come on . . . I want you to see this firsthand."

Sloan followed Garrison into the Situation Room. At least a dozen people were assembled there, and most were smiling. "We have something for you, Mr. President," Intelligence Director Kip told him.

Sloan's eyebrows rose. "Which is?"

"General Ramos cut a deal . . . And we got a lot more than we expected to."

"All right," Sloan replied as he sat down. "Lay it on me."

The lights dimmed, and video appeared on the main screen. It began with a picture of Ramos. His name and rank were visible below the photo. The time, date, and location of the interview could be seen as well.

Then Ramos appeared. His hair was nicely cut, his clothes were clean, and a bottle of water sat inches from his right hand. "Please state your name and rank," a disembodied voice said.

"I am Major General Matias Ramos, Mexican Army," Ramos said.

"Now," the voice said. "Please tell us how the alliance between Mexico and the New Confederacy came into existence."

Ramos shrugged. "I wasn't present during the initial negotiations. But, according to what President Salazar told me, a deal was done."

"What kind of a deal?" the voice wanted to know.

"The essence of the agreement was that the New Confederacy would provide Mexico with two tons of gold, plus the states of

California, Nevada, Utah, and Arizona in return for our assistance in winning the war. And that's what I call one helluva good deal."

Kip pointed a remote at the screen and the video froze. *"So?"* she demanded. "What do you think?"

Sloan was stunned. Suddenly, the whole thing made sense. They'd been aware of the gold. One ton of it anyway . . . Which never seemed like enough money to buy four divisions of troops. Especially troops that had no aircraft to speak of and were under-equipped.

But a *huge* chunk of land? Land that once belonged to Mexico? Yes. That kind of payment would make political sense. Salazar would be elected president for life. "It's amazing," Sloan said. "And a measure of just how desperate the Confederacy is."

"That's true," Besom agreed. "Which is why we should make the video public."

"I don't know," Sloan temporized. "Will people believe it?"

"Some won't," Besom admitted. "But lots of people will because it makes sense. Some of the rebs will accept the deal as a necessary evil, but others will be appalled, and the blowback could cost Stickley her job. A sudden change in leadership would be helpful right now. The timing is perfect."

"Skeptics will claim that we made the whole thing up and forced Ramos to say it," Sloan countered.

"Sure," Kip agreed. "But what if we give Ramos some money and the freedom to move freely? He's a playboy . . . And his activities will generate a lot of press coverage. That could go a long way toward countering the torture theory."

"True," Sloan conceded. "But the Mexicans would send assassins to kill him."

"So?" Kip inquired. "Why do I care?"

There was a pause while Sloan gave the matter some thought.

"Okay," he said finally. "Release the video *and* Ramos. But keep him alive."

Kip made a face. "Do we have to?"

"Yes," Sloan said. "Because we're different from the people we're fighting."

NEAR NEW IBERIA, LOUISIANA

The Mexicans were holding their positions in New Iberia, as were the Confederate troops, who had been rushed in to help block the Union advance. The result was something akin to a living hell. Dark clouds hung low. Flashes strobed them from below—and man-made thunder rolled across the land.

In trenches reminiscent of WWI, men and women from both sides sallied forth in often futile attempts to claim a few additional yards of mud, their progress marked by the waves of bodies left behind. Engines roared as tanks rolled in to support the infantry.

But the mechanical monsters were met with a hail of AT4 rockets, or targeted by the 155mm howitzers located twenty miles behind enemy lines, and reduced to piles of burning scrap. Soon thereafter, Predator drones would prey on the 155s, or ground-to-ground missiles would seek the batteries out, leaving *another* crater to mark where they had been. That's when *more* weapons would be brought forward, and the cycle would begin again.

That was the horror to which Mac and the convoy called Road-Runner-Three had to go in order to deliver the supplies they'd fought so hard to bring from New Orleans. The location Mac had been given was in the nonexistent town of Duboin. "Nonexistent" because she couldn't see any sign that a town had ever existed there as the MRAP passed the wasteland of overlapping shell craters, muddy trenches, and sandbagged bunkers that Union soldiers called "Camp Fuckme."

And Mac could tell that at least some of the complex was within range of the enemy's artillery because 155mm rounds were falling a quarter mile to the north. Each shell produced an audible thump followed by a geyser of mud. Was the attack producing a meaningful impact? It was impossible to tell. But there was reason to worry because once the enemy drones spotted the convoy, the rebel field artillery would almost certainly shift its fire to them.

But the way was clear, and the ground equivalent of a JTAC was riding Green hard. "Hurry up, Road-Runner-Three . . . Let's get those rigs down and out of sight. Over."

MPs waved them toward a well-graveled ramp that led down into a hastily excavated subsurface supply depot. All sorts of directional signs could be seen, some of which were in Spanish.

The MRAP came to a stop, and as Mac jumped down onto the ground, a lieutenant colonel came forward to meet her. He had blue eyes, thinning hair, and the manner of the college professor that he normally was. "Hello, I'm Colonel Breeson. I believe you already know my number two, Captain Wu."

"I do," Mac said as she gave Wu a hug. "She's the best supply officer I ever had."

"I concur," Breeson said. "She *is* quite competent. Especially where midnight requisitions are concerned. What happened to your convoy? It looks like someone used it for target practice."

"Partisans attacked us last night," Mac replied. "Truck three caught fire, but we put it out. Most of the cargo is undamaged."

"Did you bring us some ammo?" Breeson asked hopefully.

"Yes, sir," Mac replied. "About a third of each load consists of ammo."

"Thank God," Breeson said. "We're running low. Captain Wu . . . you know what to do."

Wu left to get the unloading process under way, and Mac took the opportunity to ask a question. "What about my battalion, Colonel? Does Mac's Marauders still exist?"

"It does," Breeson assured her. "Although I haven't been able to find any Strykers for you. I suggest that you report to Colonel Tompkins. He's the XO." Breeson turned. "Sergeant Omar! Take the major over to HQ."

Breeson turned back. "You'd never find it without a guide," he explained. "This place is like a maze."

Mac thanked Breeson and keyed her mike. "All military personnel will report to me. And bring your gear. You won't be back. Over."

Rather than ask Breeson what to do with the soldiers under her command and run the risk that he'd take control of them, Mac had decided to assume they were hers. Would the strategy work? Time would tell.

Omar led them up a ramp to the surface, through a muddy trench, and past a busy mortar pit. Mac was struck by the amount of litter on the ground. There were ration boxes, some in Spanish, and bloody bandages, and items of clothing lay everywhere.

Eventually, they entered a bunker that led to another bunker, and that's where Omar left them. Mac turned to Carey. "Wait here. If anyone asks, tell them that you report to me."

Carey's eyes widened. "So you aren't sending us back to New Orleans?"

Mac chuckled. "Fat chance. No, someone will grab the detachment, and it might as well be me."

"I'd like that," Carey said. "'The best of the worst.' That's what they say."

Mac smiled. "That's because it's true. Keep everyone together. I'll be back as soon as I can."

The bunker *beyond* the outer bunker was guarded by two Rangers and a dour-looking master sergeant. "Good morning, ma'am. Do you have an appointment?"

"No," Mac replied. "I just arrived. I'm Major Macintyre. Is the XO available?"

The noncom had bushy eyebrows. Both of them rose. "*The* Major Macintyre? Sergeant Major Price was a friend of mine. He told me that you are the best fucking officer in the army. No offense, ma'am . . . That's how *he* put it."

Price had been killed in action, and Mac missed him. She felt a lump form in her throat. "No apology is necessary, Master Sergeant. That's how he would say it all right. He was an outstanding soldier."

"Hold on for a second," the noncom said. "I'll see if the colonel can fit you in."

He was back a minute later and offered a big paw. "Master Sergeant Oliver, ma'am. Let me know if you need anything."

"Done," Mac said, as they shook. "Thank you."

The command bunker was equipped with lawn furniture that looked as if it had been "liberated" from a Home Depot store. A skeletal rack supported six flat screens, each of which featured a different scene. And there, standing on two shipping pallets, was Colonel Tompkins. For reasons known only to him, Tompkins was wearing an army blue uniform rather than camos.

When Tompkins spoke, it was into a headset as his eyes scanned the screens in front of him. "Pay attention, Roach-Four . . . Kill that battery, and kill it now. Baker-One-Eight . . . watch your left flank. They're trying to do an end run on you. Nice move, Alpha-Six. They won't forget that."

Then, after a quick glance at Mac, his eyes returned to the

screens. "Welcome to the 32nd, Major . . . A brigade of jarheads is going to travel up the ship channel and land here in about six hours. Our job, *your* job, is to clear a spot for them to land and hold it. Then we're going to push the enemy back and win this fucking war. Do you have any questions?"

Mac had to admire the precision with which Tompkins delivered the briefing. "No, sir. No questions, sir."

"Good," Tompkins said, as his eyes continued to scan the screens. "Then why are you still here?"

NEAR PECAN WELLS, TEXAS

After parking his rental car in a grove of trees two miles away, and hiking cross-country on foot, ex-general Bo Macintyre had climbed to the top of the promontory that locals called "Goat Rock." Bo had chosen the spot because he'd been hunting in the area and was familiar with it. The vantage point also allowed Bo to look out over the surrounding countryside and see everything that moved. He could see a hawk riding a thermal, a yellow school bus driving up the highway, and a pickup truck headed in the opposite direction. All of which was wonderfully normal.

Bo settled into the shadow thrown by a pinnacle of rock, put the rifle aside, and shrugged his way out of the day pack. Then he looked at his watch. It was 0732. Assuming they followed his instructions, Bo's guests would arrive at 0800.

He glassed the cabin below. It belonged to a friend. A general who, if he was lucky, would survive the war. In the meantime, Bo was going to use the structure for a few hours before putting the key back above the door. There was nothing to see around the structure except the hop, hop, hop of a rabbit.

Was the government searching for him? Maybe, but maybe not, since Stickley was up to her ass in trouble. Ramos had spilled his guts, just like Bo figured he would, and the Union was riding the bastard like a horse. They had released a video of Ramos shooting his mouth off about the true nature of the Mexican-Confederate alliance, and it was getting lots of play.

Bo was staying at a motel in nearby Gatesville. And he'd seen hours of the blah-blah. Was Ramos lying? Had he been tortured? Did that kind of deal make sense? How could the Confederate government countenance such a thing? On and on it went as people who didn't know jack shit pretended that they did.

The *real* truth was that the "territorial concession," as some commentators called it, had been part of a larger strategy. A daring plan to double-cross the Mexicans, and take their miserable country over, along with all of the land down to the Panama Canal.

And had it not been for a strange confluence of events, it would have worked. But no one, Bo included—had been able to anticipate the abduction, the storm, and Sloan's decision to attack.

I should have thought of it, Bo thought. *I underestimated Sloan. And he made me pay.* The failure weighed heavily on Bo's mind. *Focus on the future,* he told himself. *Do what you can do.*

Bo opened the pack, removed a thermos, and poured himself a cup of black coffee. Paper rattled as he stuck a hand into the bag of chocolate-covered doughnuts and selected one. "You'll get fat." That's what Kathy would have said. Her absence was a hole that couldn't be filled.

The doughnut tasted good. A gulp of coffee washed it down. Bo was about to take a second bite when he noticed a flicker of movement south of the cabin. A deer perhaps? He brought the glasses up. No, it wasn't a deer. A man or a woman, he couldn't tell which, was kneeling in some scrub glassing the cabin!

Had the government located him? No. They would have arrived in force, thrown a cordon around the area, and locked it down. This person was one of his guests. And a cautious one at that.

Bo finished his doughnut as the person circled the cabin, climbed the stairs that led to the porch, and read the note on the door. Then, after looking around, he or she went inside.

The second guest arrived in a pickup truck with a government logo and a light bar on top. Was it stolen? Probably. And Bo approved. He wanted to hire people who were imaginative and willing to take risks. Like pretending to be a game warden.

The first guest came out to greet the newcomer. They shook hands and went inside. Bo gave an involuntary jerk as something cold nudged the back of his neck. "Good morning, General . . . Chocolate-covered doughnuts! May I?" The pressure disappeared.

Bo managed to maintain his composure, but just barely. Somehow, the operative had been able to spot him, climb the back slope without making a sound, and get close. *Very* close. Was he getting old? Or was the op that good? Bo had to admit that both things were true. "Of course," Bo said as he turned. "Help yourself."

Bo had never met Corporal Jimmy Gatlin before, but Victoria had been high on him and liked to tell stories about the operative's exploits. Gatlin was thirtysomething, and not much to look at. He had brown hair, brown eyes, and a perpetual grin. As if life were a joke, and he was in on it. "Don't mind if I do," Gatlin said as he sat on a rock. Paper rattled as he took a doughnut. "I like the view . . . Is everyone here? My guess is 'yes.'"

"What makes you think there are others?"

Gatlin's eyes narrowed. "Your daughter is dead, your wife is dead, and the Confederacy is dead. Or it will be soon. And you are a survivor. A man with a plan. But you need help. So who you gonna call? The people that Victoria trusted. Am I wrong?"

"No," Bo allowed. "You're right. I have a plan, and I need help."

Gatlin sipped coffee straight from the thermos, wiped a dribble off his chin, and grinned. "I don't want to die with a bunch of Mexicans. There's a place in Brazil. A town called Santa Bárbara d'Oeste. After the first Confederacy fell, hundreds of Southerners went there rather than live as Union slaves. And their descendants still control the area. That's where I plan to go. But I'd like to live in comfort if you know what I mean."

"I do know what you mean," Bo assured him. "Come on . . . Let's go down and talk to the others. Maybe they'd like to live in Brazil, too."

NEW IBERIA, LOUISIANA

The industrial complex located south of New Iberia was home to drilling companies, a shipyard, and a host of related businesses, many of which bordered the shipping channel. It was the *same* channel the Marines were going to use.

The Marauders were situated in the shipyard across the waterway from a Mexican Army unit. And in order to join them, Mac and her soldiers had to jog west along Earl B. Wilson Road. It was defended by a mobile C-RAM unit that included both a tracking system and a 20mm Gatling gun.

The weapon swiveled, appeared to sniff the air, and fired. There was an ominous buzzing sound as the cannon threw a curtain of shells into the air. Flashes signaled a series of hits as incoming mortar rounds were destroyed. That was comforting, but what lay beyond the C-RAM wasn't.

Side channels led away from the waterway to serve specific businesses. And once the soldiers reached the end of the road, they were confronted with a badly damaged ribbon bridge. The span had taken a lot of hits during the fighting and was listing to the right. But it led to the peninsula where the Marauders were dug in. That meant Mac and her soldiers had to cross it or swim.

As Mac led her troops across the high side of the bridge, she was conscious of the fact that the enemy drones could be, and probably were, watching from above. And the truth of that assumption became evident as artillery shells began to arc overhead. The C-RAM was able to intercept most of them, but one round got through. It landed twenty yards south of the span and sent a column of muddy water soaring high into the air.

Mac felt a sense of relief as she left the bridge for solid ground. The feeling was short-lived, however, because she could hear the battle raging nearby. The chug, chug, chug of a .50 caliber machine gun could be heard in the distance and served as a counterpoint to the sharp crack of exploding rockets and the persistent bang, bang, bang of rifle fire.

"Hello, Major," a voice said, as a ragged-looking soldier rose from the protection of a shell crater. "Welcome back."

Mac stared. "It's *me*," the soldier said. "Private Temo. The captain sent me over to bring you in."

Mac didn't remember Temo but pretended that she did. "It's good to see you, Private . . . Even if you look like hell."

Temo laughed. The sound had a slightly hysterical quality. "We all do, ma'am . . . Please follow me."

Temo led the column along a pathway, through a badly holed warehouse, and into the shipyard. A large ship had been removed from the channel and was perched at the top of a ramp-like spillway. Its superstructure was riddled with holes.

A brisk firefight was under way as the Marauders fired across the waterway, and the enemy responded in kind. "This is it," Temo said, as they arrived at an open hatch. "Our HQ is located in the space down below."

Temo disappeared down an aluminum ladder, and Mac followed. Lights dangled here and there, shadows played across the walls, and screams could be heard. "Sorry about that," Temo said apologetically, as if Mac might find the sound to be offensive. "The aid station is over there . . . It gets noisy sometimes. Come on . . . I'll take you to the captain."

The headquarters group was working out of what had been a storage room. Munson stood as Mac entered, and a sergeant yelled, "Atten-hut!"

"As you were," Mac said as she looked around. "What a shithole . . . Where's the bar?"

Munson smiled weakly. His eyes were rimmed with red, his face was smeared with dirt, and he smelled like a goat. "I'm sorry, Major . . . I'll submit a requisition for one."

Mac felt a surge of concern. It didn't take a degree in medicine to know that Munson was teetering on the edge of exhaustion. And that meant the troops were hurting, too. "Apology accepted," she said with a grin. "Thanks for keeping the outfit together. Colonel Tompkins said a lot of nice things about you."

That was a lie, but, judging from Munson's expression, it was the *right* lie for the occasion. "That's good to hear," Munson said. "But our soldiers deserve all of the credit."

Mac nodded. "So what's the situation?"

"The enemy controls the west side of the waterway," Munson replied. "And we haven't been able to push them back. That means the Marines will land under fire."

Mac had no difficulty understanding the nature of the problem. It wasn't enough to shoot at the enemy. The Marauders needed to cross the channel, push the Mexicans back, and hold the newly captured ground in order to create an LZ. "So you tried to cross?"

Munson nodded. "Hell yes, we tried to cross. *Three* times. We never made it out of the boats. Some of us had to swim back. A lot of people died. Now we're out of time," Munson added.

"We're *almost* out of time," Mac said. "But it ain't over till it's over. Have we still got our wrench turners?"

"Most of them," Munson answered.

"Call them in," Mac ordered. "In fact I want you to call *everyone* in. Tell them to pee, eat an MRE, and take a half-hour nap. All except for one platoon that is . . . Their job is to convince the Mexicans that the battalion is still engaged. And when we cross, we'll leave them behind. Got it?"

Mac could imagine what her XO was thinking. Maybe the CO had an idea. A *good* idea. Or maybe she didn't. But he was off the hook . . . And that felt good. There was newfound hope in his eyes. "I'm on it, Major . . . It's good to have you back."

It took an hour for the battalion to prepare. And Mac was issuing final instructions to her company commanders when Green appeared at her side. "Colonel Tompkins is on the horn, ma'am. He wants to know what's taking so long."

It wasn't the first such message from Tompkins, and Mac felt a rising sense of anger. "Tell him I'm doing my nails, but not to worry because I'll be done soon."

Green's eyes grew larger. "Seriously? You want me to say that?"

"Yes, I do . . . And you can leave the radio here. I don't have time for his bullshit."

Mac opened her mike and spoke over the TAC frequency. "This is Marauder-Six . . . The Marines are counting on us to do the heavy lifting for them. Let's get the job done. Over."

Shouts of "Hooah" could be heard from all around as Mac led Alpha Company up the stairs that led to the 146-foot-long seagoing tug. The metal scaffolding shook as dozens of boots pounded up through three flights of switchbacking stairs, and smoke poured out of the ship's badly damaged superstructure. What would the enemy make of *that*? Would they conclude that the tug was on fire?

Mac didn't know and didn't care. The purpose of the smoke was to hide her troops and their movements. The soldiers responsible for detonating the smoke grenades soon joined the troops who were moving toward the stern. Bravo Company had climbed the stairs by then and was following along behind. A sergeant had been assigned to board last and give the word. "This is Bravo Two-One. Phase one is complete. Over."

"Roger that," Mac replied. "Six to the hammer crew. Turn her loose. Over."

By that time, the battalion's mechanics had removed all of the tie-downs except for the cables that connected the ship to four massive shackles, each of which was secured with a large metal pin. To free the vessel, the soldiers had to remove the pins using sledgehammers. Metal clanged on metal as wrench turners went to work. The reports came in quick succession. "One, clear." "Two, clear." "Four clear." "Three clear."

"Hang on!" Mac said, and hurried to obey her own command.

Nothing happened. Mac couldn't believe it. The ship weighed thousands of tons, and it was sitting on a steep incline. What the hell was wrong? Then a loud groan was heard. The tug shuddered and began to move. Slowly at first, then faster. Metal screeched on metal as the vessel slid down the ramp, hit the water, and threw a curtain of spray to the west.

And that was just the beginning. With plenty of inertia to power it, the smoke-wreathed vessel slid across the waterway and ran aground. Soldiers armed with light machine guns opened fire on the Mexicans from the stern.

Meanwhile, Mac and lead elements from Alpha Company were jumping down onto the embankment. "Push them back!" Mac shouted as she ran forward. "Kill the bastards!"

The unexpected arrival of two hundred Yankee soldiers, plus the ferocity with which they fought, threw the enemy soldiers back. "This is Six . . . Don't let them get comfy! Keep pushing!"

Counterfire sparkled all along the expanse that fronted the Marauders. And that might have been enough to stop the attackers if it hadn't been for phase two of Mac's plan. She turned to find Green crouched to her right. "I told you to leave the radio behind."

"Yes, ma'am."

"But you brought it."

"Yes, ma'am. You need it."

"And the colonel? Did you pass my message?"

Green shook her head. "No, ma'am. I didn't think that would be wise."

Mac laughed. "I'm going to put you in for a medal when this is over. Get Steelrain on the horn . . . Tell them to fire."

Mac opened her mike. "This is Marauder-Six. All troops cease firing and take cover. Some serious shit is about to fall out of the sky."

The coordinates had been fed to the missile battery half an hour earlier, and it was on standby. The unit was located seventy-five miles to the east, so there was some travel time, but not much. Two MGM-140B guided missiles plunged out of the overcast, struck the ground two hundred yards forward of Mac's position, and exploded.

As each missile disintegrated, it sprayed 275 M74 submunitions in a 360-degree radius. The subs were similar to hand grenades.

And each one of them was packed with incendiary pellets that were equally effective against equipment *and* personnel. The results were devastating. The combined payload of 550 submunitions slaughtered the enemy troops.

That left the Marauders free to take more ground, dig in, and hold it. They did.

The Marines arrived one hour and forty-two minutes later. They came ashore without firing a shot. Some waved to the scarecrow-like figures as they passed through the battalion's lines. Others shouted friendly insults. The Marauders were too tired to respond.

IIIIIIIIIIIII

That was the beginning of what the media called "The Big Push." But it was more like the big rout. Entire divisions of disillusioned Mexicans turned toward the border. The war-weary columns clogged the freeways and the secondary roads for days while they made their way home. And they would have been easy meat for the Union A-10s, Apache gunships, and fighter planes.

But Sloan ordered all military units to let the Mexicans go so long as they didn't fight or loot. The outfits that did were obliterated. Most people agreed that the policy made sense. Killing thousands of troops just to kill them would be stupid . . . And capturing them would create a huge burden.

The rebels were different, however. Many Confederate units refused to surrender and were determined to fight to the death. Where they could, Union officers put a cordon of troops around the Southerners and settled in to wait them out. That saved the lives of soldiers from both sides and served to prevent the sort of Alamo-like massacres that would make postwar reunification more difficult, if not impossible. Mac understood those strategies better than most and agreed with them.

Subsequent to the battle in New Iberia, the Marauders were sent west, but not in the lead. They spent most of their time showing the flag in small towns. Not the Union flag, which Sloan had retired, but the *American* flag—more and more of which were being taken out of storage and flown by Southern patriots.

So the city of Houston had already been secured by the time Mac arrived. In an effort to find out what fate had befallen her father, Mac made her way to his office in the southern command and control center. It had been trashed. The Intel people had been there . . . And once they left, sticky-fingered soldiers had gone through the stuff that remained.

But there were some items that neither group cared about, including two photographs. One was a picture of a woman who Mac believed to be Bo's second wife. As for the other, that was a photo of Victoria. And she was smiling.

CHAPTER 15

There is no hunting like the hunting of man, and those who have hunted armed men long enough and liked it, never care for anything else thereafter.

—ERNEST HEMINGWAY

NEAR BAR HARBOR, MAINE

It was dark. The boat's twin engines produced a throaty rumble as the thirty-six-foot cabin cruiser left the calm waters of Southwest Harbor, passed Sutton Island, and began the run up to Bar Harbor. The bow rose and fell gently as it cut through the long rollers that chased each other in from the Atlantic. As Bo stood in the stern, he could see the multicolored lights that followed the coastline. The blackouts that had once been common were over as was the war itself.

More than a month had passed since Houston had fallen, and President Stickley had fled. Some said she was living in the Caymans. Others claimed that the politician and her loyalists were somewhere in Africa. Bo didn't give a damn. He was on a mission, his *last* mission, and the one that would put him in the history books. Not that historical notoriety was Bo's goal. He wanted to kill Samuel T. Sloan for personal reasons.

After assembling the hit team and sending them north one at a time, Bo had been forced to wait. Sloan had so many bodyguards that it was impossible to get anywhere near the bastard under normal circumstances. But people, presidents included, can and do make mistakes. Sloan was no exception.

Samuel T. Sloan and Major Robin Macintyre announced their engagement only weeks after the New Confederacy surrendered. Very few people were surprised.

But the press release caused a stir nevertheless, especially when it became known that the couple were going to share a prenuptial holiday on a private island located near Bar Harbor, Maine. And *that* was going to give Bo the opportunity he needed.

The boat began to roll uncomfortably as it turned north. One of the new team members, an actor named Posey, was seasick. Rather than stick around and watch Posey barf over the rail, Bo entered the spacious cabin. An ex–navy bosun named Trey Sims was at the wheel. The African-American was built like a linebacker—and stood with his feet spread.

Gatlin, along with an ex-op named Misty Estrada, and a one-time Confederate Intel agent named Ricky Costas were seated at the table.

Bo reached out to steady himself as the boat rolled. Gatlin grinned. "It's hard to believe that some people do this for fun. We're going to play a few hands of poker. Would you care to join us?"

Bo had nothing better to do and figured it would be good for morale. But rather than the penny-ante game that Bo was expecting to take part in, the others began to place stacks of gold coins on the table. The same coins they'd been paid with.

Did it make sense to play poker with the money they hoped to retire on? No. But all three of them were risk takers and egomaniacs. Each believed himself or herself to be smarter and more capable than the rest of the people on the boat.

But there were things they didn't know . . . One of which was that Bo was broke. All of Victoria's stash had gone into giving the team half their pay up front, equipping them, and renting the yacht. Bo smiled. "I'd love to sit in. Are IOUs okay? My money is waiting for us in Canada."

The relationship between the United States and Canada was still quite rocky. So the claim was credible, especially since the team had been led to believe that a helicopter was going to pick them up after the assassination and take them north. "Sure," Costas replied. "We know you're good for it."

The next hour passed enjoyably, and by the time the boat crossed the Mt. Desert Narrows, Estrada had amassed a substantial pile of coins and IOUs. She had a narrow face, hungry eyes, and hollow cheeks. "Thanks, suckers . . . I'm going to think of you while I spend your money."

"We're twenty minutes out," Sims announced from his position at the helm.

"Okay," Bo said. "Let's get ready."

"Yes, sir," Gatlin said as he slid off the seat. "I'll check on Posey."

One by one, the team members brought their duffel bags to the cockpit and stacked them on the starboard side. Bo was on the flying bridge by then, standing next to Sims, who preferred the topside controls for docking. The cruiser's running lights were off, and the cabin was dark.

Bo brought the night-vision binoculars up to his eyes and

scanned the island ahead. Having viewed the area on Google Earth, Bo knew that Bowtie Island was actually *two* oblong islets linked by a sandbar. The main house was located on the south end of what Bo thought of as island two. There was a separate cottage as well. That was where the island's only permanent resident lived.

But what if Secret Service agents were on Bowtie? That would be a disaster. The presidential visit was days away, however . . . And, having been privy to such things in his role as a general, Bo figured the Secret Service wouldn't move in for another day or two.

Everything Bo could see confirmed that hypothesis. Had security been in place, armed Coast Guard boats would have come out to warn the yacht off.

"The target looks the way it should," Bo announced. "Take us in." Sims nodded and nudged the throttles forward.

Each member of the team was equipped with a headset, radio, and night-vision gear. Bo keyed his mike. "Heads up . . . We're going in. Sims and Estrada will remain with the boat. Everyone else will follow me. Posey will be last. Over."

The team responded with a flurry of clicks as the yacht nudged the floating dock and Estrada jumped onto it. She secured the stern line as the others made their way up a ramp to shore. They were dressed in TAC gear and armed with suppressed pistols.

Bo was on point and pleased to discover that the old habits were still there. He knew that the trail led to the cottage, the heliport, and the house at the far end of the island. The caretaker's residence became visible two minutes later.

Bo checked his watch. It was 2022. With any luck at all, George Owen was asleep. Bo knew the caretaker's name thanks to reviews posted online. "Mr. Owen was wonderful!" "Thank you, George!" And crap like that.

Bo waved the team forward. A light was visible within the cottage. Because Owen was still up? Or was it a night-light? They were about to find out. Bo pointed to Gatlin, then to the door.

Gatlin nodded and, like the pro he was, tried the knob before resorting to force. The door opened smoothly. Owen felt safe on Bowtie Island. That was about to change. Gatlin entered first, with Bo behind him. Costas and Posey were on sentry duty outside. A visitor was unlikely. But if one appeared, they would deal with it.

The front door opened onto a small foyer. The living room was on the left—and a soft murmur was coming from the TV. A recliner was positioned in front of the set, and Bo could see that the back of a man's head was visible. Was Owen awake? Or was he asleep? Gatlin circled around the chair, stopped, and pushed the barrel of his pistol up against the caretaker's forehead. "Rise and shine, sweetheart."

Owen jerked awake and attempted to get up, but the gun barrel kept him from doing so. "Who? What?"

"There's no reason to be frightened," Bo lied. "Just stay where you are for the moment. Posey? You can come in now."

Posey arrived moments later. He'd been chosen for his ability to play a part, but more than that, because he was about Owen's age and had a similar build. Posey removed a digital camera from a cargo pocket and began to snap pictures. Owen blinked as the flash went off. Later on, when the time came, the photos would help Posey to apply his makeup. "There," the actor said as he took a final shot. "That should do it."

"Good," Bo said. "Okay, Mr. Owen, stand up. You're about to take us on a tour. During the tour, you will tell Mr. Posey everything he needs to know about how to do your job. That includes the routine maintenance chores that you perform each day, the kind of problems that might crop up, and everything you know about the island's history. If you do that, and do it well, I will allow you to live. Agreed?" Owen was terrified. His head bobbed up and down.

The tour lasted for more than three hours. Posey recorded everything Owen said so he could review it later. The sky had just begun to lighten in the east as Gatlin escorted Owen down the ramp and onto the yacht. The duffel bags had been transferred onto the dock by then, and the boat's engines were running.

"Well, I'll be damned," Gatlin said, and pointed. "Look at that!"

Owen turned to look, and Sims shot him in the back of the head. There was a thump as the body landed on the deck. "Okay," Gatlin said, "let's haul him below. You know what to do after that."

Sims nodded. "Take the boat out, drill lots of holes in the hull, and row the dinghy back."

"Exactamundo," Gatlin said cheerfully. "We'll hump the duffel bags up the ramp while you're away."

Sims took the yacht out and returned forty-five minutes later. The rest of the team was waiting at the top of the ramp. "Okay," Bo said. "Stage one is complete. Stage two begins now. Mr. Posey, or should I say Mr. Owen, will start to play his part now. That includes showing the members of the Secret Service advance team around the island when they arrive.

"The rest of us will spend the next couple of days camping in the ruins on island one. There's a basement under what's left of the lighthouse, and that's where we'll stay. Are there any questions? No? All right then . . . The hard part is over. The rest will be easy. We'd better get going before the tide comes in over the sandbar."

ABOARD MARINE ONE

Even though Mac had been on Marine One before, it felt strange to ride on a helicopter that didn't have door gunners. That was another reminder that the war was over, and the killing had ended. But the country faced a different kind of challenge now. After suffering multiple meteor hits, and the extensive damage resulting from a civil war, the reconstituted United States of America faced a rebuilding project so immense that it boggled Mac's mind. And that was why President Samuel T. Sloan continued to work twelve-hour days. He was on a phone call and winked as their eyes met.

That was emblematic of the way in which things had changed. As the war came to an end, their relationship blossomed. Sloan wanted to get married. And, after giving the matter an hour's worth of thought, Mac realized that she did, too. So they were engaged. Even if it seemed to confirm past rumors and gave the president's critics something to carp about.

But for the most part, Sloan was quite popular, in the North at least, and why not? He was the Fighting President. The man who had won the war. But could he win the peace? That remained to be seen since millions of Southerners hated him and resented the troops who patrolled their streets.

Sloan was determined to ignore that, however . . . And to earn the Southerners' trust, if not their affection, by convincing Congress to enact the sort of even-handed initiatives that would help the entire country to recover. Sloan's decision to reintegrate the military was a good example. Mac thought the measure was risky, but brilliant, too, since the only thing worse than having a quarter million ex–Confederate soldiers *in* the military—was to have them sitting around with nothing to do.

As for Mac, she couldn't remain in the army while engaged to the commander in chief. So she had requested a transfer to the inactive reserves. And that was likely to be helpful in another way as well . . . In spite of her impressive war record, there were those who sought to link Mac, and therefore Sloan, with her fugitive father. Where *was* he? Mac wondered. In Africa? Like some people said? Or down in South America? Not that it made much difference. The authorities would find Bo Macintyre and put him on trial for war crimes. And, once that day came, it would be best if Mac was back in civilian life.

Mac looked out the window as a layer of wispy clouds dissipated, and an island was revealed. Two islands, really, which when taken together and viewed from above, looked like a bowtie. Three days. That's what Sloan had promised her. With very few phone calls to interrupt their time together. "A penny for your thoughts," Sloan said.

Mac turned to discover that the phone call was over. "Only a penny?"

He laughed. "All that I have then."

Mac smiled. "I guess that will have to do."

Marine One swooped in for a perfect landing. Secret Service agents were present, but only one person came forward to meet the helicopter. He was the island's sixtysomething caretaker. "Mr. President . . . Major Macintyre . . . This is an honor. My name is George Owen. Welcome to Bowtie Island! My job is to make sure that you enjoy your stay. Did you bring any staff?"

"No," Sloan replied, as the two men shook hands. "We're going to do our own cooking."

"Which means *he's* going to cook," Mac interjected. "I don't know how."

Owen chuckled. "Let me know if you change your minds. I can bring a cook and a maid in from Bar Harbor if you want me to. Please follow me. I'll give you the tour."

Mac had seen the four bedrooms, three bathrooms, and chef's kitchen online. So she knew what to expect. Fortunately, they didn't have to share the house with the Secret Service. Three shifts consisting of eight agents each were going to commute in from Bar Harbor.

Once the tour was over, Owen left them alone. Groceries had been brought in the previous day, and Sloan made good on his promise to prepare what he called, "A great American lunch." It consisted of grilled cheese sandwiches, Campbell's tomato soup, and a veggie plate—all of which was delicious. "You're a master chef," Mac assured him. "What can I expect for dinner? A Totino's pizza?"

"Wouldn't you like to know?" Sloan said as he swept Mac off her feet and carried her away. The master bedroom was large, and beautifully furnished. Mac landed on the white bedspread first—immediately followed by Sloan. They kissed.

"You have soup breath," Mac noted.

"And you are delicious," Sloan countered.

What followed wasn't the first, but it was the *best*, and deeply satisfying. A nap came next. Mac awoke first and was drinking a cup of coffee in the living room when Sloan appeared. He made the white tee and jeans look good as he padded over to give her a kiss. "You let me sleep."

"You needed it."

"I guess I did. Would you like to go for a walk?"

"Absolutely."

A narrow path circled the island, and they followed it. The sky was gray, gulls rode the incoming wind, and waves crashed below. Sloan's hand felt warm. *Here,* Mac thought, *with him. This is where I want to be.* And for the first time in her life, Mac knew what it was to feel complete.

After the walk, some drinks, and a long conversation about

their future plans—it was time to eat dinner. Sloan rose to the occasion. Much to Mac's amazement, he served Parmesan-crusted halibut, along with broccoli and wild rice. Dessert consisted of a scoop of coconut ice cream accompanied by a vanilla wafer. Coffee followed. "That was amazing," Mac told him. "You're hired."

Sloan laughed. "Good. Now, if you'll excuse me, I have to make a call. Then I'll be back." And he was. They snuggled, watched a comedian do his best Sam Sloan imitation, and went to bed.

Sloan fell asleep within minutes, but Mac didn't. She lay there for a while before getting up and making her way into the living room. Maybe it was the coffee. Or maybe she was keyed up. Her life was so completely different from what it had been.

The house wasn't entirely dark thanks to the strategically placed night-lights the owners had put in place. And Mac saw no need to turn on more lights as she passed the kitchen and entered the living room. Huge windows provided sweeping views of the Atlantic. The moon was up and only partially obscured by a thin layer of clouds.

The vista had a ghostly feel—like something in a storybook. And as Mac looked out across the front deck, she saw a figure appear and pause to look around. A uniformed Secret Service agent? Yes, judging from the assault weapon he was carrying.

Was the agent enjoying the view, too? Or focused on the job? That's what Mac was thinking when another figure appeared behind the first. A *second* agent? No, this one had a long-barreled pistol . . . And it was pointed at the first man's head! Mac was about to shout a warning when the assailant fired, and the agent collapsed.

Mac didn't wait to see what would happen next. She whirled and ran to the bedroom. "Sam! Get up! Put some clothes on . . . The house is under attack."

Sloan sat up and yawned. "What did you say?"

"I said get your butt out of bed . . . Put your clothes on. The house is under attack."

Mac's suitcase was sitting on a stand. Old habits die hard, and the Glock was there. After grabbing it, Mac cursed herself for not bringing a spare magazine.

Sloan was holding a remote. He pressed a button. "Don't worry, hon . . . Help is on the way."

Mac glanced his way as both of them got dressed. "From where? From *here*? They killed the agent who was on the front deck. I watched it go down."

"You're kidding."

"No, I'm not kidding. Get some shoes on . . . We're going outside."

Sloan hurried to obey and was right behind Mac as she led him into the hall, and from there to a guest room. Not just *any* guest room, but the one with the French door that opened out onto a walkway and the trees beyond. Maybe they could clear the house and hide while they waited for help to come.

But no sooner had they entered the room than Mac heard a key turn in the lock, and the door swung open. A man was silhouetted against the porch light. He was dressed in TAC gear. The Glock was up. Mac fired the moment the red dot settled on its target. The man jerked as a 9mm round smashed through his skull and blew some of his brains out the other side. A pistol clattered on wood as he collapsed.

"That will bring the rest of them," Mac predicted. "Quick! Grab the gun . . . I'll take his night-vision gear."

Mac was disappointed to discover that the dead intruder was female. She'd been hoping to score a TAC vest for Sloan. She ripped the woman's night-vision gear off, and was about to take her radio, when a bullet slapped the side of the house. "Get back!" Mac ordered. And she followed Sloan in.

But as they entered the kitchen–living room, a man threw himself against the French doors that opened out onto the deck. They parted, and the intruder stumbled as he burst into the room. Sloan shot him, realized that the black man was wearing body armor, and fired again. The second bullet did the job. The third was by way of insurance. The would-be assassin lay facedown on the floor.

Someone hammered on the kitchen door. "It's me! George Owen! They shot me!"

Mac went to look through the peephole, saw the caretaker, and jerked the door open. Owen stepped to one side so that another man could shoot her. He was no more than four feet away. Mac felt the small-caliber bullet hit her left arm, and brought the Glock up, knowing it wouldn't arrive in time. So she fired early, and saw the 9mm slug smash her assailant's left knee into a bloody pulp. He screamed as he fell and dropped his pistol to grab what hurt. Mac shot the bastard *again*. In the head this time.

Glass shattered as a flashbang grenade sailed in from the front deck and went off. Mac's ears were ringing, and she couldn't see a damned thing, as she brought the Glock around. "Hit the floor!" she yelled, and hoped that Sloan would react quickly enough as she began to fire.

"I think you hit him!" Sloan yelled, as Mac sensed that someone was behind her. She was just beginning to turn when something hard hit her head. Mac fell, and was staring upwards, as her eyesight returned. "Daddy? Is that *you*?"

"Damned right it's me," Bo replied. "But I ain't your daddy. *My* daughter is dead."

Sloan could see again. He raised his pistol only to feel something hard jab the back of his neck. "Drop it," Owen growled, and Sloan was forced to comply. There was a clatter as the .22 hit the floor.

"Good work, Posey," Bo said as he turned back toward Mac. "Now comes the fun part," he said. "This is for Victoria." Bo fired. Mac felt the bullet punch a hole in her right thigh. It hurt like hell. Had he missed her head? No. Bo Macintyre wanted to see his daughter suffer.

Sloan was at least a head taller than the man named Posey, and a lot younger. He threw himself backward and heard a pop as the other man's gun went off. Posey was struggling to breathe as Sloan rolled off him. Could he dispose of Posey *and* deal with Bo? That seemed unlikely. But all Sloan could do was try. He wrapped his fingers around the other man's neck and proceeded to bang his head against the wood floor.

Mac saw Bo point his pistol at Sloan's back and managed to roll into him. Bo kept his feet, but his shot went wild. The .22 came around to point at *her*. Mac had seen the angry face before. When she was a little girl. When she was bad.

"This one is for Kathy," Bo said, as his finger tightened on the trigger. Bo seemed to flinch as a .22 caliber bullet struck his temple. A look of surprise appeared on his face. Then his knees gave way, and he crumpled to the floor.

Sloan was on his feet and marching across the room as he fired Posey's weapon. "This is for Mac, you asshole . . . And this one is for the POWs in Mexico . . . And this one is for *me*!"

When the Ruger wouldn't fire anymore, Sloan replaced it with Bo's. And that's where they found him, crouched in a pool of Mac's blood, his aim shifting from door to door as the first member of the quick-response team entered the room and froze. "Give me the code," Sloan grated.

"America Rising."

Sloan placed the pistol on the floor. "Get a medic . . . And I mean *now*!"

Mac tried to protest, tried to say that she could walk, but the blackness took her down.

THE FARM, NEAR OMAHA, NEBRASKA

Thunder rolled across the land. Not the sound of artillery, though; this was different, and a harbinger of rain. It started gently. Then it fell more insistently. Tapping at first, as if checking to see what the roof was made of, before morphing into a downpour.

Mac savored the sound of it and the warmth of the blanket that was wrapped around her shoulders. She was sitting on the spacious porch of the home where Sloan had grown up. The place the press often referred to as "the farm." It had become their retreat. The place they could go to get away from Fort Knox and all of the complexities there, many of which stemmed from the coming election and Sloan's first run for office.

Three painful weeks had passed since the assassination attempt on Bowtie Island. Small though it was, the .22 caliber bullet fired from Bo's pistol had severed Mac's femoral artery and almost killed her. Two surgeries later, she was still recovering and grateful to be alive. Grateful, and a bit guilty, because she had survived when so many had died. Some at her hand, some in her arms, and thousands upon thousands in battles she had no knowledge of.

Most of them were good people. *Better* people. All because of what? Destiny? Or just plain luck? *Yes,* Mac thought. *Luck. Nothing else can account for it.*

The screen door slammed. Sloan appeared. He held a steaming

mug in each hand. “Here it is,” he said. “Just what the doctor ordered. *Instant* Starbucks.”

“Oh my God,” Mac said. “Is it my birthday?”

“No, but you’ve been a good girl and deserve a reward.” Sloan put his coffee down before leaning in to kiss her. The usual spark jumped the gap. Many things were wrong with the world . . . But one thing felt right. And, for that, Mac was grateful.

P9-DUX-348

12/22/89

Dear Mindy,

MERRY CHRISTMAS! For the thousands of times we've pondered on this question, read this book and remember our crazy philosopphical talks. Maybe none of these responses are right, and yet maybe together they're all correct. Maybe one day when your mind is jumbled into an intricate knot of deep confusion you can look at these responses + gain insight.. or maybe just laugh at your overthinking mind! I love you so much! You're the best! Read and enjoy!

Love,

Mel

P.S. Top of pg. 77
Don't forget it!!

The Meaning of *Life*

Collected by Hugh S. Moorhead

Chicago Review Press

LIBRARY OF CONGRESS
Library of Congress Cataloging-in-Publication Data

The Meaning of life / [collected by] Hugh S. Moorhead.
p. cm.
ISBN 1-556-52038-7 : $14.95
1. Life—Quotations. maxims, etc. I. Moorhead, Hugh S.
BD431.M46883 1988
128—dc19 88-22085
CIP

Permission Acknowledgments begin on page 231.

Printed in the United States of America
First Printing
Published by Chicago Review Press, Incorporated,
814 N. Franklin Street, Chicago, Illinois 60610
ISBN: 1-55652-038-7

To my daughters
Rebecca and Ann

whose lives have given
so much meaning to my own

Introduction

"How did you get this autographed book?" I've been asked that question a hundred times over the last say, twenty years. A friend or guest takes a book from my shelves, usually a title written by one of his or her favorite authors, fondles it a moment, and reads the inscription from the author commenting on the question, "What is the meaning or purpose of life?" The response may be on a flyleaf, a separate handwritten sheet, or a typed page, perhaps full-length and single-spaced. Sometimes it is in a language other than English; sometimes the author's handwriting, while intriguing, nearly renders the message illegible.

I said about twenty years, which is the halfway point from the time I obtained the very earliest so-inscribed books to today, or, from the start of a "hobby," in the early 1950s, to the realization of an eclectic "collection."

In the beginning I didn't keep any records. (Why should I?) I bought and read books for pleasure, personal interest, or for my graduate work in philosophy at the University of Chicago. Then I mailed the books to their authors and wrote them a letter expressing my appreciation of the work and asking them to please comment on the meaning or purpose of life. I packaged the books in brown wrapping paper, tied them with string (were there Jiffy bags in 1950? If so, I knew nothing of them), and sent them off to such literary locales as Oxford and Paris, Greenup, Kentucky and Tinicum, Pennsylvania. I did not buy them for a collection—I didn't even know what "first edition" meant—but neither were they poor copies or textbooks marked up by some previous reader.

I started with Arnold J. Toynbee's abridged one-volume edition of *A Study of History,* Albert Einstein's *Out of My Later Years,* Albert Schweitzer's *Out of My Life and Thought,* George Santayana's *A Sense of Beauty,* and C. G. Jung's *Modern Man in Search of a Soul.* Einstein autographed his book in minute letters, ignoring the question. Schweitzer wrote "avec mes bonnes pensées," dated 24.10.50, and Santayana's came from Rome and read, "Inscribed for H. S. Moorhead." Toynbee, somewhat to my surprise, quoted two lines of scripture. And Jung chose to acknowledge rather than answer the question—thus offering an answer of sorts. (I am grateful that the ratio of two "answers" to my question out of five replies did not indicate a pattern. By the same token, I was always elated to receive the returned book and valued it, whether or not the author also complied with my unique request.)

Only two times in the past thirty-odd years have I been told off by an author. Once because I failed to enclose return postage (unnecessarily eager to get the book off, I planned to reimburse him). The other remonstrated me for not knowing that he had arthritis in his hand, that he did not have time, etc. He returned the package unopened.

For most of the lost books (at least fifty) one cannot know the reason. With the vagaries of the mail, some reached the author, others did not. I suppose some ignored the matter, but others must have never received the book in the first place. Even with my lengthy acquaintance of this nature, I hesitate to generalize about publishers: Do they or do they not (their address often being all I had to go on) forward mail to their authors? No doubt it entails some effort and expense. But the worst case of all would be this: the writer received the book, appreciated my letter, and did "answer" my question, but the book suffered misdirection or destruction in transit (especially probable for those expected to cross the seas). One author marvelled at the speed of the transatlantic mail—only to notice that the June 17 date on my letter (he replied on June 26) was from the previous year!

My question was considered "too tough," as well as, presumably with tongue in cheek, "too easy." Another asked if I didn't have "any tougher ones." It was deemed to be "largish," a "ball-breaker," and a difficult "assignment." There were denials that turned out to be answers: the answer is "in the book" or "in my books." Some quote other writers, other philosophers. Or the very title of the book reflects the author's thoughts on the question. Another offers a multiple-choice answer—"check one." An internationally known, controversial writer let me know via a postcard that he hadn't received the book and anyway he couldn't answer my "conundrum," only to return the delayed book shortly thereafter with a more deliberate "answer" duly inscribed in it. A scientist did want to put down his thoughts on the question but just couldn't take the time because of a deadline on another book.

Some ambiguous ones defy eradication of the ambiguity and a few, written too hastily, defy interpretation. And what does one make of "I can't answer your question"? Now, or never? There are jokes, anecdotes, mottos, proverbs. A "fellow seeker" says I should let him know when I find the answer ("send me a postcard") and is balanced by a well-known literary figure who, if he knew the answer to my question would have already announced it to the world. While another, in undue homage to my being a philosopher (more correctly in my case a person who tries to teach students how to philosophize), responds to my challenge with the rebuttal that I of all persons should *know* the answer!

There have been many humanistic aspects to my venture, some of them bittersweet. Amidst celebrations of life there are intimations and occasions of death. A notable novelist and short-story writer suffering from a serious accident *apologized* for the delay in responding, while another writer, ailing from a crippling disease, dictated his reply and subsequently had the typist hold the book so he could at least scribble his name.

I received a letter from a woman whose husband was critically ill and in a London hospital, profusely thanking me for writing. My letter had done much more for him than all the pills and saline drops he was getting there and, "please God," he would be happy to oblige me at a later date. Regrettably one of the weekly newsmagazines briefly noted his death shortly thereafter. Another wife courteously returned the book, unsigned, attesting to her husband's passing.

I hope it won't sound presumptuous if I admit that I like to think I have contributed in some small degree to their work, their lives. I received numerous thank yous for my comments about their writing. One was so grateful for my commendatory words that he called me a "collaborator," an overstated compliment of course. There was another who wrote, "I want you to know that to me one of the greatest rewards of writing is to receive a letter such as yours." Another lamented that he didn't have a copy himself anymore, and I tried subsequently in my regular visits to used bookstores to locate one, though without success. On several occasions I sent, later, a book that I thought a writer would appreciate seeing, one that related to his or her particular interests.

I have both enjoyed and benefited from my special association with these authors, though it has called for no little labor of love on my own part. There have been multifarious emotions, ups and downs, as well as a varying of procedures of procurement, of the more than two hundred and fifty responses reproduced herein. Seeking permission to print them proved arduous, but rewarding. Every day for months I eagerly searched the mail for the prestamped and addressed, green envelopes that sent cheerful compliances and some refusals. All along there was the logistical problem of finding addresses, an especially difficult matter for the long deceased, where the estate or trustee had to be found to authorize printing the response. Others were never located or did not reply. Worst of all, however, were the three green envelopes that arrived with flaps unglued and sides torn, empty. Who were these from?

Often I am asked whether or not my collection includes this or that famous novelist, erudite philosopher, or engaging columnist. Sometimes I can gratify the questioners with a yes and produce the inscription; sometimes I disappoint them. After all, the collection reflects my own interests. And I appreciate the story of the woman who, with her nose raised, asked, "Mr. Emerson, have you read all these books?" gesturing to the thousands of volumes in his Concord home. "Madam," he replied, "I have read some of them twice." (This forces me to admit that once I knew my collection would be published some day, I bought more than one book for just this purpose, risking the loss of books at 1980s prices.) So no, I have not read all of them, but yes, I have read some of them twice. Not long ago I read again *Out of My Life and Thought,* while, come to think of it, I never did really read the Toynbee.

I am happy to say that although I cannot match Emerson's number, I do have about seven hundred books, approximately half of them with the requested inscription. The remaining some three hundred and fifty contain a personal note or an autograph. Then there are several hundred others of all kinds, many of them textbooks. I value them all: with or without jackets, they grant elegance to my shelves, many retaining the distinctive aroma of one of Chicago's used bookstores, the haunts of my graduate school days.

Many who have seen or know about the collection have asked me to name my favorite inscription. But I can't do it. So I confess that I have many "favorites," and without intending to be either flippant *or* less than serious, I ape one of America's greatest writers, Mark Twain, who said: "Man is the only animal that has the true religion—several of 'em!" Meanwhile I continue to hear about and read new books by talented writers. I keep a list of those authors who I hope will expand my collection and increase my number of "true favorites."

Since I cannot think of any human creation greater than a good book, I am pleased that so many good books have contributed to this one. It didn't occur to me back in 1950 that my interest in various authors' comments on the meaning or purpose of life would turn into another book, one "written" by so many of those fine writers. That idea came only some years ago, as the collection grew and more and more of those who perused it urged me to share its contents.

I am delighted to do so here.

Hugh S. Moorhead
Chicago, 1988

Please comment on the question, what is the meaning or purpose of life.

♦ *Edward Abbey*

Down The River

The question implies the answer: life has no given meaning, existence no purpose. This precisely is what makes our situation so interesting.

August 5, 1987

♦ *Dean Acheson*

A Democrat Looks At His Party

You ask me to write a few lines in this book on what is the purpose of life. I suppose the purpose of life is to live. If this seems too simple, I can cite high authority for the view in John 10:10.

March 16, 1956

♦ *Mortimer J. Adler*

Dialectic

The end of life is the complete perfection attainable by the nature of the living thing.

♦ *Edward Albee*

Seascape

The meaning of life, you ask?
Being aware of it, I should say.
1980

This copy signed for Hugh Moorhead
(1981)

SEASCAPE

A PLAY

by

[signature]

The meaning of life, you ask?
Being aware of it, I should say.

EA

♦ *Fred Allen*

Treadmill to Oblivion

Nietzsche said: "Life is an unprofitable episode that disturbs an otherwise blessed state of non-existence."

I say: "Life is a slow walk down a long hall that gets darker as you approach the end."

HUGH S. MOORHEAD

NIETZSCHE SAID:
"LIFE IS AN UNPROFITABLE EPISODE THAT DISTURBS AN OTHERWISE BLESSED STATE OF NON-EXISTENCE."

I SAY:
"LIFE IS A SLOW WALK DOWN A LONG HALL THAT GETS DARKER AS YOU APPROACH THE END."

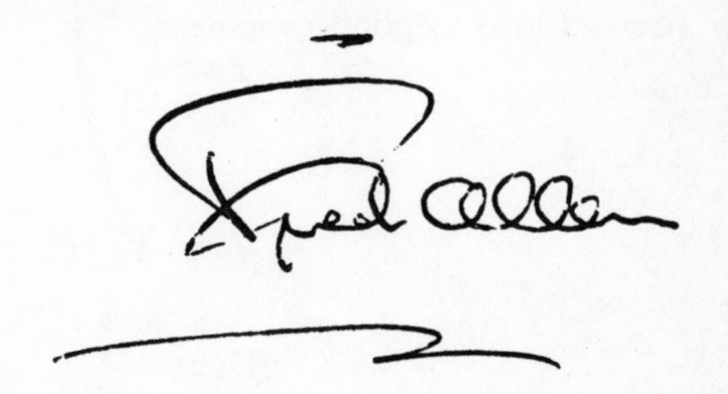

♦ *Steve Allen*

The Funny Men

There is no reason to assume that life has only *one* meaning. Da Vinci's life may have meant something other than that of Charles Manson.

♦ *Lisa Alther*

Other Women

I'm afraid your guess is as good as mine!

April 29, 1986

♦ *A. Alvarez*

The Savage God

"To chose, is to do; but to be no part of any body, is to be nothing." —John Donne

I don't really believe there is a "meaning" to life. I think life is simply a fact which we have to accept, for better or for worse. It is up to us to provide meanings implicitly through our work and our behavior and our affections and our pleasures. Sometimes they seem enough, sometimes they don't. It is, above all, a question of patience.

July 11, 1977

THE GREEN MAN

Kingsley Amis

~~*Kingsley Amis*~~

Harcourt, Brace & World, Inc.
New York

for Hugh S. Moorhead

The longer one lives, the more important it becomes not to venture statements on the meaning of life

♦ *Kingsley Amis*

The Green Man

The longer one lives, the more important it becomes not to venture statements on the meaning of life.

♦ *Michael Anania*

The Red Menace

I don't want to retreat into the justly despised positivism, but the question "the meaning of life," proposes its own answer. "Life" includes "meaning," or at least the aspiration toward meaning. *Life,* if you think of it as an assertion of meaning in process, always exceeds assigned meaning. To offer a parody of technical language—the set of all meanings is included in life, which is an additional meaning so expands the set by a hypo-set, and so forth. So any statement—any such question, expands the frame exponentially. What I'm saying in a nutshell is the meaning of life is meaning.

♦ *George Anastaplo*

Human Being and Citizen

. . . who shares the realization that one of the purposes of life is to examine the purposes of life.

♦ *Max Apple*

The Oranging of America

I wish I could respond to your question about the meaning of life—I admire you for not being afraid or ashamed to ask. All I can tell you is that I ignore the positivists too . . . keep asking.

April 17, 1981

♦ *Richard Armour*

My Life with Women

From one who believes in the two-sex system as he believes in the two-party system, who is aware of the fact that ("life") ("live") spelled backward is ("evil,") and we should therefore go forward, and who thinks that the important thing about living is to live fully and keep to the last an interest in all other living beings, human and non-human (animals, birds, fish, insects) . . .

August 1975

♦ *Isaac Asimov*

In The Beginning

As for the meaning of life in general, or in the abstract, as far as I can see, there is none. If all of life were suddenly to disappear from Earth and anywhere else it may exist, or if none had ever formed in the first place, I think the Universe would continue to exist without perceptible change.

However, it is always possible for an individual to invest his own life with meaning that he can find significant. He can so order his life that he may find as much beauty and wisdom in it as he can, and spread as much of that to others as possible.

July 13, 1987

♦ *A. J. Ayer*

Language, Truth and Logic

I do not think there can be any general answer to the question, what is the meaning of life? Our individual lives have whatever meaning, or meanings, we succeed in giving them.

October 22, 1953

♦ *Hazel E. Barnes*

An Existentialist Ethics

To create meaning where there has been none,
To make one's life significant in a Universe not made for us,
To recognize that human solidarity must be based on reverence for the need of every individual.

♦ *Thomas Berger*

Killing Time

Having pondered on this matter for longer than half a century, I now suspect that the meaning or purpose of life is probably not that which could be addressed by the question, "What is the meaning or purpose of life?"

♦ *Leonard Bernstein*

The Joy of Music

As to teleology and/or ontology, consult Kant, Spinoza, Plato, et al. As for me, the purpose of life is to live it as fully as possible, and to be grateful every day for the privilege of sharing it.

♦ *Wendell Berry*

Clearing

No leaf falls there that is lost;
All that falls rises, opens,
sings; what was, is.
May 12, 1986

No leaf falls there that is lost;
all that falls rises, opens,
sings; what was, is.

Inscribed for Hugh Moorhead
with good wishes, 5/12/86.

Wendell Berry

♦ *Arthur E. Bestor*

Educational Wastelands

Men think so that they may get bread. This is the practical argument for education—a valid argument, but not the basic one. To get at the ultimate reason for education, one must reverse the statement: Men get bread so that they may think.

January 31, 1958

♦ *Max Black*

Language and Philosophy

A philosopher once said to a fish, "The purpose of life is to reason and become wise." The fish answered, "The purpose of life is to swim and catch flies." The philosopher muttered "Poor fish." Back came a whisper, "Poor philosopher."

January 3, 1953

♦ *Joseph Blotner*

Faulkner

I wish I knew the meaning of life. Given to us as it is, one sees those for whom it is a blessing, those for whom it is a curse. Perhaps its meaning lies in the chance it gives us to know all we can, be all we can, and to express and live however much we can the message of all the great teachers: love.

August 22, 1984

To Hugh S. Moorhead

.... on life

I have no easy answers!

To me life is a precious gift

Treasure each day

Look back without regrets

Find pleasure in your work

Laugh at yourself, at your world

Love hard —

Enjoy!

And thanks —

Judy Blume

Nov. 1978

◆ *Judy Blume*

Wifey

I have no easy answers!
To me life is a precious gift
Treasure each day
Look back with no regrets
Find pleasure in your work
Laugh at yourself, at your world
Love hard—
  Enjoy!

◆ *Erma Bombeck*

If Life Is a Bowl of Cherries—What Am I Doing in the Pits?

To me the purpose of life is to know enough about it to enjoy it—but not enough to take it too seriously.

◆ *Robert Boswell*

Crooked Hearts

My guess is it is to find beauty, or at least to look for it.

◆ *Ray Bradbury*

I Sing the Body Electric

Life? Why life is for *living!*
Glory Hallelujah!!!

February 21st
Apollo Year One!

♦ C. D. Broad

Ethics and the History of Philosophy

I have written on the front page something which was said by an Anglo-Saxon nobleman at the court of King Edwin of Northumbria when, in A.D. 627, the king held a council to consider whether or not he should accept Christianity. I think that that old heathen Anglo expressed my feelings on this matter better than I could do myself.

"The present life of man, O king, seems to me, in comparison with that time which is unknown to us, like the swift flight of a sparrow through the room wherein you sit at supper in winter, with your commanders and ministers and a good fire in the midst, whilst the storms of rain and snow prevail abroad. The sparrow, I say, flying in at one door and immediately out at another, whilst he is within is safe from the wintry storm. But, after a short space of fair weather, he immediately vanishes out of your sight into the dark winter from which he had emerged. So this life of man appears for a short space; but of what went before or what is to follow we are utterly ignorant . . . ."

—Anglican nobleman to King Edwin of Northumbria, A.D. 627. From Bede's *Ecclesiastical History of England.*

June 7th, 1953

♦ *Denis W. Brogan*

The Era of Franklin D. Roosevelt

"There's nothing worth the wear of winning
But laughter and the love of friends" —H. Belloc

♦ *Pearl S. Buck*

Kinfolk

"It is better to light a single candle than to curse the darkness."
—Chinese proverb

"It is better to light a single candle than to curse the darkness."—Chinese proverb.

Pearl S. Buck

♦ *Frederick Busch*

Rounds

I have no secrets about life's purpose—Sorry.

♦ *Steven M. Cahn*

Fate, Logic, and Time

The meaning of life is invented, not discovered.

♦ *Erskine Caldwell*

This Very Earth

From a writer who must leave to others a way to find the meaning of life.

♦ *William H. Calvin*

The Throwing Madonna

As I understand evolution from Big Bang to big brain, the only discernible purpose to life is to create yet more complex and capable life forms. If we can indeed invent a computer which is smarter and wiser than we are (and lacking our tendencies to destroy ourselves and our environment), we will be carrying on this bootstrapping tradition.

June 1, 1984
Seattle

♦ *Ron Carlson*

Betrayed by F. Scott Fitzgerald

Page 184 comes closest to "life" philosophy for now. I remain a sensual optimist while at the same time I hope and know that few things last.*

*From page 184: "This is life on earth, I thought, for which I have perhaps too great an affection. . . . Wearing clothes, khakis dried to their righteous stiffness on the line, oxford cloth shirts, walking around the planet, avoiding prison in its deadly mediocrity by keeping good company and committing simple deeds that reside between the legal margins: I want these things."

◆ *Rudolf Carnap*

Introduction to Semantics

I have written only my name into your book because I find that I cannot make an adequate statement on the question in a few lines. But to give you at least an indication of what I am thinking, I will here say a few words (informally and inadequately formulated). I think that our life does not have a purpose by itself. It has as much meaning and significance as we give to it. We are free to choose our aim and the principles guiding our life. Life gains significance by our striving to fulfill the freely chosen purposes. The purpose may lie in our individual life or, on a higher level, in the development of humanity in a certain direction to which we wish to contribute. In either case the aim is human; there are no supernatural goals.

February 6, 1952

♦ *Eric Chaisson*

Cosmic Dawn

As I see it currently, the role of life in the Universe is to reflect on the Universe, to grant the Universe itself a consciousness of sorts. Without life, galaxies would twirl and stars would shine, but no one would appreciate the grandeur of it all. Thus, the Universe strives to create life, and to develop intelligence, so that the Universe itself can be known, appreciated, and perhaps loved.

◆ *Stuart Chase*

The Tyranny of Words

The purpose of life, as I see it, is to live. At the limits of one's capacity. Which means coming to terms with one's environment in nature, and with one's fellows.

May 1953

◆ *Arthur C. Clarke*

The Exploration of Space

I'm afraid I've no concrete ideas on the purpose of life, but ask me again in about ten thousand years, when Chapter 17 is ancient history.*

December 31, 1952

*Chapter 17 is titled "To the Stars."

◆ *Preston Cloud*

Cosmos, Earth and Man

Does life have a meaning? I would say rather it has a great potential for meaning. It is we who create the meaning. It is we who endow it with purpose, or fail to do so.

◆ *Cyrus Colter*

The Rivers of Eros

In *The Brothers Karamazov,* Father Zossima, on the eve of his death, speaks to his followers as follows: "Fathers and teachers, I ponder 'What is hell?' I maintain that it is the suffering of being unable to love."

March 12, 1973

COSMOS, EARTH, AND MAN

A SHORT HISTORY OF THE UNIVERSE

Preston Cloud

New Haven and London
Yale University Press
1978

Does life have a meaning? I would say rather it has a great potential for meaning. It is we who create the meaning. It is we who endow it with purpose, or fail to do so.

P.C.

♦ *Barnaby Conrad*

Matador

Do what thy manhood bids thee do—
From none but self expect applause,
He noblest lives and noblest dies,
Who lives and keeps his self made laws.

Do what thy Manhood bids thee do —
From none but self expect applause,
He noblest lives and noblest dies.
Who lives and keeps his self made laws.

Best regards —

Barnaby Conrad

♦ *Norman Cousins*

Who Speaks For Man?

You ask what I think the meaning and purpose of life are. I'm not sure what they *are,* but I think I can indicate what I think they *should be.*

First, I think we haven't begun to explore human potentiality—that we are, in this respect, living in a primitive period of our life on earth. Certainly one main purpose of life is to give every human being a chance to unfold fully, and in doing so to enrich the common life.

Secondly, I think war is the greatest single obstacle to the flowering of human life and personality. And the idea of unfettered national sovereignty that flows into it, it seems to me, is the greatest current impediment to the human future. The creation of a rational world order should therefore, I believe, be a major life-purpose of every sentient human being . . .

August 1970

♦ *Malcolm Cowley*

A Second Flowering

Life: Accept! Rejoice!

♦ *Harvey Cox*

The Seduction of the Spirit:
The Use and Misuse of People's Religion

The purpose of life is to glorify God and enjoy Him forever.

♦ *Robert Creeley*

The Island

To live.

♦ *Michael Crichton*

The Andromeda Strain

The survival value of human intelligence has never been satisfactorily demonstrated.

♦ *Francis Crick*

Life Itself: Its Origin and Nature

If there wasn't anything at all, we wouldn't be here.

♦ *A. J. Cronin*

Shannon's Way

"Experience is an arch—to build upon."

♦ *E. E. Cummings*

Poems, 1923–1954

Vide page 189, poem xxxiii, line 20*

*The line reads: "not for philosophy does this rose give a damn."

♦ *Roald Dahl*

Charlie and the Chocolate Factory

. . . what I would not have done is comment on the meaning and purpose of life. I wouldn't have felt qualified to do so.

♦ *Arthur C. Danto*

Nietzsche as Philosopher

I have no thought about the meaning of life to dignify the volume with. I *do* think—and it leaves me quite cheerful to think it—that life has no meaning at all. I think actions do, I think *lives* do (perhaps *all* lives) but not LIFE! But it is a topic I feel diffident to discuss, and am certain my view is of almost no interest to anyone, *least* of all to me.

◆ *Peter De Vries*

The Vale of Laughter

flattered you think any comment of mine on the meaning or purpose of life might be of interest or value to you—and unhappy to report that I haven't by any means Figured It All Out. I'm convinced at this stage, as an observer of and participant in the "horror and the boredom and the glory" of our human lot, that there is no Why, but only What. I believe Dreiser said that, or something like it, when asked to state his philosophy of life, and I'll have to string along with it. I had a character in *Let Me Count the Ways* say: "The universe is like a safe to which there is a combination. But the combination is locked up in the safe." That's it. Still we keep asking, wistfully and eternally, "Why?" Ah, that question mark, twisted like a fishhook in the human heart.

♦ *John Dickson*

Victoria Hotel

Actually I've never given the matter much thought, although I suspect that, reduced to its basics, the purpose of life is to live and/or procreate and the meaning of life is to live as an integral part of and with the universe, including everyone and everything in it. But I suppose, as a philosophy professor, you have asked the question many times without having received the same answer twice. Just because I happen to write poetry is no reason why my answer should be any more valid.

June 29, 1980

♦ *Annie Dillard*

Teaching A Stone To Talk

Alas, I don't know what the meaning of life is—I think it is to perceive and know, collectively, God's creation.

◆ *John Dos Passos*

Tour of Duty

That's something everybody has to work out for himself.

September 23, 1953

◆ *Paul H. Douglas*

Ethics in Government

For a reply to your query see pages 102–103.*

*A selected passage reads: "Since the state is but the individual writ large, perhaps the disclosures of the past years may reawaken within us a sense of our individual failure to live up to the standards we inwardly cherish. The faults which we see in government are all too often the reflection of our own moral failures. All this may dawn upon us, so that we will not only help to reform government but also to reform ourselves. If it does, the regenerative power both of democracy and of the human spirit will have won another great victory in the continual moral struggle which goes on within each of us and within society."

♦ *Peter F. Drucker*

America's Next Twenty Years

Every good gift and every perfect gift is from above, and cometh from the Father of lights. —James I:17

♦ *René Dubos*

A God Within

I do not know the meaning or *purpose* of life. But I'm convinced that mankind is engaged in a creative process of the kind that Saint Bernard had in mind for the Cistercian monks (page 171 of *A God Within).**

*The monks were considered to be "partners of God" contributing through their labors—looked upon as similar to prayer—to the creative process, and adding a human expression toward recreating paradise.

♦ *Allen Drury*

Advise and Consent

I'm afraid I'm all booked up for the next 3 years!

♦ *Andre Dubus*

Separate Flights

with the hoped that your philosophy is action, that your actions range from anger and passion to peace and a whispering harmony with the earth, a face, a hand, and that vast midwestern sky—

April 3, 1980

♦ *Will Durant*

The Life of Greece

You ask me what is the meaning of life. Nothing has any meaning except what mind puts into it. The meaning of life, to my mind, is that it provides an opportunity for our full development as individuals and as members of a group. Life will have just as much meaning for you as you put into it.

January 19, 1954

To Hugh Moorhead

You ask: what is the meaning or purpose of life?

I can only answer with another question: do you think we are wise enough to read God's mind?

Freeman Dyson

♦ *Freeman Dyson*

Disturbing the Universe

You ask: what is the meaning or purpose of life?
I can only answer with another question: do you think we are wise enough to read God's mind?

♦ *William Earle*

Public Sorrows & Private Pleasures

I wish I could respond to your question, "what is the meaning of life" except to say that I suppose its whatever you make of it, and perhaps to beware of assuming that there is only one.

♦ *Richard Eberhart*

Collected Poems 1930–1960

To your question what is the meaning or purpose of life, read all the great poems of the world and you still won't find out. But read them anyway as if you could. Life keeps its secrets.

Hanover, New Hampshire
1980

♦ *John Ehrlichman*

The Company

Today I am the grandfather of Matthew, who surely is a gift of God—as surely as the fact that life is synonymous with God—in that relationship lies all the meaning that man can comprehend—and more.

June 20, 1979
Matt's birthday!

Hugh S. Moorhead

With all best wishes,

Richard Eberhart

To your question What is the meaning or purpose of life – read all the great pieces of the world and you still won't find out. But read them anyway as if you could. Life keeps its secrets.

Selected Essays

1917-1932

Inscribed for
Hugh J. Moorhead
by T. S. Eliot

♦ *T. S. Eliot*

Selected Essays 1917–1932

Mr. Eliot says your question is one which one spends one's whole life in finding the answer for, and he is sorry he has not yet got to the point where he can sum it all up on a flyleaf.*

October 17, 1950

*Typed note from the author's secretary.

♦ *Albert Ellis*

Humanistic Psychotherapy

As far as I can tell, life has no special or intrinsic meaning or purpose. We are merely here because we are here, and I doubt very much whether the universe cares whether we are here or not, or will either cheer or mourn our eventual demise. I think that each of us humans makes his or her own purpose in life. Naturally, all of us who survive make one of our main purposes that very survival. Otherwise, we would not exist nor have progeny. But once we decide to survive, then we pick various forms of happy or successful survival and these tend to follow both biological and social norms, but include a great deal of individual differences. I personally think that it would be more satisfactory if more of these individual differences existed and were encouraged by our educational system. In any event, I think that they will continue to flourish because it is the nature of humans to have an almost infinite amount of variety among them. But whatever main goals we seem to pick for ourselves, these become our purposes in life, and we had better not insist that they also become the purposes of all or most other humans! I believe that unless we make one of our main purposes some form of happiness or enjoyment, life itself tends to become dull and hardly worth living. Therefore, the survival of the human race tends to be significantly correlated with its potential and actual enjoyments. But that still does not mean that any human or group of humans *has to* choose to continue to live and to live happily.

♦ *Sidra Ezrahi*

By Words Alone

As to your philosophical musings, I can only respond that my research over long years into the shadows cast by the darkest deeds in human history has not enlightened, but only sobered me. There seems to be a life-affirming impulse—studied even down to its biological foundations by Terrence des Pres—that is as strong in some as the life-destroying impulse in others. And we all live in the tenuous balance between the two.

♦ *Howard Fast*

The Immigrants

This business of *meaning* or *purpose* is a human invention, just as concepts of justice and fairness are human inventions, coined to make life less chaotic. Is there purpose in a rose, a cloud, a mountain?

But granting the premise of a purpose in life and in human existence, such purpose would be a concept of whatever force or mind created this universe and all it contains. We of the human race have not even demonstrated enough brains for us to stop killing each other or destroying our environment. We are not an admirable or particularly intelligent species, and for us to presume to enter the mind of the universe or the Almighty or God—call it what you will—is a presumption that is as arrogant as most of our fancy concepts of our importance.

Sorry not to be more helpful.

January 13, 1988

♦ *Julius Fast*

The Pleasure Book

Alas for any profundity on life's meaning—Nature intended all life to eat and reproduce—With man, the brain put an end to such simplicity—Now the meaning of life is in the living. Live it to its fullest, remembering always that you must live it with yourself.

♦ *Irvin Faust*

Newsreel

philosopher—who clearly believes in reaching out, *as I do.*

And we are here to *help* with whatever gift(s) we have . . .

♦ *J. N. Findlay*

Plato and Platonism

Ex umbris et imaginibus in veritatem.*

♦ *M. F. K. Fisher*

As They Were

I'm sorry to be such a coward about the type of inscription you request! It has given me much thought, of course, but I am afraid that I must join "the so-called logical positivists for whom the question itself is meaningless . . ."or *almost.* The more I think of it, the more I hide behind silly phrases, but I think that it boils down to my personal belief that life is a beginning.

September 29, 1982

*Out of the shadows and images into truth.

For Hugh S. Moorhead
— philosopher —
who clearly believes
in reaching out,
as I do.

And we are here to help
with whatever gift(s)
we have . . .

with sincere best wishes
for continuing
productivity & success —

Irwin Hasen

♦ *Colin Fletcher*

The Man Who Walked Through Time

The meaning or purpose of life? I guess I'd have to say that while you are, as you say, "in philosophy," I, "out" of it. I don't mean just that I was spared a college education. In fact, not that at all. But that at one stage I read a certain amount in the field—not deeply, you know, and often through comment rather than fountainhead—and reluctantly decided in the end that, as you seem to have decided, even the most promising and interesting paths ended in cul-de-sacs. Yes, no doubt the question "Why is there something rather than nothing?" has meaning. But I doubt that a human brain can do much with it. Can have fun, sure; and exercise, which is maybe the "purpose and meaning" of philosophy. And a very worthwhile thing, too. But not, I suspect, do much in the way of providing a chewable answer. Of course, any philosopher worth his salt would probably disagree. As to substitutes for meaning—I guess understanding that evolution applies to everything we know about (mountains, biological organisms and systems, idea systems) is something of a help in making at least a little more sense of what one observes around about. And also, very much so, a solid and lasting ability to stand outside our species and see it in a broader context. Within the human frame, there are a couple of thoughts of Julian Huxley's that I find nice. First, his definition of man as "nothing else but evolution at last become conscious of itself." Also his simple, difficult question and answer: "What are people for?" . . . "The answer has something to do with their quality." Of course, you may find that I've said just about bloody nothing. But then, who would be surprised at that?

◆ *Antony Flew*

Crime Or Disease?

I have as it happens been working on "Why is there anything rather than nothing?" for a few short paragraphs of a new book on *Philosophy* for the old Teach Yourself series. It seems to me that the crucial point is that every series of explanations must end in something which is just an unexplained brute fact: for the theist that unexplained and unexplainable ultimate is God, for me the existence and basic features of the Universe.

◆ *Robert Francoeur*

Evolving World, Converging Man

The future is what we decide to make it—we all are cocreators of the world to be.

◆ *Gerold Frank*

An American Death

I really can't do justice to your question: What is the meaning or purpose of life? It is too big. But for an off-the-cuff answer, I'd say that in the cosmic scheme I see neither meaning nor purpose in it.

New York
December 3, 1977

♦ *Jerome D. Frank*

Sanity and Survival

I believe that the Universe is suffused with purpose but that, as infinitesimal, almost instantaneous flashes of experience, we cannot hope to divine what this purpose is or how our lives might contribute to it. My position is best expressed by the Voice out of the Whirlwind in the Book of Job.

June 1975

♦ *John Hope Franklin*

From Slavery to Freedom

. . . with the hope that he will be one of those whose own life is fulfilled and enriched because of what he does for others.

June 5, 1970

What a question you have asked! We can only have faith that there <u>is</u> a purpose.— that we are only part of the way in the evolutionary progression towards the fulfilment of the creative will.

Yours sincerely

Christopher Fry

◆ *Lucy Freeman*

Fight Against Fears

As you know, I am Freudian so when you ask me what the meaning or purpose of life is, I can only say to be able to love and to be able to do work that one enjoys. With loving goes the ability to get married, live harmoniously with one member of the opposite sex, bear children and provide for them economically and emotionally. If one cannot give love, or allow oneself to be loved, in a mature way, not the love of a demanding infant, then, I believe, one should seek help and face some of the unconscious conflicts of childhood that are hampering one from growing up emotionally.

August 1, 1972

◆ *Christopher Fry*

Can You Find Me

What a question you have asked! We can only have faith that there is a purpose—that we are only part of the way in the evolutionary progression towards the fulfillment of the creative will.

August 20, 1982

♦ *Martin Gardner*

The Ambidextrous Universe

"I trust God knows, but not I."

♦ *William H. Gass*

The World Within The Word

There is no meaning to life. It is not a sign.

♦ *Theodore Geisel (Dr. Seuss)*

The Butter Battle Book

Life would be improved were there less Yookery and Zookery.*

*The "Yooks" and the "Zooks" represent the two warring factions in *The Butter Battle Book.*

With Kindest Regards
to Hugh S. Moorhead,
who believes, as do I,
that life would be improved
were there less Yookery and Zookery.

♦ *Elmer Gertz*

A Handful of Clients

Its meaning, to me, is that we are here and that we must make the most of it, harming neither ourselves nor others.

Chicago
February 3, 1972

♦ *Gail Godwin*

Dream Children

Maybe the meaning or purpose of life is for us to keep looking for its meaning or purpose.

March 8, 1983

♦ *Harry Golden*

For 2¢ Plain

The purpose of life is to live as long as you can.

October 5, 1960

♦ *Rebecca Goldstein*

The Mind-Body Problem

The reason I took so long to respond to you is that you asked me to comment on the meaning of life, and the only thing that I am quite certain about as regards that question is that it demands an answer as serious as it is a question, and everything I can dream up in response seems far too flippant. I think perhaps that the thing which gives the most meaning to my life, (but I'm hesitant to universalize it), is the process of making progress—or, more precisely, the sense that I'm making progress, whether or not it is really so.

February 13, 1984

♦ *Edward Gorey*

The Loathsome Couple

I doubt if there is one.

♦ *Lois Gould*

Final Analysis

The purpose of life is to leave one's mark upon the cave. The *meaning* of life is revealed at the point where all our marks converge.

December 1977

FINAL
ANALYSIS

To Hugh Moorhead:

The purpose of life is to leave one's mark upon the cave. The *meaning* of life is revealed at the point where all our marks converge.

With warmest wishes—

Lois Gould

December 1977

For Hugh Moorhead

With best wishes from a
man who has not the slightest
idea about the meaning of
life. Carpe diem.

But enjoys it immensely,

Stephen Jay Gould

♦ *Stephen Jay Gould*

The Panda's Thumb

. . . who has not the slightest idea about *the* meaning of life. But enjoys it immensely. *Carpe diem.*

♦ *Shirley Ann Grau*

The Black Prince

We are born with a need to know, a desire to understand ourselves and our world. The best of us devote their lives to that pursuit, the rest of us adopt their discoveries as our own, and all our lives wear other people's thoughts, like ill-fitting clothes, wrapped around us.

December 15, 1987

♦ *Thom Gunn*

Touch

"A cat in gloves catches no mice."

—Nineteenth century English proverb

November 1979

◆ *A. B. Guthrie, Jr.*

The Way West

If there is meaning in life maybe the purpose of life is to find it.

Lexington Kentucky
March 7, 1952

◆ *John H. Hallowell*

The Moral Foundation of Democracy

Without God life is a nightmare of terror, with God a pilgrimage of love.

March 4, 1955

For Hugh Moorhead Jr.

If there is meaning in life
maybe the purpose of life is to find it.

A.B. Guthrie Jr.

Lexington, Ky.
March 7, 1952.

THE LANGUAGE OF MORALS

Purposes are *people's* purposes; meanings are what *people* mean. Therefore *I* cannot give a general answer to your question 'What is the meaning or purpose of life?' *My* purpose in life is to help as many people as *I* can to think unconfusedly about *their* purposes.

R M Hare.

♦ *R. M. Hare*

The Language of Morals

Purposes are *people's* purposes; meanings are what *people* mean. Therefore I cannot give a general answer to your question "What is the meaning or purpose of life?" *My* purpose in life is to help as many people as I can to think unconfusedly about *their* purposes.

♦ *Sydney J. Harris*

Strictly Personal

"Man is but a reed, the weakest reed in nature—but he is a thinking reed." —Pascal

October 1, 1955

Inscribed for Hugh S. Moorhead, Jr.
with the best wishes of
S. I. Hayakawa
Chicago
March 10, 1952

"A civilization that cannot
burst through its current
abstractions is doomed to
sterility after a limited
period of progress."

A. N. Whitehead

♦ *Jim Harrison*

Legends of the Fall

Re: life, philosophically—no comment.

♦ *Charles Hartshorne*

Man's Vision of God

To live now and enrich future living is the "meaning of life." Future living means, all that can be enriched by this present living. The only future living that can be enriched by the full quality of our living is the divine Life as subsequent to the present. My reward is to serve God knowingly. Thus the present self has its reward.

♦ *S. I. Hayakawa*

Language in Thought and Action

"A civilization that cannot burst through its current abstractions is doomed to sterility after a limited period of progress."

—A. N. Whitehead

Chicago
March 10, 1952

♦ *Joseph Heller*

Good As Gold

I have no answers to "the meaning of life" and no longer want to search for any.

May 21, 1979

♦ *William Herrick*

The Last to Die

My best answer is contained in my most recent novel, *That's Life* . . . . Really, what a novelist thinks about the meaning of life is the stuff of which his entire body of work is made. A short note about it would only shortchange you.

Old Chatham, New York
April 20, 1986

♦ *John Hersey*

Hiroshima

"The crux of the matter is whether total war . . . is justifiable, even when it serves a just purpose. Does it not have material and spiritual evil as its consequences which far exceed whatever good might result? When will our moralists give us a clear answer to this question?"*

September 1978

♦ *Gilbert Highet*

People, Places, and Books

I think it was Samuel Butler who said "Life is like playing a difficult violin solo in public, and learning the instrument as you go along."

October 1953

*Hersey cites the book, pages 117–118.

♦ *Edward Hoagland*

Notes from the Century Before: A Journal from British Columbia

Life is a matter of cultivating one's six senses, and an equilibrium with nature and its subdivision, human nature (trusting no one completely but everyone at least a little), remembering almost daily that our individual lives are short.

♦ *Paul Horgan*

The Thin Mountain Air

. . . he cannot briefly answer this, and hopes you may find suggestions of an answer as you read further in his works.*

December 1977

*From a typed letter by his secretary.

◆ *Henry Beetle Hough*

To the Harbor Light

Max Eastman wrote in his narrative poem, "Lot's Wife": "Life's first commandment is that we should live it." What is most important, Thoreau said, is what imports most to me. And it is no use ploughing deeper than your own soil. At the end of "The Nigger and the Narcissus," Conrad asked, "Haven't we, together all upon the immortal sea, wrung out a meaning from our sinful lives?" The unanswerable question upon which we all turn our final page.

December 7, 1976

♦ *Irving Howe*

Celebrations and Attacks: Thirty Years of Literary and Cultural Commentary

If I knew what the meaning of life was, I'd have let the world know by now.

August 12, 1979

♦ *William Humphrey*

Proud Flesh

I cannot comment on the "meaning or purpose of life." I am a novelist, not a philosopher, and while all novels set out to answer the question of the meaning of life, only the bad ones succeed.

♦ *Aldous Huxley*

The Perennial Philosophy

. . . with the reminder that, in the words cited on page 103 of this book, "disquietude is always vanity, because it serves no good."

1951

♦ *Julian Huxley*

Evolution in Action

There is no purpose in living matter as such, but one of the significant facts about life is that during its Evolution it has generated purpose, and that in man, conscious purpose can become a dominant factor in further Evolution.

May 1955

◆ *John Irving*

The World According to Garp

The meaning of life? "We are all terminal cases," but I find that no surprise and no cause for cynicism or despair. It's all the more reason to live purposefully and well.

◆ *Christopher Isherwood*

A Single Man

You ask "what is the purpose or meaning of life?" Here's the best answer I can manage *

*The author enclosed a copy of his book, *An Approach to Vedanta,* in which the above is inscribed.

"The meaning of life?
"We are all terminal
cases," but I

The World
According to Garp

found That no
Surprise and
no cause for
cynicism or despair.
It's all The
more reason to
live purposefully
and well.

♦ *Elizabeth Janeway*

Powers of the Weak

I don't and can't pretend to have any answers for the question you ask. I have fudged a bit in what I say here but not really very much. If there is any purpose in our presence in a universe that we make out, after all, in a dim and biased way (biased by our senses, and by trends in our thinking processes that will never be knowable)—if there is any purpose or progress, it seems to be one of search and questioning. I distrust teleological ideas; at the same time, I am not fully persuaded that nothing operates on us beyond external circumstances. Well, maybe that is true; but by this stage of development, we operate back, somehow. This is muddled, I know. But life speaks of diversity and richness and interaction. I think we can take that into account without having to believe that Something wills it so. If it just happens—then the external circumstances AND a will toward diversity run on the same track.

December 1980

♦ *Karl Jaspers*

Way to Wisdom

Möchten der gute Wille und der verlässliche Freiheitswille des Amerikaner sich (sic) begegnen mit der Innerlichkeit der europäischen Philosophie,—beide würden einander ergänzen. In fruchtbarer Spannung könnten sie dem Reichtum menschlicher Möglichkeiten Raum geben.*

Basel
February 2, 1952

*May the good will and the reliable will for freedom of the American meet with the intrinsic values of European philosophy, —both would complement one another. In fertile tension they could give room to the wealth of human possibilities.

perhaps Carlyle knew

yet is the meaning of
Life itself no other than
Freedom, than Voluntary
Force; thus have we a
warfare

Thomas Carlyle

do you think so

Diane Johnson

♦ *Diane Johnson*

Lying Low

perhaps Carlyle knew:

"Yet is the meaning of life itself no other than Freedom, than Voluntary Force; thus have we a warfare. —Thomas Carlyle

do you think so?

♦ *Josephine W. Johnson*

The Inland Island

I cannot answer your question about the meaning or purpose of life except to say that each of us best serves life by realizing and fulfilling ourselves—by using "that one talent which is death to hide,"—whatever it may be.

February 15, 1970

♦*C. G. Jung*

Modern Man in Search of A Soul

Really—I don't know what the meaning or purpose of life is. But it looks exactly as if something were meant by it.

May 1951

♦*Abraham Kaplan*

The New World of Philosophy

for whom also the meaning is in the search . . .

Haifa
March 24, 1976

Really – I don't know what the meaning or purpose of life is. But it looks exactly as if something were meant by it.

May 1951

C. G. Jung.

◆ *Bel Kaufman*

*Up The Down Staircase**

a quote from Horace Walpole: "Life is a comedy to those who think, and a tragedy to those who feel . . ."*

◆ *Susan Kenney*

In Another Country

What is the meaning of life? If I knew, I probably wouldn't be writing books.

December 3, 1984

*The author took the quotation from her second novel, *Love, Etc.*

♦ *Ken Kesey*

One Flew Over The Cuckoo's Nest

Living is the purpose of life, and meaning can be found therein. *I* finds *Thou. Thou* becomes *it.* And it begins again.

♦ *Emily Kimbrough*

Now and Then

Something I could not answer briefly, and something I find rather difficult to answer at all, because I could not arrogate authority to speak for anyone but myself. To me the meaning of life is an awareness and appreciation of other human beings. One day when I was about 10 years old, my Grandfather Kimbrough said to me, "I think I have never met a man who couldn't tell me something I hadn't known before." As I have grown older I've come to realize that is what I've lived by and have learned something from everyone I've met.

♦ *Galway Kinnell*

Black Light

Back in the University College days, I might have attempted to answer—Ignorance has caught up with me, or consciousness has caught up with ignorance, however—in the meantime—

♦ *Russell Kirk*

The American Cause

To know God and enjoy Him forever; that, I believe, is the purpose of human existence.

October 25, 1969

◆ *Peter Klappert*

Lugging Vegetables to Nantucket

"The meaning of my existence is that life has addressed a question to me. Or, conversely, I myself am a question which is addressed to the world, and I must communicate my answer, for otherwise I am dependent upon the world's answer." —C. G. Jung

June 16, 1980

◆ *David Krause*

Sean O'Casey

I can only agree with Sean's advice to you, "Life is an invitation to live," advice that he always followed himself in his great good way—but with another one of his typical survival games: "A laugh is a great natural stimulation, a pushful entry into life; and once we can laugh, we can live."

September 1980

JUNE 16, 80

FOR Hugh Moorhead
with Gratitude
Peter Ustinov [signature]
ALEXANDRIA

"The meaning of my existence is that life has addressed a question to me. Or, conversely, I myself am a question which is addressed to the world, and I must communicate my answer, for otherwise I am dependent upon the world's answer"
C. G. JUNG

♦*Joseph Wood Krutch*

The Measure of Man

Life cannot be meaningless as long as there are creatures capable of asking what its meaning is.

♦*Hans Küng*

Signposts For The Future

With regard to the meaning of life of Thesis 3 (page10)*

*From the book: "Being a Christian means: By following Jesus Christ, the human being in the world of today can truly humanly love, act, suffer, and die, in happiness and unhappiness, life and death, sustained by God and helpful to men."

♦ *Paul Kurtz*

The Transcendental Temptation: A Critique of Religion and the Paranormal

Human life has no hidden meaning per se in the nature of things. There is no discoverable divine purpose in the womb of nature—no ultimate salvation. Life only presents opportunities for us to realize. The meanings that we untap in life are those that we create, the dreams, plans and projects that we live for. How exciting these can be are a measure of our imagination and creativity.

November 30, 1987

♦ *Corliss Lamont*

Humanism as a Philosophy

For Humanism the meaning of life lies in the greater happiness and progress of the individual and all mankind.

1953

♦ *Louis L'Amour*

The Haunted Mesa

The meaning and purpose of life?

To *do,* and to *become.*

Many think of what they wish to accomplish; too few think of the person they would like to be when that time comes, or at any stage in between.

Each of us is given a bit of the raw material of life with which to work. We can shape it any way we wish. The time in which we live, our inheritance of traits, etc., all have something to do with what we become, but after that it is in our hands to do much with what we have. Physically and mentally we can shape it any way we desire.

Disease and accident can leave one less than one would wish but the raw material is still there. It is yours to create or destroy or simply waste away.

September 7, 1987

♦ *Charles R. Larson*

Academia Nuts—Or, The Collected Works of Clara LePage

When I find out the meaning of life, I'll send you a postcard.

For Hugh Moorhead,

when I find out the meaning of life, I'll send you a postcard.

Warmest regards,

C R Larson

C R LePage

ACADEMIA NUTS

♦ *Richmond Lattimore*

The Four Gospels

We are things of a day. What are we? What are we not? The shadow of a dream is man, no more. But when the brightness comes, and God gives it, there is a shining of light on men, and their life is sweet.

♦ *Tom Lea*

The Primal Yoke

In answer to the query in your letter: it may be that most novels necessarily are comments on the question, "what is the meaning or purpose of life?"

El Paso
November 1978

THE

FOUR GOSPELS

AND THE

REVELATION

Richmond Lattimore

ἐπάμεροι· τί δέ τις; τί δ' οὔ τις; σκιᾶς ὄναρ
ἄνθρωπος. ἀλλ' ὅταν αἴγλα διόσδοτος ἔλθῃ,
λαμπρὸν φέγγος ἔπεστιν ἀνδρῶν καὶ
  μείλιχος αἰών.

We are things of a day. What are we? What are
  we not? The shadow of a dream
is man, no more. But when the brightness comes,
  and God gives it,
there is a shining of light on men, and their
  life is sweet.

for Hugh S Moorhead
a fellow-student of
philosophy
Max Lerner

For me the essence of life is
love and work — to love
your work, to work with
and for those you love,
in order to enhance the
life's richness for
all people —
ML

Oct 12, 1979

♦ *Max Lerner*

America As A Civilization

For me the crux of life is love and work—to love your work, to work with and for those you love, in order to enhance life's richness for all people.

October 12, 1979

♦ *Edward H. Levi*

Point of View

"Life is painting a picture, not doing a sum."

—Justice O. W. Holmes, Jr.

♦ *Ira Levin*

This Perfect Day

Having minored in philosophy, I'll hazard the opinion—not original—that the search for meaning is itself the meaning.

September 26, 1977

♦ *Ely Liebow*

Dr. Joe Bell: Model for Sherlock Holmes

As for Life, I'm sure Joe Bell would agree that it's sharper than a scalpel, sweeter than ether, and as puzzling as the stories of his most famous student.

1982

◆ *Walter Lord*

The Good Years: From 1900 to the First World War

I'm not one to comment on "the purpose of life," but I do feel these were Good Years because so many people believed in living it to the hilt.

January 20, 1970

◆ *Russell Lynes*

A Surfeit of Honey

The purpose of life? Heavens! Possibly it is to enjoy (in the best sense) what you are doing & through it to enable the people you love to enjoy what they are doing.

New York
April 1957

◆ *Archibald MacLeish*

Riders On The Earth

who knows, with Buckminster Fuller, that life is a verb.

◆ *Bernard Malamud*

The Fixer

It's all in the books.

♦ *Frederick Manfred*

Scarlet Plume

When you have life, live it out to the full—after you have made your peace with a place—

February 10, 1970

♦ *John D. Margolis*

Joseph Wood Krutch—A Writer's Life

With the thought—inspired partly by Krutch's own life—that searching for the meaning of life is more distinctively human than conclusively settling upon that meaning, and that what one day seems the meaning must be revised as a result of the following day's search.

November 14, 1985

◆ *Martin E. Marty*

A Cry of Absence

I don't know if I address THE meaning of life, but I do believe MEANING IN life can be pursued with many rewards.

When I begin minimally, humanistically, I do it in the mood of Hannah Arendt in *Between Past and Future:* "The loss of authority . . . is tantamount to the loss of the groundwork of the world, which indeed since then has begun to shift, to change and transform itself with ever-increasing rapidity from one shape into another, as though we were living and struggling with a Protean universe where everything at any moment can become almost anything else. But the loss of worldly permanence and reliability—which politically is identical with the loss of authority—does not entail, at least not necessarily, the loss of the human capacity for building, preserving, and caring for a world that can survive us and remain a place fit to live in for those who come after us."

I move from there to a theological base, after Gabriel Marcel's concept of us as "pilgrims of the eternal." Eugen Rosenstock-Huessy has taught me to "respond although I will be changed," to catch meaning in life through encounter with others and the Others who change me. I try to live by a Christian view of vocation which tells me to be unburdened by yesterday, to live with little care and some hope for tomorrow, and to see today invested with meaning.

I picture meaning found not by coming at once from shipwreck to shore but from shipwreck to some floating planks out of which to craft a raft by which to stay afloat—and maybe grab others aboard—until morning light dimly comes and maybe shores are seen.

Much more could be said . . .

♦ *Peter Matthiessen*

The Snow Leopards

I have nothing to report on "the meaning of life," have you? As to the *purpose* of it—speaking for myself—I should like to so comport myself, fulfill myself, that when the time comes, I shall be ready to die.

♦ *Cormac McCarthy*

Suttree

I can't answer, really, about the meaning of life. It seems to be its own meaning and, biologically at least, the purpose of living things seems to be to procreate. Our understanding is limited by our senses as well as our sense, and there may be, as physics seems to suggest, no such thing as reality in the absolute sense. I'm sympathetic to the idea that a successful life is one that has no need to ask the question.

♦ *Eugene McCarthy*

The Year of the People

George Seferis, modern Greek poet, in his poem "Helen" who, according to the poem, "never went to Troy," asks the questions "What is God? What is not God? What is in between?" It is in the "in between," I believe, that the meaning of life is to be sought. In observing, in seeking to know or understand (nature, persons, the arts, ideas) and in communicating that understanding, accompanied by reverence to others. As Yeats wrote "to bear the soul of man to God," to achieve, as he wrote in some measure, "the profane perfection of mankind."

September 2, 1987

♦ *Mary McCarthy*

The Groves of Academe

Who doesn't know the purpose of life and thinks its meaning must be immanent.

♦ *Richard McKeon*

Freedom and History

The purpose and meaning of life will not be clarified until men learn to understand the meanings of their words and their common past.

♦ *James McManus*

Out Of The Blue

As far as the meaning of life is concerned, I can say without cynicism that je ne sais pas. But. On page 163, line 1 (herein) and page 189, lines 6 and 7 from the bottom, there are quotes that come close to the way I was feeling at the time of composition.*

*Line 1, page 163, reads: "People die." Lines 6 and 7 from the bottom, page 189, read: " 'In other words, you can never really get the whole story.' ' You got it,' says Finn."

♦ *William H. McNeill*

A World History

Life seems to me auto-teleological, i.e., exists for itself and persists as it can.

♦ *James Alan McPherson*

Elbow Room

I cannot respond to your request for the simple reason that I do not have an answer. Many years ago, when I first began to explore the world around me, I asked myself that very same question. I am still trying to answer it for myself. So that just now my only possible answer to your question would have to be a seriously intended play on words: The purpose of life is to search for the purpose of life. After all my experience, this is the best I can do.

Charlottesville, Virginia
January 12, 1978

◆ *Margaret Mead*

Male and Female

For me, the purpose of human life is to elaborate our sense of human potentialities so that members of future generations may express more of them, more variously.

July 1952

◆ *Ved Mehta*

Fly and the Fly-Bottle: Encounters with British Intellectuals

I really can't answer your question since I don't have the slightest idea what the meaning or purpose of life is. I think, though, I recognize people who lead meaningful, purposeful lives.

August 8, 1978

◆ *Leonard Michaels*

The Men's Club

You ask what is the meaning of life. In my novel, by way of an answer, you can find a little of the thing. I don't know how else to treat your question. In the beginning there was no question, just the word.

Berkeley
1981

To Hugh S. Moorhead

Life's Purpose? Can it be to create something alive?

Arthur Miller

April, 1972

♦ *James A. Michener*

Return to Paradise

Having just returned from 7 months in Japan and Korea, it seems to me today that the main purpose of life is: 1) to have a job in whose ultimate purpose you can believe; 2) to have friends whose immediate purposes you can trust; 3) to have some spot on the earth to which you can return as home; 4) to be at the same time a citizen of some larger world.

Tinicum, Pennsylvania
April 20, 1952

♦ *Arthur Miller*

After the Fall

Life's purpose? Can it be to create something alive?

April 1972

♦ *Henry Miller*

Tropic of Cancer

As to that question you pose, I would say everyone has to answer it for himself. Maybe "just to live" would be the most sensible answer.*

October 11, 1969

Sorry not to be able to answer your conundrum!**

October 20, 1969

♦ *C. Wright Mills*

The Power Elite

You ask for a motto on "the meaning of life"—I've not got one. The minimum idea of it, however, is to be a survivor.

*Written on a postcard.

**Inscribed in the book.

♦ *Jessica Mitford*

Poison Penmanship

Sad to say, I don't really know what the purpose or meaning of life is . . . do you? If so, please advise. It would come in most handy to have the answer to this question.

November 8, 1979

♦ *Ashley Montagu*

Man's Most Dangerous Myth

The function of life is to live it—its purpose is to live it in consonance with its biological requirednesses, and to give those innate needs as noble and as beautiful an expression as possible. What is nobility? What is beauty? It is LOVE—so to conduct oneself as to warm, enlarge, and increase the capacity for living thus in others.

February 12, 1953
The birthday of Abraham Lincoln

♦ *G. E. Moore*

Principia Ethica

I have been very much puzzled as to the meaning of the question "What is the meaning or purpose of life?" At first I thought that there could be no correct answer to the question unless there was something or other which was the only purpose or the only meaning of life; and I thought, and still think, that there is nothing whatever which can properly be called "*the* purpose" or "*the* meaning" of life. But at last it occurred to me that perhaps the vague words of this question are often used to mean no more than "What is the use of a man's life?" and that this again may mean no more than "Under what conditions is a man's life of some use?" And I think that to this last question a correct answer can be given, namely something like the following: A man's life is of some use, if and only if the *intrinsic* value of the Universe as a whole (including past, present and future) is greater, owing to the existence of his actions and experiences, than it would have been if, other things being equal, those actions and experiences had never existed.

I have been very much puzzled as to the meaning of the question "What is the meaning or purpose of life?" At first I thought that there could be no correct answer to the question unless there was something or other which was the only purpose or the only meaning of life; and I thought and still think, that there is nothing whatever which can properly be called "*the* purpose" or "*the* meaning" of life. But at last it occurred to me that perhaps the vague words of this question are so often used to mean no more than "What is the use of a man's life?" and that this again may mean no more than "Under what conditions is a man's life of some use?" And I think that to this last question a correct answer can be given, namely something like the following: A man's life is of some use, if and only if the *intrinsic* value of the Universe as a whole (including both past, present and future) is greater, owing to the existence of his actions + experiences, than it would have been if, other things being equal, those actions + experiences had never existed.

G. E. Moore

ONE DAY

For Hugh Moorhead

Somewhere in this novel
Adele Skopje says "Under
Scorpio, everything is highly
personal. Just remember
that."

This approximates the answer
of the novelist to your question —
what is the meaning or purpose of life — and will
explain why we have novels.
In the meantime I hope you
will continue reading those by

Wright Morris

Aug. 20, 1970

♦ *Mary Morris*

The Bus of Dreams

When I was a little girl, my father always told me that I should reach for the stars. He said that you could never reach them, but the important thing was to try. For me the purpose or meaning of life lies in that reaching. I am not sure what happiness is or if life has some higher divine purpose, but I know that when I am trying, whether in work or in love, I feel that I am achieving some greater end; this is what gives my life its meaning.

September 7, 1987

♦ *Wright Morris*

One Day

Somewhere in this novel Adel Skopje says, "Under Scorpio, everything is highly personal. Just remember that."

This approximates the answer of the novelist to your question—what is the meaning or purpose of life—and will explain why we have novels.

August 20, 1970

For me, life is a sufficient end in itself. For most men, it apparently isn't so I can only repeat: "Ultimately, only men can make life worth living."

With best wishes for your own efforts,

Herbert J. Muller

♦ *Herbert J. Muller*

The Uses of the Past

For me, life is a sufficient end in itself. For most men, it apparently isn't. So I can only repeat: "Ultimately, only men can make life worth living."*

♦ *Iris Murdock*

The Sacred & Profane Love Machine

Life has no meaning or purpose. Our duty (another matter) is to become morally perfect. Unfortunately our lives are very short.

*From page 372, *The Uses of the Past*.

♦ *Gardner Murphy*

Human Potentialities

"He feels that he has said essentially what he has to contribute on your question, 'What is the meaning or purpose of life?' in *Human Potentialities.*"*

♦ *Thomas Nagel*

The View From Nowhere

I'm afraid the meaning of life still eludes me.

April 14, 1986

*From a typed letter from Lois Barclay Murphy, Ph.D., dates June 26, 1976

Note: inscription in book was dictated by Gardner Murphy but written by Lois Murphy, due to the former's severe Parkinson tremor

♦ *Howard Nemerov*

The Western Approaches: Poems 1973–75

According to our tradition, when a man dies there comes to him the Angel, who says: "Now I will tell you the secret of life and the meaning of the universe." One man to whom this happened said: "Take off, grey Angel. Where were you when I needed you?" Among all the hosts of the dead he is the only one who does not know the secret of life and the meaning of the universe; whence he is held in superstitious veneration by the rest.*

♦ *Reinhold Niebuhr*

The Nature and Destiny of Man

I try in this volume to explain that the meaning of life both for the individual and the whole of mankind is found in the love as it is revealed in Christ.

*Here Nemerov quotes from his own work, *The Collected Poems of Howard Nemerov*

♦ *James Oakes*

The Ruling Race: A History of American Slaveholders

Life is a perpetual struggle against all forms of enslavement—physical, emotional, and intellectual.

♦ *Joyce Carol Oates*

The Wheel of Love

I've come to the conclusion that the only "meaning" of life is to survive, biologically, but that this holds little value for us as human beings, that there are many *meanings* in life, individual, unique meanings, which we create for ourselves. Perhaps we don't create them, we only discover them—cannot help but discover them— and this leads us into the consideration of the unconscious: the constellation of emotions, which we can't control at all.

February 11, 1972

To Mr. Moorhead,

Life is a perpetual struggle against all forms of enslavement — physical, emotional, and intellectual.

James Oakes

♦ *Sean O'Casey*

Sunset and Evening Star

Life is an invitation to live . . .

I don't know. All I know is that I like life—as so many like Ike—, and have lived it well as I could in sorrow or in joy, thro' foolishness and wisdom. Curious you should ask me this; for I've just done a television feature in which an old friend asks me the same question. I've lived so hotly and so coldly, so fully that I rarely asked myself what it meant; and wisely, for no one knows. Anyway, some day we shall know more. At the moment, we are anxious to know more about nuclear energy: one step at a time.

October 20, 1955

20 October. 1953.

Flat 3, 40 Trumlands Road, St. Marychurch, Torquay, Devon

Tel.: Torquay 87766

Hugh S. Moorhead, Esq.
Chicago. Ill. USA.

Dear Mr Moorhead,

As a student of philosophy you probably know more about the purpose & meaning of life than I do; a lot more. I don't know. All I know is that I like life — as so many like Ike —, and have lived it well as I could in sorrow or joy, thro' foolishness and wisdom. Curious you should ask me this, for I've just done a Television feature in which an old friend asks me the same question. I've lived so hotly & so coldly, so fully that I rarely asked myself what it meant; & wisely, for no one knows. Anyway, some day we shall know more. At the moment, we are anxious to know more about nuclear energy: one step at a time.

All the best.

Sean O'Casey

♦ *Sigurd F. Olson*

The Singing Wilderness

The Singing Wilderness, my first, is really the essence of my own belief. As to the question you raised, I would say I believe in the eternal quest for meaning and that the goal is the maturity of understanding, a cosmic consciousness in which one becomes a part of all life in a feeling of one-ness and wholeness.

Immortality to me is knowing that one's influence goes on forever and that the wonder and awe one experiences is the key to greater *Glory.*

January 10, 1975

♦ *John Osborne*

Plays for England

Wish I *could* help you over the "meaning of life."

November 4, 1977

♦ *Grace Paley*

Enormous Changes at the Last Minute

With no answers just more questions

◆ *Alan Paton*

Cry, the Beloved Country

You ask me to make some comment on the question, what is the meaning or purpose of life? I am glad you did not ask me to answer it; I could not have done that, but I could make a comment.

Many of us are tempted to think, because the meaning or purpose of life is not comprehended by us, that our own lives have neither meaning nor purpose. This puts things the wrong way round. Let us find some purpose for our own lives, however mundane or humble, and immediately much of our anxiety about ourselves and the future disappears.

We are less terrified by the changing world when we ourselves are active.

December 25, 1952

To Hugh Moorhead —

You ask me to make some comment on the question, what is the meaning or purpose of life? I am glad you did not ask me to answer it; I could not have done that, but I could make a comment.

Many of us are tempted to think, because the meaning or purpose of life is not comprehended by us, that our own lives have neither meaning nor purpose. This puts things the wrong way round. Let us find some purpose for our own lives, however mundane or humble, & immediately much of our anxiety about ourselves & the future disappears.

We are less terrified by the changing world when we ourselves are active.

Yours sincerely

Alan Paton

Dec: 25, 1952.

♦ *Walker Percy*

The Message in the Bottle

I can do no better than Chapter 6 herein, admittedly a poor effort.*

July 30, 1977

*Chapter 6 is the book's title essay, "The Message In The Bottle." The last paragraph reads: "Since everyone is saying 'Come!' now in the fashion of apostles—Communists and Jehovah's Witnesses as well as advertisers—the uniqueness of the original 'Come!' from across the seas is apt to be overlooked. The apostolic character of Christianity is unique among religions. . . . But what if a man receives the commission to bring news across the seas to the castaway and does so in perfect sobriety and with good faith and perseverance to the point of martyrdom? And what if the news the newsbearer bears is the very news the castaway had been waiting for, news of where he came from and who he is and what he must do, and what if the newsbearer brought with him the means by which the castaway may do what he must do? Well, then, the castaway will, by the grace of God, believe him."

♦ *Noel Perrin*

First Person Rural

Life has no meaning until a person or a culture (more likely both working in conjunction) create one. For me this is best done with the aid of a good many thousands of square yards of soil.

August 1979

♦ *Ralph Barton Perry*

Realms of Value

The "remote possibility of the best thing" being better than a clear certainty of the second best.

Cambridge, Massachusetts
October 1, 1954

◆ *Harry Mark Petrakis*

A Dream of Kings

Your request that I comment on the question "What is the meaning or purpose of life," is, I'm sure you understand, a ballbreaker. I am almost hesitant to try to put it down in words. I have included a copy of a column I did recently which appeared in *Chicago Magazine* and I think in a very personal way it covers the meaning and purpose of a writer's life. Perhaps you can find in it some thoughts to answer a fragment of the question.*

August 2, 1970

*A selected passage reads: "Because wherever he is hidden, in whatever sanctuary he has fashioned as an escape from the world, he cannot hide from the knowledge that the journey of man into space can never be as significant as the journey of even one man into the recesses of himself. For if we are to survive, the answer will not be found on the moon, but in the fretful, pulsing mystery of the human psyche."

♦ *George Pitcher*

The Philosophy of Wittgenstein

I wish I had something sensible to say about the meaning or purpose of life. I feel that it is a most important question that philosophers should try to answer—but unfortunately I have no answer to it. Maybe someday I shall get an insight into it.

August 13, 1975

◆ *Alvin Plantinga*

God and Other Minds

As to the meaning of life: that (as you know) is a pretty tall order. I am a Christian, however, and the best response I can make to your request is to refer you to the first question and answer of the Heidelberg Catechism:

Q: What is your only comfort in life and in death?

A: That I, with body and soul, both in life and in death, am not my own, but belong to my faithful Savior Jesus Christ; who with his precious blood has fully satisfied for all my sins, and delivered me from the power of the Devil; and so preserves me that without the will of my heavenly father not a hair can fall from my head; yea, that all things must be subservient to my salvation, wherefore by His Holy Spirit He also assures me of eternal life, and makes me heartily willing and ready, henceforth, to live unto Him.

August 11, 1975

♦ *Norman Podhoretz*

Breaking Ranks

Who flatters me by thinking that I can answer so vast a question as what the meaning of life is in a few words, but who, I hope, will find at least a few clues to what my answer might be in the pages of this book.

January 16, 1980

♦ *Karl R. Popper*

The Poverty of Historicism

What is the meaning or purpose of life? As Kant suggested, to try to help others, and if possible to make other people happy; and to try to open our own minds a little—if necessary, by breaking a few windows and letting in air.

March 17, 1958

♦ *Katherine Anne Porter*

Collected Stories

"In my end is my beginning."

Mary Stuart's Motto—Not a bad one for anybody!

July 7, 1971

♦ *Chaim Potok*

In the Beginning

Perhaps meaning is to be found more in our ability to ask good questions than to come up with "eternal" answers.

June 14, 1978

The Collected Stories of Katherine Anne Porter

To
H. S. Moorhead—
Katherine Anne Porter
7 July 1971
College Park, Maryland

"In my end is my beginning"
Mary Stuart's Motto—
Not a bad one for anybody!
Best Wishes — K.A.P.

♦ *John R. Powers*

The Last Catholic in America

If I knew the meaning of life, I wouldn't be writing books.

October 1977

♦ *Reynolds Price*

A Palpable God

Wouldn't it be the search for the purpose of life?

♦ *Hal Prince*

Contradictions: Notes on Twenty-Six Years in the Theatre

This *is* my life!

P.S.
Correction! This is one half of my life.
I keep the other half—family and friends—to myself.

June 1977

♦ *V. S. Pritchett*

Blind Love and Other Stories

It seems to me (since you ask, but it is an impossible question) that—the purpose of life is to perpetuate itself, though not necessarily in the way we happen to desire. But it helps if, quite arbitrarily, we assume our flowering moment is worthwhile.

Lines on life for Mr. Moorhead:

Life is agid. Life is fulgid.
Life is a burgeoning, a
quickening of the dim primordial
urge in the murky wastes
of time. Life is what the
least of us make most of
us feel the least of us
make the most of.

W. V. Quine

♦ *W. V. Quine*

Methods of Logic

Life is agid. Life is fulgid.
Life is a burgeoning, a
quickening of the dim primordial
urge in the murky wastes
of time. Life is what the
least of us make most of
us feel the least of us
make the most of.

♦ *Bin Ramke*

The Difference between Night and Day

As to the question, What is the meaning or purpose of life? You will find my answer on page 77 of this book.*

December 2, 1979
Columbus, Georgia

*There is no page 77.

♦ *Anatol Rapoport*

Science and the Goals of Man

The act of communication is the primary ethical act. Good is that which contributes to the effectiveness of communication among men; evil is that which impedes communication. Life is meaningful only if the bounds of the self can be transcended.

♦ *Robert Raynolds*

The Sinner of Saint Ambrose

You ask, "What is the meaning or purpose of life?" I do not know. But the wonder and the mystery of life amaze me.

January 6, 1953

♦ *Robert Redfield*

The Primitive World and Its Transformations

The purpose of life is the effort toward goodness.

♦ *Hans Reichenbach*

The Rise of Scientific Philosophy

There is as much purpose and meaning in your life as you put into it!

Los Angeles
April 1951

♦ *Jean Rhys*

Sleep It Off, Lady

As to the meaning of life I think it depends on your own experience and belief. It would be very easy to say that life has no meaning, as far as I know, but I don't think that's the real answer.

♦ *I. A. Richards*

Beyond

I cannot comment briefly on what this book is, at some length, reflecting upon.

August 30, 1977

♦ *James Oliver Robertson*

American Myth American Reality

I have not commented further on "the meaning or purpose of life" as you asked, because I think the book is comment enough.

September 27, 1983

♦ *Carl Rogers*

On Becoming a Person

"The way to *do* is to *be.*"

July 13, 1970

to
Hugh Moorhead

who searches for
the meaning of life
while I'm out looking
for a good loaf
of Fresh bread.

Andy Rooney
4/18/83

♦ *Thomas Rogers*

At The Shores

The sequel to this book, on which I'm now working, will explain the meaning of Jerry Engel's life. Even I don't know the meaning of everyone's life, though sometimes when I'm hard at work on a novel I think I do.

August 1, 1981

♦ *Andy Rooney*

And More By . . .

. . . who searches for the meaning of life while I'm out looking for a good loaf of French bread.

April 18, 1983

♦ *Eleanor Roosevelt*

This I Remember

To me life has meaning because we love.

♦ *James F. Ross*

Philosophical Theology

Man is the rational animal capable of life with God; earthly life is locus in which one develops sensitivity and appetite, in accord with our nature, for that everlasting life.

November 4, 1980

Inscribed for Mr. Hugh S. Moorhead

with good wishes

Eleanor Roosevelt

To me life has meaning because

we love.

Richmond 4750

41 Queen's Road
Richmond
Surrey

Jan. 10. 1952

Dear Mr Moorhead

Thank you for your letter. I enclose the leaflet, but I have not written on anything about "the meaning or purpose of life": Unless you assume a God the question is meaningless, & like Laplace "je n'ai pas besoin de cette hypothèse".

Yours sincerely
Bertrand Russell

♦ *Leo Rosten*

The 3:10 To Anywhere

My view of Life will be found in the final half of the last chapter of *Captain Newman, M.D.*

♦ *Bertrand Russell*

The Philosophy of Leibniz

Unless you assume a God the question is meaningless, and like Laplace, "je n'ai pas besoin de cette hypothese."*

January 10, 1952

*I have no need for that hypothesis.

♦ *Dora Russell*

The Tamarisk Tree: My Quest for Liberty and Love

Human beings are, so far, the most gifted of animals. The purpose of their life should be to take care of themselves and, through them, of everything on their beautiful earth.

♦ *Gilbert Ryle*

Plato's Progress

I'll gladly autograph it for you, but I am certainly not going to write you an essay on "what is the meaning or purpose of life?" I regard this as a "gas" question.

June 1970

♦ *Carl Sagan*

The Cosmic Connection: An Extraterrestrial Perspective

(There may well be no "purpose" . . .)

♦ *Jonas Salk*

The Survival Of The Wisest

Life is. Its meaning and purpose are as unknowable as meaning and purpose of the cosmos.

February 14, 1978

♦ *Andrew Salter*

The Case Against Psychoanalysis

"Life is beautiful and strong only to him who during his whole existence strives toward the always desirable but ever inaccessible goal, or who passes from one purpose to another with equal ardour." —Pavlov

♦ *Helga Sandburg*

Children & Lovers

"And I thought he loved it so."—page 204

October 1976

♦ *May Sarton*

A Reckoning

The purpose of life, as I see it, is to become oneself so that one may use one's talents to the fullest and be able to give.

March 1979

♦ *Susan Fromberg Schaeffer*

Falling

What is the meaning of life? Don't you have any smaller questions? I can say this with certainty—the meaning of life is not to be found in a fortune cookie. I seem to be celebrating having just this moment finished a new novel called *Love* by writing this note.*

February 1, 1980

The meaning of life is written inside the fortune cookie with the blank slip in it.**

February 22, 1980

♦ *Jonathan Schell*

The Fate of the Earth

. . . in the hope that human life—whatever it now means and whatever it turns out to mean in future centuries—endures.

May 1982

*Written on a note sent ahead of the returned book.

**Inscribed in the book.

Falling

For Hugh,

The meaning of life is written inside the fortune cookie with the blank slip in it.

all the best,

Susan Fromberg Schaeffer
February 22, 1980

The essence of life, as I see it, is in striving, not in achievement. No basic problems are ever really solved. The good comes from the continuing struggle to try and solve them rather than from the vain hope of their solution.

Arthur M. Schlesinger, Jr.

20 September 1954

◆ *Paul Arthur Schilpp*

Kant's Pre-Critical Ethics

The ultimate purpose of man is to become, in truth and reality, a man. To be a man, in the best sense of the word, is to achieve a high development and integration of reason, of morality, and of spirituality—and to commit one's self to a cause greater than one's self. Tell me what your cause is, and I will tell you who you are.

Evanston, Illinois
March 1, 1955

◆ *Arthur M. Schlesinger, Jr.*

The Age of Jackson

The essense of life, as I see it, is in striving, not in achievement. No basic problems are ever really solved. The good comes from the continuing struggle to try and solve them rather than from the vain hope of their solution.

September 20, 1954

◆ *Nathan A. Scott, Jr.*

Mirrors Of Man In Existentialism

That's a question that defeats me.

March 3, 1980

◆ *Richard Selzer*

Confessions Of A Knife

Of "the meaning or purpose of life" I do not presume to know anything. Each day I work and so reenact the Creation itself. At rest, I ponder and am grateful.

October 9, 1979

♦ *Max Shulman*

Rally Round the Flag Boys!

Life is:
a) a watch, a vision, between a sleep and a sleep;
b) a long lesson in humility;
c) a bowl of cherries

(CHECK ONE)

June 13, 1977

♦ *John Simon*

Paradigms Lost

I don't know what the purpose of life is, but the purpose of the question "What is the purpose of life?" is to be larger than any answer can encompass, and so teach us three things: relativity, humility, and wonder.

♦ *Neil Simon*

Barefoot In The Park

Every time I come up with a philosophy of life, I find that my circumstances in life change and I have to come up with a new philosophy. Therefore, I have decided to drop the philosophy and to continue with my life.

June 24, 1978
Los Angeles, California

♦ *George Gaylord Simpson*

The Meaning of Evolution

You ask "What is the meaning or purpose of life?" Each of us must choose his own answer. This whole book is my answer.

Dear Mr. Moorhead,

Every time I come up with a philosophy of life, I find that my circumstances in life changes and I have to come up with a new philosophy. Therefore, I have decided to drop the philosophy and to continue with my life.

Sincerely,

Neil Simon

June 24th 1978

Los Angeles, Ca.

♦ *Isaac Bashevis Singer*

Shosha

The answer: I don't know. But we should enjoy it anyhow.

♦ *Philip Slater*

The Pursuit of Loneliness

Life is a Baggie.

♦ *David Small*

Almost Famous

You lay a heavy question on me: *What is the meaning or purpose of life?*

It seems to me to be the only question worth asking and one that probably a person ought not spend too much time answering. Answers tend to be passing responses, somehow, to the business of life. What we need is not more abstraction but something specific. What is needed is to *do* something. I myself have chosen writing. Others will choose medicine, literature, business. All well and good. So long as we don't get lost in the *minutae;* so long as we keep on trying to answer the haunting question with good works. Obviously I think that work can answer the question. I think love can answer the question. And so on and on. Multifarious the answers, all of them good and workable. All of them calling for extraordinary courage in face of the facts. As always . . . the answer is to be found all around us.

July 18, 1982

♦ *Huston Smith*

The Purposes of Higher Education

If you wake up to Reality you will know that you are nothing and, being nothing, that you are Everything.

♦ *Raymond Smullyan*

5000 B.C. and Other Philosophical Fantasies

In answer to your question: "What is the purpose of life?" I would say that the purpose of life is to get to the stage when one no longer asks: "What is the purpose of life?"

November 8, 1983

11/08/83

For Hugh S. Moorhead --

In answer to your question: "What is the purpose of life?" I would say that the purpose of life is to get to the stage when one no longer asks: "What is the purpose of life?"

Best,

Raymond Smullyan

♦ *C. P. Snow*

The Masters

The question you ask is one that all serious people live with, and none of us finds a general answer. I doubt if there is one, except for those who are shielded by a metaphysical arch, or more exactly, an arch of faith. For those of us who haven't such protection, I suspect all we can do is find a working answer for ourselves.

January 13, 1970

♦ *Gilbert Sorrentino*

Aberration of Starlight

la vida es sueno*

*Life is a dream.

la vida es sueño —

THE UNEASY CHAIR

For Hugh R. Moorhead

"Art is man determined
to die sane." B. De Voto.

Cordially
Wallace Stegner

♦ *Wallace Stegner*

The Uneasy Chair: A Biography of Bernard DeVoto

"Art is man determined to die sane." —B. DeVoto

♦ *Richard G. Stern*

In Any Case

Who, I'm afraid, has very little insight into "the meaning or purpose of life."

For Hugh Moorhead —
a student of philosophy
who knows therefore that
there are things we can't
know — hence faith —

Adlai E. Stevenson

Chicago 1954

♦ *Adlai E. Stevenson*

Major Campaign Speeches of Adlai Stevenson

There are things we can't know—hence faith.

Chicago 1954

♦ *Irving Stone*

Clarence Darrow For The Defense

The purpose of life is to write and read books, to teach from them and learn.

August 1, 1973

♦ *Mark Strand*

The Monument

If life has a purpose it hasn't been revealed to me. If it doesn't have a purpose it hasn't revealed that either. I haven't even tried to invent a purpose. I eat and drink as well as I can. And, of course, I write, which is a little like having a dialogue with the void. Etc. Etc.*

♦ *Leo Strauss*

The Political Philosophy of Hobbes

All good men whom I know, have taught me that we do not commit a grievous error if we make it our purpose to be as good as possible.

April 8, 1953

*The author has added the above, handwritten, as "53," to the *published* 52 pieces (notes, observations, etc.) that constitute the book itself.

53| If life has a purpose it hasn't been revealed to me. If it doesn't have a purpose, it hasn't revealed that either. I haven't even tried to invent a purpose. I eat and drink as well as I can. And, of course, I write which is a little like having a dialogue with the void. Etc. Etc.

◆ *Peter F. Strawson*

Individuals

What is the meaning of life?
—What is the meaning of a language?

June 1970

◆ *Jesse Stuart*

To Teach, To Love

Life is one's greatest possession. Life is one's all. And he should make every day, week, month, year count. He should live his life to the fullest. And it is wonderful to have a dream in life and to accomplish.

May 12, 1970

To Hugh S. Moorhead -
Life is one's greatest
possession. Life is one's
all. And one should
make every day, week,
month, year count -
He should live his
life to the fullest -
And it is wonderful
to have a dream
in life and to
accomplish. My very
best wishes to you,
a fellow teacher -
Make everything count.
You came from here -
Sincerely
Jesse Stuart
May 12th 1970

♦ *Roger B. Swain*

Earthly Pleasures

. . . but to discourse on the meaning of life . . . . I am at an age where I lack either the presumption of youth or the wisdom of maturity.

December 5, 1983

♦ *Katherine Tait*

My Father Bertrand Russell

The purpose of life is to make others happy and enjoy oneself doing it.

February 1975

◆ *Richard Taylor*

Good And Evil

The meaning and purpose of life is a subject I still dwell on. . . . It is very difficult for me to get much beyond Schopenhauer's pessimism on the subject.

April 27, 1978

◆ *Robert Lewis Taylor*

The Travels of Jaimie McPheeters

As to the "meaning of life," I've been seeking that for several decades. However, I'll think up something that we can hope won't be too nonsensical.

December 14, 1979

♦ *Phyllis Theroux*

California and Other States of Grace

What is the meaning of life? I am too humble with good reason, to answer that. But I give you Karl Jaspers: "Such is the idea of a great and noble life—to endure ambiguity in the movement of truth and to make life shine through it; to stand fast in uncertainty, to be capable of unlimited love and hope."

For Hugh Moorhead —

What is the meaning of
life? I am too humble writer good
reason, to answer that. But I give
you Karl Jaspers: "Such is the idea of
a great and noble life — to endure ambiguity
in the movement of truth and to make life
shine through it; to stand fast in uncertainty;
to be capable of unlimited love and hope."

Phyllis Theroux

♦ *James Thurber*

Fables For Our Time

I have never found the meaning of life—

♦ *Hannah Tillich*

From Time To Time

I don't know whether even Paul Tillich could answer your question "What is the meaning or purpose of life?"

I have a "hunch" that we will not live! the moment the question would be answered in "us."

From Time to Time

I don't know whether even
Paul Tillich could answer your
question „What is the meaning
or purpose of life" ?.
I have a "hunch" that
we will not live! the mo—
ment the question would be
answered in „us"
Thanks for a good
" encounter"
Hannah Tillich

♦ *Paul Tillich*

The Shaking of the Foundations

The "Courage to Be" takes the anxiety of non-being into itself.

October 1952

♦ *Arnold J. Toynbee*

A Study of History

'What is the true end of Man?—
'To glorify God and enjoy Him for ever.'

♦ *H. R. Trevor-Roper*

Men and Events

You must *deduce* my ideas about the meaning of life from my works!

♦ *Barbara W. Tuchman*

The Proud Tower

The meaning of life is what you make it.

◆ *Colin M. Turnbull*

The Mountain People

And in the belief that life is more than has been left to the Ik.

June 1977

◆ *Anne Tyler*

Earthly Possessions

but alas, without a grain of philosophy in my head

November 13, 1977

◆ *John Updike*

Pigeon Feathers and Other Stories

Well, my goodness, "What is the meaning of life?" you ask. What is the meaning of "meaning" in your question. And whose life? A worm's? Or yours? In any case, enjoy it.

for Hugh Moorhead

well, my goodness, "what is the meaning of life?" you ask. What is the meaning of "meaning" is your question. And whose life? A worm's? or yours? In any case, enjoy it.

John Updike

Aspen, Colo
1980

For Hugh Moorhead —

The ultimate value of life to me is a beloved partner.

Without one, life is fought on a physic battlefield and no victory brings fulfillment.

With such a partner, all pain is endurable.

Best wishes

[signature]

♦ *Leon Uris*

Battle Cry

The ultimate value of life to me is a beloved partner.

Without one, life is fought on a psychic battlefield and no victory brings fulfillment.

With such a partner, all pain is endurable.

Aspen, Colorado
1980

♦ *J. O. Urmson*

Philosophical Analysis

Is it not people who have purposes? Do they *live* purposely, or on purpose?

I'm not sure, therefore, what people who ask about the purpose of life want to know. I suspect that the question may have originally been about God's purpose in creating us. I am not an authority on that!

◆ *Paul M. van Buren*

The Secular Meaning of the Gospel

"What is the meaning or purpose of life?" is a question which is utterly worth trying to answer when it is raised in a quite specific situation. Whether asked in despair, or in genuine personal puzzlement, one who dares to answer for another would only do so on the basis of some rather personal relationship of trust or intimacy. To say anything in general to the question, as though it were a general question, seems to me to be a misunderstanding of the issue. Not knowing just what leads you to raise the question, I have no answer. I am puzzled to know in what context it could be conceived as a question on which to "comment." (Cf., comment on death.) I have known one or two persons who were also professional philosophers, who have worried or wondered about the meaning of life. They have convinced me that they were good philosophers in part by the fact that they did not seem to think they were asking a philosophical question. I took them to be asking a personal question of considerable magnitude. I hardly have grounds to expect that you await from me a personal confession, so I shall also respect the question sufficiently to refrain from commenting on it.

November 7, 1976

◆ *Mark Van Doren*

Collected Stories

As for the meaning or purpose of life, I can only rest on the poems and stories I've written; on my criticism; and on my *Autobiography*. I can't sum it up in a sentence—or six.

November 12, 1969

◆ *Eliseo Vivas*

The Moral Life and the Ethical Life

You will not discover in books the meaning of human destiny. Books may help. But you will have to go to your own experience to find out what it means.

January 15, 1952

♦ *Irving Wallace*

The Nympho & Other Maniacs

The meaning of life is to be happy, to be productive, to help other human beings, and to be useful to the human race.

♦ *Mika Waltari*

The Egyptian

Re: The meaning of life:
The older I grow, the less—I think—I understand.

◆ *Michael Walzer*

Radical Principles: Reflections of an Unreconstructed Democrat

If I knew what to say, I would write a book. . . . One of the arguments of *Radical Principles* is that life has *more* meaning for the citizens of a genuine democracy. But that this is the meaning it ought to have, I can't say. I suspect that the definite article is wrong: we must make our own meanings.

March 25, 1981

Dear Mr. Moorhead – you have asked
me to comment on the meaning of life, or
the purpose. I shy away from such
questions, and the only answer I
could give would be to say that I
see only the purpose, or meaning,
which we create by living. That's a
big enough purpose, I guess

RPW

♦ *Robert Penn Warren*

All the King's Men

You have asked me to comment on the meaning of life, or the purpose. I shy away from such questions, and the only answer I could give would be to say that I see only the purpose, or meaning, which we create by living. That's a big enough purpose, I guess.

October 31, 1953

♦ *Richard Watson*

The Philosopher's Diet

Take the main chance.

♦ *Alan W. Watts*

This Is It

You may wish to ask where flowers come from,
But even the God of Spring doesn't know.

For Hugh S. Moorhead—
With all good wishes,
Alan Watts.

欲問花來處

You may wish to ask where the flowers come from,

東君亦不知

But even the God of Spring doesn't know.

阿蘭

♦ *Edward Weeks*

My Green Age

Your letter catches me on the first morning after my return from a week of salmon fishing in Northern Quebec and the profundity of your question catches me off balance. Remembering the beauty of the Moisie River which for thousands of years has eaten its way through towering, fir-covered cliffs, my first thought was that the purpose of life is to identify oneself with the magnificent beauty of Nature, and, more personally, to discover that form of affiliation for which one is best adapted.

July 7, 1980

◆ *Jessamyn West*

The Witch Diggers

Any convictions I have about the "meaning or purpose of life" are contained in this book. Is that an unfair way of answering your question? But it's the novelists' way you know and we can't, however much we might wish to do so, become essayists and philosophers.

Merry Christmas 1953
Napa, California

♦ *William Wharton*

Birdy

In considering your question, I'm reminded of an old joke. It's a joke that can go on and on with elaborations which I'll leave out. You might enjoy it.

Harry was a successful man, wonderful wife, fine kids, successful in business. One day he asks himself but "what is the meaning of life?" All this means nothing. He divorces his wife, abandons his children, gives up his business and goes out to search for the meaning of life. After much meandering and painful search (this part can be built up) he arrived in Tibet. (Where else?) He finds there is a holy man at the top of the mountain who can tell him the meaning of life. After a difficult and dangerous climb (to be built up) he arrives at the cave on top of the mountain and deep inside sits the holy man in meditation, with only a loin cloth, sitting on a cake of ice. Harry prostrates himself before the holy man.

"Oh holy Guru, can you tell me the 'meaning of life?' "

Guru responds.

"A wet bird doesn't fly at night."

Harry says, amazed, "You mean I gave up my family, traveled all over the world, climbed this mountain and you tell me the meaning of life is that 'A wet bird doesn't fly at night'?"

The Guru stares deeply into Harry's eyes, a quizzical expression on his face.

"Perhaps a wet bird *does* fly at night?"

It's difficult to answer your question of "the meaning or purpose of life." For me, meaning and purpose are different questions. One is metaphysical, the other ethical. I'll try to answer "meaning" first. For me, at this time, always subject to change in this quantum world, the meaning of life is beyond human understanding. I don't believe we are meant to understand or know this, and if we did, it would probably take away most of the joy most of us find in life.

As to the purpose of life, it is easier for me. The purpose of life is the constant search for the never attainable "meaning," without expectation of answer, only the further refining of our questioning. With this, as corrolary, comes the sharing of our questions, guesses, with others.

It isn't a very satisfactory answer I know, but it's where I am right now. I hope it helps. Perhaps the wet bird doesn't want to fly at night, it's too cold.

January 11, 1988
1:05 p.m.

◆ *Alfred Whitney*

Essays on Education

Of all forms of education the one that is most likely to reveal the meaning and purpose of life is liberal education.

◆ *Allen Wier*

Blanco

The meaning of life? This is a theological question—rational inquiry into religious matters. The *quick*ness of the quick and the dead makes life terrifying, yet is the cause for our wonder. That we live in full knowledge of our mortality necessitates a life of willful disregard or of willful faith. Free will removes the crutch of absolutes. We are up against the crafty will of the God who gave us knowledge of our vulnerability and allows our redemption through the moral courage with which we choose to live. (God knows it's not easy.) Like any good father, God demands that we live well, that we balance the terror of being alive against the wonder of life. God makes nothing easy on purpose—we must suffer to be beautiful. My own prayer is the same as that of the man in Mark, chapter nine, who brings his demon-inhabited son before Christ and begs compassion. Jesus says, If thou canst believe, all things *are* possible to him that believeth. And the man, in tears, cries out, Lord, I believe, help thou mine unbelief.

To learn the meaning of life, we live. The meaning of life, then, changes as we live (and learn). I believe completely in transformation, the transforming power of the imagination. In the beginning was the Word. Something named becomes real, quick. A fiction writer, I interpret the obscure omens of personal experience. That I can give life, more than information, with the Word, I take as a sign. Life *is* light. The light shines in the darkness, and the darkness has not overcome it.

♦ *Richard Wilbur*

Things of This World

Though daunted by the question about the purpose of life . . . . Come to think of it, the purpose of life must be the purpose of God, from whom we came and to whom we will return: this purpose is reflected in everything human which is combinative, which helps to harmonize and salvage the world.

December 28, 1979

♦ *George F. Will*

The Pursuit of Virtue & Other Tory Notions

The meaning of life is on page 27.*

*Page 27 reads: "Only one portrait adorns my study. It is of Newman, the great theorist of university life. Newman, philosopher of man's *creatureliness,* insisted that we are smaller than we imagine. Like Darwin and Marx, he was of the generation that first internalized the idea that change is an autonomous process. This led him not to utopian optimism or social pessimism, but to a profound sense of human limitedness in a prodigious world.

Aristotle said the aim of education is to get the student to like and dislike what he ought; Newman said the aim is not to satisfy curiosity but to arouse the *right* curiosity. Education, he believed, is the thread on which received knowledge, jewels of the great tradition, can be strung. A university should be, primarily and for most students, a place that keeps people from getting lost rather than a place where they find things. A university, like any community, presupposes *some* purpose all members share. As Newman said, 'greatness and unity go together and . . . excellence implies a center.' The center of a university should be a rigorous curriculum of required studies of proven substance.

Requirements do diminish undergraduates' "freedom," as liberals define freedom: 'the absence of restraints imposed by others.' But true freedom is impossible without comprehension of, and submission to, the natural order. And the most direct path to such comprehension is through the body of knowledge that is civilization's patrimony. What has been lost is the understanding that education consists primarily of arguing from, not with, this patrimony."**

**This is the end of Will's essay entitled "Freedom, True and False," dated May 29, 1978.

for Hugh

from Nancy Willard

"My answer to your question—if there is one—is in this book. And sometimes questions are more important than answers."

♦ *Nancy Willard*

Things Invisible To See

My answer to your question—if there is one—is in this book. And sometimes questions are more important than answers.

◆ *Colin Wilson*

Religion and the Rebel

I'm afraid it's impossible to answer the question of my view of the meaning of life briefly. My own method of thinking is concerned with the *way* in which consciousness grasps meaning, and whether the meanings it grasps are objective, or merely reflections of our own needs and desires. Basically, I accept the notion that we are living in a "meaning universe." You will find the clearest exposition of my views on this subject in my latest book *The Occult,* especially the last four pages—i.e., my "metaphysics," my own guess about the status of life in the universe. Basically, I have always held the view accepted by T. E. Hulme, that evolution consists of the gradual insertion of "freedom" into matter, and much of my work is devoted to arguing against orthodox Darwinians who regard life as a kind of product of matter, and philosophers like Ryle who see no basic distinction between body and mind, or matter and life. I come closest to refuting the mechanistic case in the last chapter of *Origins of the Sexual Impulse.* But my chief interest is not so much the metaphysical question of the meaning of life, as the practical question of how human beings can train themselves to grasp or perceive this meaning, instead of having to rely on occasional "flashes" of insight, or moments of intense feeling when we operate at our correct voltage instead of suffering a permanent power-reduction.

March 1972

For Hugh Moorhead

warm regards

Colin Wilson

Mar 72

◆ *Donald Windham*

Tanaquil

I wish I were an Albert Camus and could oblige you with philosophy as well as fiction, but such is not the case. My theme here, however, is all too bluntly stated on page 287.*

February 2, 1978

*The book primarily concerns itself with the intertwining and tenuouness of love, and on page 287 Windham writes: "And with a quickening of his heart he foresaw, in a negative insight, which would become positive with time, that the responsibility of love may not be the price you pay for it but its ultimate value, which keeps you going for others when you would not continue for yourself alone."

2/2/78

Dear Mr. Moorehead

I wish I were an Albert Camus and could oblige you with philosophy as well as fiction, but such is not the case. My theme here, however, is all too bluntly stated on p. 281.

With my thanks for your interest and response

Don Windham

for

Hugh S. Moorhead, Jr

The meaning &

purpose of life?

Appreciation

The means?

Understanding.

Philip Wylie

♦ *Philip Wylie*

An Essay On Morals

The meaning and purpose of life?
Appreciation
The means?
Understanding

♦ *Patricia Zelver*

A Man of Middle Age

I wish I could answer your question—
Or maybe that would spoil the story—.

Acknowledgments

First, I wish to express my deep appreciation to our departmental secretary, Pauline Piscetello, whose long devotion to and exemplary work for its members did not deter her from taking on the additional task, willingly and effectively, of assisting me with this work. I am most grateful to her.

Also within the confines of Northeastern Illinois University, a number of colleagues helped along the way, sometimes just in casual conversations, from trying to decipher some illegible writing on the part of respondents who too hastily penned the comments I had asked for, to suggesting some background of an author's work that provided some clue toward making contact, to helping in my own effort at translation of non-English ones and getting them done for those which I could not attempt. Memory cannot, regrettably, recall all of these, but I can thank Ely Liebow, Dorothy Patton, Don Siegel, and Friederike Wiedimann for their contributions. Repeatedly I made trips to our Ronald Williams Library, especially at the reference desk, and here I express my gratitude for that staff, particularly Evangeline Mistaras and Mary Jane Hilberger.

It was necessary to contact many publishing firms, both in America and abroad, for assistance in contacting authors of theirs, or finding the estates or trustees of those no longer living. This took considerable research time. For that I wish to thank Ann Bujalski, Yale University Press; Stratford Caldecott, Routledge; Nancy Couto, Cornell University Press; Beatrice Hurwitz, Simon & Schuster; Mildred Garcia, Columbia University Press; Michael Greaves, Random House; Jean Kellet, Farrar, Straus & Giroux;

Mavis E. Pindar, Faber and Faber Limited; Mary E. Ryan, W. W. Norton & Co.; Barbara Stokes, Random House; and Nora Whelan, The Putnam Publishing Group.

A special note of thanks goes to Antony Flew, Professor Philosophy at Reading, in England, one who all professors of philosophy in America know through his many works, for his most cordial aid in my obtaining permissions from some other well-known English thinkers, or via their estates.

Finally, I will remember the initial meeting with the editors and staff of Chicago Review Press, whose immediate enthusiasm for and confidence in the proposed work, along with their conviviality and knowledgeability, encouraged me to undertake the project. Subsequent to a couple of further meetings, Amy Teschner was assigned to direct the production of the manuscript, and I extend to her my thanks for the friendly and courteous yet firm guidance throughout the many months we worked together. I would add that what the reader finds in the Introduction was made more accurate by her editing of what I *wanted* to say, small though the piece be, to the reader.

Permission Acknowledgments

Permission to print Dean Acheson's comments courtesy of David C. Acheson; Fred Allen's comments courtesy of Portland Allen Rines; C. D. Broad's comments courtesy of H. J. Easterling, Secretary of the Council for the Broad papers at Trinity College; Denis W. Brogan's comments courtesy of Hugh Brogan; Pearl S. Buck's comments courtesy of Janice C. Walsh; Erskine Caldwell's comments courtesy of Virginia M. Caldwell; Rudolph Carnap's comments courtesy of Hannah Carnap Thost; Stuart Chase's comments courtesy of Sonia C. Hodson; A. J. Cronin's comments courtesy of Little, Brown & Co.; and E. E. Cummings's comments courtesy of Marion Cummings.

Permission to print John Dos Passos's comments courtesy of Elizabeth Dos Passos; Paul Douglas's comments courtesy of Susan C. Metzer; Rene Dubos's comments courtesy of Jean P. Dubos; Will Durant's comments courtesy of Monica Mihell; T. S. Eliot's comments courtesy of Valerie Eliot; Harry Golden's comments courtesy of Harry Golden, Jr.; Alfred Whitney Griswold's comments courtesy of Mrs. A. Whitney Griswold; Sydney J. Harris's comments courtesy of Marie Maiorca; Gilbert Highet's comments courtesy of R. Andrew Boose; Henry Beetle Hough's comments courtesy of E. Blake Hough; Aldous Huxley's comments courtesy of Laura A. Huxley; and Julian Huxley's comments courtesy of Lady Huxley.

Permission to print Karl Jaspers's comments courtesy of Hans Saner; C. G. Jung's comments courtesy of the C. G. Jung Estate, Baden, Switzerland, and Princeton University Press; Abraham Kaplan's comments courtesy of Gardner Lindzey; Joseph Wood Krutch's comments courtesy of Marcelle Krutch; Richmond Lattimore's comments courtesy of Alice Lattimore; Archibald MacLeish's comments courtesy of The Literary Executor for Archibald MacLeish and Houghton Mifflin Co.; Bernard Malamud's comments courtesy of Russell & Volkening, Inc.; Margaret Mead's comments courtesy of Bronnell Sloane for the Institute for Intercultural Studies, Inc. and Mary Catherine Bateson; James A. Michener's comments courtesy of an assistant to James A. Michener; Henry Miller's comments courtesy of Henry Tony Miller; and C. Wright Mills's comments courtesy of Mrs. C. Wright Mills.

Permission to print G. E. Moore's comments courtesy of Timothy Moore; Herbert J. Muller's comments courtesy of Janet B. Muller; Richard McKeon's comments courtesy of Zahavra K. McKeon; Reinhold Niebuhr's comments courtesy of Ursula M. Niebuhr; Sean O'Casey's comments courtesy of David Krause; Sigurd F. Olson's comments courtesy of Elizabeth Olson; Ralph Barton Perry's comments courtesy of Elizabeth J. Perry; Katherine Anne Porter's comments courtesy of Isabel Bayley; Robert Raynolds's comments courtesy of Mrs. Robert Raynolds; and Robert Redfield's comments courtesy of James Redfield.

Permission to print Hans Reichenbach's comments courtesy of Maria Reichenbach; Jean Rhys's comments courtesy of the Literary Executor of the Estate; I. A. Richards's comments courtesy of Richard Luckett; Carl Rogers's comments courtesy of David Rogers; Eleanor Roosevelt's comments courtesy of Elliot Roosevelt; Bertrand Russell's comments courtesy of Christopher Farley; Dora Russell's comments courtesy of Katherine Tait; Gilbert Ryle's comments courtesy of Sir Geoffrey Warnock; George Gaylord Simpson's comments courtesy of Anne Roe Simpson; Isaac Bashevis Singer's comments courtesy of Mrs. Isaac B. Singer; C. P. Snow's comments courtesy of Elizabeth Stevens; Adlai E. Stevenson's comments courtesy of Adlai Stevenson; Leo Strauss's comments courtesy of Jenny Strauss Cray; and Jesse Stuart's comments courtesy of H. E. Richardson.

Permission to print James Thurber's comments courtesy of Rosemary A. Thurber; Paul Tillich's comments courtesy of Hannah Tillich; Arnold Toynbee's comments courtesy of Lawrence Toynbee; Barbara Tuchman's comments courtesy of Russell & Volkening, Inc.; Mark Van Doren's comments courtesy of Farrar, Straus & Giroux; Mika Waltari's comments courtesy of Satu Suomala; Alan Watts's comments courtesy of Russell & Volkening, Inc.; Jessamyn West's comments courtesy of Harry McPherson; and Philip Wylie's comments courtesy of Harold Ober Associates, Inc.